FOUND GIRL

HALEY WARREN

To anyone who wishes for nothing more than to find themselves—keep searching.
You're out there, and you're wonderful.

a Winchester Holdings novel

Dear Reader,

Thank you so much for picking up this book. I hope you find something in the final part of Charlie's story and the words on these pages. Before you start reading, there are some things you'll find in this book you should be aware of. The theme of grief, both present and past, is prevalent in Found Girl. As much as it's a story about finding yourself and finding love, it's also one of heavy loss.

This book mentions the death of a parent, previous and off page, as well as parental death from cancer on page, suicide, illegal gambling, and contains scenes of substance use and abuse.

As much as I would love you to read this book, you're more important.

Always take care of yourself.

Haley

Charlie

I was dreaming. It was a great dream. It was one of those dreams where all the pieces of my life fit with no sharp edges, nothing jutting out to poke me. They all softly clicked together, melding seamlessly. It might have been a boring dream to most people, but it was my best dream. The one where I lived with myself, made a home in this body made of muscle tissue, sinew, and ligaments. This body that had chocolate hair and forest eyes, just like my brother, my favorite human in the world. Features I was proud to share with him. Features that came from the mix of our parents' genetics, both our mother and our father. This body that had hurt people but hadn't hurt anyone as much as I had hurt my own heart.

I was at home now, though. At home in this body, in this dream. It was a great dream. And then the phone rang.

I groaned, smacking my hand against my pillow uselessly because there was only one person in my life who couldn't ever seem to remember the time difference. I popped an eye open, my hand ineffectually fumbling for my phone and propping it up to reveal my brother's name—along with a photo of him back in prep school I was particularly fond of. He had too much baby fat on his cheeks and couldn't grow a beard to save his life. But he was perfect.

"Deacon, it's three in the morning," I said through closed eyes and a mouth that felt like sandpaper. "I'm not flying back to New York because the alterations on your tux for the rehearsal dinner weren't right. *Again*. It's an egregious waste of jet fuel."

"Charlie. You need to come home. It's, uh, it's Dad. You have to come back."

I wasn't dreaming anymore. I was wide awake, and there was a new, sharp edge of life poking at me. This one jutted right through my heart.

––––––––––

My family home in Lake Forest was usually pretty empty. It bordered on desolate, save for when my father played host to some large event or another. It was far too big for four people when my mother was alive and we all lived there. And it was still far too big for just my father. There were staff, but they blended into the background of the home and that was how my father preferred it.

There were ghosts all over that house, and I had spent way too much time chasing them, straining my ears to see if I could hear any of them—the ghosts of my mother, my father, who my brother and I used to be. But it was always just silence.

Today, though, it wasn't silent. And it wasn't because there was some gala or charity event, and my father wasn't being profiled for some sort of magazine spread or article.

I couldn't remember the last time I was in my dad's room. Probably before my mother died, when Deacon and I used to run in there and spend evenings watching movies with them in that giant bed.

My father was in that same bed now, propped up, and the somewhat gray skin of his face pinched in irritation. He was wearing a full suit—save for the jacket. It was folded neatly on the chaise lounge at the end of the bed. One of his sleeves was rolled up to reveal the butterfly clip of an IV line, trailing to a pole with a beeping machine that was surely signaling something. Taylor's father stood over him, a stethoscope pressing just under the neck of my father's shirt.

"I'm not sure why your brother called you. It wasn't necessary," Steven Winchester finally spoke, blue eyes finding mine—the ones I shared with my brother, and once upon a time, our mother too.

It was the first time he spoke since I arrived in the doorway, dropping the giant and annoyingly expensive Cambridge Weekender from Swaine that Taylor bought me on the ground. She said before I moved that my other luggage was quote, unquote, "old and ugly."

"He called me, because apparently you have cancer, and you've been lying about it for God knows how long." I didn't want my voice to crack, but it did, and I think a part of me went along with it. The whole thing seemed ironic—that he and I would have just started to mend fences, and then some malignant disease would encroach and, quite literally, start to tear them down.

"He was in remission until very recently," Dr. Breen offered, extracting the stethoscope from his ears and winding it around his neck.

He looked so much like his daughter, and I usually thought of him fondly, but right now, I wanted to throttle him because he had been complicit in this whole thing, one of the culprits behind all the splintered wood that lay at my feet.

A hand settled on my shoulder before I could answer, and I knew who it belonged to by the size and weight of it. Taylor's thumb brushed against my sweater briefly as she strode into the room, all business, still wearing her black hospital scrubs. It would have been funny to see them juxtaposed like that: her father in a suit with the ever-permanent stethoscope accessory around his neck, and her practically his miniature, already beginning a physical examination on my father without his permission. I watched her narrow her eyes at my father, her sharp features tighter than usual, and the anger practically radiating off of her.

She gestured to a manilla folder I hadn't noticed on the mahogany nightstand.

"How were you in remission, and we didn't even know?" I finally asked, still refusing to leave my post in the doorway. It felt like another precipice of my life. If I crossed the threshold, I was firmly moving into the aftertimes. The before times might have been littered with disasters and holes left by landmines—some detonated by me, some by him, but if I took one more step, I'd forever be living in the time after I knew my dad had cancer.

"It wasn't important. It was caught early enough that it quickly became irrelevant. I didn't even need chemo," he said, his voice so matter-of-fact, that he might as well have been reading the most recent financial statement for Winchester Holdings.

"You elected not to undergo chemotherapy, Steven. You signed an AMA form. There's a copy of it in the folder right there." Dr. Breen's voice was terse, and he arched an eyebrow, liberally peppered with gray.

"Oh, you've got to be fucking kidding me!" My voice caught between something like a shriek and a sob, because there was no fucking way this was real life. "Don't tell me why. I bet I can guess. You didn't want to be away from the company, and God forbid anyone see the great Steven Winchester as anything but a ruthless businessman. You could never do something that might weaken you in your competitors' eyes."

Taylor was now moving her fingers down my father's neck in some sort of palpation exam; she used to practice them on me when she was in med school, but at my words, he jerked out of her reach.

"No. It was after your mother. I didn't want to put you and Deacon through it." Steven Winchester sounded earnest for maybe the first time in his life. And his eyes almost looked pleading.

"Are these the results of the first scan?" Taylor ignored the rest of us, now flipping through the folder her father finally handed her. She didn't wait for his response, holding the sheet up to the light. I didn't know how to read the results of a scan, but I could see a ribcage illuminated, and that was about it. "You removed it?"

"It was clean, Taylor. It was a very successful surgery. The margins were clean, and all harvested lymph nodes and surrounding tissue came back fine," Dr. Breen answered, those two in their own little medical world now.

"You should have had chemo." Her eyes flicked to my father for a moment before returning to the file. She was flipping through the documents again, pausing occasionally to run her finger down the pages, eyes moving at an unnatural speed. "Colon cancer is highly treatable, and the risk of recurrence is low when it's caught early like this."

Taylor was many things, but she was also unnaturally smart, and I found myself hoping that maybe, just maybe, she would find a way out of this. I wanted to look at her, maybe to beg her, to fall on my knees and tell her to find a way to keep my father because I had just gotten him back, but Steven and I were still staring at one another.

Before I could think better of it, I crossed the room and dropped to sit beside him, picking up his hand between my own. I felt his fingers tense. I couldn't remember the last time we hugged, let alone held hands. I had probably been a child, and it had probably been for a photo op.

"Where's Deacon?" I asked softly, not looking at my father but staring down at our joined hands.

He cleared his throat before sitting up straighter and adjusting his cufflinks. "Your brother isn't handling this well."

"That doesn't answer the question," I whispered, fairly certain I knew where this was going.

"Try any bar downtown. You might find him slumped in a chair somewhere." His words were clipped. "Noa's been away in Tahiti for the last week. I considered calling her but thought I would leave that up to you."

I nodded.

It was probably best that Taylor and I try to clean up after him before Noa had the misfortune of seeing him this way. Deacon had zero coping skills. He was a master of avoidance, and he had been ever since our mother died. I could only imagine what this would be like.

Taylor was holding another scan to the light, tipping her head back and forth, like she was trying to puzzle something out. "You aren't going to try to take these?"

I had no idea what they were looking at, but given my father's perfunctory silence, I assumed whatever it was, was not good.

"We could, but we're opening him up and exposing an already weakened immune system when we can't get them all. It's stage four now, Taylor. You're a doctor, and you know what you're looking at. Separate from your emotions." Her father was standing beside her now, pointing out various things on my father's scan that I couldn't, and didn't, want to be able to recognize.

"We should take these two while we can, before they grow and impede blood flow and ultimate function of the kidney," Taylor snapped, eyes on her father, before she turned to my dad. "Steven, I can get these. It's aggressive, and it's not without risk when your mets are this advanced. It's not curative. It's a palliative procedure that I hope will buy you time."

"It's not worth the risk." Dr. Breen shook his head. "I would have suggested it if I thought it was a viable course of action."

"I spend significantly more time in the OR than you do. You practically push paper for a living. I'm more aggressive than you, and I say the risk is worth it." Taylor tipped her chin upward and held her father's gaze, waiting for him to disagree.

He looked at her appraisingly, and something like pride winked behind his eyes. "Steven and I can discuss every possible option, including him getting another opinion. I have calls in at MD Anderson, Sloan Kettering, Mayo, and Cleveland Clinic. We have time, Taylor."

"Not enough," she whispered, finally breaking their staring contest and looking at me. Her face crumpled in on itself, those harsh features softening, and I swear her heart broke behind her eyes. "Why don't we go retrieve Deacon from whatever cesspool he's drowning in, and once he sobers up, we can all talk this through?"

"That would be wise." My father finally spoke, extracting our joined hands. "Duke and I need to talk."

I widened my eyes at the lack of formality. I couldn't remember the last time he addressed Taylor's father by his first name. Despite their years'-long friendship, he considered it the height of respect to refer to him by his title when he spoke about him.

My father had been aging before I left. I noticed it in little moments, realizing there were new, deeper lines stretched across his skin or that his hair was bordering on gray, not salt and pepper. But it never struck me like it did at that moment, studying his profile to see gaunt skin that was too tight across his cheekbones, the jut of more prominent shoulder blades under his shirt. He was too thin. Even his suit didn't look like it was fitting properly anymore. Taylor was right. There wasn't enough time.

Taylor held her hand to me, beckoning me forward.

I cleared my throat, blinking away tears that threatened to spill over. "You can borrow something of mine if you want to change out of your scrubs before we go find Deacon."

"Oh no, no, no. If I have to drag his sorry ass out of a bottle—I'll be doing it in scrubs as a reminder that there are many things my time would be better served doing." Taylor gestured for me to stand again, leave my father here, go into the world, and find my brother.

I paused, flipping through my phone briefly before landing on the Find My app. And there he was, a photo illuminated in a building downtown in a club called Aux. "Found him. Clearly, he doesn't want to hide that badly."

"Some might say it's a cry for attention." Taylor pursed her lips, bitterness lacing her words.

I turned, about to tell my father that I could send Taylor to retrieve Deacon alone, that I could stay with him while Dr. Breen broke down the ugly truth of his options, or lack thereof, but he shook his head and offered me a rare, albeit strained, smile.

"Go get your brother. We can discuss this as a family when you get back, and he's sobered up. He might actually be in need of one of those IV companies he favors so much." Steven Winchester looked at me as he spoke, and it felt like he was really looking at me, emoting in a way I wasn't sure he even knew how to anymore. His blue eyes looked so endlessly sad, like the precipice of all he was about to lose was staring back at him in my reflection.

"Sure, Dad," I said, offering him a smile that was really only a sad little tug of my lips. I stood and leaned forward to briefly press my lips to his forehead. I felt him start, his spine probably going ramrod straight at the second instance of physical affection from me. I didn't look at him again as I left the room, hand in hand with Taylor. I didn't want to see his gray skin, his ill-fitting clothes, and wonder how I had been so stupid, yet again—not to notice a parent slipping away before my very eyes. Judging by the set of Taylor's jaw, there would soon be another ghost gracing the halls of the Winchester household.

———

Taylor's car was stupid. The Jaguar F-Type Coupe was Carpathian Gray, and I knew that specifically because whenever I said just regular gray, she practically bit my head off. It looked like the fucking Batmobile, and it seemed grossly impractical to me when it just sat in the hospital parking garage for eighty hours a week, surely making all the other doctors who were drowning in student debt resentful. But she really didn't seem to care.

We drove in silence, my face pressed against the window to watch Lake Forest pass by in a blur because, like Deacon, Taylor was a terrible driver and had the worst lead foot of anyone I'd ever met. I wanted her to slow down, not only because I didn't want to end up wrapped around a tree, but I didn't want to get out of the car. The longer we were in here, moving along these winding roads and everything blurring around us, I was still in between. It was the aftertimes now, sure. But I didn't think it would feel real until I saw it in my brother's eyes, too.

I kept picturing Deacon at twenty-two; Deacon when he was grieving our mother and didn't even know it. I tried to joke about it, his lack of coping skills in general, but all he did was drink, fuck, and do drugs. It was okay at the time because he was young, and I was away at Brown and didn't have to sit with it face to face for so long; our father shut us out, and it felt okay to grieve alone, because it was the only option. But I didn't want to watch our father die by myself. We were finally at some semblance of normal, the three of us trying to be a family in the only way we knew how.

"We're here." Taylor pulled up to the curb, throwing the car into park so aggressively that I jerked forward in my seat. "He's leaving with us if I have to drag him out by the ends of his hair."

"You remember what he was like when our mother died. This is probably going to be that on steroids." I rolled my eyes, taking a measured exhale before following her out of the car.

Aux was a nicer club. There was bottle service and music that made your eardrums want to bleed, but the upper echelon of Chicago frequented it, and I knew that most of the young staff at WH spent at least one night a week here. I was still wearing my clothes from the plane—not bothering to change after the eight-hour flight—leggings and stupid New Balance sneakers Taylor assured me were all the rage, and an oversized black crewneck sweater that said, "The Bar" on it that I bought on Instagram. That, I actually liked.

The man standing at the door was impeccably dressed—a pressed black suit and impossibly polished loafers. His nostrils flared when he saw Taylor's scrubs, but his eyes landed on me, and all was forgiven. Another perk of being a Winchester. It didn't matter that I didn't meet the dress code.

"Miss Winchester, are you here to join your brother?" He asked, eyes and features impassive. I narrowed my own, searching his face for any sign of what Deacon's condition might be, but discretion was everything in this type of place.

"Here to retrieve him, actually," I said, feigning a polite smile. "Is he in the back?"

He nodded, raising his lapel to his mouth and speaking quietly into a small mic there. "Two for Winchester." He stepped to the side, pulling open the door and gesturing for us to go ahead in. A loud, grating sound of too-loud bass practically pushed me farther back onto the sidewalk. "Third booth to the left in the back."

Taylor's hand found mine again, and I squeezed once, twice, three times, before she could. She was many things—loyal to a fault, pretentious and fairly unforgiving, but Deacon was as much a part of her as I was. Her heart would be breaking in her chest for him as much as it was for me.

"I'm fine," she raised her voice over the annoying thump of music, but it sounded raspy.

I said nothing in return, each of us continuing to tug the other along, weaving through the crowds of suited young professionals and scantily clad college students. From the corner of my eye, I could see heads turning and necks craning in our direction, and even the occasional hand grabbing someone's shoulder for attention and pointing. That sort of thing used to bother me. While Taylor, Deacon, and Noa relished in it, I shrunk behind them. But since I moved, the odd time I was recognized in London, those feelings never came. I'm sure if I asked Taylor to dive back into her old psychiatry rotation notes, she would tell me that it was because I was finally learning to make a home in myself, finally comfortable in my own skin.

And I was. Not all the time, not every day, but I liked the home I was building in my own mind. I didn't spend much time ruminating on the homes I used to have—my favorite ever home with David, or the one I tried to build with Tripp that cracked the second there was pressure applied to the foundation—I was starting to like what I saw in the mirror.

But even after all this time, nothing would ever make my heart feel the way it felt around him; nothing would ever compare to those sparkling honey eyes that caught mine the second Taylor and I rounded the corner and saw who was in Deacon's booth.

Charlie

David Kennedy was leaning toward my brother, who looked seconds from passing out, the set of his jaw harsh as his mouth moved. A dove gray suit jacket sat beside him, folded on top of a ratty-looking duffle bag that tugged at my heartstrings. The arms of his navy shirt were rolled up, and the neck unbuttoned. His hair was still styled, pushed back off his forehead, and his hands were articulating, pointing at Deacon in a way I had never seen. David was never much of a hand-talker.

Taylor's fingers tightened around mine briefly, like she was waiting for the inevitable fallout at the sight of him, waiting for my pieced-back together heart, the fragments that were only sealed with freshly dried glue to fall apart, but that never came either. My heart dropped, doing its usual somersault, but instead of guilt, anguish, and utter despair, the feeling that accompanied it was joy. I was so fucking happy to see him.

I hadn't seen him since he showed up on my doorstep in New York. I could see it, feel it, just right there. His hair plastered to his forehead, feathering fingertips as he reached forward to kiss me. His smile above mine all night, his laugh wrapping around me and sinking into my skin—my bones.

His love all over me.

You're the universe that I'm just lucky to exist in.

A sound that might have been a scoff escaped my brother's mouth, and the nodding of his head at whatever David was saying was too slow. A solitary bottle of Macallan scotch sat in front of Deacon, and an alarming amount was gone. There looked to be only a finger or two in David's glass, and I was certain he wasn't responsible for the damage done to the six-hundred-dollar bottle.

Deacon's green eyes rolled upward lazily, and a sloppy grin spread over his face. "My sister's here. My only family. You ready to be an orphan, Charles?"

Taylor dropped my hand and stalked toward Deacon, snatching the bottle from his reach. "David, nice to see you. Deacon, get the fuck up now. We're leaving."

I tipped my head, the pieces of my heart threatening to shatter for an altogether different reason as I looked at my brother. "Deacon, we're going home. You're going to sleep it off, and you're going to face this like an adult. You didn't call me to come home because you needed a babysitter."

"I called you because you hate Dad, and I thought this would make you happy." Deacon's voice bordered cruel when he spoke, gesturing for Taylor to return the bottle.

Taylor and David both started at the same time, each with a raised voice. I said nothing, not because I needed them to defend me, but because my brother was so broken and so fucking sad that I didn't have room for anything else.

I moved forward, crouching beside him, and grabbed his hand. "You need a punching bag? Fine. It can be me, but it's not going to be your fucking liver."

Deacon tipped his head down, chocolate hair entirely in disarray, and cheeks flushed. He looked like a child, if children had glassy eyes and reeked of expensive liquor. "Bit rich coming from you, no? The queen of self-destruction? Everyone present has been your punching bag at one time or another." Deacon arched an eyebrow, snatching David's glass of scotch and knocking it back.

"That's enough." David's voice was low when he finally spoke.

But Deacon ignored him, only scoffing again before slumping down against the leather of the booth.

"Like I said, it can be me. But you're not going to drink yourself into a stupor." My voice was sharper this time, and my gaze met David's. "David looks more than willing to drag you out of here. How do you think Noa is going to feel when she wakes up on the other side of the world to thousands of mentions about her drunken fiancé being forcibly removed from a club by his best friend?"

The mention of Noa seemed to do the trick. His hazy eyes sharpened momentarily, and the usual playful, forest green darkened for a moment, like he couldn't believe I would bring her into it. Deacon swatted my hand away and stood, surprisingly steady. He brushed the front of his jacket off before straightening it and pointing at the bottle Taylor was still holding suspended. "You're bringing that with you. I paid for that."

Taylor raised her eyebrows, gesturing with her hand for Deacon to begin making his way to exit. "You go first, and the bottle can follow."

Deacon's eyes swung between the three of us, and he shook his head. He looked like he wanted to say something more, but David was staring at him now, his suit jacket back on, pointing with his duffel bag in the same direction as Taylor. By some small miracle, Deacon wasn't unsteady on his feet and managed to leave without causing more of a scene.

Taylor looked at me, her features softening for a moment before her eyes swiveled between David and me, and she followed Deacon, leaving us alone.

Saying nothing, David dropped the duffel bag to the floor and wrapped his arms around me. My face pressed into his chest, the warmth of his skin practically burning through the soft cotton and my favorite smell in the whole world all over me. I felt his chin against the crown of my head, and his hands were so tight around me that it was like he thought he might be the only thing keeping me together. His nose brushed the side of my face as he dropped his head, his lips warm against my ear. "I'm so sorry, Charlie. I flew in as soon as Deacon called me this afternoon."

"It's okay. I'm okay," I whispered, letting my eyelids flutter closed for just a moment before I pulled back. My hands pressed into the ridges of his back, fingers feathering against the muscles. "Thank you for coming for him."

"I came for you, too, billion dollar baby," he said, voice earnest. "I would have come if you called, too."

"I know." It was hard to pull my hands away from him. I could spend eternity mapping every inch of David Kennedy, even though his entire being was committed to memory now. Any time I touched him, it felt endlessly new, endlessly exciting. "We should go. You'll be stuck in the back of Taylor's tiny Jag with me. Deacon should probably have fast access to roll down the window."

David nodded at me, his lips tugged into a sad sort of smile, the slight lines around his eyes wrinkling. I loved them. They reminded me of how long we'd been in each other's lives. Watching David Kennedy age would be a distinct pleasure.

Neither of us seemed to want to break apart, but I took a tentative step back. He dropped his hands to my waist, spinning me around so I was facing the front of the club, guiding me toward the door. Back toward my real first home, the one that had shattered me, and was now making quick work of my brother.

———

My hair blew around my face, and the heels of my feet bumped against the stones as I kicked my legs. Deacon and I used to sneak out here to smoke weed when we were teenagers. The ledge looking out onto the lake had been the perfect refuge, hiding us thanks to the slope of the lawn. But the fact that we were never caught probably had more to do with the fact that our parents couldn't be bothered, and the staff never would have told on us. Most recently though, this became a pivotal location in my life. I had sat here alone, with Tripp, and with David. I was alone again, but I didn't really want to be.

"Charlie? You okay?"

Like I conjured him, wished him into being, David was jogging down the slope of the lawn. His suit was gone, his hair wet and curling around his ears, and I was pretty sure that was an Armani sweatsuit of Deacon's. Decidedly un-David Kennedy.

"Where's your suit?" I whispered, eyes roving him before crossing my arms and looking back at the lake.

"Your brother puked on it." David laughed, half a choke, as he dropped beside me.

A laugh escaped me too, but it was followed quickly by a sob. Because this wasn't funny, it wasn't funny at all. "I'm sorry. I'm so sorry. My family has really dragged you through it."

David shook his head, one hand shoved into his pocket until he fished out a pack of cigarettes. "I'd go through hell for you, Charlie."

I think he already had.

Tipping my head, my voice was soft. "You're smoking again?"

"Sometimes. Since you left." The cigarette hung from his lips, and a calloused thumb flicked expertly over the wheel of a lighter.

I wanted to scold him. To take the cigarette from his mouth, to take the whole pack and stomp on it, because there was no way I was going to be subjected to a world without both of my parents and without David Kennedy.

But I didn't. Because I hadn't seen him in months since I left for London, and he looked too perfect, too beautiful, illuminated by the moon. I said something else entirely. "Have you done anything else since I left? Started anything new?"

"You mean anyone?" David asked, those perfect cheeks sucking in and highlighting those equally perfect planes of his face. "No, no. I mean, I thought about trying. Entertained the idea of going on a date. But I've got a bit of a problem, Charles."

"What's that?" I whispered, staring at him, eyes eagerly, hungrily, tracing the dusting of stubble across his face.

That jawline, the one I would forever want to run my tongue across, was only bested by the way David pulled on the cigarette—how it looked between his thumb and index finger and the way the muscles in his neck tightened just so. It shouldn't have been earth-shatteringly beautiful, but it was.

"I can't come unless I'm thinking about you," David said bluntly, amber eyes swinging to meet mine. They looked the way they used to look. When it was just him and me, touching and biting and loving each other.

I couldn't stand it. If I looked for a second longer, I was going to throttle him. I was going to drown my grief in the taste of his skin, the feel of those hands, and him moving against me. I was going to kick down the front door of that home and never leave.

I dropped back, laying against the grass, wet from dew. And even though that wasn't funny at all, either, I burst out laughing. "I'm…sorry?" My whole body shook, the laughter dying and turning silent in my throat, mixing with the tears still welling in my eyes. I clapped my hand to my mouth, because it was basically just gasping sounds coming from me now.

David laid back beside me, my favorite grin falling into place. "Been a lonely few months with just my hand for company."

"I'd offer to change that for you, but I'm under significant emotional strain," I wiped the tears from the corners of my eyes.

"It's alright, billion dollar baby. I've got a whole host of memories of you I can draw from." David laughed again, bringing the cigarette to his lips once more before putting it out on the ground beside him.

I watched him, eyes following his jawline to the cords of his neck. "Do you have a favorite?"

David glanced at me sideways, offering up a hand to me. Without thinking, I laced my fingers in his. He cleared his throat, looking back up toward the stars. "Hard to pick just one, Charlie. But I think a lot about how I bent you over in my office back at WH in Chicago. Remember when we would have like ten minutes between meetings?"

My cheeks warmed, and I nodded.

There wasn't a single moment I had forgotten with David. Not those ones—where his chest pressed into my back, his hand clamped around my mouth to keep me quiet and our clothes still on—or any others. The quiet moments, where it was just whispers and kisses passing between us, laughter late into the night that echoed up into the stars where I hoped it lived forever, or those brief brushes from those perfect lips to the back of my neck when the early morning light started to stretch across the floor.

My heart swelled in my chest, but I said nothing because I still loved him, and I always would. It would be too easy to sink back into him and pretend the world wasn't out there.

"What about you?" David cleared his throat again, rubbing his jaw with his other hand. "Are you seeing anyone?"

I shook my head. "No, I haven't dated at all since I moved to London. Hard to learn to love yourself all over again when you're wrapped up in someone else."

"Did you want to date someone else?" David asked quietly.

There was more than one question there. To someone who wasn't us, maybe it would have seemed obvious—someone asking their old love if they had a new one. But it was a tentative question, one he asked me before we left. What would we do if I came back, and he still fit for me? What would we do if I came back and he didn't—like there could possibly be any part of David Kennedy that didn't fit for every version of me.

But it also referred to the third person in our relationship.

It also meant Tripp Banks.

"No, Mr. Kennedy. I didn't want to date anyone else. You'd be proud of me. I've been very busy dating myself." The words made me laugh, they were fucking ridiculous. I sounded like some sort of self-help infomercial. But they were true.

"I'm always proud of you, Charlie." David brought my hand to his lips, pressing them there briefly. "Can I ask if you've talked to Tripp?"

I closed my eyes, heart hurting for an entirely different reason, because despite everything—despite how abrasive all his edges were, how close to a real-life movie villain Tripp was, all the ways he let me down—my heart hurt because a part of it was for him. He was my friend and more, and his heart was hurting too, somewhere out there in the world.

"Of course, you can ask. The answer is no. I text him, I try to call, to check in. He never answers. Deac told me that he's working with his brother at the bank now. His dad still hasn't come back, but that's it."

David ran his mouth along the back of my hand again, and I felt him nodding against it. We lapsed into silence, nothing but the sound of the waves washing against the worn rocks on the shore, our mingled breathing, and the occasional hoot of a distant owl.

"I'm so sorry about your dad, Charlie." He finally spoke, tugging me closer and tucking me into the crook of his neck. "I'm going to stay in Chicago for a bit. I'll work from the office here. I'm worried about your brother. Is that okay with you? If I'm around?"

"Of course," I whispered into his skin, my eyes burning and all the unshed tears threatening to fall. "What Deacon said... it's not true. I never hated him, despite how much I wanted to. How much I hated what he did to me, how he forgot my mother. I've never hated him for a single second of a single minute of a single day in my life. I wish I could take it all back. I feel like I have no right to scream, to cry."

David pressed his lips to the side of my head. "He's your father. You can cry, billion dollar baby."

And so I did.

Deacon

I didn't make a habit of ignoring Noa's phone calls. I usually went out of my way to answer them, no matter how inopportune the time, actually. I'd paused meetings with arguably some of the most important people in the world just to hear her voice.

I used to tell Charlie my favorite sound in the world was the swipe of the Winchester Holdings' Amex Centurion. It wasn't a joke, not really. There were few things in my life I valued more than our family business. My sister. The vintage Audemars Piguet Royal Oak our father gave me when I graduated from Yale, and he told me he was proud of me for the first and only time in my life. The picture of our mother, smiling, when she was twenty-one on some random beach on Cape Cod no one knew about in my wallet.

Those were about the only things I would have run into a burning building for, having been a fairly big proponent of self-preservation at all costs. The only things I really cared more about than money.

Taylor once used me as a case study for some project she needed to present in a psychiatry tutorial or something. It was a poorly veiled fake version of me. She named the patient Beacon Hemsfield. All those colleagues of hers diagnosed "me" with a poorly developed attachment and shades of narcissistic personality disorder really fucking quickly. She and Charles had a huge laugh over it at my expense.

Apparently, I put so much value in the business, in money, because it was where I got all the validation and approval required for a child, seeing as my father certainly didn't provide any, and my mother didn't love me enough to want to live.

But it was all of those things that mattered the most to me, and then the things that mattered about the same as Winchester Holdings, and the things I loved but mattered slightly less. My sister would debate this fact, but I would burn my entire closet of custom Brunello Cucinelli suits if it meant we got to keep Winchester Holdings. It's the only thing I ever really was. A Winchester. And I thought it was the only thing I ever wanted to be.

Until I heard Noa Dahan speak. Heard her voice carry over everyone else around the table, all raspy. Saw those amber eyes light up, despite the arguably poor lighting in Catch. She was down the table from me, maybe four or five models away. It was a whole group of them. I was in New York for a meeting, and Taylor was there for a conference. She asked if I wanted to have dinner with her and some friends. It was when Charlie was back in London—for the first time. David declined the invitation when I asked him to join me, telling him it was a room full of probably the most beautiful women on the planet. He told me the most beautiful woman on the planet was currently in exile somewhere in England and hung up on me.

I went anyway, giving Taylor the perfunctory hug and kiss I always did. She was our childhood best friend, kind of like my sister, but in less of a biological way, because I'd seen her naked and been part of too many of her formative sexual experiences. She introduced me to everyone at the table, and Noa barely spared me a glance, only smiling politely and raising her eyebrows before turning back to the person across from her. They were mid-conversation about something, and Noa leaned forward, her eyes only for them and all her attention rapt.

I sat at the other end of the table and watched when she tipped her head back in laughter. It was too fucking loud—our etiquette instructor would have had a fit and died in it if she ever saw Charlie laugh like that. All throaty and her mouth open in a way that probably bordered undignified, but all it did was make me realize I wanted her to look at me like that.

I wanted her attention on me, and I wanted it all over me. It was like I just imagined her into being. Objectively, yes, she was one of the most beautiful women I'd ever seen. She still was, and always would be.

But it was everything else. The way her lips moved when she spoke, her eyes lighting up, the way her shoulders shook when she laughed. She just seemed so...alive. More than anyone I'd ever met before.

I texted Taylor, eyes wide and pointedly looking at Noa's end of the table until she sighed, rolling her eyes in exasperation and making up some excuse as to why everyone around the table needed to move. She was a commanding enough presence to make it happen. Noa ended up next to me. Taylor introduced us—making some offhand, entirely socially inept comment about how we both had dead parents, so we had a lot in common—and flitted off down to the other end of the table and left us alone.

Noa sat down, turned to me, and smiled politely, her eyes crinkling at the corner in a way that told me she loved her parents more than I ever loved mine, and that they loved her probably a lot more than mine ever loved me. And she asked me to tell her something about myself.

I started to tell her I was the vice president of finance at WH. She snorted, rolled her eyes, cocked her head, and told me to pick something real, or she'd move back to the other end of the table.

I told her there were three things I'd run into a burning building for—my sister, the watch, the photograph no one knew about before that moment.

She stayed in her seat, and I fell in love.

She became the thing I'd stop it all for, run into the burning building for—stop being a Winchester at any time for. The person whose calls I'd always, always answer.

But apparently, all that went out the window the second my father told me he was sick, had been before, and that soon I'd be nothing but an adult orphan.

My phone was ringing, Noa's face illuminated on the lock screen. Not one of the editorial or cover prints that hung in my office in New York or the one I still kept in Chicago. It was a photo she sent me—her skin covered in some sort of mud and these giant, Chanel eye masks taking up half her cheeks.

I didn't know what to say, and I hadn't since he called me and delivered the news, like he was discussing a particularly unpleasant dip in the stock market. I'd been in my office in New York, saw his name pop up on my phone and assumed it was about anything else. A secret cancer diagnosis and its recurrence hadn't been top of mind for me, but I ended up back in Chicago all the same.

Noa was in Tahiti, doing some branding shoot for a new luxury resort that had opened up there. It wasn't her main interest when it came to modeling, but she'd never been to Tahiti, and a few of her friends were doing it, too.

Instead of answering, instead of being an adult and the person I wanted to be, not only for her—but for my sister, for me—for everyone else in my life, I silenced the phone and threw it against the wall. It would probably damage the paint, maybe even the drywall, judging by the sound it made, but I didn't care.

Scrubbing my hands across my face, I fell backward onto the stupid four-poster, mahogany king bed and the impeccably pressed gray sheets tucked into it. I usually liked this bed, felt important in it as a kid, who was far too young for a bed this large—but it was just empty like most things in our life actually were.

I was too drunk to talk to her anyway. No one wanted to hear their fiancé sound like my voice surely did. I'd already thrown up on David, and he was gone when I got out of the shower. Not that it had helped. Everything still felt like it was lurching. I'd polished off half the Macallan before David arrived, and I don't know where Taylor took the bottle, even if it was probably for the best. But she better not have dumped it down the sink or something like that. She was fucking vindictive, and she had been since we were kids.

"You should answer her, Deac."

A strangled groan crawled up my throat with the taste of old whiskey, and I scrubbed my face again before sitting up, my vision shaky and blurry at the edges. David stood in the doorway, leaning against the frame with his arms crossed. His hair was still damp, and he was wearing my fucking Armani sweatsuit.

"Fuck off, David." I shook my head, pushing up, and my lip curling as I looked at him. "You work things out with my sister, yet? Let her off the mat, or you still too busy being a righteous prick?"

Tripp was right about one thing. David could be a holier-than-thou asshole when he wanted to be.

David shook his head, nostrils flaring, and I knew I crossed the line. He was my best friend, had been from the moment I met him, and he always would be—but he drew a very fucking firm line in the sand at anything that came within spitting distance of disparaging my sister.

Before he could answer and level me with what would surely be some sort of virtuous sermon on how my sister deserved better than me and always had, footsteps sounded in the hallway.

I'd know those footsteps anywhere. They were as self-righteous as their fucking owner.

Taylor appeared beside David, her lips pursed and looking entirely displeased as she held up an IV bag. "Thought you might want one of these."

If it were possible, my lip would have curled up farther. "You can fuck off, too, Taylor."

"Hey," David cut in, those eyes my sister was obsessed with narrowing in on me. "You're drunk, Deac. Sleep it off."

I understood the obsession with someone's eyes after meeting Noa. I think her eyes to me were probably what David's were to Charlie, but I wasn't about to admit that. Not when those two idiots were looking at me like I was somehow beneath them.

"You two here to tell me something about Charles? Why is it always about her? You're both here to tell me I need to be better for Charlie, to be this or that for Charlie. What about me? What if I need to be this way for me?" The words were out of my mouth before I could stop them.

I didn't believe them, not really. I thought my sister deserved the world and more, that fact would never change. But I hated the way they were looking at me almost as much as I hated the way I felt—all alone in the fucking universe.

David shook his head, pushing off the wall, looking at me before he turned away, something like pity stretching across his face. "I'm not do-ing this tonight. Not when you're like this. We can talk in the morning. I'll be in the guest wing."

"If you knew anything at all, Deacon, you'd know things have hardly been about Charlie a day in her life. And things have hardly been about you a day in yours, either. It's not a competition." Taylor arched one eyebrow, surveying me, and the disdain clear across her features before she turned on her heel and followed David down the hallway.

I pushed off the bed and walked across the room to grab my phone—the wall *was* damaged—and dropped back in a stupid leather armchair that also had no business in what had been a child's room to make a phone call that was out of spite more than it was out of anything else.

I fucking hated the way they were looking at me, but I hated myself more.

Tripp

It was generally frowned upon to live at home as an adult and certainly to move back home after a foray into the real world. At least in Beacon Hill and the circles my family ran in. But there was something uniquely pathetic about moving back home at thirty-one so you could keep an eye on your father, fresh off multiple SEC violations, to make sure he didn't stray too far past the property line and have his ankle monitor alert the neighbors that there was a felon in their midst.

And thanks to the endless reach of the Winchester arm, no one would ever know because Steven did what men like him do best and buried any inkling of the story before it was reported in any news outlet, financial or otherwise.

It didn't help that after close to a fucking decade, I was finally, finally getting somewhere with Chuck. But my dad and his penchant for investing money that didn't belong to him and colluding with too many major sports books to try and earn even more ruined that before it had the chance to get off the ground. If I actually looked at any of it with a critical eye, I'd know it was over the minute I left her in that bed when she was twenty and I was twenty-two, and it was certainly fucking over when David fucking Kennedy strolled into her life.

It was funny, ironic—whatever the word for it really was—to think about. I knew Chuck, and I knew David, and they existed in separate parts of my life. She was my forever dream, the most beautiful girl I'd ever known, the one that got away, my adolescent fascination that took up too much real estate in my mind close to a decade later. He was the one who somehow excelled at STRAT and passed all his data science exams when he'd been up drinking until four a.m. the night before and somehow skated through every single interaction with one of those grating, easy grins he was always throwing about.

It never would have occurred to me they'd become so...intertwined in their own lives, let alone that the three of us would enter into a toxic snake pit love triangle worthy of a TV drama.

Not that there was much of a triangle anymore. As far as I knew, we no longer met the definition. Chuck was in London because she preferred it to living in Oxford, taking the train in every day and pretending she wasn't as stuck up as she was, Kennedy was in New York, and I was here—in my parent's Beacon Hill home that had grown so much in value through the last two real estate booms, it was worth a cool $31 million. That alone should have placated my father, but here we were.

I could hear him from where I was in the kitchen, palms on the granite counter, waiting for the espresso machine to finish. The entertainment room, where the majority of my father's illegal betting activity took place, was just down the stairs off the kitchen.

The sounds of ESPN were hardly discernible beyond his shouting.

Exhaling, I scrubbed my face and glanced out at the stone courtyard that led out from the kitchen, barely visible against the setting sun.

I made the mistake of coming home from the office before midnight, which was usually around the time my father dragged himself from his self-imposed prison to his room on the top floor of the house. He and my mother stopped sharing a bed years ago, but they cohabitated well enough. I didn't even know where my mother was most of the time. She kept well away from the house during daylight hours, doing whatever it was she did to fill up her social calendar, and taking in more reformer Pilates than was probably recommended for someone her age.

We rarely saw one another either, save for awkward family dinners, or when there was a rare evening when we would sit upstairs together and watch Geordie Shore. It would only last a few episodes before she would smile softly, the only affection she ever deigned to show. She would lean over and pat my cheek before excusing herself and going upstairs to the rooms she kept for herself.

My brother made himself scarce, rarely coming home and lording it over everyone from his new position in our father's old office at the bank. If I didn't know any better, I would have guessed he was the one who reported our father. It's not like we'd ever been one of those families—one who supported one another, showered each other with unconditional love. It was a pretty constant state of trying to undermine everyone else to get ahead over here.

It was just me, my mom, and the sound of my father's failed dreams and addiction to ESPN. Which was getting way too fucking loud, and I had a lot of work left to do, cleaning up after one of several messes he left across too many client accounts.

Fingers tensing against the counter, I turned and started down the stairs before I could think better of it.

And there he was. The man that had ruined my life in more ways than one. It wasn't even the fact that he sat there with eyes that were unfortunately an exact replica of mine, not bothering to look away from whatever ESPN replay he was stuck on. It wasn't the way he leaned forward—the sleeves of the pressed Brooks Brothers shirt he was wearing for God knew what reason pushed up his forearms, and the tailored Tom Fords—without a care in the world that the shell of his wife, the home he built for her before he got greedy or showed his true colors—towered above him. It wasn't the thirty-one-million-dollars'-worth of real estate, or the inane way he looked far too casual on a one-of-a-kind antique leather couch. It wasn't even the fact that he looked like me. Or, that I looked exactly like him. He was obviously older, but both my brother and I were spitting images of him. Down to the unforgiving eyes, the hair that remained untouched by age, and the punchable, triangular shape to his jaw.

It was the fact that we were the fucking same. We both ruined everything we touched and wanted, all the things we couldn't have. For him, it was more money than he was entitled to, and for me, it was a girl who already belonged to someone else.

He didn't even bother to look at me as I stepped off the landing of the stairs. My eyes flicked to the TV. Football. That was his preferred bet. Shaking my head, I cut in front of the TV, and a noise of ire rose in his throat as I smashed the power button with unnecessary force to turn it off before gesturing toward the now blank screen. "Can you fucking not? You don't need to be watching the thing that caused your spectacular fall from grace at all hours."

Raising his eyebrows, he leaned back against the couch, the unforgiving leather barely buckling as he crossed his arms. "This is my home, Tripp. You don't get to tell me what I can and cannot do within it."

His home and his jail. A convenient location to face house arrest when he had rooms upon rooms to escape in. And when you're rich, it hardly matters that you can't leave the house. He could have whatever he wanted delivered to his doorstep within minutes. He was still pulling strings at the bank, puppeteering and lording over Post the way he always had.

He wore it well. A minor inconvenience at best, hardly a crease in any of his freshly pressed clothes.

"Yeah, the only reason you're here—" I gestured toward his ankle monitor, visible below the hem of those tailored Tom Ford's he had no business fucking wearing, my voice rising, "—and not rotting away behind a cell somewhere is because Steven Winchester did us all a fucking favor and didn't want his daughter tied to anything to do with you in the media."

It was true. I didn't think for a second that Steven paid whatever exorbitant amounts of money he paid to keep my father's unfortunate downfall out of the media due to any scrap of affection for me. I called him, not even for Chuck's sake. I called because I worked for WH, and I was loyal to him, despite what the majority of the staff thought about me, considering I tried to steal another member of leadership's girlfriend right out from under him—it would have looked fucking horrible.

A scoff sounded from my father's throat, and he shook his head. "I wouldn't be rotting away in a cell, Tripp. Money can do many things, and one of those includes escaping traditional incarceration."

He'd always been a fucking prick. Maybe that was where I inherited it. Bred right into me from the moment of conception. "You don't have Winchester money, nor do you have Winchester strings to pull."

"And how unfortunate for you that it also meant the end of your little tryst." My father arched an eyebrow, lips pulling into a tight line.

"Just another thing I'll add to the lengthy list of things I have to thank you for." My nostrils flared, and I felt my jaw start to tense. I pointed back toward the TV. "Turn on something else. Learn to paint. Meditate. Find Jesus. I don't give a fuck what you do—but this is how you got yourself into this mess, and I'm not going to sit here any longer while you rot."

"You're my son. You don't tell me what to do."

"You know what?" I started, but the vibration of my phone against my thigh in the pocket of my own Tom Ford's caused me to look down. Pulling it out, Deacon Winchester's name illuminated on the screen.

My eyebrows came together. We texted, often. But he hardly ever called. He wouldn't call, actually. He'd deem himself far too important for that unless something was wrong. I smacked the button on the bottom of the TV with my other hand, the sound of ESPN starting up again before I turned away from my father. "You're right. Rot for all I fucking care."

Charlie

Two IV poles sat in the dining room, each at opposite ends of the stately, absolutely ridiculous mahogany table that stretched practically the entire room. One was attached to my father, pumping God knows what into him. I hadn't asked Taylor what it was when I knew he was still refusing chemo. And the other was attached to my brother, pumping him full of his anti-hangover vitamin blend, courtesy of his old friends at Hydra-V.

They sat at opposite ends, our father staring unblinkingly at Deacon with his hands folded in front of him, waiting. And Deacon sat, irreverently slumped with one arm draped over the back of the equally ridiculous matching chairs, lips pursed and eyes glinting with ire.

Taylor sat beside me, refusing to look at Deacon in a display the likes of which I hadn't seen since we were all teenagers. David was across from me, having dropped into his seat with a soft smile just for me and a quick wink that was meant to be reassuring, but made my heart beat against my ribcage so aggressively that I thought it might break one. Taylor's father was beside him, flipping through more notes in my father's chart, like this wasn't the weirdest breakfast he had ever been to. The staff bustled around us, setting the table and pouring coffee, someone going as far as to drop a bottle of vintage Veuve and freshly squeezed orange juice in the middle of the table.

I cleared my throat and shifted in my seat, parting my lips to say something, anything, when Deacon's phone started ringing. The ringtone could only belong to one person.

The song "Sexy Can I" blasted at an alarming volume from his phone where it sat, face down on the table. Deacon never looked away from our father, thumb silencing the sound without ever breaking stride.

"Your ringtone for Noa is a song by Ray J? That song?" I said, rolling my eyes. For anyone else, it would have been unbelievable. But for my brother, it fit.

"Oh my God, you are so fucking lame, Deacon!" Taylor hissed, finally breaking her reverie to glare at my brother.

"Good one, Taylor. You speaking to me now?" Deacon asked dryly, drumming his fingers on the table and raising his eyebrows at her.

I knew it was more for our father to try and get under his skin, to get him to crack and speak first. But Steven Winchester continued to stare at his son, utterly silent.

"Only to say that." She crossed her arms stubbornly and looked away from him again. "Oh, and one last thing. You're a fucking child. Thirty-one years old and still running from your problems? Noa is a lucky woman."

"Hey!" I bit out, turning to her and widening my eyes. "Leave it. He's here now."

Her steadfast loyalty seemed to only be for me this morning; she was furious with Deacon for what he said to me last night and his seeming abandonment of me.

Deacon flashed her a cat-like grin, almost baring his teeth, but our father finally had enough, a fist slamming down on the table, signaling the end of whatever the hell was happening here.

"Enough." His voice was firm. His skin was the same sickly shade of gray as yesterday, looking even more tired and drawn. Like he hadn't slept. "It's time for us to have a discussion."

"Time might have been about a decade ago when you had cancer in the first place and decided to refuse chemo, but hey, who am I to say?" Deacon's voice was bitter, each word sharp and punctuated, ment to dig into our father, but I knew him better than anyone in the world. Those sharp edges were just pieces of a broken heart.

"I don't have to explain my decision to you, Deacon. And, in fact, I won't be explaining myself. I made a decision that was the best for my children and my business at the time. There is simply nothing more to it. There's no sense in continuing to try and goad me. It's nothing any of us at this table can change." Our father's voice was clipped, matter-of-fact the way it always was. He could have been talking about the weather.

Deacon stood, slamming both his hands down on the table with so much force that his IV line slipped out, a spray of vitamins and saline jetting out and all over the table. "Then explain this. You're one of the richest people on this planet, and you're just *accepting* this? Accepting the fact that these two told you it's over?" He gestured to Taylor and Dr. Breen, who finally looked up from my father's file.

Taylor looked poised to rip Deacon's throat out, as if it had been some sort of direct insult at her medical pedigree.

"It's not just the two of us, Deacon." Dr. Breen spoke, his voice soothing. I could picture him sitting in his office, delivering this type of news so often that it was down to a perfect little, world-destroying science. "I'm holding assessments from colleagues at Cleveland Clinic, Johns Hopkins, my former mentor at MD Anderson, and two separate Mayo Clinics. Some of the best cancer centers in the entire world. They're all saying it, too."

"Then get another fucking opinion!" Deacon slammed his hands down again, his scream reverberating off all of the perfectly polished surfaces in the room, deepening the cracks in the foundation of our family and this godforsaken house.

"Where do you suggest I go?" Our father asked, one eyebrow arched.

Deacon looked incredulous, eyes swinging wildly back and forth between Taylor, David, and me, like one of us was about to jump up and demand the same thing, demand that the malignant cells in our father's body listen to us because we were Winchesters, and we had already lost one parent. Two would simply be too many. His eyes darkened when he looked at me, a derisive snort escaping his nose. Our nose. "China. Russia. Canada. Thailand. Mexico. I don't give a fuck. Find the most brilliant oncologist in the world and fund your own clinical trial. You have the means to do something. More than almost anyone else in the world, and you're doing nothing. You're seriously going to let it kill you before you're even sixty? You're not going to fucking do anything?"

"No." Our father raised his eyes to Deacon, his gaze flat and words steady. But he looked away quickly, eyes finding my own where they softened, something like an apology there.

"Unbelievable." Deacon began pulling at the butterfly clip that was left in his vein, yanking it out to reveal a tiny spurt of blood. "You're just like fucking mom. You two deserve each other."

"Deacon!" I shouted, pleaded really, standing to reach my hand out, like he might take it the way he did when we were children. Like I could guide him back to me, sit him down, soothe him, and tell him it would be alright. That it would always be okay as long as we had each other. But his lip curled up at me, and he shook his head, snatching his phone from the table. I watched as he turned his back on me, on our father, and slammed the door to the room so loudly that the artwork on the walls rattled.

Thick, uncomfortable silence, save for the continued ringing in my ears, fell across the room. I was still standing there with my hand held out uselessly.

David cleared his throat, eyes only for me when he stood. "I'll go get him."

"He's a grown man, David. Give him enough rope, he'll hang himself." My father bit out. His gaze moved back to the door momentarily before he cleared his throat.

David glanced at me, his jaw tight and all those beautiful features strained.

I smiled softly and shrugged. "Go after him if you want. Make sure he doesn't wrap his Bentley around a tree."

David's knuckles tensed where he gripped the back of the chair, and the honey in his eyes darkened to an amber. He didn't want to leave me here alone.

I jerked my chin again toward the door. "Go, he's your best friend."

His eyes swept over me one more time before he turned, opened the door, and slipped out into the hallway.

Silence fell again, and I found myself looking at my father, and instead of the endless expanse that usually stretched between us, it was like looking at a laughing clock face; time was mocking us both, because at that very moment, his body, his soul, his very person was dying.

"I guess we should talk," I whispered. My eyes began to sting, my father's outline blurred.

He studied me for a moment, neck muscles growing taut. I watched my father open and close his mouth, words failing him for perhaps the first time in forever when he gave a nod toward Dr. Breen.

I sat as my best friend's father began to pull out various pieces of paper, photographs of my father's insides, followed by scribbled notes from world leaders in oncology that all said the same thing: no hope, no hope, no hope.

———

My childhood bedroom had changed over the years. From a ridiculous canopy bed that had no business in a seven-year-old's room, to an empty room that collected dust when my parents shipped Deacon and me off to boarding school. But it had remained the same since I left for college at eighteen. Even after the dissolution of our family, my father never altered it, preserving it like I might come back at any second.

I stood in the doorway, the bed I left rumpled and unmade this morning now neatly tucked into all corners by some staff member or another, the pillows fluffed and propped up perfectly. The bed was too big for me at eighteen, and it was too big for me now, the duvet an outlandish cloud of feather bedding, and the pillows over-large for one person. I always felt like I could disappear in there. And I wanted to disappear.

I padded across the carpet, dropping down onto the bed, and the duvet puffed up around me, practically shielding me from the outside world. Rolling my shoulders back, I pushed them into the cushion. I wanted the shield to go higher, to wrap all around me, because words like malignant, chemotherapy, nodule, and ostomy were biting at my skin, tearing in and burrowing their way into my bones. Pressing my palms into my eyes, a guttural noise that would have sent my etiquette teacher running for the hills swept from my throat. And they didn't stop coming. Warm tears were somehow escaping through the pressure of my palms, trailing down my cheeks and along my jaw, down the column of my throat.

The weight of the mattress shifted beside me, and a body settled onto the bed. I didn't have to open my eyes; I would know the exact weight and shape of David Kennedy for the rest of my life.

He said nothing, but he laid there, fingers skating over my jawline while I wanted to sink into the mattress and be swallowed whole. Maybe die like my father was dying. But he smelled like the ocean, and his skin was so warm. Maybe David Kennedy was the sun. My sun.

Gasping loudly, I scrubbed my eyes with my palms, my words punctuated with wet, rasping noises, "Did you find Deacon?"

His voice was harsh, words heavy with disapproval. "Yeah, he's working his way to the bottom of a bottle of Scotch down by the boat house."

"I don't know what to do," I whispered, finally opening my eyes and blinking. I could faintly see the blurred outline of David where he laid, propped up on one hand.

A pained look stretched across his face, honey eyes swirling with something I couldn't place before sweeping over my body. "There's nothing you can do, Charlie."

I finally turned my neck, my wet cheek sticking to the surely ridiculous thread count pillow. My eyes found his, and on impulse, I reached up, stopping midway to his shoulders, fingers waiting uselessly in space. I wanted to touch him. I dreamt about him all the time. Those were the best dreams—the ones where I was in love with myself, fully completely, but he was there, too.

David grabbed my hand, his fingers enveloping mine. He brushed his lips across them before placing my palm against his heart. "You can always touch me, Charlie. Can I touch you?"

I nodded, closing my eyes when the weight of his hand dropped to my hip. The warmth of his hand—of him—seeped down through my shirt, into my skin. My own personal anchor to keep me from drifting away. I kept my eyes closed, breathing in and out, the tears beginning to dry against my skin. I felt David's lips lightly move across my forehead before stopping on the crown of my head, his thumb brushing up toward my ribcage softly. I could have laid here forever, and it would have been the easiest thing to do, to pretend none of it was out there. But that wasn't who I was anymore, and it wasn't who I wanted to be.

"This is so fucked up," I finally whispered. "I was just getting him back. We we're just trying to fix things—I was just—"

"I know," David murmured against my hair. "I know. It's not fair."

"Why does everyone leave me?" My voice cracked. "I'm trying to be better. I'm trying to love myself and to like myself, and I just don't understand. What did I do wrong?"

"Nothing, billion dollar baby, you did nothing wrong." David's voice was strained. "You know that, logically. You deserve two healthy, happy parents, and you deserve a brother who can show up for you when you need him."

Shaking my head, I choked out a laugh. "Don't. Don't be mad at Deacon. I'm beginning to think he might be more fucked up than me."

David scoffed, and I felt his mouth move against my hair, like he was going to interject, but I continued. "You're his best friend. He needs you too."

David pulled back, finally letting go of my waist and gripping my chin. His thumb pushed my face up to his, those honey eyes not sparkling at all, but hard and endlessly serious. "You're my priority. Your brother knows that. We had it out over it already. He's not very happy with me right now, but I don't really fucking care."

"David, I don't want you two to fight."

"We aren't fighting. He agreed to sit down and talk with you and your dad tomorrow. You three need to talk about WH. You'll have some decisions to make." David tipped his head, hair curling against his forehead.

Before I could stop myself, I reached out and began to twirl one between my thumb.

A grin slid into place on David's face. "I'm going to need you to stop looking at me like that. I know this might be wrong, but my mind is running fucking wild right now. Being in your bed with you like this...this close to you."

"What are you thinking about?" I whispered, unable to help myself.

"My head between your legs," David said plainly, eyes darkening. "I think about that a lot. I'd go down on you in a heartbeat if you wanted me to."

Flames fanned across my cheeks, and for some unknown reason, I burst out laughing. I was becoming the queen of misplaced laughter because there was absolutely nothing funny about what David was offering and the way he was looking at me. "I'm sorry, I'm sorry it's not funny."

A grin stretched across his face, and his eyes glinted. "If I remember correctly, you never used to find that funny. I can show you how serious I am if you'd like."

I shook my head, tiny breaths interspersed with laughter tumbling from me. "No, no. I mean. I wish, but I can't do those things with you right now. It would be too easy."

"Are you saying I'm easy?" David asked, feigning mock indignation, the grin never slipping from his face.

"No. Despite the fact that you're offering to service me at the drop of a hat," I smiled softly at him, "I can't use you to drown my grief. To pretend the world isn't out there. It would be too easy to bury myself in you."

David tipped his head, his eyes now solely pupil. "I think I'd be the one doing the burying in that scenario, Charles. But it's just an orgasm. No harm, no foul." Continuing to grin down at me, he pushed back, and before I could say anything, his hands were on my thighs, pulling me in one fluid motion toward the end of the bed.

A tiny gasp escaped me, followed by a laugh that bordered on a shriek.

He was kneeling between my legs, looking down at me. One hand pressed into my left thigh, and the other swept through his hair, pushing it off his face. "Say the word, billion dollar baby. I'll be whatever you need me to be."

I stared up at him, the most beautiful boy in the entire world. I loved him, I loved him, I loved him. That was an irrefutable fact. No matter where I was or who I was, I would always love David Kennedy. But I wanted to love myself more. I swallowed, lips remaining parted. "This isn't real, David. Nothing's changed... I liked my life in London. Liked myself, maybe for the first time ever."

He started, his head pulling back and his eyebrows creasing. "This has always been, and always will be real." He bent down over me, elbows propping him up on either side of my face, and I could feel him pressing between my thighs. "Never doubt that. Ever."

"That's not what I meant," I whispered uselessly, staring up into the endless expanse of sparkling honey. His nose was inches from mine, and if I just tipped up my chin, my lips would have brushed his. "I never expected this. I wanted to be on my own. I was trying. I told you I was trying. And now all I want to do is touch you and love you and fuck you. And it just feels..."

"Too easy," David whispered back, understanding dawning on his face. Exhaling through his nose, he dropped his forehead to mine. "I'm sorry. I just wanted you to feel good. Even if it was just for a few moments. But I hear you. No sex."

"No sex," I echoed. "I'll drown myself in you, David."

"I can't have that. You're still my favorite person I've ever known." David smiled, his voice whispering past my ears. "But I don't want to leave you, not like this. Can I stay here? I'll keep to my side of the bed. I promise."

I found myself smiling too, pressing my forehead into his, his lips still a breath away. "You want to have a sleepover with me?"

"I think I do," David's lips brushed the top of my nose before he pushed off me. He shifted on the bed to settle against the insane display of pillows and gestured to the stupidly large TV mounted to the wall across from the bed. "We can stay up and watch a movie. Maybe one that's going to kill the hard-on I've got going so I don't try to pounce on you."

Rolling onto my side, I propped my head on my elbow and smiled at him. "Do we need to put a pillow between us? That might be for the best."

David grinned, and he held out one of those perfect, calloused hands to haul me up to sitting. Wrapping an arm around my shoulders, he pulled me flush against his chest. I could feel how warm he was, how hard all those ridges of muscle and sharp edges were that made up David Kennedy.

Dropping my head to his shoulder, I felt his lips press against my hair for a brief moment before he started flicking through the TV channels.

My eyelids were thick and heavy from all the tears. It wasn't long before the brush of David's thumb against my shoulder had them falling closed, and the whisper of his voice telling me to sleep had my heartbeat slowing and my breathing evening out.

I could faintly feel my fingers twitch against his chest, my mind swimming in that hazy in-between of not quite awake and not quite asleep, and I could have sworn the words "I love you" wove their way into my ears, all the way into my brain and added some extra glue to the fragile broken shards of my heart.

———

Something was vibrating beside me. My eyes flew open, milky light from the moon casting shadows all over my room and stretching across the white bedding where David and I were tangled in the sheets.

The TV was still playing, but he must have turned down the volume at some point. One arm was slung above my head, the other stretched across his chest with an open palm, like it was waiting for my hand.

I blinked, one hand groping for the phone, all too aware the last time I answered the phone like this—my brother had been on the other line, and it had been the beginning of the end for our father.

Flipping the phone over, a Boston area code flashed on the screen and my heart dropped. I kicked off the sheets, swinging my legs over the edge of the bed and practically sprinted across the padded carpet to the ensuite bathroom at the other end of the room. I threw open the door with more aggression than I closed it, practically bouncing back and forth on the balls of my feet, hoping the call wouldn't drop before I could answer. This bathroom was as ridiculous as everything else in my father's house, but I didn't have time to look at the matte black finish and marble in disdain. My shoulders hit the back of the door, and I slid down to the floor, finally clicking the answer button and pressing the phone to my ear.

"You okay, Chuck?"

I clapped a hand to my mouth, crying for an altogether different reason now. Because Tripp Banks was calling me, and that stupid lilt to his voice was there, just out of my reach on the other end of the phone.

"Are *you* okay?" I asked, my voice half a laugh, half a sob, a new sound that was quickly becoming a permanent fixture in my life.

That question was met with a belated silence, and I wondered if he would hang up. Or if it would just go ignored, unanswered, like all the other messages over the last months.

"I'm not the one with a dying parent." His voice was guarded, and I could picture his frozen eyes, like they were right in front of me, not the stupid glass waterfall sink in my bathroom. "Deac called me. He sounded a little worse for the wear."

"Most of his time seems to be spent in a bottle of scotch these days," I deadpanned, but I rubbed at my chest. Seeing my brother like this hurt my heart.

"I wanted to call to tell you I'm sorry. For all sorts of things." His voice was rough, and just underneath those words, I could hear the last ones he spoke to me—all hurt and anger, the two of us standing together picking at each other's open wounds on the steps of my townhouse in New York. I fucking missed that house. Tripp swallowed before continuing. "And that I love you. I've always loved you. I know you asked me to be there for you. To show you I could be reliable and wouldn't leave you. I wasn't reliable then, and I can't be reliable now. I can't come back to Chicago. And I need you to know that has nothing to do with you."

"I wish you would tell me if you're okay. Tell me what's going on. You can trust me. I wouldn't tell anyone, Tripp." My voice dropped to a useless whisper when I said his name. The other half of my heart was just beyond the other side of the closed door.

Tripp was silent, and I pushed the phone against my ear, desperate for something—anything—because I cared about him, too. I loved him, too. A low exhale finally came on the other end of the line. "Don't worry about me, Chuckles. It doesn't become of you. You call if you need me, okay? I can't promise I can be there for you in person, but I'm just a phone call away."

"You're going to answer this time?" I asked, wanting to sound bitter, but I think I sounded a bit hopeful instead.

"Yeah, I'll answer this time." I could hear the wryness, the almost-lilt to his voice through the phone, and my lips twitched at the corners. "I have to go. I love you, Chuck."

Tripp hung up before I could even think to answer, think to say anything back. Maybe he was afraid of what I might say, because he could never understand that when I left him—left David—it wasn't a choice between them. It wasn't about either of them. Before I could think otherwise, my thumbs were moving across the screen of my phone, telling him the truth as I understood it.

I love you, too.

I loved myself first. I came first, and I knew that now to be an irrefutable fact. But I loved him, and I loved David, and I wondered if my heart would always be split in two.

David

There was a time in my life when I took waking up next to Charlie Winchester for granted. It wasn't that they weren't the best mornings of my entire life—they were, far surpassing any quiet morning on the water back home, the ones I used to cherish more than anything.

I remember the first time I woke up with her. She let me stay in her bed after three bottles of wine on her terrace. The night we decided to try it for real. I had a horrible fucking headache, but I remember the weight of her. The exact way she fell into me naturally. The way her cheeks looked soft when she was asleep, her hair fanning all over the pillow, her eyelids fluttering, and keeping those fucking otherworldly green eyes hidden.

I remember thinking it was a feeling I wanted for the rest of my life.

I knew I needed to know her the first minute she walked into the office in Chicago, trailing behind her brother and father, her features schooled into a mask of bored indifference, arms crossed and surveying everything with vague displeasure.

But it was like I could see right through her, even back then. Because the second she saw anyone on staff, whether she was hugging them hello or shaking their hand for the first time, she smiled, and her eyes lit up. Her lips would part, and she would nod along, her attention entirely rapt with whatever it was they were saying. She was nothing like her brother and certainly nothing like her father.

And then she stopped at my office, uncrossed her arms, and stuck her hand out to me. She was being polite—a firm, Winchester first impression handshake—but she smiled, and my heart fell out of my chest. I knew I was going to love her the first time I saw her roll her eyes behind Deacon's back and make a face at him like she was a small child when he left her office.

There were a million other tiny moments between then and now, all the things that stitched her into me. If I looked back, it was probably the utter certainty that she was meant for me, and I was meant for her; the fact that she was all over me, combined with my complacency, and the fact that nothing bad had arguably ever happened to me, that did us in. I knew I was supposed to wake up with her forever, so it never occurred to me that I needed to work harder than I had at anything in my entire life to make sure I deserved to keep her.

It wasn't her fault. She was pretty convinced she held the dissolution of our relationship in her hands, but at the end of the day, it wasn't anything she did. It was me, and if she let me, I'd spend the rest of my life making sure I was the kind of person who deserved to be in her bed.

It's where I was now, scared to move or breathe in case I woke her. Charlie hardly ever looked real, but right now—hair everywhere and her mouth slightly parted, light breathing and her eyelids hardly fluttering—she looked like I made her up.

Early morning sunlight inched across the room, spilling in from underneath the gauzy curtains that wouldn't have looked out of place at a resort in Sumatra. For all I knew, they were from the same supplier. Winchester Holdings was the primary owner of more than one luxury resort chain. Steven always said it was good business. He wasn't wrong.

Charlie was prone to getting heated about it—claiming that a better business move would have been to invest in something that preserved natural landscapes instead of degrading them. It was one of the many things she took umbrage with or was particularly...passionate about when it came to the business.

I'd lost count of how many nights I'd spent, simply observing, while she and Deacon got into it over the investing structure and what they each thought would be better for the company. Deacon ended every argument saying people pretended to care about sustainable investing, but that no one actually believed in it.

I wasn't really sure what I believed in, but I believed in her. Maybe that's why, instead of praying to whoever might be listening, every thought I had was for her.

That I'd stay here, watching her forever. I'd never leave her again. I'd fight for her the way I was supposed to all those years ago—the way I should have. I'd tear down the pedestal she built me when we first met so we were always on equal footing.

I'd never take her for granted again.

And I would have stayed there, so fucking grateful that I was here, hoping whatever prayers I repeated to her in my head would find their way to her heart, but my phone started vibrating against the nightstand.

In another world, I would have ignored it, because there was nothing more important than where I was now. But I didn't want to wake Charlie up. She needed to sleep. I was worried about her now because of everything with her father and brother, but the truth was, I spent a disproportionate amount of time worrying about how well Charlie Winchester slept at night.

On the second vibration, I finally looked away, grabbing my phone and resisting the urge to chuck it across the room when I saw who it was. Her brother was many things—at this moment, he was the person keeping me from being here with her and responsible for almost waking her up—but he was also my best friend.

Deacon: Hey man. You stay here last night?

David: Yeah. How are you feeling?

Deacon: I've had better days but I've definitely been worse. You wanna meet me for breakfast? I'll buzz down and have someone set something out.

David: Alright. I'll see you down there in a few.

I really didn't want to leave her, but saying he would call down to have the staff make breakfast was the closest thing to a Deacon Winchester olive branch anyone would ever get. I turned back to look at her one more time, tucking a wisp of her hair that had fallen across her cheek behind her ear.

I was still in my clothes from the night before. I didn't want to move when she finally fell asleep, curled against my chest. I usually would have changed my clothes for any sort of breakfast, let alone a plated one served to me while I sat beside Deacon.

But it was almost guaranteed he would look worse than I did.

I practically slid out of the bed, trying to avoid any shift in the mattress or slide in the sheets. It felt wrong, like I was leaving her or sneaking out of her room like some fucking shitty college kid.

I looked over my shoulder at her, barely visible in and amongst the bedsheets and outrageous number of pillows—the best girl in the world—before quietly pushing open the door to step into the hallway.

A low whistle cut through the silence, and my eyes shot up to see Deacon leaning against the wall just outside the door to his room at the opposite end of the hallway. The lights were still dim, but I could tell his eyes looked dull, and what should have been a shit-eating, gleeful expression on his face was flat.

Deacon arched an eyebrow, the corner of his mouth pulling up. "That's not what I meant when I asked if you stayed here."

"There's no world where I would have left your sister alone last night," I offered, my voice measured as I tipped my chin toward the top of the spiral staircase, cutting through the middle of their hallway.

Deacon shot me a look before pushing off the wall and falling into step beside me. "I would refute that, but having seen how you behaved around her, and with her, when you had a girlfriend, I imagine you're right and that a world where you won't put her first doesn't exist."

I raised my eyebrows at him as we started down the steps. I don't think I'd ever seen him look this unkempt. His eyes were dull and his straight hair, usually perfectly gelled into place, flopped everywhere. He looked like shit. "That seems like something, as her brother, you'd be grateful for."

I watched his hands tighten on the staircase railing before he turned to me, green eyes narrowed in on me and a finger pointing toward my chest. "What I'm not grateful for is you fucking with her at every opportunity. I've said it before, and I'll say it again—cut her loose if you aren't going to tie her around you forever."

Charlie was the most important thing in my life, no matter how many times I spectacularly failed her, and he knew that. We'd spent hours, days, weeks—talking it to death. He spent extensive amounts of time concocting up insane plans, grand gestures, and all the things he thought I should be doing to permanently win her back when she was in London.

What Deacon would never understand, could never really wrap his head around, was the fact that Charlie lived most of her life for other people, whether she realized it or not. For her brother and father, trying to make them grieve their mother. For her mother's ghost, doing anything for forgiveness, absolution. To try and earn Steven's love and respect. For me. To try and deserve me. To try and mean something different for a twenty-two-year-old Tripp.

It was one of the ways I failed her—never seeing that part of her until it was too late.

I wanted her. I loved her. But I'd never prioritize that over her happiness. I wanted Charlie to be whoever she wanted to be, whoever she was meant to be, without anyone else's shadow or shackle.

He took the fact that I refused to show up at her doorstep in London, drop down on my knees and beg for her, to propose to her in some sort of gesture of unyielding commitment to mean that she wasn't my forever.

Cutting him a look, I shook my head and shoved my hands into my pockets. "I'd rather not have this argument again, Deacon. I don't really think this is about Charlie and me, either."

Deacon scoffed, and ran a hand through his already disheveled hair. "Who's really here for me? Taylor might be our childhood best friend, but her loyalty is always to Charlie. We know where your priorities lie."

"Your sister. Your sister is here for you. She dropped everything the second you called. And you know as well as I do that there's nothing in this world she wouldn't do for you." My words were harsh, but when I stepped off the bottom stair and into the main foyer of this sprawling house, the light from some pompous chandelier hanging overhead caught his eyes. He looked fucking sad, so I tried a different approach. "You could call Noa."

"No." Deacon's voice was flat, clipped even, as he stepped off the staircase, his posture casual but somehow looking like he could be stepping onto a red carpet. At least he hadn't lost the air of self-importance.

"You're being a child." I shook my head, crossing the foyer, ignoring all the ghosts—the memories of the sheer amount of times I'd stood here, black tie, waiting for Charlie to descend those same steps alongside her brother.

It made me turn back to him and try to be sympathetic because it's what she would want, and it's what Deacon deserved at the end of the day. It was funny—spending so much time with them. Every advantage in life, every privilege imaginable, and yet they both spent so much time fucking lost, wandering aimlessly and feeling utterly alone.

Deacon looked alone now, juxtaposed against that stupid, sweeping granite staircase.

I jerked my head toward the doorway that led to the breakfast parlor. "You're my best friend, Deac. She's the love of my life. I'm here for you both, and I don't think we should waste our time arguing over who gets the most attention between the two of you. You know Taylor would drop everything the second you asked. She tried last night, and you shut her down. I left Charlie's bed—I was in bed with the love of my fucking life after how long—and I left her when you asked. If that's not unending loyalty, then I don't know what the fuck is."

He eyed me for a moment, his features appraising and shrewd before he shrugged and tried to smile like he used to. "Should we toast to that then? Your sacrifice and blatant display of friendship? Mimosa? Bloody Mary?"

It sounded like some part of him was still in there somewhere, so I arched an eyebrow and grinned, shoving him through the doorway. "Well, I'm not going to let you drink alone."

Charlie

The space beside me was empty when I woke up. I had tiptoed back from the washroom, sliding in beside David, and watched his chest rise and fall, staring at how soft his face looked in the moonlight. I ran my fingers over the loosened muscles spanning his arms, and wondered while I looked at him if my phone would vibrate again, if there would be any sort of signal from Tripp that my message was received, but the words just seemingly floated in the ether. So, I watched David Kennedy sleep instead, until my eyelids got too heavy again, my head dropped to the pillow, and I was sleeping beside him.

But he wasn't there when I woke up. My text message was still unanswered, the words in the blue bubble becoming yet another string of unanswered letters and syllables. I could have thought about it, ruminated on why neither of them were there in the morning. But I didn't want to. And there was something freeing in that.

A jarring buzz emitted from the intercom still on the bedside table, followed by my father's usual clipped tone. "Charlie, when you're ready, your brother has finally deigned to bless us with his presence for a discussion. We'll be in my office."

In his office. Like this was some sort of business discussion we were having. And in a way, I guess it was. That was simply how my father looked at things, and I was starting to realize it had nothing to do with me. Unfortunately, I was coming to that realization a little too late, given that there was the literal equivalent to a ticking time bomb taking up residence in his body. But even cancer couldn't stop the transactional nature of Steven Winchester.

I scrubbed my face before giving one more cursory glance to my silent phone. That could have been a dream. The whispered "I love you" from David might have been one, too.

My luggage was sitting haphazardly on the chaise at the end of the bed, teetering on the edge. Kind of like my whole life. I arched an eyebrow. Usually, those types of found metaphors were for me, but as I grabbed a worn Oxford sweater and pulled it over my head, all I could think of was my brother.

———

The door to my father's office was ajar, but not a single sound came from it. I hesitated, only for a moment, before pushing the door open. It was almost a repeat of yesterday, but instead of my family spread around the breakfast table laden with lavish foods, my father was behind his desk, eyes on his desktop, and one hand shifting his computer mouse. There was still an IV pole beside him, lines disappearing under the sleeve of his shirt.

My brother sat across from him, no Hydra-V pole to be found this time, but he looked as disheveled as I had ever seen him. His straight hair fell in every which way, not at all pushed back, and it looked like it was actually bordering the need for a wash. Deacon tipped his head backward, giving nothing away when he looked at me. Even his eyes were dull.

Taylor was propped up on the edge of my father's desk, black scrubs practically dwarfing her, and the same perpetual air of disappointment around her as she watched Deacon with pursed lips. Her hair was pulled back into a tight ponytail, making everything about her look more severe. Her father was nowhere to be seen, but I saw his stack of files teetering on the edge of the desk.

"You sleep okay?" David was against the wall, one foot propped up against the bookcase that lined it. He tipped his head and pushed off the wall with his foot. The distance between us disappeared, and he was standing over me, looking down at me, those eyes all full of concern. He reached out, grabbing a tendril of my hair and wrapping it gently between his fingers.

I looked up at him, breath frozen in my throat. He clearly didn't care that we had an audience. He only cared about me.

I nodded softly, my words barely a whisper. "You were gone this morning."

David's eyes darkened, his lips parting, and I assumed he was about to tell me that he hadn't left me, that he wouldn't leave me, when Deacon spoke.

"Thought you were here for me, buddy." His voice was full of ire.

David clenched his jaw, nostrils flaring before he rolled his neck and looked toward my brother. His fingers were still tangled in my hair.

But Taylor spoke first. "Deacon, seriously? Shut up. I'm so done with you right now." Her voice was almost shrill, and her lips were pulled into a tight line.

I looked back and forth between them. I couldn't remember the last time they fought. And certainly not like this.

"Then why are you here, Taylor?" Deacon raised his voice and gestured around the room. He leaned forward in his chair, hair falling across his forehead now, the epitome of unkempt, and his lips pulled back as he looked at her. "No one asked you to be."

I swallowed, about to yell at my brother, to ask him what the fuck was wrong with him, what Taylor could have possibly done, when our father finally spoke.

"I asked her to be here. And, as I haven't died yet, this is still my home. You will never speak to another guest in *my* home that way. Understood?" Our father's voice was sharp, and his eyes narrowed on Deacon. "We were here to have a civilized discussion, and if you find yourself unable to do so, Deacon, you'll be asked to leave."

Deacon was sitting up straight again, and I could no longer see his face. See his nose, his eyes. My nose, my eyes. All of me reflected in my brother, who I usually thought was perfect. But I could tell by the set of his shoulders and the exaggerated carry-on gesture he made to our father that he was rolling his eyes. His irreverence was typically something I loved; it made me smile, made me feel light even. But right now, I hated it. I wanted to shake him, bring him back down out of whatever galaxy he had floated off to, and remind him that soon, we would be all that was left, that it really would be just me and him against the world.

I watched our father arch an eyebrow at him; his blue eyes looked gray, but I wasn't sure if that was just because he was annoyed with Deacon, or if they were just inching slowly toward death the same way he was. He cleared his throat, such an off gesture for Steven Winchester. Like he didn't know what to say, or maybe he was uncomfortable. But the moment passed, and he folded his hands in front of him the way I had seen him do a million times before.

"Duke and I discussed it, and I've decided to move ahead with the procedure Taylor proposed. She will remove the tumors that she and her father have selected. I'll remind you both that this is a palliative procedure. It's meant to relieve pain and...delay the inevitable." Our father delivered his statement—his decision—the same way he delivered news in the boardroom.

"So, no chemo?" Deacon asked, words bitter and biting. I watched him roll his neck and begin to crack his knuckles.

Deacon was many things, and he did many things, but he never cracked his knuckles. He never exhibited any body language that showed he was unruffled, anything he thought would make him look undignified, and I knew he thought people who cracked their knuckles were "pedestrian".

"No." Steven Winchester's decisions were always final.

Taylor's eyes had been firmly narrowed on Deacon, like she was waiting for him to erupt. But then they swung to me. They collapsed for a moment before everything about her hardened. I rarely saw her like this. She snuck me into the gallery once when she was an intern to watch her observe an appendectomy. Even though I couldn't see it, I imagined this is what her face must have been like, all seriousness and clinical precision. "And in the meantime, I'll be moving in to provide at-home care when I'm not in the hospital."

"Great. Can't wait for you to continue to wow us with your medical prowess, Taylor." Deacon scoffed, shaking his head. "And what about the company?"

"Ash knows and will be acting president and CEO whenever I'm...indisposed. We'll deliver a statement to the board later this week, and I expect you both to be there." Our father's eyes swung to me before landing on Deacon.

I was usually the only flight risk, but judging by my brother's recent behavior, it might have been a family trait.

I couldn't see my brother's face, but I imagined he was rolling his eyes again when he leaned forward to speak. "And the public? We have shareholders, Steven. The stock's going to fucking tank."

I flinched, lips tugging down and my breath catching in my throat, hearing my brother call him that. I understood now why it bothered Deacon so much when I did it.

"Which is why I expect you to act like a civilized human being in public, Deacon. So long as you're still...behaving, seen in public as the head of the New York office, and Ash steps in for the interim, the stock should remain protected."

Deacon raised a hand, an almost lackadaisical gesture, waving over his head toward me. "What about her? She supposed to come running back to Daddy now that he's sick? Give up everything she wanted and worked for because you're afraid your shareholders might sell? Going to pull her strings and have her pose like a good little heiress for the papers? You didn't give a shit about her when you didn't need her to make sure your legacy stays intact."

Taylor's eyes sharpened, her mouth falling into a flat line, looking poised to tear Deacon's throat out.

But David spoke first. His hand had found its way from my hair to my shoulder, and his fingers tightened briefly. "Back off, Deacon."

"Ah. There it is. Everything really does go out the window for you as soon as she's in the picture." Deacon leaned back, tipping his head upside down so he could see us. "Quite the pair you two make."

"I'll remind you that you're the one who called your sister, Deacon." Our father's voice was as close to a reprimand as it would ever get. "If that's all, you have one more day before I expect you back in the office. Perhaps you could use it to...dry out."

Deacon ignored him, shaking his head and pushing up off the chair. He paused to run one hand through his already disheveled hair, sending the chocolate strands into further disarray. "I'll stay here until the surgery's done. After that, I'm going back to New York."

"Deacon—" I started, lurching forward and about to grab onto the neck of his gray Saint Laurent hooded sweatshirt, but he swatted at my hand and pointed a finger at me before swinging it back toward Taylor.

"Not a word about this to Noa. From either of you." My brother barely spared me a glance as he brushed past all of us, letting the door slam in his wake.

Our father shook his head, his nostrils flaring in displeasure, but he wouldn't say anything more.

"David, I expect you'll be working from the Chicago office for the foreseeable future, seeing as my adult son is suddenly in need of supervision. I'll email Damien and have him open your old office." My father's words were short, and to David and Taylor, his voice probably sounded normal. Steven Winchester was brief and to the point almost every second of every day, but I could hear it—just the faintest hint of it. He was sad. His words got harsher when he was, another something I could add to the list of things I'd learned too late.

Maybe he could see the understanding dawning on my face, the collapse of my features and the way my shoulders sort of sagged. But he was still Steven Winchester at the end of the day—so he cleared his throat, like the evisceration of his only son, the bleeding out of Deacon's heart in this very room because of him, was nothing more than a minor irritation. "You are, of course, welcome to stay here. I'll have a room prepared for you. Taylor, I've already sent word to have yours ready for this evening when you're back from your shift."

"Thanks, Papa Winchester." Taylor smiled softly at him, wrinkling her nose before pushing off the edge of his desk. She was the only one who ever got away with calling him something as unsophisticated as that. "I have to go. I have a few patients I need to do rounds on this morning."

She paused, one hand brushing alongside my arm before squeezing my hand—once, twice, three times—and arching a wry eyebrow at David, whose hand was still heavy on my shoulder, before leaving the office with significantly more dignity than Deacon.

David's fingers found their way to my hair again, tucking the strands behind my ears. He looked down at me, eyebrows knit, and his jaw set in a firm line. "I should go, too. But you'll call if—"

"I'll be fine, Mr. Kennedy. Lots of important, ground-breaking, fancy research for me to be doing. The problems of the investing world won't solve themselves." I leaned into his hand, out of habit more than anything, and maybe a little bit because there might be a magnet in me connecting me to him—and his thumb stroked along my jawline before he turned, raising a hand to my father and following Taylor out the door.

I turned to look back at my father, but his eyes were already back on his computer. No parting words of wisdom for his errant daughter, so I smiled tightly instead and turned on my heel.

He spoke when I was halfway to the door. "I have something for you. It'll be in your mother's studio this evening."

Glancing over my shoulder, I watched him gesture vaguely toward the ever-shut door beside one of his many towering bookcases, and then his eyes were back on the screen of his computer while his phone started vibrating incessantly against his desk.

He might be dying, minute by minute, breath by breath—each one he took inching closer to the finite number he had left—his body might be slowing down, but his empire certainly wasn't.

Deacon

The hole I put in the wall of my room the night before was particularly unsightly in the morning light. An entire chunk of the crown molding was gone, the sun shining down on it like some kind of ironic spotlight.

Someone on staff had thrown open the stupid curtains, made the bed, and tucked in the custom, made-to-order Millesimo by Sferra sheets to look like I hadn't laid in them the night before, tossing and turning and pulling at the ends of my hair, wishing for the first time in my life I was anyone fucking else.

There was even a fresh vase of flowers on one of the mahogany night-stands. My lip curled up at the sight, and I sort of wanted to throw that, too. I sort of wanted to throw it all—upturn the bed, tip over that ridiculous fucking armchair, smash the windows on the French doors that led out to the balcony.

My father was a fucking prick, and he always had been. I hated him half the time for how he treated Charlie, drove her away. He was clearly instrumental in driving our mom away—but the thought of living in a world without him made me feel like I was being flayed from the inside out.

I hated him for that. For fucking us both up so spectacularly and finding a way to put one final nail in the coffin of whatever dreams of us having a normal, functional family I'd ever entertained. I hated the cells in his body that couldn't fight off disease. I hated our mother too, for leaving me alone here.

I hated myself more, though.

"You can't go back to New York, Deac." Charlie's voice was small, and I didn't have to glance over my shoulder to know she'd be standing in the doorway, arms crossed, her head tipped against the frame, and her eyes cloudy.

I might have hated that most of all. That our father was finding another way to break her heart.

My sister was my North Star. Guiding light. Whatever you wanted to call it. Before Noa, she was the only thing that ever tethered me to the ground and kept me down to earth.

But I didn't particularly like being on earth at this moment, so I arched an eyebrow at her, walking backward and holding my arms out until I felt the back of my knees hit that stupid armchair, and I dropped down. "Yeah? Watch me."

Charlie pursed her lips and started shaking her head. The ratty Oxford sweater she was wearing hid any movements of her body, but I could see her fingers peeking out the sleeves; her knuckles were white where they dug into her arms. "You can work from here. You know as well as I do if you miss this...these last weeks, months—we missed it all with Mom. We have time with him, Deac. It's probably macabre to say it's a second chance, but—"

A dry laugh caught in my throat. "You call this a second chance, Charles?"

"Yes, I do." She arched an eyebrow at me, and her features pulled into a haughty expression I don't think she even knew she could make. But she could. No one could serve bitch like my sister. "Not everyone screws it up as spectacularly as we all did the first time and gets another chance to try and do things differently."

Dropping my back in the chair, I arched an eyebrow at her and rested my head in my hand. "It's pretty fucking depressing when you're talking about second chances at getting the death of your parent right."

Charlie shrugged. "Well, that's where we are. Just me and you against the world."

It's what we'd always said—the only fact that was irrefutable.

"My life's in New York now, Charlie. You should go back to yours, too."

She looked at me, entirely exasperated with the collapse of her features that made me fairly certain if David was standing here, he would have decked me by now. I would have deserved it.

Maybe this is what she had been on about all this time—these self-destructive spirals she found herself in.

I was probably in one now, falling down an endless well toward whatever lay at the bottom, hands reaching out. Instead of grabbing for anything to give me purchase, to keep me afloat, I was just wrenching myself out of everyone's grip and careening even faster toward whatever lay down there. Whatever it was, wasn't good.

"We're going to be all that's left, Deacon, and I don't particularly want to spend the rest of my life peeling you off the floor." She rolled her eyes at me before flashing what was probably the world's most depressing smile and pushing off the door. "I'll be in my room if you want to talk or do something."

And then she left me there alone, in my room with its impractical furniture, expensive sheets, and damaged walls.

I didn't particularly care for any of that interaction—it was like I was fucking watching myself from above, horrified, but I just couldn't stop. Instead of following my sister, hiding with her from the world like we used to when we were kids—spending the day down in the theater or out on the water—I was going to go down to the cellar, steal a bottle of my father's scotch because it was all about to be mine anyway, and maybe call my drug dealer.

Charlie

The door to my mother's former studio was open. I could see it from where I stood in the doorway of my father's now empty office. The desktop was powered down, and the lights were off, save for one lamp meant to resemble a gas lantern of days gone by nestled between tomes of leather-bound books on one of my father's endless mahogany shelves. It illuminated the open doorway, and I leaned forward, one hand still gripping the wooden doorframe, like I was scared to go any farther. Like my mother's ghost might find me, suck me in, and trap me in there like some horror movie. I had no idea what my father would have left for me there.

I had seen that door open a total of one other time since she died—when it played host to endless racks of designer clothing for the family Forbes profile.

My lips pulled down at the memory. If I closed my eyes, I could feel the ostrich feathers brushing against my collarbone, David's hands running up and down the ridges of my spine, the breeze lifting my hair from the lake, Tripp's mouth on mine after almost a decade.

I used to think of that night as the beginning of my downfall. That was the name on the door in my mind I kept that memory locked behind. But I tentatively reached my foot forward, testing the smooth, impossibly shiny wooden floor of the office before letting go of the doorframe and finally stepping in.

My footsteps were silent across the floor, hardly an echo against the imposing shelves and rows of perfectly straight textbooks. Shadows stretched across the room, cast by the singular lamp. I paused again when I reached the sliding door, cracked open, leaving only a sliver of her studio visible. The heavy mahogany door matched every other one in the house, but this one moved on wrought-iron rungs built into the wall.

The last and only time I had seen this door open since she died, I didn't look long enough to see if there were any parts of her still in there, hidden amongst the racks and racks of clothing. I swallowed, my breath catching in my throat when my fingers feathered against the smooth wood of the door.

I didn't think there was anything left in there that could hurt me, not when I was well and truly on the precipice of being alone. No mother, soon to be no father, and likely nothing to be left of my brother.

Pushing the door back, I waited for some loud, ominous creak, like you might hear when opening a sealed tomb, for stagnant, stale air to engulf me, for motes of dust to float through the air, suspending around me, like tiny snowflakes under a streetlamp.

But there was none of that. It was just a dark room.

I flicked the light beside the door, and the hanging, horrifically ostentatious vintage chandelier flickered to life.

The room was almost entirely empty—save for the long, gold brocade mirror that still took up half the wall and an ornate, brushed copper trunk in the middle of the room. An unopened wine bottle sat perspiring in a stainless steel bucket on top, with an envelope propped up beside it.

I frowned, crossing my arms. Maybe this really was a horror movie, and my mother's ghost really was going to climb from that trunk and take me with her.

"What the fuck," I muttered, nose wrinkling and footsteps light until I settled cross-legged on the floor in front of it.

My fingers twitched toward the envelope. I could see my father's shockingly untidy scrawl across the front. I recognized the trunk; it had been in here once, amongst all my mother's things. The studio used to be full—full of furniture, things, art, *life*.

All those things—her easel, a desk that matched my father's cluttered with endless papers torn from sketchbooks, dried paint flaking on palettes—had been gone for years. I don't know what my father did with them, and I never asked.

Tentatively, I reached forward, fingers shaking as I grabbed the envelope. I had no idea what would be in here—what my father could have possibly left me in this empty room. I don't think even the ghosts lived here anymore.

It wasn't sealed, and I pulled the folded letter out easily.

Charlie,

You may remember that your mother used to keep her favorite art pieces in here. She had this trunk her whole life. It was where she kept her projects and anything half-finished hidden away.

It was the first time she showed me her work. She was on break from school, and I went to visit her at her family home in Connecticut.

It still belongs to us. It became mine after she died. Perhaps you and Deacon can go someday. It will be yours, after all.

Some of her art is in here—my favorite pieces of hers. I enjoy looking at them sometimes.

I thought you might as well.

Steven Winchester

My snort came out significantly less dry than I anticipated.

Something akin to a sob snuck up my throat when I was reading, and I barely had it in me to laugh at my father signing a personalized letter about my dead mother with his full name.

He *had* kept pieces of her. They existed in this very trunk, right in front of me. Setting the letter down carefully beside me, I pulled the perspiring wine bucket and the upturned crystal wine glass off the top of the trunk. A corkscrew hung from the side of the bucket, and I used it to shred the foil before twisting it down and working out the cork.

It was an Italian white I didn't recognize. My father never drank white. But I did. And he had cared enough to at least send someone down to the cellar and bring it up for me. To leave it here, with these pieces of my mother.

Steven Winchester had a heart after all. Who knew.

I eyed the trunk shrewdly, pouring into the glass. This was what I had wanted, what I had begged for all those years ago. For my father, my brother, to remember her. I assumed he purged her from this house the moment she died, threw her out, discarded her. It turned out he had just locked her away.

I wasn't angry like usual. I hadn't been angry at him over her in a long time. Not since he finally said her name all those months ago in New York, finally pressed his lips to the mouth of her ghost and breathed air back into her lungs. He was probably already dying at that point, malignant cells doing whatever it is they do to a body. Taylor had given me a million and one clever analogies for cancer over the years, and I could never really understand it the way she could. People grew pensive and remorseful when they were dying. It was probably some sort of Steven Winchester attempt to make things right, grounded in appeasing his conscience. But it didn't make me mad. Not really.

There was just something horrifically sad about it all now.

I took a sip before setting the wine glass down, with shockingly steady fingers unlocking the heavy brass latch of the trunk. It sprung open with surprising ease.

And there she was. Parts of her, anyway.

My lips parted, and I leaned forward, hands clasping the cold edges of the trunk as I peered into it. I could feel my eyes widen, greedily mapping and cataloging every piece of canvas, paper, and dried fleck of paint.

My fingers shook when I picked up the piece sitting on top. It was an old, worn canvas, all swirls of bright, abstract colors. That was her thing. I didn't know anything about art, but everything she did was abstract; all great swirls of color and hidden meaning usually surrounding one central focus in the middle of the painting, the drawing, whatever she was creating.

I tipped my head, really looking at the four distinct swirls of forest green in the center, and I wondered if they were supposed to be our eyes—mine and Deacon's. The whole thing felt childlike, exuberant, and playful—the way we used to be.

I don't know how long I sat there, sipping from my glass, filling it up without ever looking away from what I was doing—studying each piece, trying to understand her, as more and more surrounded me on the floor when there was a gentle knock on the door.

I turned my head, hair fanning around me and eyes finally breaking from the sketch I had been staring at, trying to understand. David was leaning in the doorway. His freshly showered hair curled across his forehead and around his ears, over the nape of his neck, and parts of his gray shirt stuck to his skin intermittently, doing nothing to hide the stretch of his muscles. He must have just gotten back from the office. I hadn't seen him, or anyone, since this morning, holing up in my room and working on papers like I was a regular student, not one who had been summoned home to watch the dissolution of a dynasty.

"Hey. I was just going to head out, and I saw the light. Thought I'd see if you were okay?" David tipped his head, pressing it against the door frame, hands shoved in his pockets.

I nodded, taking a sip from my wine and gesturing with my other hand at the gallery growing at my feet. "He left me some of her art. I was just looking at it."

David smiled softly, eyes creasing in the corners. "I'll leave you to it then. Call me if you need me, Charlie."

"You can come in if you aren't on a tight schedule," I whispered softly, looking up at him imploringly.

His lips pulled to the side before he swallowed and started to shake his head. "I don't want to intrude. I just wanted to see how you were and let you know I was heading out for the night."

I couldn't think of anyone else I would want to share this with more.

"You're not intruding." I shook my head, patting the minimal space beside me. "But I only have one wine glass. You're welcome to share as long as you don't mind my germs."

David grinned—the trademark easy grin that could fall into place at any moment and make my heart stop beating—before pushing off the doorframe and coming to sit across from me. "I don't think there's any other germs I'd rather share."

The sight of it made me want to laugh—impossibly broad David Kennedy, sitting cross-legged with me, like we were children whispering secrets.

I smiled at him, holding out my wine glass, and watched as he took a sip before setting it down.

He cocked his head, studying the art spread across the floor. "She was really talented."

Nodding, another small smile, altogether different, tugged at my lips. "She was. She went to the Rhode Island School of Design, actually. She studied painting. Met my father one spring at one Grand Prix or another. Finished her degree, they got married, and here I am almost thirty years later."

David finally broke away from staring at the art, all these pieces that had been my father's favorite, to look up at me. "They say artistic ability is hereditary. Are you holding out on me, billion dollar baby?"

A snort escaped me, and I shook my head, taking a small sip of wine before answering. "Oh, I don't have an artistic bone in my body, Mr. Kennedy. Deacon can draw, though, believe it or not."

"Of your brother's many, many talents, I wouldn't have pegged him as an artist." He leaned forward, picking up one of the paintings beside me. I think it was of our family home on Cape Cod, some form of abstract take on it anyway. All the colors were there. The seagrass, the rolling dunes of sand. He held it up, honey eyes swinging back to me. "She could have done it professionally. Did she ever pursue it after school?"

I shook my head, shrugging and puckering my lips. She hadn't, at least to my knowledge. "No. What's that saying? Why do rich kids always choose art? She was always happiest just doing this. Creating just for herself. I always thought it was enough, but maybe it never was."

David reached out, calloused fingers brushing over the back of my hand for a moment before taking the wine glass from me. His eyebrows creased, and I wanted to look anywhere but at him while he sat here, leaning forward with eyes that were only for me, and his damp hair curling around his neck, his t-shirt clinging to every cord and stack of muscle.

My resolve was moments from crumbling, and I would drag him out of this room and drown in him.

Drowning in my once-in-a-lifetime love didn't sound so bad.

But I didn't want to drown anymore. I wanted to stay on dry land. Swallowing, my eyes swung around the room—trying to focus on anything but him and all that he was.

"Do you want to get out of here, Charlie?" he asked, and I finally looked at him. And there they were, sparkling honey eyes and the light on the front porch of my first home. "I was heading downtown. A friend of mine I used to surf with. His band's playing at a bar tonight. Said I would stop by."

"Surfing and a band? Do you have a secret life, Mr. Kennedy?" I tipped my head, voice chiding. "I'm not sure I should. If my dad needs—"

David leaned forward, his forehead almost touching mine. "Taylor's staying here. She took the Hippocratic Oath. She's not going to let something happen to your dad to spite Deacon because they're fighting."

I wished they weren't. I hated when Deacon and Taylor fought at the best of times, let alone when our father was being eaten alive by malignant cells, and Deacon's liver was surely on the way out.

David's nose brushed mine, just one breath away. He was just a kiss away, and I could feel his lips move, right above my own. "Let's get out of here. Do you want to come with me, billion dollar baby?"

"Anywhere with you."

Charlie

The soles of Taylor's chunky white Gucci sneakers stuck to the floor of the bar intermittently as I wove behind David. She had quite literally thrown them at me before I left, saying I needed something to make me look less like Kurt Cobain.

I stopped in her room before we left, and my outfit was evidently not to her liking. She had always liked my old leather jacket and liked it even more when I wore it to WH, because it would piss my father off. But apparently, that coupled with the wide-leg Frame jeans and the oversized white VTMNTS college t-shirt, was too much for Taylor.

She had thrown back the covers of her bed to stand, rolling her eyes and shaking her head while she pilfered through her bag—the same Swaine bag she gifted me—until she found the shoes and tossed them at my feet.

But her features had softened, a tiny knowing glint in her eyes, and she wrapped her arms around me, pressing her lips to my cheek briefly and telling me to have fun, before she said *to promptly get the fuck out of her room* because she had a surgery in the morning.

David's hand was warm, his fingers loosely gripping mine, guiding me through the crowd to the platform that seemingly doubled as a stage. Even under the low light, I could see the stitching on his Tarheels hat was starting to fray. Blond waves curled from underneath the beak where it was turned backward, and the muscles in his shoulders tensed as he moved through the throngs of people.

The band had already started when we walked in. The bar was small enough that David had raised a hand when the lead singer looked up, fingers still deftly moving across the strings of his guitar, and he had tipped his chin in acknowledgment before continuing with the set. He looked sort of like a shaggier, smaller version of David. He bordered on skinny, with messy brown hair, but his skin was golden in the same way David's was.

We stopped just to the right of the stage, a wooden ledge jutted out from the wall, with stools haphazardly lined up underneath it. David set his perspiring beer bottle down on the worn wood, hands gripping one of the stools and pulling it out for me.

"Billion dollar baby, sitting on a wooden stool in some dive bar in Chicago, listening to shitty punk." David raised his eyebrows at me when I hopped onto the seat, tipping my beer bottle back to take a sip.

I arched an eyebrow at him, bottle still poised at my mouth. "I did grow up here, you know."

David grinned, hands grabbing the wooden ledge at my side. He still towered over me, but he angled his head, wisps of still-damp hair peeking out from under the seam of his hat. I could feel his arms on either side of me. He stared down at me for a moment, eyes moving across my face—across my cheekbones, the straight bridge of my nose before landing on my lips. When he finally spoke, his voice was low, entirely too rough, and somehow wholly inappropriate for a crowded bar. "You grew up in Lake Forest."

"Okay, Figure Eight." I rolled my eyes.

He didn't move, he just stayed there, all around me and taking up all the oxygen in the bar.

I said nothing, lips parted and breath lodged in my throat, heart beating so erratically I thought it might bust through my ribcage and ruin my shirt.

Without looking away, without taking his eyes off me, David grabbed his previously abandoned beer and brought it to his mouth, tipping it back and raising his eyebrows before finally pushing off the ledge. His shoulders tensed under his shirt, and I felt mine rolling back, a small breath escaping me, as if I could shake him off.

As if David Kennedy wouldn't be all over me for the rest of my life.

I angled my head, studying the way the objectively shitty lighting somehow managed to sharpen all the planes of David's face, his perfect jawbone dusted with stubble that I could still feel after all these years against my skin if I just closed my eyes—all the way down the column of his throat as he tipped his head back to swallow his beer.

My eyes roved over him, the way they always did, watching the pull of his t-shirt against his skin, the arms lifting ever so slightly to reveal the somehow golden all-year-round skin of his biceps—

The arm of David's t-shirt pulled up, and the edges of black ink peeked out.

I paused, my own beer pressed against my lips. "Mr. Kennedy!" I started to smile behind the cool glass of the bottle. "Don't tell me you got a tattoo? That *definitely* wasn't there before." I reached forward, fingers tugging on the arm of his shirt and yanking it back across his skin.

Narrowing my eyebrows, I tipped my head, gaze moving across the untidy lines.

It was my signature.

My head snapped up, fingers still pressed into his skin.

David's lips tugged into a resigned smile. "It was your brother's idea, believe it or not. He took your signature for something you signed for WH. It was after you left. We got drunk, and he thought it would be some sort of grand gesture—you know how he gets, hand waving wider and wider, getting louder and louder, and then he was bribing some artist Noa knew to come to the apartment to do it."

"That's illegal," I whispered, eyes flicking down to the tattoo again, before I looked back up at David. "I'm on your body."

David smiled at me, just a small one. Not his usual grin. "Always have been. I think the whole thing was built for you anyway."

Before I could think better of it, I hopped off the stool, barely able to hear the music. But I wasn't sure we needed words anymore. Wrapping my arms around David, I pressed my cheek into the soft cotton of his shirt, right above his heart.

His chin dropped to my head, his hands finding my waist for a moment before I pulled back and smiled up at him, entirely overlarge and causing my cheeks to burn. But not a fake Winchester smile. A real me smile.

There would have been a time that I might have fallen to my knees, begged for his forgiveness, for the chance to be someone who might deserve him. There was a time I would have screamed at him, for trying to hurt me, for what I thought might be abject cruelty, for burning me alive on a funeral pyre when his hands were on someone else.

But I didn't want to, and I didn't need to. My forgiveness, and his, was inked on his skin.

David looked down at me, honey eyes anything but sweet.

It would usually be impossible to look away from him, not when he was looking at me like that. But when I pulled away, turning and resting my shoulders against his chest, the warmth of him all around me, all over me, in my body and my blood, it wasn't. Because he was right there behind me, and he wasn't going anywhere.

I tipped my head back, resting it against David's chest. His arm wove around me, and I wrapped my hands around his forearm. I could vaguely feel his heartbeat against my back beneath his shirt, all the way through my worn leather jacket. I could feel my own, too.

It was beating its old, familiar mantra.

Home. Home. Home.

———

David's friend, whose name turned out to be Chase, really did look like a shaggier version of him when I got up close. No sparkling honey eyes to stop my heart, but rather friendly blue ones with more lines wrinkling around them than David's. His skin had that look of someone who lived almost permanently outdoors—what was clearly a year-round tan but hardly weathered. Taylor would kill for his skincare routine. I assumed it was probably due to the fact that he lived permanently covered in Zinc and a UV-resistant wetsuit, but I knew a lot of people who would pay an exorbitant amount of money for that complexion.

"Kennedy!" His voice was slow, almost a deliberate, lazy drawl. Chase looked up as David and I pushed through the dispersing crowd toward the stage. His guitar case was open, but he jumped down from the stage before he closed it, arms open for David. "Great to see you, man. Thanks for coming out. You like the show?"

David grinned, dropping my hand and holding out his own arms. I was waiting for them to do that thing that all men seem to do, where they hug and pound one another on the back like they're going back to Neanderthal times. I'd seen David hug my brother and Tripp that way, shaking hands and clapping one another on the back for extended periods.

But it was a real hug. Albeit, a brief one. It reminded me of the way I would hug Taylor. The way you would hug someone who's known you your whole life. Who knew all the different parts of you.

David pulled back, one hand still on Chase's shoulder. "It was great. Thanks for calling me and letting me know you're in town. I'm not usually in Chicago, I'm glad it worked out. This is Charlie."

Chase turned to me, smiling wide and recognition flaring in his eyes. He looked back to David for a brief moment, lips pulling back and a smile stretching across them. "You're kidding?"

David laughed, pulling his hat off and running his hand through his hair before shaking his head. "The one and the same."

Chase's gaze darted between us for a moment, the smile still pulling at his features before he extended a hand toward me. "I'd hug you, but I'm really fucking sweaty, and I think your clothes are probably worth more than my car."

My mouth popped open, and a strangled laugh caught in my throat. But I was smiling when I held my hand out to shake his. "What kind of car do you drive?"

"Not a good one." He smiled at me, hand gripping mine.

It was a nice smile, a genuine one. Everything about him looked entirely real. The sunlit skin, dirty blond waves that were matted with something that was probably sweat, the stacks of rope and beaded bracelets on his wrists, the oversized gray t-shirt that was very in fashion right now but definitely wasn't designer, and the khakis that had seen better days.

David pulled me flush to his chest, dropping his chin to the crown of my head as soon as we dropped our hands.

My eyes flicked down to his arms when they wrapped around me, the cords of muscle and the dusting of light hair across his forearms. Veins traipsed across them— if I bent down, I could kiss one. Kiss the piece of his body that moved all the blood through it and allowed his heart to keep beating. My favorite heart.

"So, this is her, huh? The one who's had you so strung out for the past three years that you can't even catch a fucking wave properly?" Chase raised his eyebrows, still grinning. "Hopefully, that's in the past. You coming home for S-Turns?"

David said nothing, but I felt his arms tense around me before his shoulders lifted, something like a noncommittal shrug. "We'll see."

I narrowed my eyes. It wasn't like David to be evasive—he was entirely to the point about almost everything. He had no problem saying exactly how he felt, answering any question with absolute David Kennedy honesty.

Chase ran a hand through his hair, lips pulling to the side. "Ah, man, that's shit. Not going to be the same if I'm not competing against you."

I tipped my head against his chest, about to ask what he was talking about when Chase continued speaking.

"It's a charity surf competition. Runs every year. Kennedy usually wipes the proverbial floor with everyone."

"Oh?" I looked up at David, only able to really catch the profile of his jaw to see how it was set. He looked sad to me. "That doesn't surprise me. He took me out once when we were visiting his family. I was terrible, but he looked great."

Chase grinned, nodding his head and looking entirely good-natured. Nothing hidden below the surface. No ulterior motives to be found. "Sounds about right. Could have gone pro. Anyway, we've gotta jet. We're playing in Detroit tomorrow night, and decided to head out after the show. You'll call next time you're home? A North Carolina winter with the surf is a hell of a lot better than a freezing fucking winter in the Midwest."

David stepped away from me, his arms dropping, and despite the heat of the bar, the warmth of the crowd, and the sweat starting to slick my skin under my leather jacket, I shivered.

Having his body wrapped around mine, being able to casually touch David again, like we had never stopped, was something I didn't think would happen again. I thought my body would miss his for the rest of my life. He was barely gone, and I wanted him back, all around me. Even if those small, casual touches of comfort and love were all we were sharing.

I loved sex with David; I loved everything with him. But I loved this—the casual intimacy of it all—more than anything. It reminded me how far we were from the people we used to be.

He was hugging Chase goodbye, who held out his hand for me one more time. I smiled at him, a smaller one this time, but real all the same. He represented this whole other life, this person David used to be. I could picture them, younger, scrawnier versions of themselves, salt water beading on their sun-warmed skin and heads tipped back in laughter, sand sticking to their wetsuits, and boards abandoned beside them on the beach after a day on the water.

It was a David that existed once upon a time. And maybe somewhere in the multiverse, he was still that person. The grown up, filled out version of the David Kennedy that stood before me, tanner, maybe more lines around his face from so much time outside, who spent more time in a wetsuit than Tom Ford. Who went to random bars to see random indie bands play because he knew the lead guitarist, who surfed in char-ity tournaments and always took home the trophy, who probably still smoked and ended the day with a perspiring bottle of beer watching the surf roll in while the seagrass swayed in the breeze around him. Still the same backward Tarheels hat and the same honey eyes.

I would have loved that David, too. I loved all versions of him—out there beyond the stars; infinite and echoing across the universe.

It was like finding sea glass, something special and rare, when you got to learn something entirely new about the person you loved with your whole heart, more than the stars in the sky.

I reached out, shaking Chase's hand, promising that I would go out with them if I was ever back in North Carolina. He was another piece of David I wanted to collect, to tuck away and keep forever.

I watched David under the light of the bar after Chase turned away, finally closing his guitar case and helping some of his bandmates. He tugged off his hat, running a hand through his hair before smiling tightly at me.

"Would you win?" I peered up at him, a muscle in his jaw ticking.

David glanced sideways at me, lips pulling tight and eyebrows rising. "It's not very big swell that time of year. It's for charity."

It made me sad to think about. This whole other dream he had, an entirely different life he could have been living. David loved his parents. He loved his life. I don't think he was sorry for how it all turned out. David Kennedy didn't have room for things like resentment in his heart. He accepted most things as they were.

But my heart hurt as I looked at him. "That doesn't answer my question."

He studied me for a moment, eyebrows creasing. "Yeah, billion dollar baby. I'd probably win."

"Why won't you go?" I reached out, my hand wrapping around his wrist.

David's eyes flicked down to my hand. He extracted his wrist from my grip and interlaced our fingers, callouses brushing the palm of my hand. It might have been my favorite feeling in the world. When he looked back up, his lips pulled to the side, and his nostrils flared when he exhaled. "It's a while away. We'll see. But it's a few days long, and I don't want to leave you."

I opened my mouth to tell him he should leave me, not because I didn't think I deserved his love, his support, his companionship, but he deserved to go home and do something he loved for a while. Steven

Winchester would probably live forever based on sheer will and determination alone.

But David interrupted, bringing the back of my hand to his lips briefly before smiling at me. "You want to go get something to eat?"

I nodded softly instead and followed him out into the night.

David

Charlie and I used to do ordinary shit like this all the time. Random food from a truck somewhere downtown after we'd spent all night wrapped up in each other at one of our places. Fucking and laughing and touching. She'd stop me eventually, because I would have happily spent all night buried in her, saying we needed to remember to eat, or we'd wither away.

What I should have told her and made sure she knew, was how important she was and how much she mattered—that I could easily exist on her, her attention, her smile, her laugh, for the rest of my life. I probably didn't need food or water anymore—my survival depended solely on her.

They were nights not unlike this one, when we walked through the empty streets, the wind practically unbearable, but we never got very far before I had her up against the wall of whatever building was closest, and we were all over each other again.

I could feel her eyes on me now when I leaned down to take a bite of one of the burritos we'd ordered. I was starving—I didn't have time for lunch at work, covering for Deacon's continued absence. He took Steven's advice and stayed home, but whether he was taking his "dry out day" seriously was another matter. The burrito wasn't even that good, and I didn't even realize I made a noise until she spoke.

"You know," she started, her voice taking on that goading tone it only ever really did when she was teasing me, "of all the things I have memorized about you, Mr. Kennedy, I had kind of forgotten that you make sex noises when you really like food."

"Oh, come on." I tipped my head back, laughing. "The noises I made with you must sound different than that."

Charlie shrugged at me, a tiny smile pulling on her lips. "Shockingly similar."

A grin split across my face when I looked at her, and it wasn't just because of what she said, it *was* funny—she was always funny. But the streetlights shone down on her, and she looked radiant standing there—that worn leather jacket, both hands clutching her burrito, because it was too big for her, chocolate hair whipping around her face in the wind coming off the lake. "Billion dollar baby, best sex of my life, and burritos. Who knew."

She raised her eyebrows at me, green eyes sparkling before she rounded the corner, stopping suddenly and her shoe catching on the sidewalk. They didn't look like shoes she would ever wear, the giant Gucci G emblazoned on the side. They looked like something Taylor might wear, and if they were hers, she'd kill Charlie if she scuffed them.

"Charlie?" I stopped, reaching out before following her gaze and seeing it—her old townhouse, those familiar, worn steps. I palmed my jaw, exhaling.

She turned to look at me, her eyes blurring at the edges. I watched her wipe at them with her wrist, her burrito coming dangerously close to her hair. Her voice was small when she spoke. "It's just a house."

It wasn't.

"Some of the best nights of my life happened in that house."

Coming to stand behind her, I dropped my chin to her head and wrapped my arms around her. It was true. I felt her push back against my chest and a sort of weary breath leaving her.

It wasn't just my best nights that happened in that house. It was where she started to make a life for herself, with Deacon, with Taylor; the walls probably stretched thin, unable to contain their laughter.

It was where we fell in love, and it was where the wheels started to come off, too. Where she fell asleep with Tripp—shared a bed with him—after I hurt her that night by prioritizing politeness and formality, and seemingly Victoria, over her.

At the end of the day, I tore the wheels off the cart, not her. I left her when I should have stayed.

I tightened my arms around her, trying to fold her into me, into my chest and my heart where she lived, because it was just us out here, arguably shitty burritos, the streetlights, and a townhouse that was apparently our beginning and our end.

But it wasn't the end, because here we were, three years later.

She tipped her head back, offering me a soft smile. Her eyes were cloudy, not as iridescent as usual, and that broke my heart. "You want to go home?"

"Sure, billion dollar baby. Let's go home." My voice was low, and I dropped my lips to the side of her head for a moment before grabbing her hand.

I'd go anywhere with her.

A faint light emanated from under Deacon's doorway. There was no noise coming from that end of the hallway, but that didn't really mean anything. It wasn't a regular hallway, and it certainly wasn't a regular house. There wasn't even a lock on the door. There was a fucking mechanical keypad there instead. God forbid Steven Winchester use something as banal as a key.

The distance between Charlie and Deacon's rooms stretched longer than most apartments and bordered cavernous. The idea of them both existing here as children was almost laughable—and I knew from Charlie it hadn't changed since then. They were always giant rooms with imposing beds, too much sitting space, and inappropriate furniture for children, with ostentatious ensuites with bathtubs that would never fill up, and French doors that led to balconies overlooking the back of the property.

I hadn't spent much time here when we were together, nothing really beyond our expected appearances at events, and only one or two nights. They both avoided it like the plague, and I could never really understand why. My family home was one of my favorite places on the planet—but I was starting to realize it was full of things that had probably never existed in these halls.

Charlie paused at the top of the stairs, her lips parting when she noticed the light at the end of the hallway.

Reaching forward, I grabbed her hand and brought it to my mouth, out of habit more than anything. "I should go check on your brother."

"Please." She smiled, and I could tell she meant to sound dry, but her voice cracked. "Make sure he hasn't gone through too much of the scotch reserve."

I nodded, brushing my lips across the back of her hand one more time before dropping it gently and rolling out my shoulders. It took about all my restraint, every hour of the day, not to be all over her all the time, and I wasn't doing either of us any favors. "You should get some sleep. I can stay—"

"No," she interrupted, shaking her head. "You can stay with me. I promise I'll keep my hands to myself. The pillow wall can remain up. I'm going to shower but just come in whenever you're back."

She wasn't the problem, but I didn't say that. I just watched her walk backward, her eyebrows waggling at me until her back was against the door, hand searching for the doorknob. She smiled, raising her other hand in a tiny wave before disappearing into her room.

I waited for a minute for the light to turn on under her door—like I was waiting for her to get home safe. Even though I wasn't sure anything in this house was safe—before turning and walking down the hallway to knock on Deacon's door.

I didn't wait for him to answer before swinging the door open—who fucking knew what he was doing in there.

He was sitting in the fucking dark, save for one lamp that illuminated him where he sat in an armchair in the corner, holding a glass of scotch, like a movie villain.

"Jesus Christ, Deac." I palmed my jaw, shaking my head, tempted to storm across the room and grab the glass from his hands.

He arched an eyebrow at me, swirling the glass before leaning back even farther in the chair, one arm thrown over the back, and his hair somehow more unkempt than it had been this morning.

"Want a glass? This bottle of scotch was recovered from the seafloor. Some fucking pirate ship or another smuggled it way back in the day. Quite literally the only one of its kind."

"No," I answered, my lip curling up. Something looked off about him. I squinted, leaning forward. I could see them from here—his pupils were fucking blown. "Are you fucking high?" I glanced at the table beside him—and there it was, his Amex Centurion sitting askew on an ornate silver tray, a rolled-up bill, and unmistakable lines of coke residue across the shiny surface. "Deacon, are you—"

"Spare me the indignant outrage, like you've never done blow." Deacon shook his head, knocking back a measure of the scotch, before grabbing the bill and swiping his nose across the tray.

"I've never railed lines alone in my room in the dark. I'll tell you that for fucking free." My lips were still curled back and I watched him in what I could only describe as abject horror. "What are you doing, Deacon?"

He looked up at me, thumb finding his nostril and a loud snorting noise following. "Not a fucking clue, man. But I know what you should do. Walk back on down the hall to my sister. She needs you more than I do."

I wasn't sure that was entirely true, but I crossed my arms, eyes narrowed in on him. "I'm not sure this is what Steven meant when he said take the day to dry out. You have to be at the office tomorrow."

He nodded, barely sparing me a glance as he dropped the bill and started pouring himself another glass of scotch. "Board meeting. Wouldn't miss it."

We stared at one another. My best friend. Charlie's brother. The most important person in the world to the love of my life. My brother-in-law in another universe, if things had worked out differently. "I'll be just down the hall if you need me."

He shrugged before leaning down again, another godforsaken snorting noise following. "Don't need you."

I shook my head, raised my eyebrows, and took a measured exhale before closing the door. I don't think anyone had ever needed anyone as much as Deacon Winchester needed someone right now.

Tripp

My mother had a penchant for changing the furnishings in the house at least once a year, so I supposed it was a boon that my childhood room looked nothing like it did when I was eighteen.

A new rug she had imported from Italy stretched across the cherry hardwood floors. She'd changed the bed, too—what was surely a custom, cream-colored, cushioned headboard towered against the wall, and the navy Ralph Lauren sheets tucked in tightly.

The ornamental fireplace was still in the wall—changing the structure of the house was likely beyond her reach—but the brick had been painted an almost identical color to the headboard. There was a bar cart against the wall now—glass and laid out with three different bottles of scotch and two Waterford Heritage whiskey glasses, ready and sparkling. I wasn't sure if that was a pre-moving home addition, or something she put in for me.

It was the only type of motherly gesture she knew how to make—the furthest she would go in acknowledging that maybe things would be difficult with my father—ensuring there were multiple options for a glass of top-shelf scotch at the end of a hard day.

Yanking at my tie to loosen the knot before unbuttoning the jacket of the BOSS Slim Fit Houndstooth Virgin Wool suit, I went straight for the cart. It *had* been a particularly difficult day; Post paraded around the office in his ridiculous fucking pinstriped Armani suit—even I wouldn't wear something that pretentious. It wasn't even the suit. It was the shit-eating grin that had taken up permanent residence on his face. Our father siphoning money and making illegal bets with it couldn't have worked out better for him.

He was president of wealth management at Boston United about ten years earlier than he anticipated. And I was schlepping it as his underling in his former position as the divisional director of private clients.

The absolute minefield that Winchester Holdings was about to be when people found out that Steven was sick would have been preferable.

Grabbing the already open bottle of Glengoyne, I tipped it over one of the glasses, watching the amber liquid pour from the neck of the bottle. I let it go for too long, the glass full beyond an acceptable pour for scotch, before taking it and dropping down on the freshly pressed sheets of the bed.

I felt my phone vibrating on the inside of my jacket when I was about to turn on the TV that hung across the opposite wall—there was actually a game that I wanted to watch, and I wouldn't risk doing it in the entertainment room where my father was probably lurking.

Chuck's name lit up my screen, covering a photo of us that probably shouldn't have still been there. It was from one of the nights when we stayed up at that sterile rental I had in the financial district in New York, watching shitty TV and eating too much takeout. She was wearing one of my sweaters, a gray Hugo Boss that practically drowned her. Our heads were tipped together, she was smiling—one of those dumb Winchester smiles—and my expression was purposely flat, but I could see the lines around my eyes that I did my best to combat. I was fighting a smile. Hers was the first number I put in my phone when I moved home and got a new phone, and apparently, I was feeling particularly masochistic at the time when I set this as the contact photo.

It wasn't a number I'd intended to use, until her brother called me.

But it was also a number I'd probably always fucking answer.

"Hey." Her voice was soft, but I could hear the surprise there.

Like she couldn't believe I answered her, and given my track record over the last few months, it was a valid assumption.

"Hey," I offered, dropping my head back against the headboard, letting the words hang between us.

Her next words were the equivalent of her taking one of her Jimmy Choo's and hacking open my chest cavity with it before skewering my heart on the heel.

"He got a tattoo for me."

She didn't need to tell me who. There was only one him for her. I didn't particularly like how it felt—knowing that Kennedy had inked her permanently on his skin. But it was the hope in her voice, the tiny spark that probably only a handful of people in the world would be able to hear—that caused whatever was left of my heart, impaled and held in her hands, to metaphorically spurt blood all over me, my designer suit, and the custom headboard.

It would have been utter carnage, if any of it was real.

I blinked before rolling my shoulders and forcing the lilt back into my voice she hated so much because it got under her skin—a place I'd gladly live forever. "I'd get a tattoo for you, Chuckles."

"Well, did you?" Charlie's voice was petulant.

"No." And I probably wouldn't. I had no interest in permanent body modifications and didn't particularly relish the idea of injecting my skin with ink. That particular sweet, yet rough-around the edges-gesture, had DK written all over it. I palmed my jaw, offering a shrug, even though she couldn't see me. "Kennedy was always the better man anyway."

"You're not a bad man, Tripp."

She was always fairly resolute in her defense of me, even when it wasn't deserved.

Laughing, I shook my head and took a too-large sip of the scotch before answering. It burned, and I wanted it too. "Don't get soft on me, Chuck. We both know there's a difference between not being bad and being good."

And there was. I'd never really considered myself to be bad. But I certainly wasn't fucking good.

Case in point—I had no problem kissing Chuck, telling her I missed her, all in pursuit of clearing my name and having what I'd wanted for years. I'd thought it was all fine, completely okay, because Kennedy didn't understand her how I did, didn't have the shared history, and what did anyone else matter if they were my way?

It was another uncomfortable truth that looking in the mirror of this fucking house had been. My father was horrifically selfish.

So much so that he didn't care what he left in his wake. My brother was the same, happy to step over all our father's casualties and wrongdoings for his own purposes. Maybe selfishness was an inherited trait, genetic.

I was no fucking better than them.

I could practically hear her rolling her eyes when she answered. "Wouldn't dream of it. Will you tell me what's going on?"

"Family stuff. You don't need to worry about the inner workings of an elitist East Coast family. Speaking of, did you know Mr. Banks is sitting on over thirty million dollars'-worth of real estate? Does that make my real estate portfolio more impressive than yours?"

A short laugh, something between a bark and a scoff, came from the other end of the phone. "Goodnight, Tripp. Love you."

Her voice was soft, and I could hear her smile. It was practiced; they sounded like well-worn words she tossed my way all the time. Friendly.

Entirely different than how they sounded when you said them to someone you were in love with.

I could tell the difference because I'd heard what those words sounded like, changed by the way her lips curved upward, the way her heart spilled out from her chest with them when she said the same thing to David Kennedy.

Swallowing, I gripped the back of my head for a minute before answering. "Love you, too."

She didn't mean it how I did, that was for fucking sure.

Charlie

The impulse to call Tripp had been sort of like the impulse to call Taylor—to tell my best friend something, *anything*. Whether it was good news or bad news.

I had actually wanted to go to her room, to whisper to her that David had stamped me permanently on his skin. I was about to—when I checked my phone and saw that she got a page and had to go back to the hospital for a few hours.

So, I called Tripp instead.

I wasn't even sure why I did it; half to make sure he was living and breathing, that he was okay, and the other half maybe because we were friends once upon a time, too.

Wiping the condensation from the shower off the bathroom mirror, my eyes fell to the unmarked skin of my inner bicep. There was significantly less muscle there than what was found on David's arms and on his body in general. I'd always been certain he was a permanent part of me, in the very roots of who I was, but it was intangible. Nothing different about me to the naked eye that marked me as his.

But now there was something about him, visible for all the world to see, if the sleeve of his t-shirt lifted just so—something to tell everyone he belonged to me.

Tugging on my pink Big Feelings pajama tank top, I pulled it down across my damp skin toward the waistband of the matching shorts. There wasn't much skin on display, but when you were trying to have a platonic sleepover with the love of your life, a man that quite literally inked your name on his body, any little bit was too much.

The stupid chandelier-style light was off, the curtains thrown open, and moonlight inching across the floor. My side of the bed was empty, the duvet turned down and waiting for me, David on the other side.

One of David's hands was under his head, resting against one of the many pillows stacked against the headboard, the other splayed across his abdomen, which, unfortunately for me, was bare and on display.

He looked particularly pensive, staring up at the ceiling and his honey eyes dark. His jaw was tense. I could tell by the set of it that he was angry or frustrated. Something had probably happened with my brother—Deacon could give Tripp a run for his money when it came to being an antagonistic piece of work.

But I didn't really want to know what happened between them. They had their own thing, and this version of David, bare and ready for sleep in my bed, my signature etched onto his inner arm, this version was just for us.

He glanced over, offering me a grin as I padded across the carpet and crawled into bed beside him. There was no pillow between us, but the years and all the things we had done to one another stretched out there, just waiting to rear up and sink their teeth in.

"I've never asked you...it didn't feel like my business," I started, studying the way his hair curled at the nape of his neck and the striations of muscle running along his shoulders where they were stacked against the pillows.

"Everything about me is your business," David said plainly, one hand still resting under his head and the other still on his stomach.

I suspected I should bring back the pillow wall—more so for me than for him. The stacks of muscles across his chest and abdomen were all illuminated by the light streaming through the open curtains. The sheet rested just below his waist, tapered obliques disappearing beneath the impossibly high thread count.

"Why were you with her?" I whispered.

I wasn't sure why I asked, why I even wanted the answer. It didn't really matter at the end of the day. But David Kennedy was mine, just like I was his, and it seemed almost impossible to me that there was a time when we belonged to other people.

A muscle jumped in David's jaw, and his lips pulled tight for a moment before he rolled to his side. He propped himself up with his hand, staring down at me, eyes dark. "I wish I had a good answer. Something meaningful to say. Something salient that makes me less of a jackass, but I don't. I was just trying to survive without you."

"I'm sorry I was something you needed to survive," I offered, fingers feathering against the duvet. I wanted to reach out and take one of those rogue waves between my fingers.

"I'm not." David shook his head and wrapped his hand around mine, closing the distance between us—those calluses lovingly scraping against my skin—and brought our joined hands to his lips.

They were warm, but a shiver ran down my spine.

We stayed there for a moment, his eyes on me and his lips against my skin, before he brought our hands down to the bed. He let go, and as it always was when David Kennedy stopped touching me, I felt entirely bare, my skin missing the feel of his. But his fingers found mine, playing with them, thumbs making gentle, soothing strokes across them.

"Can I ask you about Tripp?" David's voice bordered on hesitant.

My heart crumpled, cleaving in two for a moment, because he looked hurt. I could see it in the tightness across his jaw, his mouth. I didn't regret what I did, but I would always regret causing David pain.

I didn't regret Tripp, not for one minute, not anymore.

Whatever it was between us was love; it always had been, and we'd been lucky enough to have more than one kind of love. I loved him—I did. But not the way I loved David.

I could feel it—it was intangible. Just something that took root in me, growing and blooming, decaying and dying, and ultimately poking through the soil of me again. I knew when I looked at David, how whatever time of day it was, he somehow constantly looked more beautiful to me. I used to think that dusk was what David was made for—but there was something about the way the moonlight threw shadows across all the planes of his face, the stacks of muscle and endless stretches of perfect skin—maybe it wasn't so much about the time of day, where the sun or the moon sat in the sky, and the way the light made him shine.

Maybe it was the fact that after all this time, he was just across from me, his fingers playing with mine, in my bed. There were years stretching between us, laughter and love, anger and heartbreak, and sadness. But here we were at the end of the day, just me and him again, entirely stripped bare and seeing each other the way we always had.

It was almost ethereal, found in the quiet moments and the silent understanding.

I nodded, finally speaking. "You can ask me anything, David. In and amongst all the time I spent in London trying to date myself, I realized I'm not a terribly honest person. Maybe not intentionally...but I tend not to share a lot of what I'm feeling or thinking, and it's been to the detriment of me and everyone around me."

David's fingers stilled, and he stared at me intently, seemingly weighing his next words. "What was it like with him? Different than us?"

Exhaling, I tipped my head against the pillow. "I'm not sure I have a good answer for that, David. It was different. But different doesn't mean better."

"No, it doesn't," David answered. His gaze dropped to our hands, and he moved my fingers between his again.

Swallowing, I wrapped my hand around his wrist, stilling his movements. "I've spoken to him on the phone since I got home. Twice. He finally returned one of my calls the first night because Deacon called him to tell him about Dad. And I called him earlier tonight to see how he was."

"You don't owe me an explanation. I don't want you to think you need to tell me every little thing you do, Charlie. I meant it when I said I forgive you. I'm not—"

I cut in, fingers pressing into his wrist. I could feel his pulse beneath them. "It's not about that. It's about me, and the holes I've dug with dishonesty and lies by omission. I just want you to know. He's in my life, and he probably always will be, in one way or another."

He nodded, lips pressing together. He didn't look angry; he just looked thoughtful. "What did you talk about?"

"Well, tonight, I told him about your new ink." I offered him a small smile. "He himself hasn't dedicated part of his body to me, but he did confirm you were always the better man, anyway."

It was meant to be an affirmation, confirmation that David had the most important place in my life and always would. It was inked on his skin, but his features pulled back into something like a grimace. "Is that all I am? A good guy?"

"What's wrong with being good, David?" I asked softly, eyebrows knit.

His eyes flicked down to where my fingers wrapped around his wrist before he finally looked back at me. "There's nothing wrong with being good. I just want to be more to you."

I wanted to tell him the truth—that he was always more, had always been more, and he would always be. I once thought he was the entire earth, and I was just a star lucky enough to be in his atmosphere, his universe. It took me too long to realize that I should be my own Earth, that I deserved that. And I think I was now. At home in my own skin, my own planet, anchored down by my own atmosphere instead of someone else's.

But he was still the sun. Would always be the sun—the brightest, most important star in my sky; what kept me warm, lit up my life with honey eyes and a grin that was just for me, would always be what I wanted to tip my chin upward to, to be bathed in all of him.

I didn't say any of that, because if I did, and he smiled at me, looked at me, and God forbid, any of his hair fell onto his forehead, my no-sex rule would be out the window.

Instead, I brought his palm to my mouth and pressed my lips to it.

I closed my eyes briefly, before I gently placed his hand back down on his side of the bed. Looking up at him, I smiled. "Thank you for tonight. I liked being normal with you."

"Oh yeah?" David asked, raising his eyebrows before he turned, laying back with one hand under his head again. "I like being normal with you, too, billion dollar baby."

Turning onto my back, I settled into the pillow. Shadows moved across the ceiling, and I watched them for a moment before asking a question I had always wanted the answer to. "Do you think there's a world where we do stuff like that? Where even if my father were dying, the biggest concern wouldn't be public perception and stock value?"

David's voice was low, but I could tell he was smiling when he answered. That was one of the best things about knowing one another the way we did, in the quiet moments. It was easy to notice those subtle things. "What other things do you want to do? Go to more shitty bars, drink shitty beer, and smoke cigarettes with me?"

"I don't know. We could sail around the world, just me and you. We could sit in the box at a Cubs game and have no one take our photograph. We could go bowling," I offered, shrugging. The list of things I wanted to experience with him, both normal and entirely grand, was endless.

"One of those things is not like the other." David laughed, and I could feel the movement of his shoulders against the bed.

I felt myself smile, a small laugh catching in my throat. "I suppose you're right. I'll have to dream up some other things for us to do. Goodnight, Mr. Kennedy."

"Goodnight, billion dollar baby. Try not to get too carried away and dream about joining a bowling league."

Bowling with David Kennedy. It sounded like the best dream.

Charlie

"He seriously got a tattoo of your signature? Permanently stamped you on his skin? And it was Deacon's idiotic idea?" Taylor raised one eyebrow, eyes flicking up from her laptop.

"That's what I said, yes." I would have narrowed my eyes at her, I had to repeat myself more than once while she typed away, but my face was currently being contoured, poked and prodded at for a *no-makeup* makeup look, and my already straight hair was being pulled in every direction with a flat iron.

Taylor pursed her lips, looking down at the screen again, hardly breaking stride in whatever she was typing. "And then you went for a romantic little stroll with burritos, reminisced about your old townhouse, and came back here—to your room—and he told you his last relationship was just for revenge, entirely about you, and then you slept in the same bed and you didn't fuck?"

"No, Taylor, we didn't fuck," I answered, voice flat. "We aren't even having sex."

If the woman currently attacking my face with an angled brush and the man pulling at my hair found this line of conversation to be off, they gave no indication. The makeup artist's face remained impassive, all glowing pillowy cheeks and flat eyes, and there was no sudden tug at the back of my head, no smell of burning hair.

Anyone who came into this house for any sort of service like this signed an NDA, anyway. Sabine was always bringing in different people to do my hair or makeup, depending on the day and the event. But Rebecca always made sure they signed off on the proper paperwork. Secrecy never seemed as important as it did right now, not when the man at the helm of the next great American dynasty was being eaten away from the inside.

Taylor's nostrils flared, and she shook her head. "Your signature is really ugly. You should definitely bone him for that alone."

I rolled my eyes. One of the few things I had inherited from my father was his messy penmanship. "Okay, thanks for that. Pretty sure doctors have notoriously messy writing."

"It seems a little...edgy for David. Mr. North Carolina, what with his say-it-like-it-is, address any problem head-on, mature communication, and his manners? He seems too nice to mark his perfect, tanned skin permanently."

"David isn't that nice," I interjected, cheeks heating.

He *was* nice. Entirely more mature and more emotionally available than anyone I had ever met. But there were plenty of things only I got to see, memories that were just for me—when it was just us, alone in my room, alone in his apartment, alone anywhere really—when he was anything but *nice*.

"Oh, that's right. I forgot he was a bit of a freak in the bedroom. All domineering and filthy. I really love that for him." Taylor continued to type away, barely sparing me a glance, and the set of her features sharp as always.

I said nothing; she was hardly paying attention anyway. I watched her while my face was dusted with powder and the last strands of my hair were framed around it until she finally looked up, snapping her laptop closed.

Taylor waved a hand, and I noticed how red, how dry, her skin was. She had a hard time keeping her skin from cracking in the fall and winter with the constant washing, sanitizing and scrubbing in for surgery. But she said she would be spending more time in the OR, observing and assisting, or in the lab to prep for whatever surgery she was going to be performing on my father. She was already trying so hard. For me, for Deacon, for him. Quite literally tearing her skin off just to try to give us a bit more time with our last remaining parent.

"What's all this about, anyway?" She gestured to the hair and makeup artists before turning to look at the rack of suits Sabine wheeled in earlier before promptly disappearing to ensure Deacon was dressed.

I raised my eyebrows, grateful that everyone had finally stepped away from me. "WH Board meeting today to announce the half-baked plan to keep our father's terminal illness a secret."

Taylor stood from the chaise lounge, pursing her lips while she shoved her laptop into her Saint Laurent computer bag. "Why do you need your makeup and hair done for that?"

I snorted as Sabine traipsed through the open door, her black patent Louboutins sinking into the plush carpet while she beelined for the rack of suits. "Probably because Deacon smells like a fucking brewery, and my father looks permanently gray. So maybe they're hoping if they trot me out like a little doll, no one will notice."

"Well, you are very pretty." Taylor shouldered her bag before brushing her hands down her thighs, smoothing out some invisible wrinkles in her black scrubs. "Text me when it's done? I don't think I'll be back tonight."

I nodded, about to tell her how thankful I was. And I was endlessly thankful for so many things where she was concerned—her enduring friendship, her love, her support, her unwavering loyalty, her tenacity in trying to scrape any more time she could for my father's life, when my brother appeared. He was dressed and looking almost entirely put together, save for the bags under his eyes and the untidy sweep of his hair.

Deacon walked through the open doorway, features cold and eyes cutting across the room. "Where's David?"

I flicked my eyes up at Deacon, one brow rising. "How am I supposed to know? Last I checked, he worked for you, not me."

Deacon scoffed, ire rising in his eyes. "We both know that's not true. He didn't sleep here last night, then?"

I said nothing, ignoring the bait. Deacon wanted a punching bag, and it could be me. I would rather it be me than anyone else. But I didn't feel like playing. Not when he was talking about David.

Taylor seemed to have no problem, though. She stalked forward, crossing her arms over her chest and her features looking decidedly predatory. Her nostrils flared, and she leaned forward, the tip of her nose practically brushing the seam of Deacon's chalk-striped Brunello Cucinelli blazer. She tipped her chin up, her hair swinging in its uncharacteristically sleek ponytail. "New cologne?"

Deacon jerked back, eyes narrowing at Taylor. "What are you talking about? I've been wearing the same cologne since I was sixteen."

It was true. Deacon had been wearing Tom Ford Ombre Leather since he and his prep school roommate shared a bottle in their dorm room.

"Hmm. Smells like scotch." She shrugged, turning back to me and her gaze softening momentarily. "Text me after."

I widened my eyes at her. I really wished those two would knock it off. I *needed* them to knock it off. They had fought over the years—we all had. But never like this. Those two, their bizarre magnetism and seeming inability to stay away from each other had always concerned me, but it had never really been an issue.

I remember Taylor losing her virginity to him—like it was yesterday, unfortunately. Our families were in Mykonos for the summer. My father stayed on the phone the entire time; Dr. Breen constantly needed to be near a computer so he could review images for any consultations that came his way. Taylor's mother was a vapid thing, and mine was long dead behind the eyes at that point.

So it was just the three of us, a precursor of what was to come—when we wouldn't just be *alone* but practically forgotten.

Taylor and I were sharing a room—her whale noises were already required and annoying me to no end. The three of us stayed up way too late drinking alcohol that we had no business drinking, but our parents certainly weren't paying us any attention. I went to bed—ready to leave those two to their own devices. But I remember her telling me the next day, waking me up, one hand shoving at my shoulder and her teeth chewing at her lower lip.

Taylor never worried. She had always been blissfully confident, certain everything would work out.

She didn't want it to change anything. Not for me and her, not for me and my brother, not for the three of us and what we were to one another.

It was an on-again-off-again thing we all pretend never happened. Until it wasn't anymore. I didn't know the last time they were together, and I didn't really want to, because the three of us had just fallen into what we were. The only family I ever really had and ever really needed.

"Oh, fuck off, Taylor." Deacon rolled his eyes, shoving his hands into his suit pocket.

She arched an eyebrow at him, her lips curling up in triumph. Taylor turned, features only softening for me as she raised her hand in goodbye before her Hoka-sneakered feet carried her from my room.

Deacon watched her leave, his own lip curling back in distaste. He shook his head, one wisp of hair moving across his forehead before he stalked across the room, ignoring Sabine and the two stylists who were packing up and dragging the chaise lounge from the foot of my bed across the stupid, high-pile carpet.

"She needs to get off her fucking high horse. She went to Northwestern. She didn't go to fucking—"

"Stop. What is the matter with you? " I cut him off, eyes flicking up and watching as the words died on his lips.

I waited for Deacon to scoff, for some ire-filled remark to come from his lips, or for the usual boyish indifference to take over. Instead, his features collapsed on themselves, all that fake bravado and that mask he wore disintegrating before my eyes—eyebrows falling together and his lips parting. He looked like a little boy again, the one I loved with my whole heart—too much baby fat on his cheeks and a softer jawline. "Who do you think is here for me?"

I pulled my head back, wrinkling my nose. "David flew in the second you called."

Deacon shot me a look, a barely restrained eye roll.

"Convenient how my sister also happens to be the love of his life. And Taylor? *Your* best friend."

"*Our* childhood best friend." I reached forward to grab his hands, but he pulled back.

Deacon shook his head, his palms raised in the air. "Everyone's here for you, and they're all fucking on me about how I need to be better for you because you deserve this, and you deserve that. And don't get me wrong—you do, you fucking deserve better than a brother whose blood alcohol level is questionable at any given time, but I just feel so—"

"Alone?" I interjected softly, grabbing his hands from the air.

Deacon's jaw tensed before he threw me a noncommittal shrug.

"You're not alone. I came here for you. I'm here for you. And besides, we both know a Winchester is never really alone." I offered him a tiny eye roll, and his lips twitched when I gestured behind us to the endless racks of designer suits, where Sabine was sifting through them.

We both watched her make a triumphant sort of tapping gesture on one of the hangers before pulling it down and turning to us. "Charlie? Are you ready? I have the pinstriped Alexander McQueen pulled for you—"

"Can I wear the Vince instead?" I gestured helplessly toward the rack, where a camel-colored suit spilled from an open bag. "Wool makes everyone itchy."

Sabine pursed her lips, shaking her head. "Too casual."

She glanced back at the racks, her eyes narrowing on another open bag, where houndstooth pants were visible. "We'll put you in the Favorite Daughter. The houndstooth is nice for fall."

My lips parted, and I looked back to my brother, whose face had lit up. "Favorite Daughter?"

Deacon's mouth split into a grin, and for a moment, he almost looked like he used to—when nothing could touch him and nothing hurt him. "You can't make that shit up."

"No, you can't," I whispered, my smile stretching and holding onto this little moment where it was just me and him against the world, where as long as I had him, nothing could hurt me, either.

Charlie

I hadn't set foot in the Winchester Holdings' Chicago offices in almost three years. The last time I was there, my father effectively fired me. I gave him back the ring that was meant for me in another lifetime, and I had steamrolled my entire life. It was just me—alone—save for a security guard who looked like they were half-asleep when I walked out through those lobby doors that day, and walked away from my life.

Today, those same lobby doors were being held open for me, for my family, the next great American dynasty, while my brother and I walked behind our father the way we always did—three steps back and one to the side.

I wondered if the marble flooring, shiny as always, would feel different under the soles of my beige Aquazzura Bow Tie Pump 105s. I used to skate over this floor, outfits not unlike the one I was wearing today, expensive material billowing around me, and go up the elevator, stepping into a life that wasn't really meant for me.

But the floor felt how it always did when I crossed the lobby in perfect Winchester formation—as if the man at the helm of this demented triangle wasn't slowly dying, being eaten away from the inside, as if my brother wasn't given breath spray for the inside pocket of his suit, along with strict instructions from the family publicist to use it every ten minutes to stave off the smell of stale scotch.

I glanced sideways at Deacon, Ray Bans still pulled down over his eyes, despite the fact that we were inside. Both hands were shoved in the pockets of his suit. He walked with purpose behind our father, seemingly not a care in the world beyond making sure he didn't catch the toe of his Gucci loafers on anything.

"Rough night?" I asked, as the elevator doors opened, and we stepped in behind our father.

We didn't stand in front of him, like he was fucking Moses parting the Red Sea, my brother and I stepped around him, each taking our respective spaces on either side behind him. God forbid an elevator door open and Steven Winchester not be front and center. Certainly not when said elevator opened right in the middle of the executives' floor of the company where he liked to play God.

Deacon leaned back, dropping his head against the mirrored wall of the elevator, and rolled his head to look at me. "Could ask you the same question. David being back in your bed and all."

I gave him a flat look. "Not many brothers are this interested in their sister's sex lives."

"Yeah, well, not many sisters make their way through half the leadership team at their family company, either."

My lips parted with indignation, and I was about to ask him what the fuck was wrong with him, when our father spoke. It was only one word, harsh and biting in the tiny elevator. He rarely intervened between us, and it never went very far. This wasn't an exception.

"Enough."

I couldn't really see his face; it was distorted in the shiny metal of the elevator doors, but the set of his shoulders seemed unbothered. My father's humanity only showed in small, seemingly insignificant moments. Apparently, going to the 35th floor of a building to tell the Board of his company, his entire life, and universe, that he was dying didn't make the cut.

I looked back over to Deacon, head still tipped back and one strand of chocolate hair brushing his forehead. It was longer than he usually kept it, all slicked back save for the one piece. He wouldn't say anything in front of our father, so I pulled my phone from the beige leather Saint Laurent top handle Sabine had shoved at me before I walked out the door.

> **Charlie**: Don't push me away. You can hit me all you want—but leave David out of it. Leave Tripp out of it.

I watched as he seemingly felt the vibration of his phone in the pocket of his suit jacket, one hand fishing out the phone and his head tipping down to read the message. He shot me a look, mouth tightening before his thumb started moving across the screen.

> **Deacon**: You're right. I'm sorry.

> **Charlie**: Did something happen? I'm here with you, Deacon. Me and you. Not alone.

> **Deacon**: Noa texted during the car ride over. She has to go straight from Tahiti to Japan for another week or two.

Before I could answer, the elevator came to a halt, and the doors slid open—revealing our father and his presence to the entire executives' floor and revealing Winchester Holdings to me.

I swallowed, eyes peering beyond my father. It looked the same—marble flooring, admin assistants, and their mahogany desks stationed in front of offices behind heavy wooden doors, save for two. One glass door at either end. My father's office and the one that was mine.

Deacon pocketed his phone, gesturing for me to step out after our father, who had already strode out of the elevator. He reached out, fingers wrapping around my wrist, and I turned to him, sunglasses finally pushed off his face. His features were soft, and his eyes almost looked like mine again. His voice was quiet when he spoke. "They're just memories. Nothing that lives here, nothing that you did when this was your life, deserves to hurt you."

Wrapping my hand around his—our father would look back any minute now, wondering why we weren't trailing behind him like well-trained dogs—I pressed my fingers into his skin. "Me and you against the world."

"Me and you against the world, Charles." Deacon smiled, but it didn't meet his eyes, and he took his hand from mine, knocking his fist against my chin briefly before shoving both hands back into the pockets of his tailored, three-thousand-dollar suit and walking onto the floor like he didn't have a care in the world.

I tripped the last time I walked out of this elevator, my heel snagging when I saw my father sitting behind my desk.

Unbidden, my eyes swung to the left. The office was almost empty, save for the standard furnishings. The desk I had bought and put in there, all my furniture was gone, still collecting dust in storage some-where. I liked it all, each piece carefully curated to make my office feel like me, to try and make Winchester Holdings feel like me. But I didn't want any of it back.

I followed behind my father and brother, heels clicking on the stone. The stretch of floor to get to his office and the conference room just beyond it never felt long enough. It always went too fast when I would make my way across it, stomach churning, and simply never enough time to prepare and steel myself for what I might find, the father I might get when I stepped into those rooms. But today, it felt like it went on forever. No one looked at my father or Deacon, but there were a few curious glances at me. I didn't recognize anyone here anymore. The leadership team had been rebuilt after I decimated it.

But there were doors, offices, spaces I recognized, ones that meant something to me.

Tripp's old office was unceremoniously occupied by a woman I didn't know, but I could see her sitting behind the desk that had once been his—dark hair pulled back and severe features set as she typed at an almost impossible speed.

The door to David's old office, where we had fucked, fallen in love, and fallen apart, was open. It wasn't the space, the proximity, and the ghosts that made my heart stop.

It was David Kennedy, sitting behind that same old desk, hair pushed back and honey eyes sweeping across the screen in front of him. The blazer of his suit was discarded on the back of his chair, the top buttons of his shirt undone, and the cotton stretching across his chest and shoulders. My favorite eyes in the world flicked up, and then he was looking at me. Back here where we first met, a scene not unlike this when I walked in on my first day.

I blinked and could see it, remembered exactly what it had looked like, what the silk of my blouse had felt like against my skin, what his calloused hands had felt like when he reached out to shake mine. The first knock on the door to a home you don't live in, not yet—but you're thinking about renting.

By the time his hand dropped, I was ready to buy it. To supplant myself there and never leave. I would have grown roots there, stretched out there for eternity, had the roots of my own heart not been full of decay, rot that needed to be cut out from the inside out before anything could really bloom.

His grin—my grin—stretched across his face, and he winked at me. I raised a hand, just enough for him to see it, a tiny little wave of hello to a life gone by, to an old home that I loved, but not one I wanted to go back to, at least not the way it used to exist.

Major renovations were required, major renovations concluded.

That's what it felt like to me—to be here, the two of us staring at one another. Nothing felt heavy, nothing hurt.

Maybe I could go home again.

I could have stayed there forever, but Deacon was looking over his shoulder at me, fingers poised a moment away from snapping, and our father was already through the door of the conference room.

David jerked his chin toward the other end of the office, toward the boardroom, winking at me one more time before dropping his eyes back to his computer.

Deacon had stopped, waiting for me a few feet from the entrance to the conference room. Our father wasn't in there—Steven Winchester was—shaking hands and moving his way around the table to greet each board member sitting there, seven men and five women, and the total cost of their suits likely more than most people made in a year, pretending just hours ago he wasn't getting nutrients from an IV.

My brother and I looked at one another for a moment, us against the world, two small children again who had both parents and lived in that impossibly big house, before we ever knew anything about the world we lived in before we followed our father to play dynasty.

———

I could count on one hand how many WH board meetings I had been required to attend over the years. It was always a Deacon duty—the heir to the face of the whole thing. I was never really important in the grand scheme of things, because Deacon and our father outnumbered me when it came to shareholder power, and they were always aligned. I never mattered to the board members—I didn't hold enough stock to be a problem if I decided to stage a coup. Apparently, there was a time my lack of interest alarmed the majority of board members, and there was a certain level of pressure on my father to bring me into the fold, to make sure I would fall in line and never cause a problem.

But I was about to become very, very important. Because when Steven Winchester died—stopped breathing, left the Earth—everything he owned was going to be split right down the middle.

The revelation that he was sick, secretly dying, had been alarming to the Board. Faces paled, lips tightened, and one or two of them even had to wipe their eyes.

But what really bothered them—caused mouths to part, eyes to widen, displeasure to radiate across features and voices to be raised—was the announcement that his assets, every single one, including the company, would be split down the middle.

Right between the faithful heir—the next great Winchester patriarch, who despite his irreverence and penchant for flashy suits, had always fallen in line—and me. The once missing, irrelevant, forgotten daughter who steamrolled the entire leadership, and who was deemed a PR liability and had her whole portfolio dissolved.

It was always going to be that way—written into my father's will from the time I turned eighteen. I had wondered if he made any changes over the last three years; it wouldn't have surprised me. Not after everything. I'm sure he had been advised to do so by legal, by the people in this very room. But he hadn't changed a thing.

"What if she marries Kennedy? He has shares and decision-making power. They marry, and they outnumber you." Scott Sabean, one of the longest-standing board members, sat across from me and pointed one finger toward my brother.

Once upon a time, Scott had worked for our grandfather. A permanent, scowling figure at all our family events and a perfunctory invite to anything, and also, apparently, a not-so-secret misogynist.

"Watch it." Deacon's features were a flat line, and his voice sharp. He leaned back in his chair, arms folded. He hadn't so much as blinked when our father delivered the news, resolute and unwavering in his solidarity and support for me.

I usually wouldn't rise to the bait, content to let them argue over things they weren't going to change. Steven Winchester was steadfast and resolute, and his decisions were final, even here. I wasn't even planning on addressing the blatant sexism; he wasn't worth my time or energy. Not when it would be utterly wasted. But it was the implication that David might do something untoward that had me speaking.

"Women can do things aside from getting married," I offered, one eyebrow rising.

Scott's eyes flashed, and there was a barely restrained eye roll that was almost comical when it was coming from a sixty-five-year-old man with white hair and a custom Ralph Lauren suit. "What can you do, Charlie? You've worked at the company for less than—"

"She can have you fired, Scott," Deacon cut in, slamming his hands down onto the table. A muscle in his jaw twitched. With his disheveled hair and the bags under his eyes, he almost looked deranged. "How does that sound?"

It wasn't exactly true either. Our father, or a vote of non-confidence by the rest of the Board, could fire Scott.

I certainly couldn't, and neither could Deacon.

Scott knew that, and he clearly didn't heed the warning written all over my brother's face, the future CEO of Winchester Holdings, he turned to our father instead. "Steven, be reasonable. If it gets out that you're sick, and your contingency plan is your son, who spends more time chasing supermodels than he does at work, and your daughter, who has fraternized with multiple members of your staff before you were forced to relieve her of her duties—"

"And now you're relieved of yours."

Our father's voice was clipped, pointed, matter-of-fact. He didn't blink, didn't so much as twitch a single muscle fiber. Steven Winchester sat at the end of the conference table without so much as a crease in his tailored, navy Milano Slim-Fit Check 1818 Suit from Brooks Brothers. Sabine had been right to dress him in navy—it brought out the blue in his eyes and detracted from the general pallor of his skin. His hands were folded, almost demurely, atop a yellow legal pad.

He hardly looked sick. If he hadn't told the entire board room, he probably could have gotten away with saying he had a poor night's sleep. He looked like the Steven Winchester of years gone by, the man at the helm of a multi-billion dollar holding. Sitting there, entirely unblinking and unfeeling, hair liberally streaked with gray, clean-shaven—he looked like he was watching a particularly dull weather report.

He certainly didn't look like he had just fired one of the longest-standing members of the Board. One of the first employees when his company was nothing more than an infant in the grand scheme of things.

"Steven—" Helen, the ever-present, ever-matronly head of Legal started, her eyes widening behind her wire-framed glasses.

But my father cut her off with a simple sideways glance. It wasn't even a cutting one. He looked back to Scott, his face blank. He didn't blink, simply staring at him while Scott's eyes widened.

"You may go." He arched an eyebrow, like he couldn't believe Scott was still sitting there with the audacity to take up space in one of his ridiculously expensive boardroom chairs.

I glanced at Deacon from the corner of my eye, expecting to see his gaze volleying back and forth, a grin spreading on his face. He lived for drama. But he wasn't smiling. His features were harsh, a muscle jumped in his cheek, and his eyes narrowed.

If it would have made a difference, I would have told my father not to fire someone who had been in his life for its entirety, someone who, in theory, had always done what was best for business. But judging by my lifetime of experience with my father, and the way he was staring, still unblinking like a robot, at Scott while he shook his head, scoffing and shoving everything back into, what was in my opinion, a hideous embossed Salvatore Ferragamo briefcase, it didn't matter.

I should have said something anyway, but I didn't, because a part of me was still a small child, and she was mollified, smiling from ear to ear, heart beaming entirely because her father chose her, defended her, above all else.

Scott said nothing, but his lip curled up in displeasure when he threw me one last, scathing glance. He shook his head, like the idea that he couldn't get away with it—that Steven Winchester would have chosen an innate defense of his children—was so unbelievable.

And it was. But maybe there really was a first time for everything.

"Leave the door open, Scott. It can be a nice reminder for anyone else at the table what happens if they speak ill of my children." Our father didn't even bother looking over his shoulder when Scott threw the door open; the only sound in the room was the heel of his ridiculous Oxfords against the echo of the floors.

Steven Winchester looked up, one salt-and-pepper eyebrow arched. "Anyone else?"

It was a rhetorical question. The rest of the Board said nothing, practically bowing their heads in deference and pulling out their papers, the annotated agenda, and various briefing notes, looking anywhere but at the still-open door. Looking anywhere other than at the man who was slowly, but surely, dying. The man who had given them all their fortunes and had let them inside to all of this.

The only world that mattered.

While he was still living, still breathing, it was his world. And in his world, his word was final.

Charlie

I missed the desk that I put in this office. The white one, glossy and lacquered, entirely out of place and probably an entire month's rent, but still cheaper than the rest of the boring, mahogany desks that dotted the executives' floor.

The sound of my heels against the floor reverberated louder than it would have three years ago, because the office was empty, nothing left but one of those standard, ugly Winchester Holdings' desks.

Crossing my arms over my chest, hiding the low cut of the Favorite Daughter blazer—surely not an outfit that helped to garner the Board's faith in me—I crossed the floor, stopping in front of the desk. I reached my hand out, fingers brushing across the smooth wood.

I had a habit of doing that, I realized as I looked at the empty walls and bare office. A pattern that I had probably been repeating for longer than I knew. Trying to find a home. It was terribly ironic that my father owned more real estate than multiple families combined—than was likely owned across some countries.

But this office had never been home, never would have been home—no matter how many pictures I hung up, how many pieces of myself I dragged across the marble floor.

It wasn't a place; it wasn't a person. It turned out to be entirely intangible—just me. Forest green eyes that I shared with my brother, hair that could never be styled much to the chagrin of every professional ever staffed by my father, and a mind that had a propensity for running.

Home was me.

But I found things here, that brief period of time when Winchester Holdings was my world, when these four walls with the glass door were a home I was trying on for size—things in this building, this floor, this office. I collected them. Things that I think I would hang up on the walls of me—my heart, my mind, on the inside of my lungs to help me breathe.

Honey eyes. Calloused hands. Hands that held me and all that I was. One rogue wave of blond hair across a forehead. A head tipped back in laughter to reveal a perfectly constructed neck. Broad shoulders and arms that I'd die for.

My brother's laugh. His entirely inappropriate suits. Wisps of straight chocolate hair. His preposterous shrieking when things went his way.

A friend. A best friend—entirely unthawed. Frozen across an expanse of time, but a best friend just the same.

Not a home but wooden trusses, shingles laid down, flooring. Nails into the drywall to hang the artifacts of a life lived.

"It's been empty since you left."

I whirled around, my hand coming to my chest.

My father stood in the doorway, glass on either side of him, and the inner workings of his universe visible just beyond him. If the rest of the staff had any idea that his impromptu board meeting was to announce his impending death and subsequent firing of one of the longest-standing members, they didn't let on.

"Couldn't find another director of charitable givings?" I asked wryly, leaning back against the desk and crossing my arms again.

My father considered me, eyebrows creasing and narrowing in. "I'm not sure that was ever the correct title."

"Oh?" I arched an eyebrow.

He cleared his throat, such a human moment and gesture he rarely made. "No. To my understanding, to do it correctly, you would have to dismantle much of the existing structure here and what's embedded in the institution. Giving you a small platform, a different title than everyone else around the table...I might as well have asked you to push a boulder up Mount Everest with one hand."

My eyes widened. Steven Winchester never admitted to being wrong. The portfolio itself hadn't exactly been a disaster; it was more to do with the collateral damage and fallout from my disastrous decisions in my personal life. But he was right. It wasn't a sustainable model, and it never would have been, regardless of whether or not I stuck it out.

My eyes burned, and I focused on a point just beyond his shoulder. He looked decidedly uncomfortable. I was uncomfortable, the silk of my blouse sticking to my clammy skin. I could count on one hand how many human, father-daughter moments we had. It was better between us, light-years away from what it was after we finally talked about my mother. Each performed CPR on her corpse, our acknowledgment of her breathing life back into the lungs of her ghost.

But I still wasn't used to this. And judging by the ticking time bomb festering away somewhere in his body, I never would be.

"Where'd you get that idea?" I finally asked, blinking and swinging my gaze back to him.

My father raised his eyebrows, blue eyes impassive. "Your most recent paper. It was quite fascinating."

"You read my publications?" I had meant for my voice to sound dry, incredulous, and lighter than I felt. But it cracked instead, and the edges of my vision blurred.

Steven Winchester exclusively read the Tribune, the Wall Street Journal, and his own financial statements. He did not read his daughter's publications, journal articles, op-eds, and general commentary about sustainable investing and economic development from her various forays into academia.

Except, apparently, he did.

He nodded, saying nothing as his eyes swept around the empty office, taking in one of my many abandoned homes. "You made some compelling arguments in the last one, particularly the notion that continued traditional investing structures leave the industry vulnerable for decline if we aren't moving toward a state where ESG factors aren't wholly considered economic ones."

I blinked, lips parting again, but no words coming out. I didn't have anything to say. In all of the worlds I dreamed of, where my family was whole, and my father approved of me in all the ways I wanted him to, it had never crossed my mind that he would agree with me on something like this. That he would be almost prideful when he spoke about it.

"Perhaps we can discuss it further over breakfast next week after my surgery." He continued, assessing me as neutrally as ever, before his gaze dropped to his wrist. There was some Audemars Piguet watch or another there—his preferred brand. "I have another meeting. But Damien will reach out, and we can schedule a day."

It was comical. Even steps from his deathbed, my father was still having his assistant schedule a breakfast in our family home with his own daughter. But that wasn't what I focused on, what my heart swelled and snagged on. "You want to talk investment structures with me over breakfast? Are you sure you aren't mixing me up with Deacon?"

My father glanced up from his watch, the other hand having already started typing away on his phone. He looked troubled. Like he could see just how much damage had been done and it stretched between us. So far and so vast that I couldn't even believe he would be interested in talking to me. "Your brother is far more intelligent than he lets on and is excellent at his job. But you bring an entirely different set of skills and type of intelligence to the table. We can discuss it further at another time."

"Sure, Dad." I smiled tightly at him, quickly wiping at my lash line before placing my hands on the edge of the desk. I didn't feel particularly steady.

His lips pulled together tightly, and his nostrils flared before he turned on the heel of his polished Oxford, leaving me alone in this place I once tried to make a home. Just me and the approval I had been waiting my whole life for.

All I had ever wanted and not enough time.

"Rumor has it you got Scott Sabean fired."

David leaned against the doorframe, head resting against the mahogany trim. He grinned at me, honey eyes entirely alight, all my favorite stars winking at me. The top buttons of his Isaia-striped cotton shirt were undone, and the sleeves pushed up his forearms. He had ditched the jacket of his gray slim-fit Hugo Boss suit somewhere, the wool pants clinging to his muscular thighs and tapering down his legs.

I rolled my eyes, pushing up farther against the stacked mountain of pillows. My computer was open on my lap, an article I was working on with Dr. Batra illuminated on the screen. I ran my hand across my chest absentmindedly, palm brushing the knit cotton of my heather gray SKIMS rib tank top I was wearing with the matching lounge boxers—a gift from Taylor so I could "study in style". She got the black for herself.

"I don't have the power to fire Scott Sabean," I offered, fingers pausing over the keyboard.

David grinned, fingers drumming against his bicep before he pushed off the door and strode ever so casually across the room. Instead of going to the opposite side of the bed—the one that had effectively become his—he came and stood beside mine. I looked up at him, mouth drying out and heart starting to hammer erratically.

He was still grinning at me, one hand now shoved into the pocket of his suit pants while another reached out and grabbed the strap of my tank top.

"This is nice." He ran the fabric back and forth between his thumb and forefinger, his eyes tracking across my chest, my collarbone, up my neck before they landed on my mouth for a moment that stretched on far too long.

I swallowed, cheeks heating, and the paper open in front of me forgotten. "Easy, Mr. Kennedy."

David flicked his gaze back up. His grin was gone, his pupils were wide, and his jaw tensed. "Sorry, I forgot. Temporary vow of celibacy between us. Do you mind if I jack off in your shower?"

A smile split across my face, stretching my cheeks as a laugh tumbled from my lips. It wasn't funny at all. There was nothing funny, or nice, or good, about David when he was like this. Not when he wanted me. I knew if I looked down, broke away from his eyes, I'd be able to see all the evidence of just how much he wanted me straining against his pants. It never took either of us that much time when the other was involved. "I missed this."

"Missed what?" David asked, lips finally tugging into a grin. "Me stuck with a raging hard-on while you sit there, entirely unattainable, entirely the hottest person I've ever seen in real life?"

"This. Being silly, playful, irreverent with you." I grabbed his wrist, his fingers still holding my shirt. His skin was warm, as always. "I don't think there's anyone else in the world who knows just how secretly perverted you are."

David smiled, leaning down and dropping his lips to my forehead for a moment before he pulled back, fingers finally dropping the material.

My collarbone felt bare when he took a measured step backward, palms raised in defeat. My eyes roved over him while he walked around the bed, over to his side, and dropped down on top of the covers, one hand coming to rest behind his head as he turned to look at me.

"Did everything go okay? With the board meeting? I can't imagine your father would have fired Scott over nothing."

I shrugged, closing my laptop and tossing it down toward the foot of the bed, the duvet puffing up around it. There was a time when my father would have considered the insult, the slight against me, to be well and truly *nothing*. "It was fine. My father announced his plans for his shares and all his assets. Everything split entirely down the middle, and Scott seemed to take umbrage at the fact that I could easily marry you and overthrow Deacon."

"You could, you know." David's voice was rough, and he ran a hand through his hair, eyes staring determinedly at the crisp, white bedding before finding mine.

"Could what?" I asked softly.

There was something about him, the entire set of his being, that made me feel like he was about to say something monumentally important.

"Easily marry me," David answered, words low. I felt them skitter across my skin. "I could go without overthrowing your brother and stealing his empire, but if you really wanted to…"

He had a ring for me, once upon a time. My mother's ring, gifted to him by my father. I still had no idea what happened to it, or where it went after I gave it back to him. But the idea had taken root long ago when David and I were different people—two people who had never hurt one another—two people who wouldn't have dreamt of it.

There probably was a multiverse somewhere with those versions of us living in it. It was hard to fathom that there was probably a me, still in that same, ill-fitting fake home I tried to build years ago. Where we went to work together each day and became some sort of Chicago power couple. Where Tripp had never come back into my life.

I wasn't sure what I would say, how I could possibly answer him. How I could possibly tell him there was a me once who would have married him in a heartbeat, and even though he was still mine and I was his, and always would be, I felt miles, entire light-years, and maybe even universes away from that person. But I was spared, because somewhere in the multiverse, David and I were a romantic comedy playing out, constantly getting interrupted, and some of that was spilling over into this one.

My brother's voice came from the still-open doorway.

"What are you two doing?" Deacon leaned in the doorway, almost a mirror image of David, but he was already sans suit and up one glass of scotch with blue circles under his eyes. The hood of his black Theory sweater seemed like it swallowed him whole. The king cube floating in the amber liquid knocked against the crystal when he brought it to his lips.

"Staging a coup." I tried an attempt at humor, but it fell flat as my brother continued to stare blankly at me, so I shook my head, sitting up straighter. "Nothing. Did you want to do something? We could go to the boathouse or go down to the theater and watch movies?"

They were childlike suggestions, and I felt a bit like one, even though I was weeks away from thirty. I wanted to sit up even farther, to pat the space at the end of my bed and beg my brother to come sit down.

But he just looked at me before taking another measured sip of his scotch. "Taylor home?"

"She's at the hospital. She's doing something in the skills lab tonight," I answered, omitting the fact that I knew she was practicing our father's procedure on a cadaver and likely would be until her fingers started to chafe and bleed.

My brother's eyes swung back and forth between David and me. There was no judgment, no revulsion, nothing really there at all.

He just looked lonely.

I leaned forward, desperate. I shot David a look. He seemed on the precipice of rolling his eyes—a decidedly un-David Kennedy mannerism, but he was well and truly over Deacon's behavior. I sat up and looked toward Deacon. "We could order pizza or something. Nothing pairs better with a thousand-dollar scotch than a shitty Chicago deep dish."

Deacon surveyed us, sitting side by side. Me in pajamas, and David still in remnants of his suit. "Yeah, alright. I'll meet you down in the theater. But don't order in. Just ask one of the staff to make it."

I narrowed my eyes at him, lips pulling back, but before he pushed off the door and turned away, he pointed toward David with his glass. "And get out of my sister's bed."

Dropping back, I scrubbed at my face for a moment. I felt the bed shift beside me, and I knew without having to open my eyes that David moved closer. I would forever be keenly aware of him, the exact weight of him, the ocean and sunshine smell. "You want to get drunk with me and watch shitty movies while my brother spirals further into existential doom?"

"Only if someone on staff makes the pizza," David answered, his voice deadpan.

I turned to look at him, honey eyes bright, and his mouth pulled back in a grin, rogue waves splayed out against the outrageous feather pillows of my bed.

There were probably worse versions of the multiverse out there.

Deacon

Charlie never listened to me, so I don't know why I expected anything different when I threw open the door to the home theater, sequestered away in the farthest corner of the house, and saw two takeout boxes sitting there.

"We have staff for a reason, you know." I tossed a look toward her—she was sitting on one of the theater chairs, still in those stupid pajamas, with her legs thrown over David's lap where he sat beside her.

She narrowed her eyes at me before smiling tightly. "And I have a phone for a reason."

My lips pulled up before I took a sip of my scotch, quickly becoming an ever-permanent fixture of my person.

David said nothing, one eyebrow rising on his forehead, but I noticed the way his hand tensed over her kneecap, like he'd get up and throttle me the second I said anything he didn't like.

Shaking my head, I dropped down in the seat beside them. So much for being fucking here for me. "I didn't say the staff should cook to be a jackass, Charlie. I said it because we shouldn't have delivery people coming to the door. What if someone fucking saw Dad, saw Taylor staying here? There's medical shit all over."

Charlie shrugged, her lips pulled into a tight line. "Those could be your IVs, for all anyone knows. It's not like your...affinity for Hydra-V is a secret. Neither is your penchant for scotch."

David had the audacity to crack a grin, his eyes lighting up, like my sister was the second coming of a comedic Jesus Christ.

"Oh fuck off." I rolled my eyes, about to ask them what they wanted to watch when my phone started to vibrate in my sweater.

Swallowing another measure of scotch, I pulled it out, and the burning in my throat suddenly had nothing to do with the alcohol.

> **Noa**: Hi – just landed in Tokyo. Can I call when I get to the hotel? I miss your voice.

> **Deacon**: Can't – sorry. I'm at the office.

> **Noa**: Oh. You can call me when you get home. I'll make sure the set assistant knows to put your calls through.

I fucking hated myself, because I didn't want to talk to her. Not because I didn't want to hear her voice—it was the best sound in the world. I didn't want her to hear mine.

I didn't want her to see the bags under my eyes—they were fucking unsightly. So I'd rather flay myself open, because that's what it felt like, not talking to her. This was the longest we'd gone without speaking since the night we met.

And because I hated myself, the fact that I couldn't see my way clear to be a good brother, a good friend, a good fiancé, couldn't get over the fact that it felt like I'd been drowning in my own blood when my father's words that he was dying—that he was leaving me too—stabbed me, eviscerated my lungs, I decided to pour salt all over my open wounds and send the love of my life a thumbs up emoji instead of saying anything at all.

I certainly did not give anything a thumbs up, and I fucking hated emojis.

Before I could put my phone back in the pocket of my sweater, or God forbid, before I threw it against the wall, a text message from my father came in, requesting my presence in his office.

"I'll be right back." I glanced over at those two where they were sitting—entirely tangled up in each other. Not even solely in the way they were sitting—they weren't tangled at all, really.

Charlie was just sort of draped over David, one hand resting at the back of his neck, fingers twirling loosely in his hair. And David—that one hand was still on her knee, but his other arm was slung over the chair, wrapped around her but not touching her, like he'd pick her up and carry her away from it all at any minute.

But they were all knotted together, anyway.

Charlie turned to look at me, her lips parting, and something like worry clouding her eyes, but I held up my phone. "Steven summoned me."

"Everything okay?" she asked, her fingers stilling and all of her tensing.

"Maybe he's pissed about the seafloor scotch," David answered, his voice dry. He dropped his head against the back of the chair and rolled his neck to look at me. I was about to tell him to fuck off when he offered me a grin—not those moony ones he saved for my sister that seemed to set her heart on fire—just a normal, friendly one.

"Well, you had your chance for a glass, and now it's shot. He's probably going to pour it down the drain out of spite." I pushed to stand up, sending my father another thumbs-up text because apparently, that's who I was now—an emoji-sending trainwreck. "Don't do anything fucking weird in here while I'm gone."

I wasn't banking on it. They looked more like a couple now than they did when they were actually dating.

The house was dark, all the winding halls lit solely by the occasional pretentious sconce lining them. I used to like this house, liked the features that reminded me of stately old manor homes. Or the fact that it was far too big for the three of us, because it felt like that meant it was full of possibility—full of futures where it was me and Charlie against the world, and maybe our father would eventually stop being who he was and start being more of a human.

That was a secret hope—a wish if you wanted to call it that—I'd had my entire life. I pretended that I didn't care he was who he was, was the *way* he was, because I wanted Charlie to feel better about it. I did care, I was only fucking human and a pretty imperfect one at that—but I pretended I didn't, acted so aloof and lackadaisical about it because I wanted Charlie to be able to let it go, to love herself and see herself the way she deserved to.

Our father was a fucking robot, and it never had anything to do with her.

But all that armor, whatever it was I constructed around myself in the name of protecting my sister, cracked and fell apart entirely when he told me he was sick. I was an adult, thirty-one years old, and forced to grow up earlier than I was probably supposed to, but the truth was, I didn't want to be without both my parents.

The theater was in the same wing as his office—an addition put in by our mother at some point. She loved movies, even though she referred to them exclusively as films, a bit of East Coast pretension that leaked through in her day-to-day life. Her family had been pretty artsy, from what I remember. They all died before she did. My memories of my grandparents were next to none at this point.

Turning the corner, the light from his office spilled across the floor, overpowering the tiny flicker from the sconces along the wall. His door was wide open, which was odd. Summoning one of his children wasn't out of the ordinary for him, but he rarely left the door open at all, typically preferring we knock so he could grant us entry into his innermost sanctum whenever he deemed appropriate.

I looked down at my glass of scotch, eyes narrowed before swallowing the last of it. I should have taken the long way around so I could top up. He had a bar in his office, but I doubted he asked me here for a drink.

I didn't bother knocking, and I didn't bother sitting down. But there was an open bottle of scotch sitting on his desk beside him while he worked. I did bother helping myself to that.

"Am I interrupting your evening?" He arched an eyebrow at me, watching, and his displeasure barely masked as I stepped back from his desk and leaned against one of the many bookcases lining the walls.

I shook my head, shoving one hand in the pocket of my Tom Fords. "No. I was just in the theater with Charlie and David."

"I expected to see Noa arrive today." He gazed at me, and I didn't like how he looked—all-knowing, like he was somehow privy to the inner workings of my self-sabotaging brain.

"She's in Tokyo."

His eyes narrowed before he gestured to his computer. "I've emailed you a proposal about a leadership restructure I'm going to implement, should your sister agree. It officially names her as the VP of sustainable investing. She'll be responsible for revolutionizing our sustainable investing practices, liaising with the rest of the team on ESG integration, stakeholder relationships, and reporting."

I started, my head pulling back and my mouth falling open in disbelief. "They'll fucking eat her alive. You're setting her up for failure if you ask her to come back and do this without support or buy-in...you saw what Scott was like today. That's the tip of the iceberg."

He raised his eyebrows at me, pushing back from his desk far enough so he could lean back and fold his hands over his chest. The clip for his IV line poked out from the sleeve of his white Armani shirt. "Without support? Am I to take that to mean you aren't supportive of your sister returning to the company?"

He was fucking unbelievable. Knocking back too much scotch, I shook my head. "What I'm supportive of is Charlie. And what she wants. If this is what she wants, she has all my support and then some. But you can't just surprise people with this out of the blue. Your reach only extends so far, and you're not going to be around long enough to strong-arm everyone into listening to you."

He looked at me in that annoying, appraising way he did to both of his children, like he didn't quite believe what we were saying. "It will be important that you both surround yourselves with people who support you. Who are loyal to you. I won't be able to protect you when I'm dead."

"You haven't done much of that while you've been alive, so forgive me if I don't sit here on bated breath, drinking in every word of your sage wisdom." I arched an eyebrow and swirled the glass lazily in my hand.

My father gave me a flat look. "Shall I count the number of untoward stories about you I've kept out of the media over the years?"

"I'm not talking about me." My voice was low.

His nostrils flared, and his eyes widened. He had the decency of looking troubled, looking disturbed by the flagrant disregard and mistreatment he'd offered his own daughter in his quest for whatever he'd spent his life looking for. He tipped his head, his features looking soft for a brief, passing moment before they hardened again. "And I wasn't talking about you. You need your sister, if your recent behavior is any indication. And she's going to need supportive leadership. I think you should call Tripp. He was an invaluable asset to the company. David would sooner cut off his own arm than let something happen to Charlie, but I fear he's blinded by love."

"And Tripp isn't?"

He looked like he was considering the idea of it for a moment, but he shook his head, like whatever it was between the three of them, was so cut and dry, matter-of-fact, that he, Steven Winchester, could understand it as clear as day. "Not in the same way, I don't think."

"He won't come back. He's dealing with some shit at home." I shook my head. Tripp was a cagey fuck. No matter how many times we'd spoken, he never so much as alluded to whatever was going on. "Have you told Charlie?"

"She's aware I have a...proposition for her." He raised his eyebrows at me and glanced toward the door in clear dismissal. "Proposal is in your inbox. I'd like your thoughts by morning before I take this any further."

Rolling my eyes, I knocked back the rest of the scotch and dropped the empty glass on his desk. He wasn't looking at me, eyes already back on his computer. Probably looking at his own fucking stock prices. I was going to turn my back to him, the way he seemed to have no problem doing with us, the same type of disregard he clearly showed in his own life, but he rolled his shoulders and shifted in his seat.

The light caught his face in a way it hadn't before. His skin was practically fucking gray.

Here it was, right in front of me, as my sister put it. A second chance to do things right with another dying parent—because our mother had been dying. Just not in a way that any of us could see, or even bothered to recognize. Swallowing, I offered the only platitude I could muster. "Surgery in a few days. You're feeling okay?"

His eyes cut toward me for a brief moment. "I'll feel better when I know you've done as I asked."

I cringed as I pulled my phone out. I felt a bit shitty about calling Tripp—especially after what I'd just seen, those two draped over one another like that. David in her bed every night.

The poor fuck didn't stand a chance.

Charlie

Money could buy a lot of things.

I thought about it a lot, the general see-saw of hypocrisy that made up my life.

Deacon never thought about it—what money and influence could buy. He just always knew he could have whatever he wanted, whenever he wanted it.

I thought about it—how the amount of money I had at my disposal made me exactly that—a hypocrite. It was one of the main reasons I could flit from temporary home to temporary home, and why I could try all these different things on for size with no real consequence.

But I had never really considered the niche fact that money could buy you ultimate comfort and privacy in one of the most uncomfortable, sterile, and exposed environments to exist.

The private recovery suite at Northwestern Memorial wouldn't have been out of place at any of the hotels downtown, at The Peninsula, the scene of one of my many public demises.

It felt fitting to be here, in this stupidly lavish suite, sitting on a leather couch, staring across an impossibly shiny granite coffee table laid out with a centerpiece of fall flowers, at my brother—who, despite the custom Ralph Lauren suit, looked like he should be the one hooked up to an IV.

The only clues we were in a hospital were the bed I could see, just beyond Deacon in an adjoining room. It looked more comfortable than most beds you'd find in a suburban home. There were IV poles and monitors waiting to be plugged in and hooked up. But even in that room, where our father would soon be, there was art that cost thousands, if not hundreds of thousands of dollars, dotting the burnt umber walls. There was even another ornate vase giving way to a display of flowers—chrysanthemums, dahlias, and sunflowers.

The second clue, the only other indication we were in a hospital, was the small monitor mounted in the corner of the "waiting" room we were in. It read with the code, the unique number assigned to our father during pre-op: 7983SW. It listed the stage of the operation, the lead surgeon, and the OR room number.

Judging by the screen, Taylor was currently prepping to cut our father open, some sort of vertical slash straight down his abdomen that would let her peel back everything and see what Steven Winchester was really made of.

It was just us in the room, no other Winchester family left to stand vigil. Taylor hadn't stopped by, but her father had, promising he would be by again later with an update. Dr. Breen claimed he planned to take time out of his schedule—doing whatever it was the chief of surgery did—to scrub in at some point and see his daughter in action. And see inside one of his oldest friends. He said he would see how things were progressing for himself so he could be honest with us.

If either Taylor or her father thought it was weird that they would both see his insides—one of the formative male figures in her life and an old friend—see firsthand the malignant cells taking over his body, they didn't let on.

I looked over at my brother, two fingers pressed to his forehead, while he stared unblinkingly at his phone, gripped loosely in the other hand.

"Do you get used to the security?" I tipped my chin toward the sliding glass door, sealed and effectively closing us in.

Two security personnel stood, flanking either side. They were in plain clothes, entirely non-descript, save for the earpieces hardly visible beneath two plain black baseball hats. They were here to make sure no one saw the great Steven Winchester at rest in such an exposed and vulnerable state. To make sure no one found us in our private, familial moment.

Security never had much of a presence in our lives—hence the notion that the Winchesters were an elusive dynasty. But since Noa, an entirely public figure, had become a very permanent fixture in our lives, it had become more commonplace.

Deacon finally deigned to flick his eyes up, staring at me from under the fingers still pressed to his forehead. "It's never really phased me. We probably should have started using security a long time ago."

I frowned, eyes still on the back of their heads. "How do you figure?"

"Next Great American dynasty and all that." Deacon waved his hand around. "Pretty easy for someone to grab you off the street and extort Dad for millions of dollars. Pretty dangerous, being you and just walking around. WH holds the equity for a lot of public funds."

I rolled my eyes before I could stop myself. It was certainly in bad taste to disparage our father as we sat in what would be his recovery room. "Deac, we both know that would not be a ransom he paid. Steven Winchester would not stand for extortion, nor would he negotiate with kidnappers."

Deacon gave me a flat look, finally pushing back and sitting upright in the chair. I waited for him to argue, to tell me that our father wasn't as bad as I had made him out to be over all these years, that he loved me, would undoubtedly pick me over money or saving face. And he wasn't as bad as I had made him out to be.

But Deacon considered for a moment, his lips tugging down and eyes narrowed before shrugging. "You're probably right. Easier to spin a story about his only daughter's disappearance than it would be for the stock to recover."

It should have made me sad, and I think it did make this tiny part of me unhappy, that my brother was so hopelessly broken down by our father, that he couldn't see the forest through the trees.

But it felt like common ground, maybe our only common ground left. So I laughed, tipped my head back against the leather couch, and started laughing so hard I couldn't catch my breath.

It was misplaced, absurd even, and there was nothing that remotely bordered on funny. But the whole thing, our whole lives really, felt comical.

"We'd make very captivating television." I smiled, wiping my eyes, when I finally looked back at Deacon.

He smiled back at me, and it was almost lazy. The way I always thought he should smile—he always was a perfect version of himself.

It made me want to cry all over again.

But he grinned at me, raising his eyebrows. "All we need is Taylor parading around, self-righteous as fuck. Noa can be the pretty one, too good for everyone. Add David and Tripp to the mix, you've really got a show."

"What's the storyline for season one?" I asked, my smile growing. It was funny, and somehow, it was made even funnier by the fact that we were in our only parent's hospital room.

Deacon ran a hand through his hair, straight wisps of chocolate flying everywhere. "The day you meet Kennedy is the first episode, but it's juxtaposed with flashbacks of when you met Tripp. Season finale is when Dad tells you we're hiring Tripp. No—actually, it's the day he asked you in front of the entire office if David had screwed all the sense out of you."

"Excellent television. If the whole investing, finance, master of the universe thing doesn't work out for you, you have a future in production." I raised my eyebrows, crossing my arms over my striped Free People cotton sweater. The arms were huge, making me feel like a small child wrapped up in a blanket.

Deacon smiled at me for a bit longer before his eyebrows pulled together. "If I had known then, what would happen, what it would cost you...to go down that whole road with Tripp, I—"

"Don't," I interjected, swinging my legs up onto the couch and crossing them. I wore the same jeans from the other night out with David, and Taylor's Gucci sneakers that proved to be shockingly comfortable, so I didn't return them. "I wouldn't change it. Any of it."

"You don't regret it?" Deacon asked, his voice quiet. One hand held up his chin now, thumb pressed there, and index finger against his mouth.

"I regret hurting people," I answered softly, fingers starting to pull at the sleeves of my sweater. "David. Tripp. Me."

"But that's it?" Deacon asked, eyes narrowed—not in judgment, not with ire—more like he was trying to figure me out.

I nodded softly. My eyes prickled a bit, but the usual waves of nausea, anxiety, all the regret that would rake over my skin and cut me open, waiting for me to bleed out in penance, never came.

"That's it."

Deacon surveyed me for a moment longer, and I took the opportunity to really look at him—dull eyes with bags under them, and a general pallor of his skin that would indicate maybe he was the sick one. We really would be all that was left soon. We had always joked about it—us against the world, how we were all one another ever really had. Maybe it was some sort of ironic self-fulfilling prophecy after all.

"Don't look at me like that, like you're trying to figure me out, or you're feeling sorry for me," Deacon cut in, shaking his head. "We're talking about you and your tangled love life."

I arched an eyebrow. "Previously tangled love life. We could do a few minutes on you, though. Perhaps we could discuss why you won't call your fiancée home? The love of your life? It's not wrong to want her by your side during this Deacon, to want her support, to want her here."

"Like you and David?" Deacon asked, his voice harsh. "Why don't we just call Tripp to come on down, and you can have quite the little support system sharing your bed with you?"

"Why are you being like this?" I hissed, leaning forward. "Stop hitting me. Stop hitting everyone in your life, and stop pushing us away."

I watched as Deacon leaned forward, movements almost mirroring mine, but instead of locking his gaze on me, he scrubbed at his face furiously, like a small child might try to wipe away their tears. Somehow, when he looked back up at me, he looked years older and years younger simultaneously, like the inexplicable weight of it all was finally too much for even the ridiculous, irreverent Deacon Winchester.

His voice was barely a choked whisper when he finally spoke.

"Her whole family is gone—her parents, her aunt. Ours is about to be gone, too. I wish I was a big enough man to say keeping her away was to protect her, so none of this—" He paused, arms gesturing wildly, and sleeves of his suit jacket buckling under everything he was carrying, "So none of this hurt her. But it's not because I'm a fucking coward. And all I can think about is that when she takes one look at me—sees that I'm an inept child, sees me like this, sees me mean to you, lashing out, because I can't fucking take it, and my chest feels so Goddamn heavy all the time—that she's going to leave me, too."

My nostrils flared, and a wry laugh bubbled in my throat.

Deacon and I were entirely different, polar opposites in most ways, save for the physical characteristics I had also taken so much pride in because we shared them—they weren't just mine or his.

They were ours. The things that proved we were a part of our parents, a part of one another, a part of a family that was whole, once upon a time.

That's where the similarities had ended, or so I thought. But underneath it all, we were the same lost little children, so terrified we would be left with nothing but ourselves.

I pushed off the couch, rounding the ridiculous coffee table and floral display, before settling cross-legged on the floor in front of my brother.

His head was hanging down now between his arms, elbows digging into his knees. Raising his chin, Deacon looked at me, lips parted and tears tracking down from his impossibly dark eyes—woods that you'd get lost in, be told to stay away from as a child because you might never emerge, never find your way out from all those overgrown, gnarled trees.

"We're the same, you and me. So afraid of being left alone," I whispered, gathering his hands in mine and pressing them to my chest. "I'll never leave you, Deacon. Never ever."

And I wouldn't. There was no world, no life for me anywhere else if my brother was miserable, suffering so completely. I'd pick him over anything any day. He started to shake his head, eyes closing for a moment. He would argue with me, send me packing back to London the first chance he got if he thought I was going to supplant myself here.

But his phone started vibrating at an alarming rate.

My eyes immediately flicked up to the screen to see if there was an update—like it would tell me our father bled out or coded on the table.

But a strangled, wet laugh sounded from Deacon. My eyes cut back to him, and he held out his phone. "If Taylor doesn't manage to kill him, that fucking will."

And there it was. Our last family secret, splayed out for the world to see on the front page of Society News, juxtaposed with footage of cameras and reporters gathering outside the hospital.

Breaking: Winchester Patriarch, CEO and president of multi-billion-dollar holding, diagnosed with stage-four cancer

David

There was a monitor in one of the Winchester Holdings' executive conference rooms that practically stretched across the entire wall. It was usually the type of thing you'd find on a trading floor—but Steven liked to keep an eye on his empire. He had it installed after Deacon opened the New York offices. Most people would think it was a sign of mistrust, and it probably appeared that way, like he wanted additional eyes on whatever was happening across the markets in real-time.

But I always took it as a display of pride in really the only way he knew how—his son had expanded his business, his legacy—and this was his version of a photo of Deacon at graduation in his office.

I could see the numbers blinking away behind me, reflected across the impossibly shiny surface of the table. The whole team was here, sans Deacon, and certainly sans Steven, for some presentation Riya, the VP of risk management, was giving.

I wasn't listening, my fingers drumming incessantly against the table, eyes shifting to my phone every few minutes. I didn't make a habit of ignoring my colleagues when they spoke. I didn't make a habit of ignoring anyone when they spoke, actually. Deacon droned on and on about how it was part of what made me so good at my job, part of what made Charlie fall in love with me—active listening. Maybe it was what made me good at my job. I spent hours on the phone with CEOs, VPs of Finance and the like, designers—anyone whose IPO we might take public. That was intentional, something I could turn on and off.

But listening to Charlie? The second she spoke, I couldn't hear anything else. Listening to her was easier than breathing, and hearing her voice for the first time probably changed me on a cellular level, and hanging on her every word was certainly not something I could turn off.

But she wasn't here; she was in some surely lavish suite at Northwestern Memorial while Steven underwent surgery, and I definitely wasn't fucking listening.

I would have gone with her today—but Steven probably would have had a fit and died in it, even more prematurely, if he knew his company was short two VPs, and it certainly would have detracted from the whole idea that nothing was amiss.

I would say it was inappropriate for me to be sitting here on her family's dime, thinking about her, entirely consumed, but it wasn't terribly different than any other day.

"David?"

My gaze snapped up. Riya was looking at me, an irritated smile plastered across her face.

"Sorry—I'm sorry, Riya. I missed what you were saying. Can you repeat it?" I ran a hand through my hair, tugging on the ends before offering her what was supposed to be an apologetic smile.

Her lips pursed, and she blinked before shaking her head slightly and opening her mouth to speak.

But the world came crashing down before she could say anything.

Everyone's phone started at once—vibrating across the table practically in unison. All eyes dropped, and there it was—the dirty laundry, the last Winchester secret sold and out into the universe.

I stood, sending my chair careening backward, ignoring everyone else around me and the chaos I could already see starting across the floor through the glass doors.

"Kennedy, where the fuck do you think you're going?"

I snapped my head to the head of the table, where Steven usually sat, but Ash was there in his place, looking like an almost identical replica in a navy Brooks Brothers suit.

"Where do you *think* I'm going, Ash?" I arched an eyebrow at him.

He raised his eyebrows, both liberally peppered with gray now. His green eyes bordered on looking amused. "Nowhere. Sit."

I snorted, shaking my head and shrugging my suit jacket back on. "Not a chance."

"Your display of unyielding loyalty is admirable, David. I'll be sure to pass the message along to my *best friend*—that his daughter will be well loved after he's gone. But you'll be more good to her here." Ash pointed toward the chair again, still spinning from my abrupt attempt at a departure.

I didn't miss the emphasis he put on the words, the way his eyes softened for just a moment when he said it. It's what stopped me from sending the chair flying into the wall.

"Because that—" he continued, pointing toward the screen stretching along the wall, where I didn't have to look to know numbers were changing and the stock was plummeting, "is only going to get worse."

My nostrils flared, and my teeth hurt from clenching them. "Fine. But one word from her, and you can consider me gone."

Ash smiled tightly, gesturing for me to sit back down.

"Admirable—but I doubt you'll even have the time to hear said word. What's your title again? VP of mergers and acquisitions? I imagine you're about to have a whole lot of angry CEOs on the line."

Scrubbing my jaw, I was tempted to reach across the table and throttle him—this man I usually held in pretty high esteem.

He must have known, seen it all over my face, the way my jaw clenched and my fists feathered in and out, because he looked pointedly toward my phone, where it was already vibrating across the conference table. "Your phone's ringing."

Charlie

All the secrecy and careful planning—a family friend performing the surgery, arriving at the hospital at some ungodly hour under the cover of darkness, the suite located in the most inconvenient spot, a labyrinth of hallways and doors, and the security—were for nothing.

Because someone, an alleged source close to the family, had given far too many details for it to be anything but an unsubstantiated rumor.

Someone had told our family secrets. And just like our father predicted—because he did know what he was talking about when he talked about business—the wolves were descending.

"Scott—call me back as soon as you get this, or I promise you, you won't ever fucking work again." Deacon was practically screaming into his phone. He was holding it in front of his face pacing around the suite, suit jacket discarded and shirt unbuttoned, his other hand raking through his hair constantly.

It was no longer just home to us, alone in our grief and the ostentatious displays of flowers. Half of the legal department and the PR departments were at the hospital now, too. Fielding calls and trying to make a plan while our father was being carved up just a few floors below.

Helen and Rebecca, who was somehow still the WH Publicist after all these years, and not because she was bad at her job, but because it seemed utterly thankless, were both here. Helen and the rest of the legal department were trying desperately to find whoever the "source" was. Scott was the most likely culprit, having just been semi-publicly eviscerated by our father and ousted from a position he had held for decades.

"Fuck!" Deacon's phone smashed against the wall. I watched as he pulled on the ends of his hair with both hands now, the screen of his phone still illuminating from where it lay shattered on the floor. "Halton's stock price is down from 160 to 145."

Becoming the majority shareholder of Halton Entertainment had been my father's crowning achievement, really propelling him into the stratosphere. It was what landed us on the cover of Forbes, me in a dumb feathered dress, and the start of the trajectory that would change everything.

"That—is a substantial drop," I offered uselessly.

It *was* a substantial drop, entirely unheard of. But there was no obvious succession plan, the true flaw behind our father's need for secrecy. I was irrelevant, but the media seemed happy to dredge up everything they could find from my precarious personal life over the last few years. They were currently running rampant with every story they could find about Deacon, painting him as a wholly irresponsible billionaire playboy without a care in the world who couldn't mind his own money, let alone the interests of other Fortune 500 companies.

Deacon cut me a look, his lips practically parted in a snarl before he stalked across the room and snatched the smashed phone from the ground. "Someone get me a new fucking phone. Now."

"Deacon—" I finally stood from where I was sitting on a dumb leather couch while the family empire crumbled around me, moving to grip his wrists in my hands. He finally looked at me, hair flying in every direction and his almost labored.

"Deacon. Breathe. Me and you against the world. Sit down with me, and we can decide what's next together."

The phone continued to light up and vibrate in his clenched hands, and we both looked down at the same time when the song started.

Fucking *Sexy Can I.*

"You haven't changed your ringtone?" I hissed, eyes wide and lips parting. "That is NOT the ringtone of a future president and CEO. Change it before someone hears it and another source close to the family lets the press know that not only are you too immature for the responsibility, you've got terrible fucking taste in music!"

"I can't deal with this right now," he muttered, pocketing the broken phone and ripping his arms away from me. He turned on the heel of his shoe—a polished Prada derby loafer, because apparently that's what you wear to the dissolution of your world as you knew it.

"Deacon she's your fiancée—"

He whirled back to me, his palms up in the air. "Then you call her. I've got my hands full at the moment, in case you haven't noticed."

Before I could reach out to him to try to grab one of those hands that were trying to hold our whole world and keep it from crumbling, before I could try to bring him back down to earth, Rebecca was stalking toward me, the heels of her nude Louboutins sounding like a fucking war drum. I didn't even have time to peel back my lips over her crème double-breasted jacket and matching straight-legged pants from The Row because she was shoving her phone in my face, one manicured finger tapping the headline on the screen pointedly.

The heirs to an empty empire? With the recent revelation that President and CEO Steven Winchester has months to live, stock prices are dropping, shareholders are growing anxious, and all eyes look to his children, Deacon and Charlie.

I looked up from the phone, one eyebrow raised. "The heirs to an empty empire? Catchy."

Rebecca gave me a flat look, lips pursed. "You two have to give a statement. We have the media on standby for a press conference."

Shaking my head, I crossed my arms and dug my literal and proverbial heels in. An unsolicited press concern would wake Steven Winchester from the fucking dead—anesthesia would be nothing. "Rebecca—he wouldn't want that. He's going to be out of surgery in a few hours. Issue something boring and bland. It can wait until—"

Rebecca interrupted, one hand making a cutting gesture, her impossibly tight, slicked-back blonde ponytail moving with her.

"We can't put him in front of the cameras, Charlie. Not now. And we don't know how long his recovery is going to take."

I said nothing but crossed my arms tighter—like that would help. Like it could stop the tears that were threatening to spill over the edges of my eyes. Like it could stop my heart from hurting, my father from dying. Like it could stop what was left of our family from being picked apart, like a particularly abundant carcass on the side of the road.

In an uncharacteristic gesture of sympathy, one that bordered on maternal, which was ironic given the fact that Rebecca wasn't even five years older than me, she reached out, her palm cupping my cheek for a moment, and her voice much softer when she spoke.

"Hair and makeup will be here in twenty. Sabine will be by with some options for you."

Closing my eyes, I leaned into her hand, just for a moment. Just for a moment I pretended she wasn't someone employed by my family, that her livelihood didn't depend on our success, that she wasn't quite literally paid to care about my brother and me. It was only a moment, and then her hand was gone, my eyes were open, and Deacon was ripping the plastic off a box containing a new iPhone.

———

"Please turn it off. I'm so sick of seeing my own face," I whispered from behind my fingers.

The TV in the hospital suite was on, rolling footage of our press conference playing on a loop. The monitor still blinked away beside it—the only change in the last hour indicating that Taylor, or another more junior surgeon, was closing up.

Deacon was long gone, leaving promptly after the press conference to go to the office, where apparently, hell was breaking loose. The whole thing was terribly ironic—that our father would have exerted every last ounce of control his entire life, sacrificing it all to keep his business—his empire—together. And when he was asleep, under anesthesia, the whole thing would start to fall apart.

It was just Rebecca and me, sitting at opposite ends of the stuffy leather couch while I waited for an update on my father. I'm not sure exactly what she was waiting for—probably to make sure the headlines stayed on this side of positive.

"You both did great. And you look phenomenal. Very sympathetic interview. See how the headlines have changed?" Rebecca didn't even bother looking at me but pointed with one bony finger toward the headlines rolling across the bottom of the TV screen:

In a swift (and smart) move, Winchester Holdings' Board names CFO Ash Reynolds as interim president and CEO

Winchester siblings Deacon and Charlie step out at Northwestern Memorial and speak to the press

The Winchester Dynasty soon to be reduced to two—how young is too young to be alone?

Where is Noa Dahan?

Steven Winchester, rumored to be in recovery after a successful palliative procedure
Dr. Taylor Breen, surgical oncology resident, and her medical school grade percentile

"I look like a fucking vicar, Rebecca!" I blurted, gesturing to the screen. The black Khaite asymmetrical lapel jacket *did* have a severe neckline. It wasn't helped by the slicked back, high knot tied at the back of my head, making all my features look sharper than they were.

Rebecca turned to me, a barely restrained eye roll as her fingers continued tapping across her phone. "No. You look like you're about to inherit half of a company that controls some of the most lucrative corporations in America."

"Maybe the whole thing should fall apart." I shrugged, eyes burning with exhaustion. I dug my thumb into the seam of the couch. "No one should have all that money."

"Well, you do," Rebecca stated bluntly.

I watched her stand, smoothing out imaginary wrinkles in her suit.

Somehow, she managed to go through the day without a single smudge of dirt to mar the cream wool. "We'll issue another statement tomorrow, pending your father's recovery. But you're going to need to stay put. We can't have you traipsing back off to London to further your...academic pursuits. It's not a good look."

"You know I'm the easy one to jettison right? I come with more media-related baggage than Deacon does." I arched an eyebrow at her.

The snap of her clasp on her mascarpone leather Ferragamo bag echoed throughout the room. It really was a very monochromatic look she was going for. I watched her fingers wrap around the top handle, and she crossed her arms, leveling me with one last look.

"Do me a favor, and don't get involved with any other members of the staff for the next few months?" She smiled tightly before turning on her heel, leaving me sitting on an overstuffed, too-expensive, leather couch in the waiting room of a stupidly lavish hospital suite.

Before I could even flip up my middle finger to her retreating back, my phone vibrated against the leather of the couch. Sticking my tongue out with significantly less dignity than a child, I picked up the phone to see the text message illuminating the screen.

Tripp: Stock prices are down.

Charlie: You don't say.

Tripp: Saw you at the press conference. Nice jacket. Call if you need anything, Chuck.

The monitor beeped, signaling a change in status.

I looked up, grip loosening on my phone. Steven Winchester was in recovery.

Deacon

My tie felt like it was fucking choking me. On a regular day, it was usually one of my favorites—a violet geometric print silk one from Zegna my sister bought me. But today, it felt like a noose.

And I guess it was—in the proverbial sense of the word. I wasn't a fidgety person. It was incredibly unbecoming, but I found myself yanking on the knot and adjusting it more and more as the day went on, because it felt like it was inching closer and closer to cutting off my fucking air supply.

Everyone was fucking looking at me like my father wasn't being carved up by a surgeon who wore far too many sequins to be taken seriously in any facet of life. I didn't have the fucking answers for what to do. I couldn't reach into the TV or manipulate the stock exchange in real-time. I knew why it was tanking and so did everyone else in the room—Steven Winchester was a robot, and in his quest to remain so far above us all, to not be considered human, he didn't think that maybe the best plan of attack was to be fucking honest and open about a succession plan before shareholders were hit over the head with it.

And fuck Scott Sabean—I was going to ruin his life. If David didn't get there first.

He'd looked less than pleased when I blew into the office, probably because I'd just ditched my sister after the press conference—left her alone in that stupid suite to sit there and wait for the surgery to finish. And had it been any other day, had the world not literally been falling apart under our feet, I'd imagine I'd know what it felt like to have my best friend punch me in the face.

His jaw had twitched when he saw me through the glass of his office—he was pacing back and forth, hands running through and tugging at his hair before waving wildly around him as he made and answered endless phone calls.

It was killing him, slowly eating him from the inside out, not being able to get to my sister. Composed David Kennedy was seconds from crumbling.

I would have told him to leave if I didn't need him to keep doing what he did best, if Ash wouldn't have killed him, and if my father wouldn't have woken himself up from his anesthesia and dragged himself down to the office to strangle him. He might have looked like he was falling apart, coming unglued, but when I tossed open his door, despite his general demeanor and now too-messy hair, his voice was calm, and he was steady, cool, and collected when he spoke to every single subsidiary CEO and stakeholder he needed to.

I kicked open the door to my own bedroom now, and the silence of this house that usually felt so heavy felt more like weary relief—cool water on too-hot skin, a breeze through your window in the morning. Whatever fucking metaphor worked. There was no incessant buzzing, no shouting, no angry numbers rolling across a screen, and no headlines about disintegrating dynasties tattooing themselves on my retinas.

I could feel my phone in my pocket, but I ignored it, like I had been for the better part of the day, making for the bottle of scotch that still sat beside the armchair in my room. I should have felt guilty that this was some special bottle to my father—who knows what he'd been saving it for—or maybe it was just something he wanted to own, to covet. It didn't matter to me, so I poured another glass of the seafloor scotch he'd never get to taste.

But I didn't feel guilty; I felt spiteful more than anything. He was the reason that our stock was down. He was the reason I had to leave my sister and that the love of her life, the only person she really felt comfortable around, was kept from her all day—the reason she'd be surrounded by security from now until the end of time.

Steven Winchester and his malignant cells could go fuck themselves.

"Hi."

The second glass of scotch was halfway to my lips. I closed my eyes, knocking it back and pretending that my heart wasn't simultaneously standing in the doorway of my childhood bedroom and falling out of my chest.

Dropping the glass unceremoniously and without a care whether it shattered against the end table, I turned toward the door.

Noa tipped her head, brown curls piled high on her head, and her face flushed the way it only did when she was anxious or upset. She shifted back and forth, her shoes stayed planted on the ground, but I knew her better than I knew myself, so I knew she was pushing up onto her tiptoes, that her fingers were gripping to find purchase through whatever oversized sweater she was wearing, digging into her arms.

Her teeth came down to her bottom lip, and I felt myself leaning forward ever so slightly to reach out and grab her, to swipe my thumb across it, to hug her and tell her it wasn't her; it was me and my fucked up family. But the roots, or the ghosts—as my sister liked to call them—of said family snuck up through the floor and wrapped around my ankles keeping me there.

Her features sort of collapsed, like she could see them all clawing at my legs, their fingers wrapping around the pants of my custom Ralph Lauren suit.

Shrugging off my suit jacket, I threw it haphazardly toward my bed.

"When did you get in?" I turned away from her again, focusing on pouring another glass of scotch because I didn't want to see *it*.

It wasn't that I didn't want to look at her; I always wanted to look at her.

But I didn't want to see how I was hurting her.

I knew what Charlie meant now—what it was like to be so self-destructive, to see it all unfold before you and be unable to stop.

"I left Tokyo as soon as I saw. You haven't answered any of my calls. I was worried." Noa's voice was closer now.

I could feel her just behind me. I forced my eyes closed, stopping the glass at my lips and rolling my shoulders back. "The day got away from me. Stock took a crash-level dip."

I wanted to throw the glass against the wall and add some more damage to the crown molding that still wasn't fixed. There was no way Steven didn't know—the staff would have alerted him the second they saw it. The fact that it was still there was probably some sort of message I didn't care enough to decode.

Her arms wrapped around me, her tiny hands skating across the front of my shirt where I could feel them, like they were moving against my bare skin, and her head came to rest between my shoulder blades. Wayward curls escaping her bun brushed the back of my neck.

My hand tightened against the glass, hers pressed against me, and I felt myself leaning back for a moment.

But then I opened my eyes and looked down at the table, the half-empty scotch bottle sitting there alongside a rolled-up hundred that had seen better days and more coke residue across an antique silver tray I took from the kitchen than I wanted my fiancée to see.

Every single muscle in my body clenched. I wasn't sure what I was going to do, but Noa's chin came to rest on my shoulder. I could feel her behind me, pushing up to her tiptoes, hands raking over my chest.

I could hear it. Her small intake of breath, and that was enough for me, because I'd failed her like I failed my sister and my father and my mother. I shrugged her off and took a measured step to the side.

It was just a step. But she cocked her head back, and her bottom lip dropped and quivered. I might as well have stepped across the Grand Canyon.

And I stood there, entirely useless, holding a glass of priceless scotch as she took a small step forward, one of her hands flexing before a perfect finger came down and swiped across the tray.

She turned to me, cocking her head and looking at me with a question I wasn't sure there was an answer to.

"It's—"

She arched an eyebrow, and her amber eyes—those fucking eyes—flashed with thinly veiled displeasure. "Deacon, I've been modeling for the better part of a decade. I've seen cocaine before."

Noa rubbed her thumb and forefinger together before brushing her hands across her black sweatpants.

I watched her, my own lips pulling up in a grimace as she tried to wipe it all away—the person I was, who she was finally seeing.

She tipped her head to the side, her eyes searching me as her lips parted softly, and I knew she was about to say something that was going to undo me when she glanced down toward the pocket of those ridiculously giant sweatpants that I would have already been pulling off her in another life and fished out her phone. Her little eyebrows came together, and she glanced up at me before answering. "Taylor? Hi. Yeah, I just got in. I'll tell him."

Noa's eyes flicked up, and her features softened. The harsh set of her displeasure at my immaturity and general ineptitude faded away. "Your father's awake."

Charlie

The surgery was wildly successful—the mets were less advanced than Taylor, her father, and the entire arsenal of oncologists at my father's disposal thought. She was able to remove the two tumors she set out to, and when he didn't code on the table due to strain, she removed the rest she could see within her field of vision.

Clean margins, so she said. Still a palliative procedure but probably less pain and maybe more time.

There'd be more time for him to clean up the mess that his need for saving face, his inability to admit that he was fallible, just like any other person on the planet, had caused.

He still wasn't awake when I left the hospital, flanked by two security guards and subject to more camera flashes and microphones shoved in my face than someone should be in their lifetime.

I was sure it sent a message of some kind that neither of his children were holding vigil by his bedside until he woke up. Rebecca seemed to think it was a good PR move to send Deacon to the office and for me to be seen leaving the hospital—that it somehow downplayed the situation.

I wasn't sure how you could downplay a situation that would result in the same end no matter how you sliced it, but maybe that's why I wasn't in PR.

Taylor had practically pushed me out of the suite, out the front door of the hospital, claiming my father would likely be asleep all night and that the sight of all the press clamoring at the lobby doors was growing disturbing to the rest of the patients.

She had better things to do and made far too much money to sit vigil at Steven Winchester's bedside, but I knew she wouldn't leave. I could picture her sitting there, nodding off with her head in her hand and the fishtail braid she always wore at work growing increasingly frayed, while Steven slept and all his machines beeped and delivered whatever was pumping through his veins at any given time.

Deacon was probably still at office and likely would be for the foreseeable future. I heard from David only sparingly throughout the day, though he made several offers to leave the office and come sit with me at the hospital. But it wouldn't have made a difference.

The cat was out of the bag, the whatever was out of the whatever. It didn't matter. The damage was done, and we would all be lucky to get out alive.

The house was quiet, almost desolate, as I padded through the empty, winding halls. Most of the staff would have gone home for the day, and if there was anyone here overnight, they could have been anywhere.

The door to Deacon's bedroom was firmly shut, no light illuminated from behind it, no signs of life snaking out from underneath. The hallway that stretched between our rooms was abnormally long—had always been abnormally long. Too much distance between family members. Just like all the endless, winding hallways in this house were.

We had always been able to bridge the distance, but it seemed like it was stretching further and further. I should have called Noa, should have stolen his phone before he shattered it, or taken the replacement that came from God knows where. Begged her to come home, to come save him from himself.

I pushed open my door, ready to rip off my clothes and scald the hospital off me in the shower—I had no idea how Taylor did it every day. I needed to bleach the smell off my skin, the thought of tubes and wires coming from my father, and then I would call Noa, tell her in no uncertain terms that Deacon was off the rails, that she needed to come home and rein him in.

The door to the bathroom was open, the light was off but there was a flicker of something against the wood. It looked like a flame—like a tiny candle trying to light an impossibly dark room.

And David Kennedy was leaning in the doorway.

"Hey baby." David's hands were shoved into the pockets of his pants, one half of a tan wool Zegna suit I knew he favored because I knew him better than I knew my own mind. Ridiculous on anyone but him. The jacket lay abandoned on the buttoned chaise at the end of the bed.

My breath caught in my throat. *Baby. Baby. Baby.* "No billion dollar?"

"Not today," David answered quietly. He cocked his head, studying me for a moment before taking what looked like a hesitant step forward, and one hand stretching toward me, palm open.

"Shouldn't you still be at the office?" I asked, my feet tentative as I crossed the carpet to lay my hand in his.

David shook his head, thumb brushing the back of my hand. "No. More important things to do."

"What's this?" I peered around him into the bathroom, past the ridiculous black and white swirls of the marble countertop, where candles flickered, illuminated against the mirror. I watched in the mirror as David turned, wrapping his arms around me and dropping his chin to my head.

The bathtub—that stupid clawfoot bathtub that had enough room for an entire family—was home to endless mountains of bubbles. Candles were strewn haphazardly across the floor around it, and a hammered copper bucket perspired, an uncorked bottle of wine leaning against the rim. One single crystal glass sat beside it.

More important things to do.

My mouth felt dry, and words that should have been teasing just came out quiet. "Mr. Kennedy, did you draw me a bath? With all these expensive bubbles, a bottle of wine, and Jo Malone candles?"

"Yeah, I think I did." David tightened his arms around me, chin coming down to my shoulder so his lips moved past my ear. "Call me if you need anything, okay? I'm going to—"

"Do you want to join me?" I asked softly.

I wasn't sure why I said it; I knew I shouldn't have. All this touching and hugging. Sharing the same bed was one thing, but being entirely naked, entirely exposed around David Kennedy, was a whole other thing unto itself.

But my skin was hot, and my heart hurt where it pushed against my ribcage. Not the usual desperate bid to get to him, where it would almost tear itself open, where I would have torn my own heart from my chest with my bare hands and placed it at his feet if it meant absolution. Maybe it was trying to open a particularly stubborn door. Not to go home, not to leave my body, just to open a room that had been shut in a house for far too long.

I felt him swallow against the back of my neck and the low, hoarse tone of his words. "I think that would go against the rules set by the pillow wall in our bed."

Our bed.

It wasn't ours. It wasn't even mine. It hadn't been in years. But in the same way that there wasn't anything about him that wasn't about me, there was nothing about me that wasn't about him.

"You've never had a platonic bath?" I asked, with a small, teasing laugh.

David shook his head, his chin still pressing into my shoulder. "No, I can't say I have, baby."

"I don't think I have, either. Shall we lose our platonic bath virginity together?" I stepped out of his arms, watching the way his eyes tracked over me in the reflection of the mirror. I studied him for just a moment, his head angled, everything about him entirely dark.

Before I could change my mind, listen to it instead of my heart, instead of all the parts of me that wanted his skin pressed against mine—wanted him against me, on me, inside of me—I pulled my sweater over my head, losing his reflection in the mirror for just a moment. Dropping the sweater to the ground, I flicked my gaze up to meet his. I watched him swallow, watched his nostrils flare, and his eyes move over me in the mirror, skate across the nude lace of the Fleur of England Mia balcony bra, to my hair that was splayed across my shoulders, down my collarbone, and over my shoulder blades—until they landed on my fingers that were undoing the buttons of my jeans.

"Charlie—" His voice was strangled, and he rubbed a palm across his jaw.

A small smile unfurled on my lips, and I felt playful—almost giddy—the childlike way I only ever felt around him, all unbridled excitement. Kicking off my jeans, I stood, watching him watch me as his shoulders tensed and rolled back when his gaze landed on the lace of the briefs that stretched across my upper thighs. "Come on, Mr. Kennedy. Get in the bath with me."

I could see his pupils dilate from here, those honey eyes growing impossibly dark, the specific shade of amber they only ever were when he was turned on.

He was still palming his jaw, eyes wide, and everything about him tense when I reached behind me to grab the clasp of my bra. He was behind me in an instant, calloused fingers brushing over mine in permission, eyes still on mine in the reflection.

I offered him a tiny smile, fingers moving past his when I dropped the clasp.

We were still watching one another, the flickering candles casting shadows across everything, and I could feel David's fingers whisper over my skin as he unhooked my bra.

Rolling my shoulders forward, one by one, I brought my hands to each of the straps, moving them down my arms until I was entirely bare, eyes never leaving David's in the mirror.

His nostrils flared, and his eyes left mine to skate over my collarbone, down the curve of my chest, where they stopped.

Something like a groan came from his throat.

"Missed them?" I arched an eyebrow, the tiny playful smile that only ever came from being with him stretched across my face.

David shook his head, still gripping his jaw. He was still so close to me that I could hear his words, practically feel them as he dropped his hand and they whispered by me. "I miss all of you all the time."

Before I could answer, he dropped to a crouch, his hands finding my ribcage, slowly skating down until they gripped my waist. I felt those calluses, his fingertips, tense against my skin before David hooked his fingers around the sides of my underwear and slowly started to pull them down my legs.

A small shiver ran through me. Despite the fact that I was on fire, my skin pebbled and hot all over, I stepped out of the fabric pooling at my feet, and his hands traced the back of my calves and thighs before he stood.

Our eyes met again in the mirror. I tipped my chin up, words soft when I spoke. "Your turn."

"Get in the bath. You look cold." David's thumbs brushed over my shoulders.

I wasn't cold, not even close. I might have been close to combusting from the inside out. Being this close to David clothed was a challenge; him just looking at me would send my pulse skittering, making it hard to breathe.

But like this—all of me entirely exposed, not just my body—I hadn't been like this with him, with anyone, since he showed up at my townhouse in the pouring rain before I left for London.

I stared at him in the mirror imploringly, looking like I thought this situation wasn't as serious as it was. I raised my eyebrows at him. "Not until I'm sure you aren't just going to turn around and leave me in here alone."

David grinned at me, eyes dropping to my chest one more time before he raised his hands, palms up in concession. "As soon as you get in there, I'll follow."

I narrowed my eyes, raising one finger and pointing at him in the mirror, before finally turning and walking toward the tub. The mountains of bubbles hadn't gone down at all, and I raised one leg, testing the water with my toes, before I sunk my leg in and moved to sit on the ledge and slowly dropped myself in.

The water was warm against my skin, the perfect temperature and the bubbles bobbed in the water, settling around my collarbone and obscuring me from view. I raised my eyebrows at David expectantly, and he grinned, walking forward and bending down quickly to grab the bottle of wine and glass.

The muscles in his forearm stretched as he poured a glass and handed it to me.

I smiled up at him, his eyes never leaving mine again as he dropped the bottle back into the bucket, the telltale sound of ice clinking against the edge.

I wanted to tell him what this meant to me, how no one had ever taken care of me, done something just for me like this, without an ulterior motive. My father or brother had certainly never chosen me, left the office early for me on a regular day, let alone one where the future of the company, the empire, was hanging on tenterhooks.

But I wanted to pretend we were normal, just me and him, and not who we were.

So I asked an entirely normal, pedestrian question. "How was your day?" I looked up, pressing the wine glass to my lips.

David cocked one eyebrow, fingers deftly undoing the buttons of his shirt. The material fell open, revealing his year-round sun-kissed skin and the ridges of his abdominal muscle. He moved to his sleeves, unbuttoning the cuffs of his shirt before answering. "Utter chaos. You've been at Winchester Holdings when stock prices go down, or a company folds and is ripe for a hostile takeover. Imagine that but like the crash of '87 on steroids."

I took a small sip of wine while I watched him roll his shoulders back and shrug out of his shirt. "Did you take care of my big, important company, Mr. Kennedy?"

"I work in mergers and acquisitions, baby. Spent all day on the phone assuring very pissed off CEOs their businesses were safe and making sure new deals were still solid." David laughed, the noise from his belt being undone echoed throughout the room. "I'll warn you that I have a raging fucking hard-on."

"Oh?" I feigned surprise, tipping my head. "Why ever would that be? Perverted mind running away with you? Thinking about all the things you want to do to me? How to take advantage of me in my vulnerable state?"

David grinned, one hand quickly undoing his pants before he pushed them down his thighs and stepped out of them, revealing a pair of black Tom Ford boxer briefs that clung to his muscular thighs and left absolutely nothing to the imagination. "The things I want to do to you are unspeakable."

"Maybe we should change the topic. I'm worried about the lack of blood traveling to your head at the moment." I smiled at David, swirling the wine glass more for something to do as he shucked the underwear off.

He wasn't wrong. He was impossibly hard.

My mouth dried out, and he winked at me, laughter falling from his mouth. "Oh, I don't think that's going anywhere."

I felt David's laughter skitter across my skin, all over me, down to my heart, my soul, and felt it wrap around me as he stepped into the bath behind me. The water sloshed against the sides, somehow not spilling over, but the bubbles rose as he settled beside me.

I held the wine glass over my shoulder, settling against David's chest. His fingers brushed against mine as he took it. "Do you think there's a world where we do this every day? Come home from our respective jobs, whatever they are, open a bottle of wine, and we get in the bath together? Maybe not a tub as ridiculous as this one, but a tub that fits two comfortably."

"Would those be entirely platonic baths?" David asked, his arms wrapping around me, offering me the wine glass again.

I shook my head, smiling even though he couldn't see me. "Not in my preferred versions of the multiverse."

"Oh?" David's voice was low, and I felt the column of his throat move against the back of my head. "And what happens in your preferred versions of those baths?"

Before I could answer, could tell him all the things I wished we could do with one another, the ways I loved for him to touch me, to kiss me, to fuck me—all the things I wanted to do with him, had never stopped wanting to do, would never stop wanting to do, almost ready to tell him to forget the metaphorical and literal pillow wall entirely so the rest of our lives could start now—I heard the door to my bedroom slam against the wall.

"Charlie!"

I saw my brother in the reflection of the mirror before he stormed into the bathroom, suit jacket discarded, hair disheveled, and the glass of scotch clutched in one hand. But it wasn't just him. Noa trailed behind him, looking on the precipice of grabbing his arm to pull him back, to yank him out of my room. She had clearly been traveling all day. Her dark curls were pulled into a tight knot at the crown of her head, her face was bare, and she was wearing an oversized black sweater with matching sweatpants and white Alexander McQueen sneakers on her feet.

"Jesus Christ!" Deacon flung his hands in front of his face, a waterfall of scotch sloshing from his glass down the front of his freshly pressed, previously immaculate, Brooks Brothers button-down. He dropped his hands immediately, his apparent horror forgotten, and a look of disgust on his face as he pulled at his shirt. His eyes flicked up, narrowing, before he pointed his glass at us. "This is your fucking fault, Kennedy. Get out of the bath with my sister, get dressed, and then go buy me a new fucking shirt, because you ruined this one."

"Noa, nice to see you." I looked toward her, even though she was looking anywhere but at us, her cheeks growing redder by the second, before turning to glare at my brother.

"Deacon—respectfully, maybe set down the scotch for like two seconds of the day, and oh—get the fuck out of my bathroom."

Deacon scoffed, draining the rest of the scotch. "Oh, trust me. I'm never going to set foot in this room, this entire wing of the house ever again. But Taylor just called. Dad's awake. So you know, wrap up whatever the fuck this little clandestine bubble bath is."

"I'm so sorry," Noa whispered, staring determinedly at the ceiling before turning on her heel and following Deacon out the door.

I dropped my head back against David's chest, his chin coming to rest on the crown. His arms were still wrapped around me, and I wished for more reasons than I could count that the foundation of this house would finally crack open and swallow me whole.

Charlie

Seeing the great Steven Winchester, a man who lived so high above everyone else in the stratosphere, almost incapacitated, connected to so many wires and tubes, with ashen skin and in something as pedestrian as a hospital gown, was enough to disturb any subscriber to Chicago Business Weekly. It disturbed me, cleaved my heart open and stole the air from my lungs. He might have been in a stupidly lavish suite with expensive art, painted walls, and too many floral displays, but he was still my father.

The toe of my shoe—Taylor's Gucci sneaker—caught on the smooth tile floor when I followed my brother and Noa into the room. I reached out for David, fingers wrapping around his wrist.

He paused in the doorway with me, his still-wet hair curling around the nape of his neck and across his forehead.

Deacon barely spared me a glance, not even looking toward the direction of our father's hospital bed before throwing himself down onto the leather couch we sat on earlier. Something like a cringe stretched across Noa's face, and she looked at Deacon before her amber eyes swung to our father.

Staff surrounded his bed, some adjusting settings on the various machines, others listening, attention rapt as Taylor spoke to them, gesticulating wildly with her hands before pointing a finger toward my father and then at each of the doctors surrounding her.

She was still a resident, not exactly high enough to pull rank—but she was chief resident, because Taylor was never to be out done. It wouldn't have surprised me if everyone standing around her was her year, and she was just terrifying enough to demand the most respect in the room. She glanced sideways, raising her hand to me, one finger up before she turned back to them. She gestured to the chart one final time, tapping it repeatedly before she quite literally shoved it toward a very scared-looking doctor.

Her brown eyes swung back to my father momentarily, and her features softened. I could see his lips move from here, but it wasn't discernable, and I knew enough from Taylor to know that after patients were intubated or under anesthesia, sometimes they found it difficult to talk at first. Whatever she said, she nodded softly before turning away and walking through the sliding door into the suite.

"Why is your hair wet?" Taylor narrowed her eyes at me, her lips pursing.

Deacon propped his head on his fist, elbow digging into the arm of the couch. "Because she and David were having a nice little bubble bath."

Taylor's eyes went wide, and she looked pointedly back and forth between David and me, pausing where my fingers were wrapped around his wrist. "Oh, did you two finally bone?"

"Didn't look like it to me. Just wine, bubbles, and candles." Deacon supplied, one eyebrow rising. A wisp of straight hair fell onto his forehead. He had clearly found time to change his shirt, the scotch-stained button-up likely in the trash.

"Deacon." David's voice was flat, and I could see him shake his head from the corner of my eye.

Noa's eyes darted back and forth between Deacon and David, at that taut string of tension that never existed between them before.

Deacon flashed David a cat-like grin, one that was mostly teeth and usually reserved for me when I pissed him off. "Did I misspeak? You're in my sister's bed, in her bath—"

"Shut up." Taylor glanced at Deacon before rolling her eyes. "Your father asked to speak with you both when he woke up."

A singular brow rose on my forehead, about to refute that fact because there was no way the first thing Steven Winchester would ask for was his children, but my brother beat me to it.

"Before or after he checked to make sure the news hadn't leaked?" he asked dryly.

Noa came to stand behind him, running her fingers through his hair, twisting the tendrils at the nape of his neck, before wrapping her arms around him and dropping her head to his shoulder.

The tension across Deacon's shoulders, the tight cords of muscle down his forearms loosened. His hands unclenched, and he looked more relaxed than I had seen him in months. He looked like all the weight he was carrying, pressing down on him, left all at once—like he could breathe easier now.

I felt like I could breathe easier, too. Looking at him was like looking at me. Minus the flagrant substance use and abuse. I'd had questionable coping mechanisms over the years, but that had never been one, and all it told me was how broken he really was. I didn't want my brother to hurt, ever. And I didn't want to lose him, either. With Noa finally here, bringing him back down to earth, it didn't feel so much like I would.

Deacon's eyes flicked up to me, everything about him softening, and he smiled at me—a tiny acknowledgement that it was still us against the world—before he looked back at Taylor.

She gave Deacon a flat look. We all knew the answer. It was as close to a rhetorical question it could be without actually being one. But we were still his children, and I think there was a small part of us that probably hoped we didn't actually know.

Taylor's lips curled downward as she looked between us. "He asked for any updates on the business first. And then he demanded someone show him the press conference, to call Rebecca, to call Ash, and then to call both of you."

"Fourth place." Deacon nodded, lips pressed together, before looking at me.

We both laughed at the same time, everyone staring at us with wide eyes. It wouldn't make sense to anyone else—why it was funny. It would only make sense to us, Steven Winchester's children, who despite it all, understood him better than anyone on the planet.

I could feel David standing closer to me, because I always knew. I could feel it in the way my heart beat just a tiny bit faster. My shoulders shook until Deacon and I finally stopped, both wiping at our eyes.

"Could be worse," I offered, tipping my head at Deacon.

"Could have been fifth." He conceded, before pressing a brief kiss to the side of Noa's head and pushing to stand.

I turned to David—he was closer, marginally, but closer nonetheless. My eyes dropped, and I realized I was still holding his wrist.

He grinned at me, but it was softer than usual as he raised my hand and brushed his lips across it. He held it there, and everything else was gone. It was easy to believe it was just us in here. The wet hair curling against his forehead made it hard to breathe—a reminder that less than an hour ago, all of him was pressed up against me, a reminder that if I just—

"I'd say get a room, but you're already fucking doing that." Deacon's voice was dry.

Rolling my neck, I shot him a look and let go of David's wrist.

Deacon raised his eyebrows at me before jerking his chin toward our father's room. "Let's not keep him waiting and get him so worked up that he busts a fucking stitch."

"I closed up, and I promise you none of my stitches would bust." Taylor flashed a grin at Deacon, stepping to the side and gesturing toward the sliding glass door that separated us from our father.

She reached out, her hand encircling my wrist like mine had David's, offering me an uncharacteristically soft smile before squeezing once, twice, three times.

I held her hand for a moment before falling into step behind Deacon when the door slid open.

It was less disturbing, seeing him face to face and not through glass, even though all the tubes and wires and the hospital gown he probably hated remained. But he was sitting up, and Steven Winchester somehow managed to look formidable.

It might have been the way one of his eyebrows was cocked and his mouth pulled into a tight line, all the while he stared at one of the doctors, who seemed to be growing more nervous by the second, constantly fumbling with his clipboard.

Our father's eyes cut to us. They were the same unforgiving blue, but they seemed hazier than usual. He was probably the type to refuse pain meds after whatever time period he deemed appropriate, and I was sure his eyes would be as sharp as ever by the morning.

"If you'll excuse us," he interrupted, entirely cutting off the physician who was standing there to deliver him medical care, as if he owned this hospital and everyone in it reported to him. "I need to speak to my children—alone."

One of the residents, who I vaguely recognized from pictures Taylor had posted and stories she told, raised her hand like she was about to object. But Taylor leaned around the corner, hands gripping the edge of the still-open sliding door.

"We'll come back and finish up after. Let's finish post-op rounds first. Steven, buzz if you need anything, okay? It'll go right to my pager." Taylor nodded at our father before jerking her head at the rest of the doctors to follow her, and they all scurried out after her.

Deacon snorted, barely containing an eye roll before slamming his hand against the button on the wall to close the sliding door, effectively sealing us in with our father, all his tubes and wires, and what looked like an original Monet on the wall.

He said nothing, only raising one eyebrow at our father before tossing himself into one of the empty armchairs surrounding the bed. They were probably meant for functional families who wanted to be with one another.

I shook my head at him and looked back at our dad. "How are you feeling?"

"Groggier than I'd like," he answered, his voice clipped as he leaned over his bed, farther than was probably medically recommended, to grab a manilla folder sitting on the nightstand beside him. "But I've asked Taylor to start reducing the pain medication in a few hours."

I was about to ask him if he thought that was wise, to tell him that no one won a medal for suffering the most, when he began flipping through the folder, a purposeful set to his jaw until he extracted a document that looked identical to a Winchester Holdings' employment contract. And I would know, having been subjected to the unique experience of signing one and then signing the accompanying termination papers.

My nose wrinkled, and I leaned forward. "Is that—"

"The offer I mentioned after the board meeting, yes." His eyes cut to Deacon with what was probably a look of morphine-addled displeasure. It lacked some of its usual sharpness. "I would have thought in your unyielding loyalty to your sister that you'd have run to tell her the second I sent you the role breakdown and contract."

Glancing toward my brother, his eyes softened for just a moment, his cheek twitching, and he gave a tiny shake of his head like it was all the apology he could offer, before tossing a flat look at our father.

Deacon shrugged, holding both his hands up. "Hadn't gotten around to it. I was a little busy keeping your empire from crumbling to the ground, and Charlie was a bit busy in her bubble bath."

Rolling my eyes, I reached forward, hesitantly, like I was reaching out across a lifetime, back into the past maybe, to grab the contract from my father where it was in his outstretched hand.

The world's most bizarre olive branch. But an olive branch all the same.

The paper felt heavy in my hand. There were probably many reasons for that—employment contracts with Winchester Holdings were so intricate and lengthy, they bordered malignant, and I supposed, in some ways, they were. But it wasn't all the legal clauses and the citations of the privacy act and the built-in non-disclosure; it was everything else. All the things that had weighed me down my whole life. All those mistakes I made, half-built homes and half-lived-in lives. It was terribly ironic—because it was as close to approval I'd ever get from my father, and it was coming far too late. The only thing I wanted, once upon a time.

My finger traced the title on the first page, my eyes moving along with it, greedily soaking it all up, because what was I, if not a child at heart who just wanted to be loved, accepted?

"Vice President of Sustainable Investing." My words were a small whisper, hardly discernible over the various noises from all the machines hooked up to the great Steven Winchester.

"I don't have to tell you that you should read it over thoroughly before signing. Before making a decision. There are some things we need to discuss, regardless of what you choose." Our father sat up straighter, cutting a look toward Deacon again before attempting to smooth out his hospital gown, like he thought the whole thing was undignified. "It's rather opportune David came along, because I'd like you all to be here for this discussion. Perhaps that will force you all to take it seriously."

"You all?" I asked, eyes narrowing and nose wrinkling as I gestured with the contract between Deacon and me. "Don't tell me you have another child running around somewhere, and you're going to create some sort of acrimonious, tripartite leadership of Winchester Holdings?"

The look of morphine-addled displeasure was for me this time. "No. But I did make another call after seeing the concerning...dip in our stock."

"Who?" I practically spit the word out, but I had a sneaking suspicion who he was talking about, what kind of lecture or discussion he would want to impart about protecting his legacy, ensuring there was never another risk to the stock, to the company, like that again.

Our father arched an eyebrow at me, some of that haziness fading from his eyes, and I watched them grow sharper and sharper. "Tripp. His flight landed not that long ago. He should be here shortly."

Deacon scoffed, a dry laugh echoing endlessly throughout the room against all the polished surfaces, the seasonal flowers, and the out-of-place art. "Wow. We were actually in fifth."

Tripp

I thought about what it would be like to see Chuck again if I ever escaped the proverbial jail I existed in alongside my father. It was usually a far-off fantasy wherein I proved her wrong—showed up for her, didn't make a habit of seemingly abandoning her in all her times of need, didn't have a family that had fucked me up so spectacularly I didn't know the first thing about being dependable—a world where she wasn't, and wouldn't always be, wholeheartedly in love with someone else.

It certainly wasn't through a hospital window while being frisked by Winchester security, my arms up, like I was in a body scanner at the airport as they patted down every inch of me. Or, where I could barely see her through said shitty window, and she stood beside her dying father's bedside, her brother definitely didn't look that rough in any future I imagined for us, and David Kennedy certainly wasn't fucking there.

"You boys about done?" I asked dryly.

"Funny." The one closest to me raised his eyebrows, grip tightening on my arm for a second before he jerked his head toward the door. He couldn't really be described as a security guard because he looked more like a former secret service operative, with the immaculately kept, close-cropped beard, the bulging veins in his neck, and the earpiece.

Taking a measured step forward and removing the sleeve of my gray Theory cashmere sweater from his grasp, I offered him a flat grin. "Thank you for your service."

I didn't wait to see his face or hear his response, not when he had a solid twenty pounds of muscle on me. I wasn't even sure why I said it. He was just doing the job he was paid to do, and I certainly didn't look down on it. I wasn't really sure why I said most things like that in my life. Why I was always an asshole, proving everyone around me right time and time again. I probably wouldn't have to dig particularly deep to figure it out—I hadn't grown up in a warm, nurturing environment.

I knew Chuck would be furious at me. I could picture her face and the way her lips would purse, how her eyes would flash if she heard me say it. The idea of pissing her off was a welcome distraction from the general dismay I felt at seeing her again. It wasn't that I wasn't excited; it was just that nothing turned out how I'd hoped.

The sliding glass door to the suite opened. Noa and David were sitting at opposite ends of the leather couch positioned in the middle of the room.

Noa was gnawing on her fingernails with a veracity that bordered alarming, and frankly, it was quite unbecoming of anyone, let alone the biggest supermodel in the world. She stared determinedly at Deacon through the window of Steven's room, where all that was left of the Winchester Dynasty was huddled around a dying man in a hospital bed that probably had higher thread-count sheets than most homes.

She didn't notice me; her eyes were entirely focused on Deacon. Kennedy was no better, one hand gripping his jaw, a muscle twitching in his cheek while he stared at Chuck. One thing about DK that always drove me nuts—and probably instrumental in my reasoning behind half the things I'd done that were less than ideal—was how infallible he was. It was impossible to get under his skin.

But in an uncharacteristic display of frayed nerves, his left knee bounced up and down.

"Noa, DK," I offered, stepping through the door and shoving my hands in my pants' pockets.

Both of their heads snapped toward me, Noa's fingers falling from her mouth before she promptly sat on her hands, kind of like a child who had been caught doing something they weren't supposed to. David's leg stopped jumping immediately, and he pushed to stand, holding out a hand to me.

That polite fuck. North Carolina manners never died.

"Hey man." He nodded, offering me a strained smile before clapping my shoulder. "Charlie call you?"

My eyes narrowed, and I shook his hand, clapping his shoulder the same way he had mine.

I waited for it—disdain, anger, even envy to leak into his voice, but it wasn't there. David never let those fucking manners falter, but he waved his displeasure around like a fucking red flag when he was irritated with me over Chuck. But there was nothing.

Something had fucking changed between them since I last saw them.

I shook my head and jerked my head toward the room, not enjoying that particular revelation. "Steven did. He said he wanted to speak to both of us, actually."

David's eyebrows came together, and right on cue, like this was a fucking spaceship and not a luxury suite at Northwestern Memorial, the door to Steven's room slid open.

Deacon Winchester, or maybe a pod version of him because there was no way the Deac I knew would have willingly wandered out in public with bags that big under his eyes, stood behind the door, one hand holding it open. He jerked his chin at us before pointing his thumb over his shoulder.

It was a better summons than usual. He'd been known to whistle at people to get their attention.

David shook his head, shoving his hands into his pockets before closing the distance to the door.

I waited a minute before following to see if he'd stand by Chuck—stake some sort of claim, but he just propped himself up against the wall closest to the door. I didn't miss the way he took inventory of her, though—eyes quickly cataloging everything, like he was checking to make sure there was no damage since the last time he saw her.

Deacon tipped his chin toward me before looking back to his father. "What's he doing here?"

Steven somehow looked better than his son, hospital gown and all, where he sat propped up on the bed. His eyebrows came together, and his lips pursed. It was this shrewd sort of expression anyone who spent enough time around him grew used to. "I did him a favor, and now he's returning it."

"You can't just fucking extort people whenever it suits you—" Charlie's voice rose to an octave I'd never even heard before, and she whirled on her father, looking seconds away from pointing one of her bony fingers at him.

"I came here voluntarily, Chuck." I cocked my head to the side, my voice lilting the way she hated.

She spun around, her hair fanning around her with far less dignity than usual—it looked damp. She blinked rapidly, clutching what looked like a contract to her chest. I recognized the Winchester Holdings' embossment in the lower right-hand corner.

A muscle ticked in my jaw—that'd be Steven's handy work, all part of his grand plan to ensure the company didn't collapse. That's what he'd alluded to when he called. Some offer of a lifetime that would *beat rotting at the bank under my brother's leadership*. Steven's words.

He wasn't wrong.

"You're here." Her voice cracked a bit, and it looked like she wanted to smile.

One eyebrow rising on my forehead, I dropped a shoulder against the wall. "Glad to see you still possess your sense of sight."

Her eyes narrowed, like she remembered to be irritated by me trying to bait her, before swinging her gaze back to Steven. Her eyes stayed like that—dark and fairly foreboding.

"What favor?" Charlie repeated her father's words. Favors that required Steven Winchester were never good.

"Yeah, what favor?" Deacon's voice was almost at its usual dryness, the usual irreverence that only one of the richest men in the world could achieve—but not quite. It was the same way you wouldn't know Chuck was truly unhappy if you didn't know her, couldn't see all those subtle little things all over her—you'd never know he wasn't at his peak, indifferent and uncaring, because what could possibly bother him? But I knew him. I knew them both.

The way his voice tried too hard—the way his hair fell across his forehead. Maybe only the people in this room, and his fiancée just outside it, could tell.

Deacon Winchester wasn't okay, and I wasn't sure he would ever be okay again.

Steven's eyes were flat, leveling all of us with a bored look, and with a regular person, I would have said that was from the pain medication, but he was Steven Winchester. He probably metabolized narcotics at a quicker pace than the average human body. "What matters most is the favor he's returning."

Charlie's mouth parted in an indignant circle, and she looked like she was about to repeat herself when Deacon spoke again. He even sounded like shit. All the usual arrogance and bite to his tone was gone

"For the sake of everyone in this room, why don't you just go ahead and tell us what you're holding over his head? Last I checked, no one here is clairvoyant." Deacon rolled his head from side-to-side lazily before making a carry-on gesture.

My stomach tightened, and I felt my neck grow hot. It wasn't out of loyalty to my father or the Banks family name. I didn't want anyone to know; it was why I hadn't told Chuck back in New York. Maybe if I had, nothing would look the same.

But it was embarrassing to be cut from the same cloth—to share the same DNA—as a man like my father, who unlike Steven, who only metaphorically thought he was above everyone and the law. And I guess my father was because he was in Beacon Hill, not prison. I was usually quicker on my feet than this, and I was fairly adept at providing a dry retort for everything, but I just stood there, looking anywhere but at Chuck, rubbing the back of my neck. I was pretty sure that was a Monet on the wall behind her.

"Seeing as you aren't even acting CEO of Winchester Holdings, it's none of your concern." Steven barely spared me a glance, skating right by the bailout he was offering me by practically insulting his son. "There's enough intelligence in this room for you all to surmise why Tripp would be here and why Charlie would be holding that contract in her hand."

"How many degrees between everyone in this room, then? I count two Harvard MBAs, one from Wharton, a Masters in Economics and Development, and about one-quarter of a Ph.D., because you just can't resist pulling strings." Deacon flashed his teeth at Steven before shoving both his hands in the pockets of his Ralph Lauren suit pants.

I glanced over at Kennedy, and he rolled his eyes before dropping his head back against the wall, like he was hardly resisting banging it there.

"Enough, Deacon." The reprimand didn't come from Steven this time. Chuck cut him a glare that wasn't as harsh as it seemed. Her eyes were shining in the way they only really did when she was on the precipice of tears. She looked between Kennedy and me, her lips pulling into a grimace before she hugged the contract to her chest and looked back to her father.

Steven's nostrils flared for a moment as he stared at his son, but he sat up straighter in his bed against the pillows, one of the many tubes sticking from his arms and catching on his hospital gown. The muscles in his neck clenched, and he looked like he was about to rip every single tube from his arm when Charlie reached forward, dropping the contract at the foot of the bed, straightening out all the tubes, and smoothing out the side of his hospital gown.

I don't think I'd ever even seen them hug, and this felt far more intimate than when Steven gave her a perfunctory kiss on the cheek.

He didn't smile or offer her any platitudes of thanks. He simply nodded at her before looking back at the rest of us. He cleared his throat before speaking. "It will become increasingly important that Winchester Holdings has a solid, united leadership. And a loyal one. I can't think of anyone more loyal to my children or the company than you two."

Steven looked pointedly between David and me, but Deacon let out a dry, almost maniacal laugh.

"Loyal to who exactly? Not sure you can call this equal footing when they've both slept with one of us—" He pointed back and forth between himself and Charlie before cocking his head to the side. "And spoiler alert, it's not me."

"Deacon, I swear to God, I'll throw you through that fucking window." Kennedy tipped his chin toward the glass stretching behind Steven. A muscle ticked in his jaw before he dropped his head against the wall again.

Deacon's upper lip curled back. "Why don't you go run another bubble bath?"

Something had changed between them, too.

I glanced over at Chuck, and she didn't even look mad. Didn't look uncomfortable like she usually would if someone brought up our sordid history. I was expecting devastation, utter carnage at her brother's words, the only person she might love more than David Kennedy. But she just looked tired.

"Thank you for proving my point with your little display, Deacon. It doesn't take four masters' degrees and one-quarter of a Ph.D. to realize the company will get picked apart at an alarmingly fast rate when you can't even make it through a conversation without losing control. Quite frankly, I don't care who they're loyal to so long as they have the last name Winchester." Steven's words were clipped, and everything about the set of his features was exactly as I'd seen it time and time again: irritated and angry. But his eyes didn't look like they usually did. He stared at Deacon for a moment longer and almost looked like a father, sad for his child. But the moment passed, and he pointed toward the door. "You may go. Tripp, I'll have Helen file your paperwork, and I expect you in the office as soon as possible. I have calls to make."

Deacon rolled his eyes and slammed his palm against the button on the wall to open the sliding glass door, shoving the sleeves of his shirt up his forearms with a concerning amount of force.

David pushed off the wall, those annoying brown eyes sweeping over Chuck, and the corners of his lips pulling up like he just couldn't fucking resist smiling at her, before he nodded at me and followed after Deacon.

I watched Deacon yank open the door to the suite, DK right behind him. I couldn't hear them from here, but by the set of David's shoulders and the look in his eyes, Deacon was getting an earful.

"What a warm welcome you've received." Chuck came to stand beside me, eyebrows raised, and a tight smile on her face. She was hugging the contract to her chest again, and just behind her, Steven Winchester was on the fucking phone.

It was out of habit—but there was something about touching her that had always been familiar, comfortable even. Probably what it was like to really and truly have a friend who understood you and saw you. Tossing my arm over her shoulder, I steered her out into the waiting area of the suite. Deacon and David had disappeared down one of the winding hallways. "I've been on the receiving end of a Steven Winchester admonishment before, but none quite like that."

Charlie snorted, shaking her head. I waited for her shoulders to tense, or for her to duck out from under my arm like she used to, hand peeling mine away with a look of disgust on her face, or for that version of us from New York to peek through, where she'd lean into me, look up at me and smile softly.

Neither of those versions came. She didn't pull away, she didn't lean in; she just sort of...existed beside me. It reminded me of the way things used to be, back when we were just two kids, two friends. I didn't have time to think about how that felt, ruminate on how that had never been the version of her I wanted, but in this moment it didn't feel so bad—because she tipped her chin toward the door of the suite, offering Noa a tiny wave and steering us toward the hallway, empty save for the security still-standing vigil by the door.

Glancing backward, I felt myself cringe.

Noa sat there, wide-eyed and looking on the verge of tears, hands still firmly clamped under her legs. This was a fucking disaster.

I turned toward Chuck, dropping my voice. It wasn't something I would usually do—who cared if Noa heard me. Everyone could see Deacon was falling apart. But for maybe the first time in my life, I didn't particularly feel like baiting anyone. "Your brother's seen better days."

"So has his wallet. You should see the amount of cocaine residue on all of his credit cards." Charlie shook her head, raising her hand in thanks to the security and steering us down the hall toward another empty waiting area. "I have no idea where David and my brother went. Maybe Deac's off to the washroom to chalk up a line."

The soles of her shoes made a clunky thud that echoed against the sterile hall, and I tipped my head down to see the giant Gucci sneakers. They looked out of place on her—too flashy. She finally extracted herself from under my arm and dropped to perch on the worn leather couch that matched the one in her father's suite. The whole setup—flowers on a polished wood table and another original painting on the wall—screamed of understated opulence, like this part of the hospital had just been waiting for the likes of the Winchesters.

Pressing my hands into my thighs, I sat on the armchair across from her. I cocked my head and surveyed her while she stared at me, eyebrows up, waiting for me to make the first move. "What happened between you and DK while I was gone?"

"Nothing." Her nostrils flared, and she shrugged, all nonchalant, as if anything with them could be reduced to a singularity. A simple glance between those two couldn't be reduced to *nothing*.

The lilt in my voice came back when I spoke, usually reserved to annoy her to no end, but in this case, I was hoping it might bait her enough to tell me the truth. "Nothing? Nothing at all? Guy gets a tattoo for you, and you don't even kiss? You're not known for your restraint as far as he's concerned, Chuck."

Charlie rolled her eyes, waving her hands around in a manner that looked so much like her brother that it was alarming. "We are sharing a bed. But there is a pillow wall between us."

"A pillow wall," I echoed, voice deadpan.

She nodded primly, like a good little debutante might when asked a rhetorical question during finishing school.

I wasn't done, because if there was one thing I could do in all of this, it was goad Charlie Winchester into giving me an answer, maybe even convince her to smile. "What would have happened if I had been here, too? Who'd get to sleep in your bed and comfort you?"

She pursed her lips and gave me a flat look before straightening her shoulders. "But you weren't here, Tripp."

No, I wasn't. And now that distance that used to be between us, that stretched years but was primarily made up of my king bed in my stupid frat house bedroom, was wedged right back here instead of the table that probably cost more than some peoples' rent. "Answer the question. Or would the three of us be having a sleepover?"

Charlie raised her hands in defeat. "Fine. You could flip a coin."

"Winchesters don't carry coins," I answered, the lilt in my voice carrying between us.

"Amex then. Signature side up wins." She raised her eyebrows briefly, and her voice sounded like she might be hiding a laugh, and that distance might have been reduced to a double mattress. I felt on top of the world before I remembered where else you could find her signature.

Tattooed on David Kennedy's stupid fucking arm.

Silence fell between us, and she might as well have been here, and I might as well have been back in fucking Beacon Hill. A sad, small smile tugged at the corner of her lips, the ones I used to be able to kiss at will before I pissed it all away for a man who didn't give a fuck about anyone else.

Charlie wrinkled her nose, her voice quiet, and her words a tentative olive branch. "I'm glad you're back. Here, safe, away from whatever's happening at home."

I grinned at her, and I meant it, even though my heart didn't feel particularly pleasant. But staring at Chuck, even if it was across a vast, insurmountable distance, was preferable to staring at my father. "Me too. Wanna pick back up where we left off?"

She narrowed her eyes. "Friends, Tripp. That's all I'm doing with anyone right now."

Her lips parted, and she tipped her head, green eyes surveying me, tracing over all of me, like she was checking to see if I was really there. "Are you going to tell me what happened?"

Shaking my head, I pulled my lips into a grin that I knew would piss her off. "Need-to-know basis, like Steven said. You're not CEO, yet."

"And never will I be." She raised the contract, still clutched between her hands, and stood, like she was resigning herself to my lack of transparency. "We should get back before anyone thinks we're colluding to take over the company."

Pushing my hands into my knees to stand, I arched an eyebrow at her. "Would that be a legitimate concern?"

Charlie tipped her head back, a dry laugh coming from her. "You'd be surprised. Scott Sabean thinks I'm planning to steal the company from underneath Deacon."

"I read on Business Insider that Scott got fired." I shoved my hands into my pockets, and we fell into step beside one another, back toward the suite.

She paused a few steps before the security, folding her arms across the contract and her chest. "He did, in a very public display, actually. We have quite a bit to catch up on. Maybe when you're settled back in at the office, we can grab a coffee?"

A far cry from takeout in my bed before I spent hours methodologically worshiping every inch of her, but if friends was all she was offering, I'd take it.

I grinned at her, winking before I could stop myself. "It's a date, Chuck."

She pursed her lips before giving me another flat look, turned on the heel of those shoes that really didn't suit her, and brushed past the security into the suite. I wasn't far behind her when her toe somehow managed to snag on the polished floor, and she lurched forward, arms out to steady herself.

For a girl who went to finishing school, she certainly tripped a lot when entering various rooms.

Charlie's eyes went wide, and she looked back and forth, nothing more than a deer in headlights. Only Deacon and Noa sat on the couch, Noa's legs draped over him, practically on his fucking lap, her hands running through his hair in a gesture I assumed was meant to be soothing, and Steven was alone in his suite, still on the fucking phone. No sign of Kennedy.

"Where's David?" Charlie's voice rose, and it cracked in alarm.

I think whatever was left of my heart after she hacked it up with her metaphorical Jimmy Choos cracked too.

Deacon's gaze flicked up, and he widened his eyes at her. "Getting you a coffee. He'll be right back, settle down. He didn't abscond into the fucking night."

She rolled her eyes, but I didn't miss the way she swallowed, blinked rapidly for a moment, and how her shoulders and back went ramrod straight, like all her muscles had suddenly knotted together. She stayed like that as she sat down across from her brother and Noa, on the edge of her fucking seat, and every part of her practically robotic.

I watched it, like I was suspended above it all in outer space, staring down as the world imploded.

He walked back into the room, and all that tension in her shoulders just fucking evaporated, like it had never been there in the first place.

I watched as he casually strode across the room, one hand shoved into the pocket of his navy Theory pants, the sleeves of the camel-colored rag & bone cashmere sweater pushed up. I watched as he handed her that non-descript cup of coffee.

I watched her smile up at him, like he was all the fucking stars in the sky, watched her fingers brush against his stupid, calloused ones she never shut up about. I watched as he grinned down at her, and she looked right back at him, like he was the only thing in the entire universe.

I never stood a fucking chance.

David

Charlie was silent the entire ride back to Lake Forest. From the moment Deacon threw open the door to the waiting town car outside the hospital, without as much as a wave toward the press still congregated outside the lobby doors. She said nothing when she ducked under my arm, her hair shielding her face from the camera flashes and stayed that way as she sat there across from me, still clutching the contract from her father, eyes glued to the window, watching the city at night.

The irony wasn't lost on me that it was the second time I was in the back of a town car with her after Tripp parachuted back into her life. But I didn't have the luxury of closing the partition and asking her about it, not when Deacon and Noa were there, and certainly not when one of them was making their way through the tiny bottles of scotch stocked in the minifridge in the back of the car.

Granted, she had lied to me when I asked her about him in that different town car, that different life.

Tripp's presence in my life had meant different things over the years—in business school, he was a friend. He'd been an asshole then, too. But he was still my friend.

When he came to Winchester Holdings, I didn't notice anything different until it was too late. I'd considered him to be the man responsible for the reason I wasn't with the girl of my dreams, the love of my life. And then, in New York, I considered him to be in my way the vast majority of the time, even though I was in my own way. It took me way too long to realize the only person responsible for any of it was me.

It hadn't bothered me when he showed up at the hospital, Steven demanding from his literal deathbed that we all work together to keep the company from meeting an untimely end; it didn't bother me that Charlie was relieved to see him.

What bothered me was how heavy the air in this room felt. Our room. What bothered me was how I could feel Charlie fidgeting just beyond the wall of pillows. I could see her rolling her fingers over and twisting them into knots from the corner of my eye, where she stared resolutely at the ceiling.

It bothered me that she couldn't forgive herself, that she was probably sitting over there running through the rolodex of her alleged mistakes she kept at the ready in her mind and that maybe I'd only ever be a reminder of that.

"The biggest mistakes are mine, Charlie," I offered, my words low. I scrubbed my hand across my jaw before tugging on the ends of my hair. "I left you when I should have stayed."

Her fingers stilled, and I could see her lips part for a moment, but she said nothing.

"Do you think you'll ever feel free around me? Unburdened? The way you deserve to feel?" My voice was rough. I said it like it was a simple question, but it wasn't and I was fucking terrified of the answer. I wanted the world for her, and maybe that wasn't me. "Because if you won't, I'll bow out now."

I could feel Charlie's shoulders start to shake against the bed, and I was about to reach out across these godforsaken fucking pillows because she was crying—but then I heard it.

The best goddamn sound in the world.

Laughter tumbled from her lips—closer to a cackle—and her shoulders continued to shake, her words punctuated with rasping breaths. "Bow out? What, are you and Tripp going to joust for my hand?"

A grin spread across my face, and I stared at the ceiling, the shadows dancing across it. Everything felt brighter, more beautiful, when she laughed. "You never know. He *is* an elitist East Coast prick."

Her laughter continued, and I stayed there, afraid to look at her because I didn't want her to stop, when it slowly faded away into tiny, regular breaths. We laid there, side by side in silence for a few more minutes until she spoke, her voice just a soft whisper. "I'm glad you didn't."

"Didn't what?" My voice was still rough.

"Didn't fight for me," she whispered, and I didn't have to roll over to know her hands were pressed against her chest, like she could hold her own heart. "Because then we wouldn't be here."

I couldn't think of a single place I'd rather be.

***

Tripp's return to Winchester Holdings caused a media circus. And maybe that had been Steven's well-timed plan all along, to distract and allow himself to be quietly discharged from the hospital. The phones rang non-stop; Rebecca was a constant, grating presence on the executives' floor. She always wore some monochromatic suit or another, ducking into everyone's offices to remind them that, in no uncertain terms, they were not to offer commentary to any of the press who camped outside the building day and night.

Rebecca was particularly harsh on Tripp, always popping her head into his office and asking him what I considered to be relatively unfair questions about his family that were also, frankly, none of her business.

He was a fucking vault, anyway. No one was getting those secrets anytime soon.

I watched from my office through my open door and into his across the floor, leaning back in my chair and palming my jaw as Rebecca delivered what looked to be yet another sermon. I could see one of Tripp's eyebrows rise as he looked at her with one of his usual impassive stares. But as she turned on her heel—powder blue today—he yanked on the knot of his tie in frustration.

I hesitated before pushing off my desk and ducking out of my office. The whole thing should have felt weird; it probably was weird to someone else looking in. Anyone on the outside who didn't know what it was like to be entirely consumed by Charlie Winchester.

Tripp had been my friend, too, and he still was. We had a few things in common regardless of what we did: Deacon, Winchester Holdings, Charlie.

For better or for worse, he was her friend, one of her best. He was the only person other than Taylor I'd ever seen her loosen up with, laugh with like that. And there probably wasn't a fucking thing in the world I wouldn't do to make her smile, to hear that laugh.

My favorite sound used to be the ocean—the way I could hear it when the window was open back in my old bedroom at my parents' place on Figure Eight. It was my favorite sound in the world until I was twenty-nine. Until the first day I heard her laugh.

I remember it like it was yesterday because I think a fundamental part of me changed that day. My heart stopped beating to keep me alive; it started beating just to hear that fucking sound again. My heart had been beating for Charlie Winchester for three years now, so maybe it was weird, entirely fucked up, but it was easy, because even though once upon a time he was my friend, he was a part of her.

"Hey man." I leaned against the mahogany door frame of his office, shoving one hand into the pocket of my suit pants.

Tripp raised an eyebrow, eyes locked on his computer screen for a moment longer before he finally looked up. If he was surprised to see me in his doorway, he didn't let on. It was one of the more infuriating things about him. He was always wearing a mask, and it rarely fucking slipped.

His voice was flat, borderline guarded when he spoke. "Hey."

I cleared my throat before scrubbing a palm across my jaw. He looked uncomfortable, almost tense. It bothered me, mostly because I knew it would bother Charlie. There was nothing I wouldn't do, get over, get past, set down my own pride for when it came to her, and it was a lesson I learned too late. I wouldn't repeat the same mistake. "We're good, right? All that shit—I get it now, what it's like to want her, to need her and to not have her. I don't blame you for any of it, Tripp."

I didn't. It wasn't his fault, and it wasn't even hers. I had only myself to blame for the fact that I hadn't been with her these last three years. Couldn't get past my own pride. There was only one person to blame for that. And I did understand, more than I ever wanted to, what it was like to exist in a world where she was just out of reach.

Tripp's voice was clipped, dry even. He leaned back in his chair, crossing his arms over his chest. "You're the one in her bed, DK."

My nostrils flared, and I exhaled. He wasn't wrong, but it wasn't like that. I wished pretty much every day that I had a magic lamp, three wishes from a made-up genie that would send me back in time so I could be worthy of her, be the type of person she deserved.

I shook my head, crossing my arms. "It's not like that."

"But you wish it was." It wasn't a question, and Tripp continued to appraise me from behind those blue eyes that sent most people into a frenzy and had since I'd known him.

"Of course I do. She's the love of my fucking life." My words were incredulous; there was no other answer than that. But I watched him, the way that one eyebrow still arched on his forehead and the way he was studying me, like he was trying to riddle something out so he could be two steps ahead of the rest of us like always. "You don't wish it was different for you?"

Tripp's mouth pulled to the side before he shrugged. "I don't know. I look at you two now, and I have no idea what the fuck I was thinking, trying to come between you two like that...thinking I had a right to. When she's around you, the whole weight of the world is off her shoulders. You can see it—her posture fucking changes when you walk into the room. I don't know how I didn't notice it before, what it is between you two. It's intangible."

"Funny, I once said the same thing to her about you. Whatever it is...the chemistry." The words were matter-of-fact. They were true.

She had chemistry with Tripp, some sort of intangible something, and he probably wasn't the only person on the planet she had it with. I'd never been insecure, but I'd been insecure about him.

"I'm not sure chemistry can compete with what you two have—certainly not for someone who's never felt safe to be who they really are for a moment in their entire life." Tripp's words were low, and any other day, I would have assumed there was some ulterior motive, some intention to goad me hidden there.

But when I looked at him, he just looked resigned.

"You, uh, you want to grab a drink after work? See if we can keep Deac from downing a whole bottle of Macallan by himself?" I asked, palming my jaw again.

Tripp's eyes narrowed, and his suit jacket buckled where his shoulders tensed. "Why?"

"Why what? Why should we try to keep Deacon from emptying yet another bottle of six-hundred-dollar scotch? It's not for his wallet like it would be for a regular person. I think his fucking liver could use a break." I shrugged, not particularly caring if Deacon drank the river water right now, when he was so hell-bent on destroying everything in his path.

"You could do that without me." Tripp's voice was skeptical, and it bothered me.

I could almost see what Charlie was always talking about; the things she'd go on about when it came to him. He looked like it was somehow so unbelievable to him that someone might want to spend time with him. Maybe it was unbelievable that I would willingly want to, but I knew it would make Charlie happy, and there probably wasn't anything on the planet I wouldn't do for her.

I nodded. "I could, but I'd rather not bear the brunt of Deacon's shitty attitude all night. Seems like something that should be shared amongst everyone."

The ghost of a grin flashed on Tripp's face for a moment before it was gone. "Yeah, alright. Come get me when you're ready to go?"

Raising my eyebrows, I tipped my chin at him, but he was already looking back at his computer.

Charlie

The balcony that stretched off my father's room was the largest by far. I wasn't even sure you could consider it a balcony in the literal sense of the word—it was a veritable terrace. It was like the ones that stretched from my room and Deacon's. But instead of one set of French doors leading to a balcony with furniture to our tastes—Deacon's, an overly large sectional, a sheltered TV, and a dry bar he had installed when he turned twenty-one, and mine, plants I couldn't keep alive myself that I suspected the staff had either been watering or replacing at regular intervals—and a cream, circular, daybed.

But our father's balcony—it could have been another conference room. In fact, he probably had used it as such throughout his life. A sterile, walnut table with a barbecue built in stretched the length of the space with too many leather chairs tucked in around it. There was one personal touch, a tiny, white wrought iron bistro set that still sat in the farthest corner, where the view of the sloping property and the lake was the best. It was our mother's favorite place to sit, and it stayed there for all these years, constantly surrounded by potted plants, towering palms, and all sorts of flora and fauna that my father certainly wasn't caring for.

I frowned, looking at it. I wasn't sure I liked it sitting there. This reminder of my mother. It's not that I didn't think it belonged there, *deserved* to be there. But she had been a forgotten ghost. Disregarded entirely.

I didn't like seeing these tiny ways my father had tried to preserve her. He had done so silently, without ever acknowledging her to his children. But here was her favorite spot to sit, kept, and cared for. There had been a trunk of her artwork—a trunk of her, really. The things that represented her best.

But these things had been here the whole time, and maybe I had been the one who didn't want to see them.

Steven Winchester cleared his throat, and I jerked my head back to the dining table. It was inlaid with everything you would expect at a formal breakfast, minus any champagne today. There still was freshly squeezed orange juice. It was something my father had always loved. He never went without it. Another juxtaposition of him. Ruthless businessman. Ruler of his own universe. But he couldn't start a day without his glass of juice.

There was one sitting in front of him now, his hands wrapped loosely around a crystal glass, and a cup of coffee steamed beside it.

He hardly looked like a man who just had major surgery and had just been discharged from the hospital—save for the IV pole that had become his ever-permanent companion. The sleeve of his freshly pressed shirt was pushed up his left arm so the butterfly clip wouldn't come out, and his suit jacket was folded neatly over the back of his chair. A copy of the Tribune lay folded beside him.

"Thank you for joining me." He gestured with his right hand—the one that wouldn't pull on the IV line to the seat beside him.

"Sure." I offered him a faint smile, folding my arms over my chest. My steps were tentative, socked feet arching against the cold balcony floor.

It was early enough—you could see the chill in the air over the lake from here. The haze that always settled in when fall hit Illinois. It felt like it came earlier out here than it did in the city. He probably shouldn't have been out here, but I wasn't sure if there was any truth to that. I could have called Taylor, or buzzed her on the stupid intercoms that were in all of the bedrooms to ask, but I didn't want to wake her up. She didn't get home until late, and she had to go back to the hospital in the evening.

The chair scraped against the wooden rungs as I pulled it out. The whole picture would have been serene—a father having breakfast with his daughter, the mist on the lake, and the immaculately kept property—had it not been for the IV pole and the fact that I was formally invited to this breakfast through an Outlook calendar invitation.

"How are you feeling?" I asked, looking over at my father as I tucked my legs beneath me and sat in the chair beside him.

"Hm?" His eyes were already back down on the paper.

He usually read the business section exclusively, but I could see our last name in big block letters. I didn't need to reach forward to grab it to know it was the equivalent of an entertainment page. It was upside down from where I was sitting, but I could see a black and white photo of Deacon and me at the press conference. Breaking News—our pain was media fodder now.

Maybe it always had been.

"How are you feeling?" I repeated, leaning forward and flipping up the white porcelain mug that was waiting there for me. Steam rose from the French press beside it, and it warmed my hands as I poured a cup.

"Fine." His tone was clipped, but it wasn't directed at me. I knew what he was going to say before he said it. "I'd be better if I could get back to the office. Stock has stabilized since the press conference. It's rebounded slightly, but I think it would do better if I showed my face to demonstrate there was an appropriate handover happening, but Rebecca thinks—"

I paused before I could take a sip of the coffee, interrupting him before he went on for too long. "Ash has been at the company since before you took it over. It'll be fine, Dad."

He raised one eyebrow, the silver hairs even more stark against the pallor of his skin. "It was a smart move to name Ash as acting president and CEO. Was that your idea?"

Deacon had been far too frantic—pulling the ends of his hair, making great, slashing movements and gestures with his arms to appear like a credible choice. It was supposed to be his—the heir to the great empire. But he wasn't even interested when Rebecca offered to prepare a statement for him, a speech, as if he had won a presidency. He had shrugged her off, telling her to make someone else do it.

"It was both of ours," I lied. I wasn't about to tell him that the child he had spent his life preparing, laying in wait for the keys to the kingdom, didn't seem to want them at all anymore.

His eyes narrowed momentarily. He had never been a terribly present parent, both before and especially after our mother died—but part of his business acumen had always been knowing exactly when people were lying.

I waited for it, ever permanently feeling like a child who had been caught doing something they weren't supposed to, but my father schooled his features and took a measured sip of coffee instead. "You were exceptional at the press conference, as well. I was proud of you both. The way you carried yourself." He eyed me from behind his porcelain mug.

I could see it, just beyond the faint steam of the coffee—that glow of pride behind his eyes. So entirely rare coming from Steven Winchester that Deacon and I were trained to spot it miles away.

"Well, you can thank yourself for that. Media training and etiquette lessons as a child." I offered him a tight smile.

It was shocking, really, how often I had managed to make a very public mess of things, given the fact that I spent more time in private lessons like that than I did kicking a soccer ball around a field like a normal child.

It wasn't meant to be a dig, not really. But it probably was. I wished I could take it back, but my father wore an impenetrable shield around him, and if it bothered him, he didn't let on.

Instead, he said something that felt like he had taken a pair of garden shears and started plucking out all the barely healed stitches that were patching me up—the things I had worked on so hard to heal. "Tripp is back. And David seems to be staying in your room."

I felt myself flinch, those invisible shears moving down my sternum and flaying me open. I thought we were past this, but maybe we weren't. Not when his business was teetering on the edge of a proverbial cliff, and its once biggest public image threat was back all around him.

The headlines when I moved to London were probably some of the worst I'd ever seen about myself, or anyone really. There was a particularly cruel nickname that floated around on some messaging platforms that played on the fact that our name started with a W, a poor alliteration with the words "Winchester" and "whore" the internet seemed to find far too clever.

But I didn't care, not really. I was building a new home, brick by brick, in my own body, and my own heart. But maybe my father still did.

Before I could say anything, Steven Winchester uttered a string of syllables, letters, and words, the likes of which had never come from his mouth before. "Do you know the difference between a twin flame and a soulmate?"

"Do you?" I asked incredulously, lips pulling back. "You've been spending too much time with Taylor."

"Neither is better. They're just different. I'm told a twin flame...is like the same soul split in half. Soulmates are separate, but you come together, complement one another, and support one another. One is meant to teach you something, a lesson, maybe. But those connections—they burn entirely too hot. You tend to be meant for one and not the other, despite the...intensity of it all. David and Tripp are different."

Chewing on my lips, I shook my head slightly. "You don't want to hear about this, Dad."

He arched an eyebrow, taking another sip of his coffee before setting the mug neatly down on the matching porcelain saucer. "Don't I? I don't have all the time in the world, and I wouldn't mind getting to understand my daughter a bit better."

He wasn't ripping open an old wound, cutting open barely healed sutures and stitches. He was asking me a question that was meant to help it close over entirely.

"David was the first time I felt like I was really me, you know? Not Charlie Winchester. Not your daughter. Not Deacon's sister. Not half an orphan. Just...me." I tipped my head back, watching clouds tumble across the clear sky as I sunk back into my chair and folded my arms across my chest. "And Tripp. He's my friend. Maybe my favorite friend. Someone who existed with me in all the shitty, messy parts of life. Popular literature would say I should pick the toxic one, but I don't know. I spent so much time with David worried I wasn't good enough, so much time with Tripp hating who I was." I shook my head, nostrils flaring, and tears started to spill down my cheeks. I wiped at them, they were cold against my skin. "But when I'm with David, I don't think about him. But when I'm with him, I think about David. I think I'm always thinking about David Kennedy. How pathetic am I?"

"You're not pathetic." His voice was sharp, and I could see it in the usually distant, cold eyes—it hurt him, caused him a sort of visceral, flinching pain to hear me call myself *pathetic*. His hand twitched where it was sitting beside his coffee. "For what it's worth, I don't think either of them are toxic. I think they see and hold different parts of you, and that's okay. That one of them, and I think you're smart enough to know which, is a lifeboat—one you've clung to when you didn't like what was happening in your life, your head, or your heart. And the other...your lighthouse beam that guides you home. But what matters at the end of the day is who you want to be, Charlie."

Who I wanted to be.

I think I had an answer to that after all this time.

I wanted to be me. Me exactly as I was. Who I had always been. Maybe someone who was more careful with her own heart, with other people, but me all the same.

"Do you miss Mom, Dad?" I whispered, lips parted and my features on the verge of collapse.

He looked at me, and there wasn't a fraction of hesitation, not a single twitch of muscle fiber. "Every day."

My voice was childlike when I spoke, just a sad little whisper from a tiny child who would soon be without both her parents. Unmoored, unanchored. Lost when she wanted nothing more than to be found. "Are you scared?"

His eyes flicked to the IV line, to the clip in his arm, and he frowned like it was nothing more than an inconvenience. He considered it for a moment longer before looking back at me. "Of dying? No, I'm not. Perhaps it's simply the next great thing for me to conquer. I do find that I...worry I've wasted too much time. With you. With your brother. Scared, possibly, that you'll never forgive me. That you and Deacon won't be happy the way you both deserve." His voice was quiet when he spoke again, barely discernible. "But I greatly look forward to seeing your mother again. Truly, I do."

I cocked my head back. This might have been the most shocking revelation of the entire conversation, so at odds with the man I thought I knew. "Don't tell me the great Steven Winchester, ruthless businessman, patriarch at the helm of the Next Great American dynasty, believes in heaven?"

He studied me, his words low when he spoke. "Don't tell me the curious, brilliant, daring Charlie Winchester doesn't believe in anything?"

"Wow. When did you get to be such a philosopher?" I whispered, my voice thick with tears. Everything blurred, even the edges of his IV pole. It looked softer, and it didn't feel as sharp like it was poking into my skin and jutting into my heart.

A dry snort escaped my father, and Steven Winchester looked at me for a moment, his features softening impossibly before he gestured to my abandoned coffee. "I'll have someone bring you up a fresh press."

"That's not necessary, Dad." I shook my head, offering him a quiet smile before wrapping my hands around the mug again.

It had grown cold; he was right. But everything else about me felt warm.

He nodded, one of his usual curt ones, but the lines around his eyes were soft when he picked up his paper again, speaking before disappearing behind it. "I'd still like to talk to you about coming back. I think the new role is...worthy of your talents and skills. But perhaps we can save that for another day? I'll ask Damien to schedule us another breakfast later this week."

Another day. Another breakfast with my father. I think I wanted all the awkward, bizarrely formal Outlook invitations he had left to extend.

Charlie

Early morning light—all crisp and clear, the way it only ever was in Chicago when it was the precipice of fall—streamed through the paned windows that lined the hall between my room and Deacon's.

The door to my room—our room—was wide open. David was nowhere to be found, it was still early but well into his day by now.

But someone, a member of the staff most likely, had been in the room. The bedding was made, far too immaculate to be done by David, tucked in impossibly tight to all corners, the pillows fluffed and propped up across the head of the bed, and a solitary white daffodil sat on the nightstand in a tall, glass vase that I didn't even want to begin to think of the cost. I usually left my room closed on the rare occasions I stayed here because I didn't see the point in having someone turn it over every morning, like it was a fucking luxury hotel. David must have left the door open—I didn't see him last night. I'd fallen asleep in Taylor's room while she watched surgery footage.

Or, maybe someone on staff thought it would be a nice thing to do for me. Dead mother, soon-to-be dead father. Maybe someone just wanted my room to look nice.

Deacon, on the other hand, always left his door wide open, an invitation for all of his things to be cleaned and pressed, tucked in, and pulled tight. But this morning, his door was almost closed, just a tiny crack left open where the lock wasn't secured.

On tentative feet, I padded down the hallway, raising a fist to knock gently. The heavy door creaked open at my touch, the whole room still under shadow.

I peeked my head around the door, fingers gripping the edges, and a cloying, horrific sense of fear began to gnaw at my bones.

I had survived without my mother. How effectively was questionable, and I was fairly certain I would survive without my father, even if I didn't want to.

But life without my brother—without Deacon—that was a world I don't think I would even try.

But there was no horrific scene waiting for me on the other side of the door. The curtains were drawn, blocking out the morning sunlight, but there was a single source of light.

It was coming from Noa's phone. Her amber eyes flicked up to me, and she smiled softly, but for the first time since I had known her, she didn't look entirely put together. Blue circles rounded her eyes, and her lips were downturned.

She had propped herself against the headboard, against far too many pillows, with her hair piled on top of her head, curls escaping the knot around her forehead and ears. One hand held her phone loosely, and the other twirled Deacon's hair between her fingers.

He was curled against her, almost like a child, head on her lap, and his arms wound around her waist. I could see his back rise and fall, low, steady, and even breathing. From the hunch of his shoulders, the way they curved inward—he looked exhausted. I couldn't see his face, but I could imagine it. Softer than ever, hair falling onto his forehead, and everything sharp about him dulled entirely.

I cocked my head, they were in kind of an odd position, but it looked like he fell asleep with his head buried in her chest. How a child might fall asleep on a parent—seeking comfort from everything around them.

Noa's ministrations continued, and I studied the way she twirled his hair between her fingers, never slowing, like she couldn't bear to stop soothing him. But she tipped her chin toward the end of the bed.

"He's asleep." Her voice cracked, and she raised her eyebrows, pointing her chin toward the edge of the bed again. "He won't wake up. He was out with David and Tripp last night."

My nose wrinkled. "That's quite the group."

Noa shrugged, gently setting her phone down on the bed. "Did you want to get out of here, go for a walk? Down by the river? I could use a change of scenery."

Like I was afraid to disturb Deacon too, I tiptoed into the room and stopped at the side of the bed. "What? The empty halls of the Winchester fortress aren't doing it for you?"

A tiny smile tugged at her lips, but it didn't meet her eyes, and up close, I could see that they were bloodshot. "It's...cavernous in here. I can see what you mean when you say it's lonely."

My heart hurt, a visceral pang in my chest at the thought of it—that she would be so lonely here when she wasn't alone. She was living with her fiancée, who usually was so exuberant he could fill any space, no matter how big.

Glancing down at the ring on her finger, it hurt even more.

The three-carat Harry Winston sat askew on her slim finger, tipped to the side, like the diamond was weighed down by so much more than its sheer size.

"I suppose it would be," I whispered, the backs of my eyes starting to burn. I wasn't sure what time it was, but I knew it was well beyond when Deacon felt he needed to be at the office, no matter his state the night before. "Why don't you wake him up and just come get me when you're ready?"

Noa shook her head, fingers finally stopping their gentle sweep through Deacon's hair, the chocolate strands now more mussed than usual. I watched as she carefully pushed up before cradling his head and sliding her legs out from under him. His back still rose steadily with his breath, in and out, and Noa pulled the sheets up to cover him before dropping a kiss on the top of his head.

She turned to me, offering me a weary smile. "I'll let him sleep a while longer. Let me just get changed, and I'll be ready to go."

"I don't think he'll be thrilled he overslept, no matter what shape he was in last night," I whispered, a cringe settling across my face.

And he wouldn't. Deacon was many things, and right now, he was certainly a disaster, but he would hate to lose face in front of everyone at the office.

"It'll be fine." Noa shook her head, one of her small, manicured hands waving me off.

That ring, weighed down by everything that hung around us, caught in the rays of early morning sunlight streaming in through the windows and made everything sparkle for a minute, look beautiful and other-worldly, like this house wasn't about to be home to at least one more ghost.

***

The oversized taupe KHAITE x Oliver People's sunglasses were doing their job, keeping Noa's fairly recognizable face from being noticed as we walked side by side along the busy avenues of The Loop.

My face was half-hidden behind a pair of black and gold Bottega Veneta pilot sunglasses.

It was either the sunglasses preserving our anonymity, or the fact that the November wind was bitter, biting at any inch of exposed skin as it blew in off the lake, keeping almost everyone but tourists inside. There were still plenty of those—people spilling out across the steps in Millennium Park and taking selfies in the mirrored reflection of the bean.

Noa said she'd never seen it, only in photos. It definitely wasn't the type of place my brother would frequent; he'd never think to show anyone something as cliché, but the neighborhood itself was full of young professionals, and Winchester Holdings was only a few blocks away.

Her hands were shoved into the pockets of what I considered to be a fairly ridiculous coat—a BOSS down-filled jacket with taupe teddy panels, accompanied by black and white ones—but I knew Taylor would love it.

My coat wasn't that different—a shiny black vegan leather and sherpa down Sam coat with a white shearling hood—but there were no giant color blocks stretching across mine. It made me feel like it was more understated than it probably was.

Noa started up the steps, moving closer to the small clusters of tourists taking photos of their reflections. "Have you ever taken a photo here?"

"Do you think I've ever taken a photo at any tourist monument in the world?" I asked, nostrils flaring with a small snort.

Noa cut me a sideways glance from behind her sunglasses, her brown cheeks pink from the cold. "Not even for the family photo albums?"

"Winchesters don't have photo albums. Just oil paintings to commit our likeness to canvas." I raised my eyebrows at her.

She stopped, mouth parting and a small laugh tumbling out. "Don't tell me there's a wall somewhere in the house just lined with creepy, posed portraits of all of you?"

My lips tugged up into a smile, and I shook my head. "No, there's not. Thank God. That house is depressing enough. That's the last thing we'd need."

Noa tipped her chin up as our reflections came into focus, stretched across the surface of the bean. She was only a bit taller than me in real life, still on the shorter side for a runway model, but on the mirrored surface, her usually willowy body stretched out even farther.

I watched her tilt her head from side to side in the reflection before she turned to me, reaching forward and grabbing my hand between hers. "I don't know what to do."

Her voice was endlessly sad, each syllable of each word cracking, and all the worries she had been keeping close to her chest spilling out and into the world.

Before I could answer, Noa wiped at her cheeks underneath her sunglasses, her next words almost a quiver. "Was he like this when your mom died?"

"He was—" I started before shaking my head and tipping my chin up toward the sky. Clear blue, not a single cloud. A perfect day if you weren't standing beside an ostentatious tourist trap, if your father wasn't dying, and if your brother wasn't headed toward his own destruction. Swallowing, I looked back at Noa and tried again.

"Deacon is the way he is *because* our mom died. He was different before. The same irreverent, carefree Deacon, but the inability to address anything and the astounding ability to compartmentalize—that came after. He's never even dealt with her death. He took off, buried his head in a pound of cocaine, and went on with his life, like she was never in it."

A tear trickled from underneath the rim of Noa's sunglasses, and she somehow managed to look unfairly beautiful, standing there crying in public. Her tears looked like fucking diamonds. "I thought this was something he and I would be able to do together...I know what it's like to lose your parents, to feel like you have no one. Deacon has so many people in his corner, and it's like he can't even see it."

"My brother is my favorite person on the planet. I don't care how far he falls. I'll never leave him." I could feel the tears welling behind my eyes spill over, tracking down my cheeks. I couldn't make out my reflection in Noa's sunglasses, but I'm sure they didn't look like diamonds.

Noa pulled her hands from the pockets of her ridiculous coat, her long fingers fluttering for a moment before she reached forward and grabbed my hands in hers. "He's not the only one grieving. He always says it's you two against the world, but I feel like he's left *you* all alone in this."

My lips parted, mouth drying out as I blinked rapidly. I was at an odd crossroads in my life—I liked myself for maybe the first time ever, liked my life, and all these pieces of the puzzle sliding into place. The one for my mother would always be missing, but I'd thought for one brief moment that maybe the pieces for my father, my brother, the pieces of me, could have come together all around the hole she left. Soon, all those malignant cells in my father's body would cause his puzzle piece to crumble to dust, and I wasn't sure what was happening to my brother's, but it seemed like it would disintegrate all the same.

Noa's fingers tightened around my hands. Her nose wrinkled, and her voice was steady when she spoke, like she was coming to some sort of resolve, like she didn't care that people were taking selfies beside us, that we might end up in the background of one—our pain captured there forever. "If you could have anyone with you, anyone holding your hand through this, who would it be? And you can't say David."

A wet laugh escaped me. "How'd you know I would have picked David?"

"Because I've seen the way you look at each other. Pick—if you could have one person holding your hand through this, who would it be?" Noa's voice dropped, and a soft smile pulled at her lips.

My heart hurt, not because of all the scars and stitches stretched across it, but because its other half was out there, breaking. "My brother. I'd pick my brother."

Noa let go of my hands, not before squeezing them one last time, wiping at her cheeks. "Come on, we aren't far from the office. We can bring Deacon a coffee. He didn't stumble in until two a.m. I can't imagine David and Tripp are feeling much better. I've never seen the office, either. It'll be like we're two regular people, and you're just showing me around the city you grew up in, all the sights."

"Oh, yes, Millennium Park, the bean and the main attraction of Chicago, the Winchester Holdings' office." I tipped my head back, a real laugh spilling from me now, still not a cloud in the sky—but maybe another piece of my puzzle, a different type of family that I didn't expect, walking alongside me in a ridiculous coat and designer sunglasses.

Deacon

"Rough night?"

Ash was leaning in the doorway of my office, a look of thinly veiled displeasure etched across his features. He arched an eyebrow, crossing his arms over the jacket of his pinstriped Ralph Lauren Purple Label suit. He looked every part the acting president and CEO of a multi-billion-dollar holding, the salt and pepper hair, light green eyes that were friendly enough but could be sharp when they needed to be, down to the perfectly polished cap-toe Cole Haan oxfords on his feet.

I, on the other hand, had seen better days.

For many reasons—the fact that I'd overslept for the first time in a decade, since my fiancée didn't bother to wake me up and was nowhere to be found in the morning. The navy Canali wool suit and unbuttoned white dress shirt I wore were both in desperate need of a dry clean. No tie, and certainly no pocket square. I didn't even notice what shoes I shoved on when I was rushing out the door; all I knew was that they were loafers, because I couldn't be bothered to bend over and tie up any laces properly. And I only owned black loafers, so they most certainly did not match the rest of my suit.

Not my finest work.

I said nothing, offering him a flat look and turning back to my desktop, which was taking it's sweet fucking time powering up too. Slamming my hand down on the keyboard like that would make any difference; I was tempted to start grinding my teeth into a fine powder if it weren't for the fact that I took oral hygiene seriously.

I could still see Ash in my periphery, standing there in the doorway. Flicking my eyes up, I raised my eyebrows at him expectantly. "Do you need something?"

Technically, I was being insubordinate—even though my last name was engraved on the awning of the building, monogrammed on all the corners of the stationary. But he was acting president, and I was in his old role. I really just wanted him to fuck off. I needed our shared assistant, Nika, to bring me a coffee immediately so I could shut my door and draw the blinds and pray that the fucking pounding behind my eyes would subside.

Ash shrugged, surveying me with an annoyingly bland expression. "I don't remember the last time I've seen you at work without a tie."

Flashing him a grin that my sister told me often looked like I was baring my teeth, my words were sharp when I answered. "My dry cleaning didn't get returned on time."

He raised his eyebrows, his lips pulling down. "That's unlike any staff of yours."

"Yeah, I fired them." The lie rolled off my tongue easily.

It was something I would do, but I hadn't even remembered to send my dry cleaning out. Since one of the staff walked in on me doing coke alone the night after I put the hole in my father's crown molding, they were sticking to the standard activities in my room that primarily included turning down the bed and setting out fresh towels. No one was going through my suits to make sure they were freshly pressed.

A resigned look settled over his face, and he exhaled in a measured sigh. "You can tell me if you need some time off, Deacon. You can work from home. You can do whatever you need. You're like a son to me, and I don't say that just to say it."

"How convenient for me, seeing as I'm about to be short another parent. I'll keep that in mind. But if you don't need anything, I have some reports to review." I looked pointedly back at the blank screen of my computer.

This stupid fucking monitor still hadn't turned on.

I could see Ash shake his head before pushing off the doorway, like he finally realized what a lost cause I was. But I heard him greet someone, the deep timber of his voice saying "hello," followed by a much lighter one that, on a good day, I might tell you sounded like the first notes of the best symphony in the world.

But today, it was my worst nightmare. I'd woken up alone, late, with a pounding headache, schlepped my fucking way over here only to be hounded by reporters screaming in my ear about how I was doing, how my father was doing, whether Ash's move to president was only temporary. It was like being a carcass. Ready to be picked apart every single day while the rest of the world watched on, waiting to see what they could salvage from the carnage.

Noa smiled brightly at Ash just beyond my office, her perfect, small hands wrapped around a coffee cup, and her engagement ring sitting askew on her ring finger. She wrinkled her nose at something he said, too low for me to hear now, before coming to stand in the doorway where Ash had been moments ago.

She smiled softly at me, her eyes bright and cheeks pink, like she'd been outside. A pair of sunglasses kept her hair pushed off her face, save for the usual curls that escaped. "Hi, you. I brought you coffee. Americano. The way you like. I thought you might need one."

Taking a measured exhale, I pressed my fingers to the bridge of my nose. "What I needed, Noa, was to be at work on time."

"I thought—" she started, her small shoulders rising in a shrug that I could barely see under her teddy jacket. Any other day, I would have pushed her up against my desk and told her how cute she looked with all those different panels of color in that fuzzy jacket, her hair curling around her face. That was one of the things I fell in love with first. She *was* beautiful—one of the prettiest women on the planet, according to Vanity Fair, but she was so fucking adorable.

But she didn't get it. No one, except maybe my father—the ultimate irony—would get it.

Clenching my hand into a fist, I brought it to my mouth, my teeth digging into my knuckles and all my restraint slipping. "I don't really care what you thought when every fucking reporter out there saw me coming in over two hours later than I should be. Do you know what that looks like?"

Noa's eyes went wide, and she brought her fingers to her lips. She was about to start biting them before wringing her hands together instead. "You were up so late, and you were drunk and sad. I thought you'd be tired this morning."

"That's what cocaine is for." I raised my eyebrows at her in an attempted deflection. I needed her to smile like everything would be okay and leave this office. But she pulled her head back, and her nose wrinkled. "It's a joke."

It wasn't.

"It's not funny." She blinked rapidly, followed by a tiny sniff. "Why don't you come home with me? We can talk, maybe you could have lunch with your father—"

"What aren't you getting?" I smacked my fingers to my temple, my voice rising beyond what was appropriate for an office setting when your door was open, let alone when speaking to your fiancée, before I gestured widely around the office. "What you don't understand is that every moment I'm not on, that I look like I'm less than—that I'm falling apart—they will eat me alive. They will rip me apart, and then they'll strip this company down to *nothing* and sell it for parts. Is that what you want? If I don't have this—if I'm not this—I'm nothing. I'm *no one* without this. That ring certainly isn't on your finger, and you can say goodbye to the fucking multi-million-dollar wedding at The Pierre."

Noa shook her head, her stupid beautiful fucking upper lip trembling and those fucking eyes refracting every inch of light in this office because they were full of tears. "That's not true. You're *you.* You're the boy who loves his sister more than anything, who carries a secret picture of his mother around in his wallet. The boy who played hide and seek with me in my apartment and spent all day in bed with me, who laughs and chases me around and talks to me in different accents. Don't reduce yourself to this singularity. You're so much more than this. I need you, Deacon. Charlie needs you."

Losing all pretense, I slammed my hands down on my desk. I was so fucking sick of hearing about everyone else who needed me. "What about what I need? Who's here for me?"

"Me." Her voice quivered, and everything about her seemed small.

"Convenient you turn off my alarm, you spend all morning with my sister, and then come in here to lecture me about how much she needs me." I dropped my head into my hands, scrubbing my face. My stubble scratched against my palm. It was uneven and unkempt, longer than I ever kept it. "Just go, Noa. Please. We'll talk at home. I have a lot of work to do."

A small sob caught in her throat, and she turned on her heel, quietly closing the door to my office. The absence of a slam, what I would have deserved, echoed louder, and the silence made me wince.

I looked more like my mother than my father, but it was his reflection I could see staring back at me in the still-dark computer screen.

Charlie

Noa left Winchester Holdings crying. It wasn't the first time someone left those offices in tears, and it likely wouldn't be the last. It was also usually my father making people cry, not my brother.

David and Tripp had been in meetings, so I'd supplanted myself in Ash's office to say hi. I'd barely seen him since I came home, and I wanted to talk to him about my father's proposal, his grand ideals for a reimagined WH leadership based solely on Winchester loyalty. We'd barely gotten past the boring formality when Deacon's yelling echoed across the office. My heart broke before I even saw Noa try to walk across the marble floor without bolting for the elevator, her shoulders shaking the whole way. It broke when I heard what he was yelling. He sounded like our father.

I'd debated throwing open the door to Deacon's office, not to reprimand him or yell at him.

Even in my worst moments, he'd never done that to me. My brother had always accepted those broken parts of me, entirely unflinching. I used to think nothing could ruffle Deacon Winchester. But he was clearly very fucking ruffled. I thought about going in there, dropping to my knees and begging him not to do this, not to do what I did to everyone I loved.

But I was beginning to suspect Winchesters just came with an automatic self-destruct button that turned on whenever our nervous system sensed danger.

I followed Noa instead, because I'd been chased out of that office by a Winchester too.

I caught up with her at the elevator as she was frantically pushing the close button, a sob sneaking its way out of her throat. I didn't have the heart to tell her those were just for show.

We didn't say anything, but I held my palm open for her the way Taylor would for me, and we held hands all the way down to the lobby and all the way through the throngs of reporters still camped out there.

We stayed that way, hands joined as she silently cried beside me in the back of the town car, and all the way back to that too-big house full of too many ghosts. I'd offered to spend the afternoon with her, listed off a whole host of things we could do in the Winchester fortress, down to taking out one of Deacon's sailboats that was docked down at the boathouse and getting drunk. But Noa had smiled at me when we reached the top of the stairs between my room and Deacon's and shook her head, saying she was tired, and she wanted to be alone.

If I thought it would make a difference, I would have gone to my father's office where he was holed up, evidently not dissuaded by Rebecca's urgings that he not work at all and begged him to do something, but I wasn't sure what he would do anyway. Our father had always operated at a distance, never really interfering with our affairs until they interfered with his.

Instead, I sat on my bed, a proverbial list of pros and cons spread out in front of me. On my right, my laptop open with a paper I was still working on for Dr. Batra—all my dreams of academia—and to my left, the heavy, imposing contract for WH with that shiny new title stamped across the front.

The two things I'd ever really wanted for myself, side by side, spread out on Winchester quality, impossibly high thread count sheets—my father's love and acceptance on one hand and to be me, entirely free and unburdened in a different life somewhere, on the other.

It wasn't really that simple; there were many more nuances and threads running through each of those lives, but my brother's ship was sinking at a faster rate than even I'd ever achieved. It needed to be reduced to the most base singularity for me to make this decision.

I stared all afternoon, resorting myself to using those stupid intercoms to call down to the kitchen and ask for someone to bring me lunch.

It was certainly not one of my finer moments.

I was about to admit defeat, chasing around the last lettuce leaves from a garden salad that had been left outside my door on a ridiculous ornate silver serving tray, when the door was unceremoniously tossed open, followed by a dramatic moan and a head of messy blonde hair ducking through the doorway.

"Hi, I feel like I haven't seen you in days." Taylor's voice was practically a whine as she kicked off her Hoka's and threw herself down onto the bed in front of me, still in her scrubs, arms splayed out and knocking my laptop off the bed.

"Jesus, be careful! The last thing I need is for that to break right now." I widened my eyes at her and pushed to sit up against the pillows. "And you just saw me last night. I fell asleep listening to you drone on about resection techniques. It was the worst sleep of my life."

Taylor snorted, propping her chin up on her hands. "Oh, I'm sorry. I forgot you couldn't afford one."

Leveling her with a flat look, I glanced pointedly toward the laptop where it fell beside the bed until a strangled groan left her, and she crawled across the bed to retrieve it.

"Happy?" She threw it back toward me, where it landed with a dull thud beside the contract, the duvet puffing up around it. Her nose wrinkled, and her eyes cut to me. "Have you thought about what you're going to do?"

I puckered my lips and shook my head, tempted to bang the back of it against the velvet headboard, covered in far too many pillows to cause any significant damage. "I've been thinking all afternoon. Help me make a pros and cons list. You're great at reducing things to singularities."

"Easy." Taylor pushed up, reaching forward and grabbing the Winchester Holdings' contract. "Same city as me, tons of money, and two very impossibly hot men who are both at your beck and call."

Reaching forward, I grabbed the contract from her hands.

"Speaking of, knock next time. David could have been in here."

Taylor pursed her lips and narrowed her eyes. "I've never not been able to just walk into your room."

"Well, it's not just my room anymore, Taylor." My words were tentative, tiny little things. Scared that if they were too loud, something out there might hear and squash the hope in my chest that grew each day at this idea of a life with David Kennedy.

One eyebrow rose, and her eyes started to sparkle. "Remind me why you're not boning him?"

I leaned forward and smacked her shoulder with the contract. "Can you stop saying *bone*? I can't say I'm a fan of this new addition to your vocabulary."

She raised her eyebrows expectantly, holding out her hand like she was still waiting for my answer.

Rolling my eyes, I crossed my arms across my chest, like I could keep my heart safe from all of my terrible habits. "Because I have a habit of ignoring my problems through other people. Drowning in them, if you will."

"Is that what you think? You don't drown yourself in David Kennedy. You've drowned yourself in Tripp." Taylor's words were slow, deliberate, and she tipped her head studying me before shaking her head softly. "You couldn't drown with him, Charlie. He wouldn't let you."

My lips parted, and my heart beat irregularly in my chest—not the usual desperate bid to get to David, snagging and tearing itself bloody against my ribs, but a gentle, softer type of beat—like everything in my body liked those words. Before I could answer, a tentative knock came from the door, and I flicked my gaze to Taylor before tipping my chin toward it. "See? That's how you enter a room in modern society. Come in."

Noa slipped through the door, her clothes from earlier gone—her body now engulfed by one of Deacon's Saint Laurent sweaters, her tiny legs shoved into black leggings, and her feet covered in a giant pair of socks. Her skin was bare, and instead of looking luminous like usual, she looked exhausted. Her eyes were even devoid of their usual color.

"Are you okay?" Taylor asked, lips pulled back as Noa carefully sat down on the edge of the bed.

"I haven't had a chance to fill her in yet." I practically winced, my face scrunching up. "Deacon was in fine form today. He was late for work and seemed to think that Noa was at fault for letting him sleep in."

Something akin to a cat-like growl rose in Taylor's throat, and she pursed her lips. "He needs to get his fucking attitude in check. I'm sick of him parading around here, like he's the only one suffering."

Noa looked down at the duvet, saying nothing for a moment, drawing patterns with her hand before looking up at me, her eyes shining. Worrying at her lip with her thumb, that diamond ring still sitting askew, her eyes found the contract I still held, and her voice shook when she spoke. "I've been thinking about it all afternoon, and I just...I don't know what to do. I know you need him, Charlie. But I think he needs you more. Please?"

There were probably very few things in this world that I wouldn't do for my brother.

Deacon

I hesitated outside the door to my room. It was closed, but there was a light emanating from underneath it. That made me at least hope Noa was in there, that she hadn't taken the next flight out and went straight back to New York after this morning. I wouldn't have blamed her. I hadn't texted her all day, and she'd maintained a stony silence. I couldn't blame her for that, either. But it had been a relief, avoiding the inevitable confrontation for a bit longer.

I was a fucking coward.

Reaching up to loosen the knot on my tie, I remembered I wasn't wearing one, thanks to my fucking mad dash out of here this morning. I'd never rushed to anything in my life, because most things waited for me, and I didn't want to make a habit of it—ravenous reporters aside.

Scrubbing my jaw, I felt the stubble against my palm again, and irritation raked across my skin. No matter how disastrous things felt, one thing I took pride in was my ability to keep it together on the outside. Apparently, the looming threat of being an adult orphan was enough to crumble any facade I tried to maintain. Before I could think better of it and give in to the temptation to go down to the cellar and drown in another bottle of irreplaceable scotch, I reached forward and opened the door.

Noa sat in bed, propped up against the headboard by too many pillows, my Saint Laurent sweater barely visible above the duvet. Her hair was still damp, tied back into two braids the way it usually was after she washed it, and she barely spared me a glance, her eyes only flicking up from her phone before she looked back at it, swirling the glass of red wine she held in her other hand.

"Baby." I forced a grin, running a hand through my hair so some of it fell onto my forehead the way she liked. "You know how I feel when you're wearing my clothes. How I like to take them off."

A derisive snort came from her, and she flicked her eyes up again, giving me a flat look. "Nice try. You won't skate your way out of this one with the charming little billionaire boy act."

"It was worth a shot." I blinked, palming my jaw before crossing my room to where that bottle of seafloor scotch sat beside the armchair, only the dregs left.

I didn't think Noa would be particularly inclined to share her wine, so I'd have to settle for that. I could feel her eyes on me as I rolled my shoulders and shrugged out of the suit jacket, throwing it haphazardly onto the chair beside me. I usually hung my suits up at the end of the day, exactly where I found them, by designer and color in my closet, but not only was this suit in desperate need of a dry clean, I was tempted to throw it in the trash. It felt like I'd been wearing all my failures around all day.

Pushing the sleeves of my shirt up, I undid the third button. I'd undone the top two in the afternoon, trying to look like I was going for something more casual at work as opposed to the trainwreck of not even knowing what I'd thrown on this morning.

And then fucking Tripp had walked into the conference room—pressed black Armani suit and a white Ralph Lauren shirt unbuttoned, actually pulling the look off the way it was intended—and I gave up on trying to find anything salvageable about the day. So I spent the afternoon yelling at new traders on the investing floor, because it made me feel better for about two minutes before I remembered everyone heard me fucking lose it in front of my universally loved, supermodel fiancée as I kicked her out of the office.

I poured the last bit of the scotch into a new Waterford glass before throwing it back. I could tell it was new, because the crystal detailing was different than the one I drank from yesterday, so clearly someone on staff was trying to keep things in some semblance of order.

"How was your day?" Noa's voice was clipped, and when I finally turned around to look at her, my heart felt like it fell out of my chest. She was so fucking beautiful, even when she was looking at me like she'd like to take one of Taylor's surgical knives and eviscerate me.

I never really understood why my sister was always going on about never deserving David. It didn't make sense to me, because I thought she deserved the world and was far more than the sum of her mistakes, but looking at Noa right now, I got it. Looking at the person that I loved more than anything—that I somehow managed to fail so spectacularly—was almost comical and probably worse than having my limbs hacked off one by one.

"Not great. Turns out, when all your colleagues hear you yell at your fiancée, it sours them to you pretty quickly." I crossed the room, tossing myself down beside her, one arm behind my head to prop myself up. I rolled my neck, offered her another grin, like nothing was really wrong, but it was just another buckle to lock my deflection armor in place, and held out my hand for her glass of wine.

A tiny, indignant puff of air came from her flared nostrils, and she took a measured sip before pulling the glass out of my reach.

"You aren't going to share with me?" I baited, dropping my voice the way I knew she liked. I owed her an apology, and I would gladly spend all night making it up to her, but I didn't want to talk about it. I didn't know how. I didn't know how to tell her that there must be something so fundamentally wrong with me if my own mother willingly left me and my father didn't love me enough to try and live.

Noa tipped her chin up, but it looked like there might have been the hint of a smile pulling at the corners of her lips. Her full bottom one quivered slightly, like it only did when she was trying not to laugh. Her voice was stubborn when she spoke. "No, you were mean to me."

Leaning forward, I brushed my thumb across her cheek before holding her chin and tipping her head back down so she had to look at me. Her amber eyes were beyond their usual hue, which meant she had spent the day crying. "I'm sorry. It wasn't about you. I was frustrated."

And I was sorry. In my spiral of self-destruction, she was the only thing that really mattered, the only person I really cared about shielding from any collateral damage, and I'd failed at that.

Everyone else was stuck with me no matter what, mostly because they were stuck in my sister's orbit. Charlie would take anything I threw at her the way I would for her. Taylor was sewn into the fibers of who we both were, so she could act all high and mighty and pretend she was above it all. But she was never leaving Charlie, so she'd be stuck with me too—and David and Tripp were never going to let her go either, so it didn't really matter what I threw at them.

It mattered what I threw at Noa. I cared. I didn't want to hurt her. But I wasn't sure if I was the type of person capable of being anything else now.

Noa swallowed, and I tracked the movement of all those delicate muscles down her neck. Everything about her was perfect. She shook her head, closing her eyes briefly before finally handing me the glass of wine she was holding hostage. "I know that. But it's still not okay. You're allowed to be upset. You're allowed to grieve, Deacon. But I need you to let me in—all the way. You can scream, you can yell. We can stay in bed and fuck it all away or get so drunk we both need one of your stupid IVs. But please don't leave me all alone. Talk to me. Please."

"I don't want to talk right now," I said, each word punctuated with a stubbornness that felt like the only thing keeping those bits of my armor on, keeping her shielded from whatever the fuck lived in me now. "Can't we just play hide-and-seek and fuck in the closet?"

A snort escaped her, and she clapped her hand to her mouth, like she could shove it back in. I grinned at her as I brought the glass to my mouth and took a sip.

I might not be good at much these days, but I was still good at making her laugh. I'd wear that like a badge of honor when it all fell apart—the next time I fell apart.

"Tomorrow then. We can talk tomorrow." Noa smiled softly, bringing her lips to the corner of mine for a brief moment before carefully extracting the glass from my hand. "I'm taking this back. I've changed my mind. Go pour your own."

I wondered how many tomorrows I had left before she finally got sick of it and left me, too.

Charlie

I liked watching David do just about anything.

But I think the thing I liked watching him do most, maybe the best view in the entire world, was the view from my bed, in this room that had effectively become ours in a house that used to haunt me, where I sat propped up against too many pillows, hands around a nondescript white coffee mug that probably cost a fortune, while he got dressed for the day.

The staff had taken to leaving a tray with a steaming press outside my door and Deacon's, which I think was supposed to be some sort of comfort. I repeatedly told the head of the kitchen not to bother, but they kept showing up, and today, I was grateful because watching David Kennedy get ready for work made my heart sing.

He was conventionally handsome in the same way my brother and Tripp were, but where they both could have walked off the pages of any menswear magazine at any given time, there was something a bit more wild about David, intangible in what made him so beautiful. He looked like any boy you'd fall in love with on a summer vacation, who you'd sneak out of the family beach house to see night after night—one that would stay etched in your memory, carved into the chambers of your heart all those years later when you settled into your life.

Except he was standing in front of me, shrugging on a light blue BOSS slim-fit shirt, his calloused fingers deftly doing up the buttons, hiding the ridges of his abdomen and all that year-round tanned skin from view, one wave curling over his forehead while he smiled down at me in the early morning sunlight.

Maybe I'd get to keep my beautiful summer boy after all.

"You're very, very, hot. Has anyone ever told you that?" I raised my eyebrows, taking a small sip of my coffee and tipping my head to study him.

David jerked his chin toward his side of the bed. "Yeah? Hot enough to tear down that pillow wall?"

Glancing over at the pillows, now dented and practically flattened because David always found a way to touch me at night, whether it was his arm thrown over me, wrapping around my chest, one hand on my shoulder, or his fingers at the nape of my neck, I looked back at him, biting my bottom lip and shrugging one shoulder.

My eyes went wide when his hands moved to the button of his charcoal Emporio Armani suit pants before I realized he was only undoing them to tuck his shirt in. My teeth dug further into my lip.

David grinned, dropping into a crouch beside the bed, one of those perfect hands coming out, his fingers tugging on a strand of my hair before landing on the strap of my Ginia India Ink lace trim tank top. A shiver skittered across my skin when his fingertips brushed my collarbone. His voice was rough when he spoke.

"When you finally let me back in your bed, we won't be leaving."

"Oh?" I asked quietly, my cheeks flaming and my heart stumbling over itself.

"No, baby. And you won't be walking straight for about a week." David's breath whispered past me as he leaned in, lips hovering right above mine and those eyes fully dark.

He was right there—it was all right there, the life we could have together, the people we were now instead of the people we used to be—just a brush of my lips and the desecration of a pillow wall away.

But that stupid fucking intercom sitting on the bedside table went off, a muffled voice I could hardly discern coming from it. "Your father requested your presence for breakfast out on the terrace."

David dropped his head, a strangled groan coming from him before he looked up and grinned, one hand wrapping around the back of my neck, and his lips roughly finding my forehead. "And when that day finally comes, we will be far, far away from fucking Winchester intercoms."

Narrowing my eyes at him, I brought my coffee to my lips more for something to do, because my heart was beating far too erratically to be healthy and pointed at him. "No more taking my brother out until way too late so he sleeps in and blames his sweet fiancée for his own shortcomings."

He held his hands up, walking backward with that stupid grin that made me feel like I was the only person in the world. He winked at me, grabbing his suit jacket off the lounge at the end of the bed and shrugged it on before turning towards the door.

I might even like watching him walk away now, because I was certain he would always, always come back.

———

The breakfast table on my father's terrace looked exactly the same as it had yesterday. So did he, but today, it was a crisp white Eton button-down rolled up to avoid catching on that same IV pole that had become his steady companion.

And instead of the Tribune or the Wall Street Journal, it looked like the most recent copy of Chicago Business Weekly was in between his glass of juice and steaming mug of coffee. There was a photo from the press conference on the cover, alongside our estimated net worth with yet another pithy title: Orphans or Heirs?

My footsteps were muffled by the UGG Tasmins I'd shoved my feet into. Pulling out the chair beside my father, I settled into it and tugged the sleeves of my Oxford sweater down over my fingertips. It would be too cold for us to keep sitting out here soon. "Morning. To what do I owe the pleasure of a repeated Steven Winchester breakfast invitation?"

His eyes flicked up to me, hand pausing just as it wrapped around his coffee mug. "Can't I have breakfast with my daughter?"

I tossed him a flat look, tipping up my mug and pouring a cup from the still-steaming press sitting there. He might be having some sort of resurgence of his conscience now that he was officially a dying man, but I knew my father, and he didn't do anything without a motive.

He shook his head, the ghost of a smile beckoning at his lips before he schooled his features. "I heard your brother put on quite the performance yesterday."

"Ah. There it is." I offered him a tight smile. "He did indeed."

He arched an eyebrow at me over his mug, ignoring the ongoing beeping from his IV, waiting for me to continue.

I usually wasn't in the business of ratting my brother out to our father, but he wasn't usually in the business of caring, so I shrugged, inhaling before taking a sip. Steam rose off the coffee, visible against the chilled fall air. "He went out the night before with David and Tripp. He came home late, and Noa made the perhaps misguided decision to turn off his alarm and let him sleep. She thought he needed it."

His nostrils flared, and his lips pulled into a tight line with a tiny shake of his head. I waited for him to offer some vague reprimand about his only son's lack of coping skills, immaturity, or irresponsibility, but he said something else entirely. "He should consider himself lucky that there's someone who cares enough about his sleep to turn off his alarm."

I pulled my head back.

Before I could say anything, he took a measured sip, swallowing slowly. "Your mother used to try to show me similar kindnesses. I didn't see them as such until it was too late."

"Oh," I whispered, hands tensing against the porcelain. I kept it suspended there, more for something to do as I watched my father. My eyes traced his silhouette against the backdrop of the sloping lawn, the boathouse in the distance, and the lake, fall mist hanging above it again. I blinked, hoping that maybe it would be burned into my retinas forever. There would only be so many more mornings like this.

Raising his eyebrows, he straightened the copy of Chicago Business Weekly just on the other side of his place setting. "I worry about you leaving him after I'm gone."

I smiled softly, exhaling before leaning back in my chair. "Me too."

My father surveyed me, his features entirely impassive. "What do you want?"

"To be happy." The words tumbled from my lips, and the corners of my eyes started to blur his silhouette—that outline I wanted to memorize forever before time slipped through my fingers yet again. But that's all it really was at the end of the day. It wasn't one life on one hand, all my choices reduced to singularities.

"Were you happy in London?"

Chewing on the inside of my cheeks, I tapped my thumb against the coffee mug and watched the steam rise off it before looking back to my father. "I liked myself, maybe for the first time ever. I liked school. I liked research. But happy?"

I tipped my head, considering his words before taking another sip. "Can you be happy if part of your heart lives elsewhere?"

More than one part of my heart, if I was being honest. It wasn't just David who took up all the space in there. My brother lived there, so did Taylor. So did Tripp.

My father clasped his hands in front of him, maneuvering deftly around the clunky IV line, like it had always been a part of him. Steven Winchester was nothing if not resilient. "I don't think you deserve to punish yourself forever. To deprive yourself of the kind of love you two have."

"I don't want to hurt him." My voice cracked, and all that worry poured out of me.

Tripp had hurt me, let me down impossibly, more than once. But it had never really been a true choice between the two, never really a tug of war. I'd always loved David, and I'd never stopped, even when I loved Tripp too.

Wiping at my eyes, I choked out a laugh. "Besides, Rebecca told me to do her a favor and not get involved with anyone in leadership for a few months."

"Well, you're welcome to fire Rebecca after I'm gone," he offered, his words matter-of-fact as he picked up the magazine and folded it open in front of him.

A smile split across my face, the tears cool on my cheeks. "Was that a joke, Dad?"

Without looking at me, Steven Winchester shrugged, but it looked like a smile might have flitted across his face, too. "I suppose it was."

I leaned back farther in the chair, hands warming against my coffee, watching the mist on the lake rise and change while my father read an article about his own business. The uncomfortable silence that used to fall between us was long gone, and I liked the way it settled over us now. It was one of the many things I wished would never end.

I wasn't sure how long we sat there. I left my phone in my room, but my head was tipped back, face being warmed by the sun, my legs stretched out, and my feet propped up on one of the spare chairs when I heard the door creak open.

"Morning, Papa W. I wanted to check on your IV before I head in for the day. I won't be back tonight—I have another surgery, but the home care nurse will be here." Taylor's voice carried, and my eyes opened, watching her cross the tiled terrace toward us.

Her hair was tied back in a messy fishtail braid, black scrubs already on, and her eyes glued to her phone until they finally flicked up and landed on me. "What are you doing out here? I thought—are those my Gucci sneakers? I've been looking for them everywhere."

"It doesn't look like you need them today." I looked pointedly toward her Hoka's and kicked my feet out. We both knew she had more shoes than almost anyone, save for my brother, and she certainly hadn't been missing these.

She narrowed her eyes at me, a look of feigned annoyance passing over her features. She dropped one hand to my shoulder and squeezed gently before unwinding her stethoscope from around her neck to start whatever daily examinations she did on my father.

"What are you doing today?" She murmured, tucking the end of the stethoscope under the collar of my father's shirt.

His eyes cut to her for a moment before going back to the article. They were a well-oiled machine.

The tears had dried on my cheeks, but I felt my eyes start to well again. My best friend in the entire world, doing the absolute most to give my father every millisecond of time she could, and my father, who sat there, unyielding as always, and hardly looking sick.

But all I could see when I looked at him were all those lost years between us—mine, and his. I wondered if my brother would look at all like him as he started to age. But Steven Winchester wouldn't be around to see what either of his children would become.

It was sad how much time we wasted.

I blinked, turning to Taylor, whose eyes were still on me expectantly as she moved her fingers around my father's neck and under his jaw. "Can you drop me off at the office on your way to work?"

Charlie

I dropped the signed contract off before I had a chance to change my mind. It wasn't that there was a danger of that necessarily, but if I thought too long about what I was giving up, thought too long about what waited for me in another try at a life at WH, which included yet another dead parent and a brother who couldn't really tell up from down at the moment, I worried that my propensity for running from my problems would kick into full swing.

During the drive into the city in that dumb Jaguar, Taylor whipping through the streets at a speed that bordered alarming for someone who had probably seen several car crash victims in her lifetime, I thumbed through the contract one more time with significantly less of an eagle eye than my father would have expected. She told me to think about it not so much as giving something up, but exchanging one life for the other.

Pros and cons to both, but there were so many more things my heart was gaining back in this one.

The elevator doors slid open, announcing my arrival on the executives' floor in a significantly more anticlimactic way than if my father was stepping his Oxford's onto that marble flooring. Maybe they possessed some sort of otherworldly signal that moved through the floor to let all his staff know he had arrived.

No one even looked up when the heels of my Stuart Weitzman boots touched the ground. To be fair, most doors were closed, because most people who worked up here were incredibly busy and actually earned their money.

I raised a hand to Damien, still my father's assistant but currently on loan to Ash, and a bright smile stretched across his face before he rolled his eyes and pointed to the headset firmly clamped over his ears.

The echo from the heels of my boots against the floor was drowned out by the constant background noise. I used to keep my door firmly closed during working hours, Deacon's laughter and out-of-place noises of toxic masculinity when something went his way annoying me to no end. But when I'd been alone in my office at Columbia or Oxford, I found the silence too heavy. I missed it.

The sounds of a shark tank, chaos, and too many people who thought they were far too important.

My brother's door was firmly closed, but I could see a shadow moving from underneath the heavy mahogany door. But the door to the office beside his was open.

Stopping in the doorway, I leaned my head against the thick frame. "Hey, Mr. Kennedy."

David looked up from his computer screen, where he'd been staring intently, and he rolled his shoulders back, grinning widely at me. "Baby. To what do I owe the pleasure? Here to make sure Deacon's alive? Don't worry. I checked for a pulse when I arrived. He was already in his office when I got here."

"I'm not here for him." I wrinkled my nose, offering him a small smile. That wasn't entirely true. My brother had been a primary motivator in the decision I'd made today. But so was the man sitting in front of me, all broad shoulders, tousled blond hair, and honey eyes that weren't all that sweet. "I wanted you to be the first to know, aside from Taylor,

I guess, seeing as she drove me here in her death trap of a Batmobile knockoff—I said yes. You're looking at Winchester Holdings' inaugural Vice President of Sustainable Investing."

David's eyes darkened for a moment. "This is what you want? You chose this, right? Steven didn't strongarm you into saying yes?"

"He was surprisingly silent on the matter." I raised my eyebrows. "Mr. Kennedy, I have to say I expected your levels of elation to be significantly higher."

"I just want you to be happy." David's voice was low, his eyes tracing my face, like he was looking for any sort of hesitation, and when he didn't find any, he started to grin again. "And if this is what makes you happy, then I'm the luckiest man on the fucking planet to get to sit across a conference room table from you again."

The phone in front of him started vibrating across the table, and I tipped my chin toward it. "I know you're very busy taking care of my big, important company. I was actually going to see if Tripp had time to grab a coffee. But I'll see you at home?"

David nodded, eyes narrowing at his phone screen before he looked back at me, another real, just-for-me grin stretching across his face. "I have to take this. But let me take you out to dinner to celebrate. I'll duck out early. Eight?"

Smiling, I nodded, raising one hand as he picked up the phone, winking at me before answering, his voice easygoing when he leaned back in his chair. "Hey, man, yeah, good to hear from you. We were getting a bit worried there was some hesitation on your end."

I stayed there for just a moment longer, leaning my head against the doorframe, and my nose scrunched up when David started tossing a pen in his left hand and catching it. I'd seen him do that countless times, but it was like a mirrored version of the first time I saw him again back in

New York, through that glass wall surrounding a conference room when we were worlds apart.

This wasn't a world I would have imagined for myself, not just the fact that I was returning to WH and the circumstances surrounding it, but a world where I hoped that maybe all these parts of my past and present could coexist.

Pushing off the door frame with one last look at David, I turned on my heel and realized Tripp's old office was otherwise occupied, which meant he would have been in one of the only empty ones toward the end of the hall, where my old one used to be.

We'd be side by side.

The door was open just a crack, and I wondered if he was even in yet—my father had mentioned that he was flying back and forth most days—when I pushed it open slightly and peeked around the corner.

He was there, behind the standard-issue WH desk, eyes frozen over as they skated across his computer screen. With more stubble than he usually walked around with, but this was like looking back in time, too.

But looking at him now wasn't painful, not like it used to be.

"Hey," I whispered, my fingers still gripping the door as I leaned around it.

Tripp's eyes cut to me before he leaned back in his chair, one eyebrow arching. "Chuckles. What brings you in?"

"Do you have time for a coffee?"

That annoying smile he seemed to save just for me slid into place alongside the lilt in his voice. "Are you asking me on a coffee date, Chuck?"

Rolling my eyes, I pursed my lips. "If you call two people who are just friends getting coffee a date, then sure, a coffee date."

Tripp appraised me for a second longer, his impassive features giving my father's a run for their money, before he finally answered. "I'll always have time for you. Just give me a minute to finish this up."

Wind nipped at my exposed cheeks, and out of habit, I tugged my leather jacket tighter around me. Strands of my hair whipped around my face, and I batted them away before pulling my nondescript black beanie down farther over my ears.

The heels of my boots reverberated against the worn stones of the Riverwalk, echoing alongside the heels of Tripp's polished Tom Ford Oxfords.

The Riverwalk was usually teeming with tourists, and the spillover from the business district, taking in one of the many coffee shops, restaurants, or bars. It was quiet today, the wind whipping across the lake entirely unforgiving, even for a Chicago fall.

I studied Tripp from the corner of my eye.

He almost looked the same as he did when I left on that tarmac—tried to leave my life behind—before it clawed me back.

Almost the same but endlessly different. The same sharp angles and planes to his face, down to the stubble dusting his jaw that somehow seemed harsher, firmer, like he spent so much time clenching it or grinding his teeth. Same ice-cold eyes—entirely frozen over with hair a bit longer than usual, artfully tousled and pushed off his face. There were more lines of age around his eyes—but only a few. I knew Tripp had a carefully curated nighttime routine, and he would have added a retinol into the rotation the second he caught the hint of a wrinkle.

He strolled alongside me, seemingly not a single care in the world, hands lazily shoved into the pockets of the Elk single-breasted Theory wool coat, with a slate gray cashmere Brunello Cucinelli scarf draped over his shoulders.

"See something you like, Chuck?" He glanced sideways, one brow rising ever so slightly.

"Nice scarf." I shrugged, a smile tugging at the corner of my mouth.

Tripp looked down, plucking at the scarf and rubbing the material back and forth between his fingertips. "It's Brunello Cucinelli. My mom bought this for me."

"Sorry to Mrs. Banks, but it makes you look like—"

He shot me a look, dropping the scarf. "Don't say Patrick Bateman."

Holding up my palms, I puckered my lips. "If the shoe fits."

"Like your brother or Kennedy wouldn't put a cashmere scarf on if it was cold," Tripp said, voice dry.

A laugh, more like a bark, escaped me. "Deacon, yes. Absolutely. He probably has that same scarf in every color. But David wouldn't be caught dead in a scarf."

A grin pulled at Tripp's lips, and that made my smile wider, and my heart sing too. Because it felt sort of like it used to—like we might really be friends. "You're probably right. Too neat and tidy for the somehow rough around the edges golden retriever with a penchant for secret cigarettes."

My smile grew and stretched at that. "That might be the best descriptor for David I've ever heard."

"Kennedy mad you're taking a little lunchtime stroll with me?" Tripp's eyes cut back to me, and I could see him swallow, the column of his throat moving, like he was worried, nervous even, waiting for my answer.

"No," I answered plainly. I hadn't asked. I didn't need, nor did I want David's permission to do anything. But he hadn't seemed phased when I'd said it and told him I'd see him later.

I think this version of us—of me really—might be my favorite. The one where I didn't fear the truth, all the secrets of who I was spilling out unfettered—all those messy parts of me I tried to stitch together, to hide.

"Well, like I said, he was always the better man. Turns out he's the bigger man, too." Tripp tipped his chin toward a coffee cart set up at the end of the Riverwalk. "I'm sure it helps that he's in your bed every night, and I'm on a crowded commuter flight back to Boston."

I cut him a look before rolling my eyes. "*Friends,* Tripp. And don't pretend you're slumming it in coach. We both know you sit in business."

Tripp rolled his neck, grinning at me. "Business or bust, Chuck."

"That's a terrible fucking motto." I shook my head, but I was still smiling at him, that tiny seed of affection, the one that would always be there as far as he was concerned, ever-blooming in my heart, my lungs, my whole body.

"Spare me the self-righteous bullshit. I'm not the one on the cover of Chicago Business Weekly with a big old number stamped next to my photo." Tripp stopped in front of the coffee cart, turned, and looked pointedly at me.

It was funny—the subtle differences between him and David. They were polar opposites in huge ways, living on entirely different planes, light and honey and home—a golden retriever with a penchant for secret cigarettes and the villain who wouldn't bat an eye at any of your misdeeds but would never touch a cigarette because of the possibility of skin damage.

But it was the small things, the quiet things, that really separated them.

Tripp didn't know how I liked my coffee. David did.

I blinked up at him, and he raised his eyebrows expectantly. They were unfair comparisons—maybe in another life, he would know that on a regular day, I liked my coffee black, and on a bad day, it was a latte with nonfat milk and one pump of vanilla syrup.

Maybe in another life, my mother never died, my family stayed whole, and Tripp never got tangled up in the worst parts of me, all those things I did when I was just a little lost girl.

But that wasn't this life.

"Uh, sorry. Medium black, please." I looked away from Tripp, smiling politely at the barista who was so bundled up, down to gloves covering her long fingers, and only a fleck of pinked brown cheeks visible between her scarf and hat. She nodded, eyeing my leather jacket with an abject horror.

I smiled. It was warmer than it looked.

My eyes cut back to Tripp, watching as he ordered a bone-dry cappuccino, which felt so pretentious—so him—that my cheeks started to hurt from poorly restrained laughter.

I was still smiling, everything entirely warm, barely able to feel the wind at my cheeks, blowing the strands of my hair everywhere. When he handed me the cardboard cup, steam rose from the lid.

"Black coffee?" Tripp shoved his free hand back into the pocket of his coat, tipping his elbow up to the tables scattered around the river's edge. "How terribly boring of you, Chuck."

"Not boring." I wrapped my hands around the cup, offering him a tiny smile and a shake of my head.

Maybe it was boring in the grand scheme of things. But he was my friend, I think, after all this time. I wasn't running, I wasn't lost. I certainly wasn't whole—especially given the circumstances surrounding my life in general, but maybe I was found.

A boring order in the grand scheme of things—but a good day nonetheless.

Tripp loped down the stone staircase toward the table, looking like he just strolled off the pages of GQ with his stupid scarf and wool coat over his suit, bringing his equally stupid bone-dry cappuccino to his lips. A breeze even picked up off the river, lifting the wisps of his hair across his forehead.

I trailed behind him, that same breeze knotting the straight strands of my hair. But mine kept whipping across my face, sticking to my lips and looking far less dignified than Tripp. Puffing my cheeks, I exhaled forcefully as the metal legs of the chairs scraped across the stone when Tripp pulled them out.

He waited for me to sit, one hand grasping the wrought iron back of the chair, eyebrows raised, like I was taking too long.

"Thank you," I offered, pointedly settling into the chair. The metal was cold against the back of my legs, biting at my skin through the thin wool of my tights.

Leaning back, I watched Tripp toss himself down into the tiny metal chair with that lazy air he always had when he was doing anything, and he threw his arm over the back of it.

Those frozen eyes, endless expanses of ice, surveyed me as I took a small sip of my coffee.

"Thank you for the coffee." I pressed my lips to the lid.

Tripp grinned widely. "You're welcome. You should probably be the one paying for mine, but I'm willing to let it slide."

"How chivalrous."

He angled his head. "So, Deacon's a fucking disaster. Who would have predicted he'd be the one to throw it all away?"

A small snort escaped my nose, and I shook my head. "Any psychiatry textbook could have riddled this one out. But seeing as I doubt Deacon has ever opened one of those, I don't think he saw it coming."

Tripp chewed on his lower lip, eyes skating across the river. The boats still bobbed along where they were tied off, people walked hand in hand with coffee cups between their gloves, or sat outside the pubs and wine bars with chilled glasses, with jackets not unlike his lifting in the breeze. He glanced back at me. "I always hate when they dye the river green for St. Patrick's Day."

"You're right, it's kind of ugly." I nodded, tilting my head and studying him against the gray, fall day. "But that's a few months away. Do you think you'll even be here then?"

Tripp gazed at me impassively, swirling the coffee cup in his hand, like it was scotch, before narrowing his eyes down at it. "I hope so. Maybe full time. We'll see."

"Even with the looming, ugly green river?" I asked, teasing.

I didn't want him to leave. I didn't know what anything was going to look like in a few months, if my father would still be breathing, but I didn't want him to go home to Boston, to whatever he had been running from, whatever ghosts were there.

He belonged here, at least to me.

"Even with the looming green river." Tripp drained the rest of his drink, setting the empty cup down on the table. "And what about you? Will you still be here?"

"That," I started, thumb picking absentmindedly at the cardboard sleeve of my cup, "was not an easy question to answer, but yes. My dad wanted me to stay...to come back. You saw the contract at the hospital. A whole new position, just for me. Not even at the lowly director level."

I tipped my chin up at him.

Tripp's brows furrowed, lips pulling down.

"You don't remember?" I leaned forward, planting my palms on the table, the metal cold against my skin. "Three years ago. The Supper Club.

Dinner with David, Deacon, and me. You made a comment about how I was only a director."

Tripp pulled back, lips still turned down before palming his jaw. "Wow, what a fucking asshole I was."

"You really were." I offered him a small, fond smile. It didn't hurt to think back on who he was, who he used to be.

Tripp shifted in his seat, hand still rubbing at his jaw. He looked uncomfortable, frozen eyes bordering on sorrowful. I didn't want him to think that I regretted anything with him. I didn't. Not anymore.

Clearing my throat, I leaned back and wrapped my hands around my barely warm coffee. "But yes, I was finally offered a coveted VP position—an entirely new department and financial structure. Sustainable investing comes to Winchester Holdings. Who would have thought?"

"Me." Tripp's voice was quiet, and his gaze flicked up to me. "I would have thought. And I'm pretty certain Kennedy would have bet on you, too."

My lips parted, and I debated saying a few different things—laughing him off, refuting it. But he was right. They had both believed in me in their own ways.

Tripp cleared his throat, his hand finding his empty cup, thumb tapping against the plastic lid before he looked up at me. "What made you say yes? You've spent so much time trying to get away from this place."

I exhaled, chewing the inside of my cheek. It wasn't a simple question, and there wasn't a simple answer. "Noa practically begged me to stay. Not for the company, not for Dad, but for Deacon."

"And that tipped the scales for you?" Tripp's question was measured.

"For my brother, you'll find there are very few things I wouldn't do," I answered softly. "I'm glad you're back, Tripp. It wouldn't feel like home without you."

Tripp stared back at me—just a tiny crack in the ice—before he grinned. "Don't let anyone hear you say that. The last thing you need is someone sending an anonymous tip to the press, and the next thing you know, all of Chicago thinks we're colluding to take over the business together."

A smile split across my face. "We can't have that. Should we head back?"

He lazily extracted a hand from his pocket, eyes flicking to his wrist and the Rolex that sat there. "I have a few more minutes on my lunch, courtesy of the Winchester Holdings' payroll."

"Oh fuck off." I rolled my eyes, a laugh spilling from my lips. I pushed to stand, pointing in the general direction of the office. "Back to work."

"Alright, Chuckles. Back to work." Tripp was still grinning when he stood, shoving both hands back into the pockets of his coat, voice low and dry.

It was nice—to be his friend.

David

My idea of celebrating with Charlie hadn't originally included her brother and Noa. It also hadn't included Taylor and Tripp, but I invited them anyway because I thought it would make her happy, that it might be fun to have her favorite people there to celebrate her.

Taylor was stuck in surgery but sent me a lengthy text message about how she was going to rip Deacon's balls off if he misbehaved, and Tripp was as mysterious as always, saying he absolutely had to be on his commuter flight back to Boston because he'd been gone for two days.

It definitely didn't include the version of Deacon that sat across from me at Barclays, half-drunk when we got here, and no better now that the first bottle of champagne had arrived at the table.

It was one of those days-gone-by, prohibition-era restaurants that littered Chicago that Charlie tended to hate, but it was dimly lit, and the staff were in Steven's pocket. She picked it for that reason. None of the staff would so much as let someone with a camera inside, and it wasn't the type of place where you'd put your phone on the table.

Deacon didn't seem to have any such reservations, slouching down in the padded, walnut leather chair, tossing both his personal and company phones onto the table and kicking back, like he was at home in a fucking recliner.

Charlie's lip curled up, and she glanced over at me, rolling her eyes before taking a measured sip of champagne. Even with the low lighting, her eyes were striking. All of her was. She was only wearing a simple, black Helmut Lang cut-out dress that went down to her mid-calves. The only reason I knew that it was anything other than just a black dress that made every inch of her look otherworldly was because she had Taylor on speakerphone when I got back to the house as she rifled through her closet. Taylor had tried to convince her to wear some sort of shiny heels with a giant gemstone stuck to the front that I'd hoped was fake, before they compromised on something called Aquazzura 105s in an iridescent leather.

The toe of her heel kept brushing my knee, where she was aggressively jiggling her leg underneath the table, watching Deacon with poorly veiled displeasure. This probably wasn't the version of her brother she wanted to have dinner with, either.

Even Noa didn't look particularly keen on him, unable to keep herself from glancing sideways every ten seconds. Her lips pulled down, and her eyes looked like she might burst into tears at any moment.

I was about to ask Charlie a stupid fucking question about what she was most looking forward to about her new portfolio, maybe even going as far as making a stupid toast, when someone in a neatly pressed black suit, who I assumed was the manager, stopped at the table. He inclined his head, his coiffed hair unmoving and pushed off his face. "Miss Winchester, Mr. Winchester. I didn't realize you'd be joining us tonight."

Charlie's foot stopped moving immediately, and she leaned forward on the table, placing her palms there, tipping her chin up at the manager with a bright smile. On Deac, it would have been a performance meant to earn him more good faith for any future endeavors.

But Charlie was unfailingly polite and friendly. She loved talking to people. "Please, Sal. Mr. Winchester is our father. You can just call us Charlie and Deacon."

"Not for long," Deacon muttered, barely audible under his breath.

Noa's eyes went wide for a moment before a smile slid into place, and she hastily grabbed her champagne flute.

Charlie's eyes cut to her brother for a moment before she looked back up at him like nothing had happened.

To his credit, Sal offered her a good-natured smile, rocking back and forth on his heels before dropping his voice. "How's your father? I was so sorry to hear the news."

"He's well. Thank you, Sal." Charlie smiled politely at him, her chin propped in her palm now, even though her etiquette instructor would have considered it highly inappropriate to have her elbow on the table. But she looked the picture of casual.

Deacon snorted, emptying the crystal champagne flute in one gulp. "He's shit."

"Deacon," Noa hissed, grabbing the sleeve of his light blue suit jacket that looked like it should have been run over a few times with an iron. Her engagement ring illuminated by the low-hanging chandelier above our table, sending out a million little rays of blinding light.

I wished it would fucking blind me so I didn't have to watch the trainwreck that was Deacon Winchester.

Sal continued smiling, like Deacon hadn't just thrown propriety out the window, before turning to focus solely on Charlie, the only Winchester really worth talking to at the table. "Your father was particularly fond of the champagne cake, if I recall. I'd love to send some home with you."

"Oh, that would be wonderful. Thank you so much." The corners of Charlie's eyes crinkled, and her voice cracked. She watched, unblinking as Sal nodded, turned on his heel, and walked to greet another table.

I knew things like that bothered her—these human moments of Steven Winchester. The fact that he liked a particular type of cake, kept her mother's artwork, apparently couldn't start his day without a glass of juice. She'd told me once she had difficulty understanding how he could have been one way with her practically her entire life, and gave away all those small moments of humanity to virtual strangers.

Rolling my shoulders back, I dropped one hand to her thigh and brushed my thumb along the top of her dress. Most days, I couldn't believe I was lucky enough to even look at her again, let alone that she'd be back in my life every day.

She turned, a tiny smile on her lips, before she plucked her champagne flute from the table and arched an eyebrow at her brother. "Jesus, why don't you try laying off the scotch when you get home from work?"

"David drinks after work." Deacon shrugged, still leaning so far back in his chair I was worried it would tip over.

My hand tightened around Charlie's thigh. He was my best friend in the entire world, but I spent most days wanting to put him through one of those paned windows at the back of their house. Seeing as I didn't have a paned window, and unlike her brother, I didn't make a habit of fucking ruining everything for her, I smiled tightly at him. "Not quite the same, man."

Deacon waved his hand around in the air before leaning forward, grabbing the champagne bottle from the perspiring silver bucket on the center of the table, and topping up his own glass. He didn't bother offering any to anyone else before he dropped it back in, splashing water from the melting ice across the table.

If I wasn't so angry at him for the new heights of selfishness he seemed to reach every day, I would have been at peak levels of concern. Deacon Winchester did not pour his own drinks.

Noa's lips parted for a moment before she chewed on the inside of her cheek, staring at him like she could hardly recognize him. She blinked rapidly before turning to Charlie and offering her a weak smile. "So, tell me about the new role. How's it different from your old portfolio?"

Charlie smiled, one of her hands dropping on top of mine where it still rested on her thigh, and I felt her squeezing my fingers. It was something I noticed she did with Taylor a lot when she needed reassurance. Flipping my palm up, her fingers skated across the sensitive skin on the inside of my hand before lacing through my own.

Her lips had hardly moved when Deacon cut in. "I can't believe he fucking manipulated you into coming back. You *hated* working at WH."

"I didn't hate it," Charlie answered stubbornly, her shoulders shifting as she sat up straighter and stared at her brother.

Deacon's lip curled back, and he paused the champagne flute before taking a sip, scoffing loudly. "Yes, you fucking did. You've spent the last three years saying the company—and Dad—were personally responsible for your downfall. And somehow, he convinced you to come back to the scene of the crime? Come on, you know better than to let yourself be manipulated by Steven Winchester."

"Deacon," I cut in, voice thick with warning. There were no paned windows, but this table would have to fucking do.

He tossed me a look, disdain etched on his features, and looked back to Charlie, his eyebrows rising expectantly.

Charlie continued to stare at him, unflinching, only angling her head to the side, her slicked-back low ponytail dropping over her exposed shoulder. "He didn't manipulate me, Deacon. Give me some fucking credit. The choice was my own."

Deacon shook his head, rolling his eyes in a display that could have rivaled Charlie's. "Bullshit. Steven deals in manipulation daily. It's probably what he fucking eats for breakfast. So, it's either that—he got one over on you after all these years where you claimed you could see right through him—or, you finally curtsied at his feet and decided to play good little heiress because he's dying."

"Incorrect on both fronts." Charlie tipped her chin up, everything about her resolute. I was closer to losing my mind than she was. She looked like she could have been discussing the fucking potholes across the streets of Chicago.

He leaned forward, his lips pulling back and all his perfectly white teeth on display. "How fucking pathetic. Just admit it, Charlie. You wanted Daddy's approval—"

"Stop." Noa's voice cut through Deacon's, thankfully stopping him in his tracks before I reached across the table and snapped his neck. Her nostrils were flared, and all the muscles in her jaw were tight. Both her hands were pressed into the table, knuckles turning white against her brown skin. "It was me. I asked her to take the job and come back."

Deacon

I blinked. I lost count of how many times. It was fucking undignified.

My hands tightened around the stem of the champagne flute, and my voice dropped. "You what? Say that again."

Noa straightened her shoulders, chin tipping in the air while her hands pressed into the tablecloth. "You heard me the first time, Deacon. I won't repeat myself just because you're angry and want to make some sort of show of throwing your weight around."

She didn't blink, but her eyes were catching in the light from the chandelier more than usual, all that amber hidden under pools of unshed tears. It was unfair really, that she was about ten times more beautiful when she cried. It had ended more than one argument in our relationship prematurely.

But I'd spent the entire day furious. I doubted there was any stopping me now. I saw the email with Charlie's signed contract come through my inbox earlier this morning, copied on it by Helen when she forwarded it to Ash.

She signed it off with her congratulations, saying how excited she was to have Charlie back at the company. I wasn't sure what she was fucking congratulating me about—the great achievement of having two dead parents before I turned thirty-two? That our father was such a master fucking manipulator with no regard for the actual wants and needs of his children, he somehow managed to drag his only daughter back to the place she hated more than anything? That he spent his last weeks on this earth pulling strings?

I'd thrown my phone and smashed it again, having to send Nika out to get me another new one at lunch.

I'd spent all day hating him, more than I did on an average day now, for willingly choosing not to even try and live for us, for letting this be it, what our lives would be reduced to. All we were as a family was a series of fucking mistakes and pain everyone tried to hide, and all Charlie and I were was the great culmination of his prioritization of his business and empire. He didn't give a shit that he was leaving us without a parent. He only cared that his legacy was intact.

But it wasn't just our father that was a colossal failure.

Apparently, I was too.

I'd failed my sister and everyone around me so spectacularly that the person who was supposed to have my back throughout anything—to quite literally love me through sickness and health—thought I was so incapable of functioning that she did this behind my back. Without even asking me what I wanted, with no regard for what my sister might want. I wasn't even allowed to be fucking angry and grieve without someone passing judgment on the way I did it.

"You think I need a babysitter?" I leaned forward, voice incredulous and my lips pulling back at Noa. "This is the type of thing we should talk about."

"But you don't want to talk, Deacon!" Noa's voice was shrill, and she looked like she might clap her hand over her mouth in embarrassment before she wrung her hands together. Heads turned around the restaurant, but I couldn't be bothered, and apparently neither could she, because her next words were punctuated with something that verged on a sob. "You have been a *shell* of a person since I got here. You won't let me in, you aren't interested in listening to anyone, you treat everyone hor-ribly. The way you speak to your father and your sister. And apparently all you do now is drink scotch."

"And apparently, all *you* do is go behind my fucking back, Noa!" Losing all pretense and the last little semblance of control I had, forget-ting who I was and all the eyes on us, I smacked my hands to the table.

I also forgot I was holding a delicate crystal champagne flute. When I smashed my hands down, it shattered underneath my palm. Blood soaked through the ivory tablecloth surrounding my hand, and when I pulled it back, there was a sizable chunk of glass sticking out of my skin. Tiny shards were visible across the rest of my palm, glinting in the low light from the chandelier, and rivulets of blood bubbling out and barely contained by the glass trying to hold it in. A scoff left my throat.

I think I felt like my hand looked.

"Jesus, Deacon!" Charlie's voice rose, and she reached forward with-out a care in the world, dunking her napkin into the perspiring cham-pagne bucket to get it wet.

Noa lurched forward, her tiny hands reaching out for mine, but I wasn't sure there was much difference between this version of me and the one who first lost a parent at twenty-two, so I jerked it out of her grasp in a childlike display of I don't know what. Droplets of blood flew from my hand, peppering the tablecloth and the front of my suit jacket.

"Why don't you run off to Taylor and tell her I need medical atten-tion? You're good at that. Interfering when you aren't fucking needed." I bit out, all that anger I had for myself leaching into my voice and directed at the person I loved more than anything.

Her eyes went wide, and she jerked her head back, actually clapping her hands to her mouth this time, but I heard the sob before she pushed off the table and ran from the fucking restaurant.

My sister barely bothered to toss me a look of disgust before she threw the wet napkin across the table and ran after Noa. It hit my chest and left a watermark on my jacket. I usually would have cared; this suit was dry clean only. But the whole thing was fucking ruined anyway.

"What the fuck is wrong with you?"

My eyes cut to David. He didn't even look mad. He looked exhausted. Palming his jaw before he scrubbed his face, something that sounded like a groan came from him. His eyes came back to mine.

I held up my hand, blood pouring from it and a chunk of glass that probably cost hundreds of dollars sticking out of my palm. "At the moment, I think I'm in need of a few stitches."

"I'll leave you with the bill. God knows you can fucking afford it." David shook his head, pushing to stand as staff from the restaurant finally converged on me with ice for my hand and a broom for the shards of glass at my feet.

I thought he was going to walk right by me, but he stopped, one hand shoved in the pocket of his suit pants, the other dropping to my shoulder in what was probably supposed to be a comforting gesture, but it just made me feel more alone. "Keep it up, and all that money will be the only thing you have left."

———

"Care to explain?" My father's voice was even, but anyone who knew Steven Winchester knew that was when he was at his most dangerous.

He tossed a special Saturday issue of Society News onto the table in front of me, his IV clip flashing in my periphery as he pushed it alongside him. I didn't know what was in any of the various bags that hung from it at any given time, and I didn't really want to know. It wasn't chemotherapy drugs, and that was all I cared about. I didn't have to look at the headline to know what it was about. You weren't supposed to take photos at Barclays, but everyone did it anyway, and I'd put on quite the show last night.

I shrugged, reaching forward and trying to grab the handle on the porcelain coffee mug in front of me without wincing.

I'd barely slept. Not even because I came home and Noa wasn't in my bed—I always slept significantly better when she was there—but because my throbbing hand kept me up all night.

I'd foregone a trip to the emergency room and took a Vicodin my drug dealer left me instead. It hadn't fucking worked. I could hardly bend my fingers this morning, and my nostrils flared with a loud exhale as I grabbed the mug.

He didn't look at me as he pulled out the carved mahogany chair, careful not to catch the tubing sticking out from underneath the gray Tom Ford button-up he wore. A copy of the Tribune sat folded beside the place setting, waiting for his breakfast order. He might have been one of the only people left in the city, possibly on the fucking planet, who still read the paper in that medium. His voice was clipped when he spoke. "Did you even bother to get your hand checked?"

"Does it look like I bothered?" I muttered, wishing someone would hurry up and come ask what I wanted for breakfast so I could get the fuck out of here.

I didn't even know what wing of the house Noa slept in; the room choices were endless, but I didn't want to spend my morning hunting through these godforsaken halls for her. I was planning on going into the office; it would be quiet. Tripp was in Boston, and David probably wouldn't leave my sister's side, so if I got lucky, it might just be me.

His blue eyes, usually pretty fucking flat and cold, flicked up over his paper, now folded open between his hands. "Your disregard for your legacy was concerning enough, but the sudden disregard for your own life and wellbeing borders alarming."

Something between a scoff and a snort—frankly a sound I hoped I never made again—came from me. "That's fucking rich."

His nostrils flared, and his mouth tightened into a straight line. "Is there something you'd like to say, Deacon?"

"I think I've said it all." I leaned back in my chair, the legs scraping against the polished wood flooring as it tipped up.

A look of displeasure flashed across his features. He might be dying, sure, but he still cared about the integrity of his flooring. "You should have Taylor look at your hand. I saw her this morning, and she said she had some work to do before she went to sleep for the day."

"She's a surgical oncologist. What the fuck is she going to do about a half-healed cut on my palm?"

Half-healed might have been an exaggeration. It looked like it could weep blood at any moment.

"The question you should probably be asking is, what the fuck are we going to do about your little display last night? Halton's stock dropped again this morning, as did many other subsidiaries. It seems your little stunt had its own viral moment on some Chicago society Instagram page." Steven finally set his paper down, steepling his hands together and peering at me over the peaks of his fingertips, like some sort of movie villain.

"Sue them." I shrugged, like I didn't have a care in the world. But I think I might have had too many.

Breathing was growing harder each day, my lungs constantly feeling like they were shredding each time I inhaled, my heart threatening to fall from my chest every time it beat, and my brain wishing to God I was a different person each time I spoke.

My father was no stranger to admonishment, and he rarely tolerated anything that bordered on insubordination at work and certainly not at home. This usually would have been the point in the conversation where he raised his voice and tore into me when his eyes and everything about him would look entirely unfeeling.

But when he looked at me, if I didn't know any better, I would have said he looked sad.

A muscle ticked in his cheek, and he swallowed, like he was steeling himself to say something.

The heavy door separating the breakfast parlor from the winding hallways swung open, and whatever words he might have said died on his lips. He looked past me and inclined his head before picking back up his paper. "Ah, Taylor, impeccable timing. Please take a look at my son's hand."

Taylor and my sister stood in the doorframe, the former still in her scrubs from the night before. I was starting to suspect she did that on purpose, just to remind us that while we were all arguing over more money than you'd ever need, she was saving lives. As if she didn't drive to work in a car that cost more than most people made in a year.

My sister had her arms crossed, wearing that ratty Oxford sweater that had certainly seen better days. But she'd been proud, quietly so, to wear it. To belong there and to work there. Now she was trading that in for a shiny new Winchester Holdings'-embossed business card. She offered me a small smile, and I think sympathy shone there. She was no stranger to causing a scene.

Granted, she'd never screamed at her fiancée and sliced up her hand in a public forum.

Taylor pursed her lips and strode across the room, roughly grabbing my hand. Wincing, I tried to yank my hand back, but her bony thumbs just pressed even harder into my skin. Her eyes narrowed as she looked at the angry cut. "I can't stitch this. It's starting to heal already, and it's not down to the muscle. Put some steri-strips on it, and I'll write you a prescription for an antibiotic."

"How about something for the pain?" I finally yanked my hand back, grimacing up at her.

She arched one eyebrow. "No."

Rolling my eyes, I grabbed my coffee with my other hand, wishing someone had left out champagne instead of just coffee and juice. Taylor walked the long way around the table, eyes skating over the machine on the IV pole before patting my father on the shoulder, and settling into the chair beside my sister, who seemed to have no reservations about this being an alcohol-free breakfast and was currently pouring coffee for the both of them.

"Where's David?" I asked, looking everywhere but at my father or Taylor. It didn't grate as much when I looked at my sister.

She might have been furious at me, she might have given me shit for how I was acting at all hours of the day, but I think she at least understood why. That underneath it all, she was right; we really were the same.

Charlie glanced up at me as she poured milk into Taylor's coffee. "He's been on the phone all morning trying to mend fences with some angry shareholders."

I cleared my throat, my voice lowering, words hesitant. "And Noa?"

"Somewhere far, far away from you," Taylor offered, the edges of her lips curling up and making her look like the fucking Grinch.

I flashed my teeth at Taylor, but before I could answer, my father cut me off. "I spoke to Rebecca this morning."

Charlie snorted, offering our father a saccharine smile that usually would have earned her a reprimand too. "Oh, great. Do she and Sabine have a sequinned monstrosity they'd like me to wear? Some hospital steps they'd like to trot me out on?"

But he only cut her a look before continuing. "She had several suggestions for how we can...restore the family image and present a united front. I'll be hosting a charity event at a new art gallery opening downtown in a few weeks. You will all attend, and you are all expected to be on your best behavior."

"We aren't children." Charlie arched an eyebrow, kicking her feet up and tucking them under her on the chair. Highly inappropriate breakfast table decorum, but here I was, slouched back in my chair.

I cocked my head, widening my eyes at her. "And how have the last few Winchester-sponsored charity galas gone for you, Charles?"

Flicking her middle finger up without even looking at me, she continued to stare at our father.

Had he been someone other than Steven Winchester, he looked like he was tempted to roll his eyes, but he cleared his throat and unfolded his paper again. "On a more personal note, I'm having the house on Cape Cod prepared for Thanksgiving."

Charlie's face paled, and her coffee slipped in her hand before Taylor reached out with annoying catlike reflexes and steadied it before it smashed to the ground. We hadn't been back there since before our mother died. I was surprised he didn't have it fucking condemned.

Eyes wide and lips pulled back, I looked over at him. "What the fuck do we have to be thankful for?"

Our father's eyes darted back and forth between Charlie and me before going back to his paper. His voice was hardly even a murmur. "A great many things, whether you can see them at this moment or not."

Tripp

Finding David standing in my doorway at some point throughout the day had become a fairly common occurrence.

Sometimes, we talked about sports, which generally wasn't my favorite topic. I'd grown a bit averse to organized athletics when my father couldn't seem to stop betting on them to the detriment of everyone around him. But it was nice to have common ground.

Sometimes, we talked about the dumb things clients did.

Sometimes, we talked about Deac.

Sometimes, he just stopped in to say hi.

But today, we talked about Chuck.

I heard him before I saw him, my eyes having been glued to my phone, trying to decode the latest text from my brother. I was likely reading into it, there was never much to decode as far as Post, or the rest of my family, were concerned. Post didn't give a shit I left the bank prematurely; if anything, it probably made him feel like he had free reign to do whatever he wanted, and my father certainly didn't miss me hiding the remote and unplugging the TV.

"Hey man, how was the flight?" David asked, leaning in the doorway and crossing his arms like he usually did.

Glancing up, I tossed my phone onto the desk before shrugging. I didn't mind the commute. I would have preferred to be living back in

Chicago or New York full time, and I probably would have preferred to be with Chuck, but neither of those options were exactly within reach. I was still going home every few days, mostly to make sure my father hadn't bet our house, leaving my mother with nowhere to live. But the more I went back, I wasn't really sure why I did. There was nothing for me there.

I wasn't sure there was anything for me here, either. But DK had shown up day after day, so at least I could count on friendly conversation. There was none of that at home.

"It wasn't bad," I finally answered, tipping back in my chair. "Morning crowd in business is as you'd expect. What's up? Are you looking for those numbers on—"

David cut me off, an incredulous look pulling at his features. "Believe it or not, some people might just want to talk to you to talk."

"Not." I arched an eyebrow, my voice dry as I looked at him.

He was fucking frowning. Like the idea that I didn't believe that bothered him. If the roles were reversed, I wouldn't give a single shit what happened to him. I'd meant what I said to Chuck—he was the better man and probably always had been.

"I don't swing by your office with ulterior motives every day." David's voice dropped, and he rolled his shoulders back. "But I did want to talk to you about something."

I stilled, hands tensing against the arms of my chair. I'd been waiting for this ever since Chuck signed that contract. It was her first day back, and despite her swearing up and down they were just friends, he was sleeping in her fucking bed every night. Kennedy didn't strike me as terribly territorial, but he had punched me in the face over her before, and that was tame.

"Charlie's birthday is in a few days."

My eyes cut to the bottom corner of my computer screen where the date and time were stamped. He was right. Glancing back up at him, I arched an eyebrow. "You here to make sure everyone in the office sings to her? Can't imagine she feels much like celebrating turning thirty."

David rolled his eyes before scrubbing a hand across his jaw. "No. I thought we'd do something. The six of us."

He said that like there *was* a "six of us." Like we were some ragtag group of friends brought together by common elements and tragedy. Which, I supposed we were, in the loosest sense of the word.

"There's a bowling alley out in Lake Forest that let me rent the lanes on either side of the one we'd be using. It's probably a shithole, but I doubt it's overly crowded. She's never been bowling." David shrugged, shoving his hands in his pockets.

"She's never been bowling?" It was my turn to sound incredulous.

David gave me a flat look. "Do you think Steven was throwing themed birthday parties when they were growing up?"

"Can't imagine the Winchesters' childhood birthday parties were terribly fun for children." I nodded, eyebrows raised. "Yeah, alright. But I'm not putting on fucking bowling shoes, and I can't imagine Deac will be too keen on the idea."

Taylor probably wouldn't enjoy trading in her Manolo's for unflattering, used, peeling leather shoes either.

David looked amused for a moment before his features hardened, the muscles in his neck tightening. I was positive his traps were tensing under the shoulders of his light gray Canali Milano wool suit jacket. "Speaking of, I'm sure you saw, but Deac put on quite the show at a dinner that was meant to be for Charlie the other night."

"Pretty sure everyone with a cell phone saw that one," I offered dryly. The muscle was still jumping in his neck, and he looked like he might kill someone at the drop of a hat.

Clearing my throat, I continued, "I can be on Deacon duty for this one. I'll go talk to him and make sure he'll be on his best behavior after my call at nine."

He blinked, pulling his head back. "Why would you want to do that?"

"You said it yourself. It's a burden that should be shared by more than one person." I shrugged again before looking back at my computer screen. "And I doubt Helen wants to deal with the paperwork that would result if you snapped his neck in the office."

David raised one hand, the other still shoved in the pocket of his suit pants, pushing off the door frame and walking back onto the executives' floor.

I wasn't sure when I became the type of person who would willingly fall on the sword for someone else, which is exactly what it was like putting yourself in Deacon's path for longer than necessary now. Chuck was probably the only person I would have been willing to make that type of sacrifice for, and here I was, offering myself up to the person I was pretty certain I'd lose her to forever.

I might have been able to get under her skin, but I never would have thought to take her bowling.

The door to Deacon's office was closed, but that was nothing new. He hid in there most days now, only coming out when he needed to yell at someone to make himself feel better. That was far below my pay grade, and he usually went down to legal or the investing floor for that.

I thought he might leave the door open, seeing as it was Charlie's first day back, but he hadn't, and she'd been in a meeting with Helen and Ash all morning, only waving at me and scrunching her nose when she walked past my open door earlier.

I'd seen some of the other staff, with the exception of David, hesitate outside his door, rocking back and forth on their Tom Fords or Jimmy Choos, hands raising a few times before they worked up the courage to knock. Fortunately, I wasn't scared of Deacon fucking Winchester.

More than anything, I thought we might have more in common right now than we ever had before.

Rapping my knuckles against the heavy door, I didn't wait for him to answer before pushing it open. "Working hard, I see." I jerked my chin toward his computer. It hadn't even been powered on.

His eyes flicked to me, a bored look hardly masking the poor pallor of his skin. One thing Deacon and I did have in common was a carefully curated skincare routine, and he'd clearly been neglecting his. Tipped back in his chair, one hand held in front of his face with a bandage wrapped around it, the other behind his head, he could have looked the picture of casual to anyone who didn't know him.

His hair was unkempt, but it almost looked intentional. And the simple, black Zegna suit would have looked classic and understated on anyone else. But Deacon Winchester wasn't understated.

Closing the door behind me, I crossed the room without waiting for an invitation and pulled out the chair on the other side of his desk.

Deacon opened and closed his hand, flashes of angry, red skin and the start of a hideous scab visible across his palm. He rolled his neck, head lolling as he looked at me. "Let me guess which one sent you in here to give me shit. My sister, hoping you'll lend me a sympathetic ear, all the while convincing me that I need to make it up to Noa?"

"DK, hoping you won't ruin the cute little plan he has for your sister's birthday," I answered coolly, ignoring what was probably a poor veiled jab.

I wasn't someone Charlie could rely on to get anything done for her, and I never really had been.

He leaned forward in his chair, neck stretching, so he could eye the phone on his desk. "Huh. My only sister's thirtieth birthday is only a few days away, and I forgot. I'll add that to the list of failures." Deacon crossed his arms, and a look of discomfort flickered behind his eyes before they fell flat again. "What does that self-righteous fuck have planned?"

Arching an eyebrow, I paused before telling him the grand plans. There was a time I'd have jumped on those words, agreeing wholeheartedly. But I was starting to see David more as a generally good person as opposed to just being a holier-than-thou prick who existed just to piss me off.

Swallowing, I tossed Deacon a dry grin. "He wants to take her bowling. For the six of us to go, too."

"I've never been bowling," Deacon muttered, frowning a bit and staring at his hand again before looking back at me. "You ever going to tell me what this favor my father did for you was? The big secret you're so intent on keeping?"

"I'll tell you mine if you tell me yours."

A real Deacon Winchester grin flashed across his face. "I thought Steven manipulated Charlie into coming back here somehow...turns out my fiancée went behind my back and begged her to stay. My worst fucking nightmare man...my sister stuck back here where she hates it because I failed her."

I didn't think that was how Chuck would see it. She'd told me herself there was nothing she wouldn't do for her brother. Anyone with a pulse could see that. But I studied Deacon and wondered if his heart was barely beating to begin with.

I shrugged, like it wasn't the thing that had cost me Chuck, or at least ended whatever it could have been prematurely. Time with her was all borrowed, anyway. "Your dad kept my dad out of jail."

A low whistle came from Deacon, and he nodded. "SEC violation?"

"Multiple."

Deacon blinked before he tossed his head back with a harsh bark of laughter. "What a fucking cliché, man. He's every dying man with regrets, just trying to make amends left and right."

"If he's offering, maybe you should accept and say thank you. Enjoy what you have left." Pushing off the chair to stand, I raised my eyebrows at him. "Can I tell Kennedy you're coming? That you'll be on your best behavior?"

Waving me off, Deacon leaned forward, finally sitting straight in his chair and powering on his computer. "I'm not wearing the fucking shoes, though. I still have some dignity."

Charlie

There were still spots of light in the corners of my vision, despite the photoshoot ending over an hour ago. I hadn't been given any notice about it, but I wasn't surprised when Sabine and Rebecca trotted into Helen's office, a photographer from *Chicago Business Weekly* in tow.

Sabine had pursed her lips, tipping her head to the side, impossibly slicked-back curls hardly moving as she studied my outfit—a dark, almost black, oversized Navy pinstripe wool blazer from Nili Lotan with matching pants, and a pair of patent leather Louboutins—and offered a tiny nod of approval before leaving the office.

I didn't see it, but I was sure there was a rack of outfits waiting somewhere should she have deemed my clothing inappropriate for the photoshoot.

I hadn't really been listening when Rebecca told me what the feature would be. It was something meant to detract from Deacon's glass-smashing, which was still doing the rounds on the internet, and demonstrate that the Winchesters still maintained a modicum of control over the far reaches of their empire, despite stock yo-yoing up and down. It wasn't just Halton that was fluctuating. Even some of our more stable subsidiaries, the luxury resort chain Deacon was particularly fond of, and some sort of engineering firm that made engines for race cars that had once upon a time been owned by my mother's family, were suffering.

It wasn't the first time there was a Winchester photoshoot to save face, and it probably wouldn't be the last. Usually, they bothered me. I typically sat down in one of the pretty wing-backed chairs, my stomach tight and smile wholly faked, and left feeling empty.

But it didn't bother me today. My smile wasn't even fake as I leaned forward in the chair, arms propped up on my knees and hair tucked behind my ears in what was a much more casual pose than I was usually allowed. The photographer was around my age and turned out to have a penchant for designer clothes that could have rivaled Taylor's. It had been fun, and though that was probably a stroke of luck more than anything, I decided to take it as a sign of good things to come.

I didn't put much stock into vibes or signs, but Taylor did, and she informed me this morning that she had a great sense of inner peace at the idea of me ditching academia once and for all to return to Winchester Holdings. It hadn't hurt my heart when I emailed Dr. Batra my withdrawal forms. I felt guilty—but only a little bit. It wasn't what I predicted, and it definitely wasn't how I thought my life would turn out, but these halls and this old office didn't really hurt the way it used to, either.

It wasn't so bad to be here again.

I was tentatively hopeful about it, if I was being truly honest. There was an Excel spreadsheet stretched across my computer screen that I was particularly excited about. I'd stayed up until two the night before, pulling together a list of companies we could explore for our first foray into sustainable investing.

David had stayed up with me, propped up beside me against the headboard of the bed, his own computer open on his lap. Whatever he was working on seemed far more boring than what I was doing, but he was more than willing to look away from his screen and lean across the pillow wall to look at mine, whatever I was pointing out to him. It had been fun, just us and the light from our respective screens casting shadows across the bedding. David looked like he always did, like he was hewed from stone, conjured up from the secret part of my brain that wanted a boy who was beautiful, safe, and wild all at the same time—damp hair curling against his neck and one wave across his forehead, all broad shoulders tapering down to golden skin and seemingly endless ridges of abdominal muscle.

I loved him, I loved him, I loved him.

And I'd never stopped.

I was due in Ash's office in about ten minutes to present to him. I'd wanted to run it by my father first, but he had to go to the hospital with Taylor for a scan. A normal parent might have sent a text that wished their child good luck, but Steven Winchester sent one that instructed me to be prepared to present to him at breakfast the following morning.

I'd left my door open in an attempt to embrace the veritable lion's den of the executives' floor, and I saw David and Tripp as they left the former's office. David talking animatedly to Tripp, whose hands were shoved into his classic, black slim fit Calvin Klein suit, before they came to stand in my doorway.

Crossing my arms, I tipped back in my chair. "Have I died and gone to hell? Because this must be what purgatory is—the two of you, blocking my path to all that waits for me in the wonders of sustainable investing at Winchester Holdings."

David grinned, stars in his eyes coming alive, while one eyebrow rose on Tripp's forehead, his voice a dry lilt when he spoke. "Already saddled up that high horse, and she's been here for all of five minutes."

Pursing my lips, I narrowed my eyes at him before making a continue-on gesture with my hand.

Still grinning, David dropped his head against the polished door frame. "Your birthday's in a few days."

It was. I hadn't really thought much of it. It wasn't one of those cliché moments in the movies where I looked over, suddenly saw the date, and realized my birthday was only days away. My birthday was mostly a non-factor in my life. When I was in school, my sorority sisters used the excuse to throw one final party before Thanksgiving break, and it was never more than a passing acknowledgement from my father after our mother died. I usually celebrated with Deacon and Taylor, and that was that.

"It is, indeed, the formal exit of my twenties. I hope to enter the next decade with more grace than I possessed in this current one."

"How do you feel about making your bowling debut? You can start your thirties by honing a new skill," David said, his voice teasing. "What do you say about the six of us at some shitty bowling alley in Lake Forest? I reserved the lanes on either side of us just in case, but I can't imagine a reporter from Society News will be hiding out there."

"Deac will be on his best behavior. I have his word." Tripp's voice was low and his features impassive, as always.

Tipping my head back, my derisive laugh echoed across the still-bare office. I didn't have time to hang anything or bring in new furniture. "Were his fingers crossed when he said that? Oh wait, that might be difficult, seeing as his hand is practically still bleeding."

"Don't worry about Deacon. Worry about learning how to throw a bowling ball so it doesn't break your dainty heiress fingers." Tripp grinned, and for a moment, his eyes looked like they could be coming alive again in a spring thaw.

Flicking my middle finger up at them both, I smiled tightly. "Fine. We can usher in my thirties in a seedy bowling alley. Now, if you'll excuse me, I have work to do. Not everyone here gets to manage such low-maintenance portfolios."

"Well, that's just rude." David laughed, his eyes dancing before he cut an incredulous look toward Tripp. "We work very hard."

"Really? Could have fooled me." I smiled, jerking my chin toward the hallway beyond them. "I'm serious. I have a meeting in less than five minutes. Go away, both of you."

David took a measured step back from the door, holding both his hands up, while Tripp narrowed his eyes on me before pointedly rolling them and turning on the heel of his Prada derby loafer.

Winking at me before shoving his hands in his pockets, David turned around, falling back into step with Tripp.

They'd both walked away from me before, left me behind, and I guess I'd done the same to them. It had broken my heart each time, the respective pieces that belonged to each of them—these boys that had shaped and molded me, making my life all that it was.

But watching them walk away together, the way Tripp leaned his head in toward David, how he tipped his back in laughter before clapping Tripp on the shoulder and going back to his own office, my heart swelled, stretching, stretching, stretching, all those glued together fragments melding themselves back together one piece at a time.

———

"Ew," Taylor hissed, gripping my arm and trying to pinch me through the sleeve of my leather jacket. "This place looks like a staph infection waiting to happen."

Rolling my eyes, I glanced sideways at her. Dropping the sleeve of my jacket, she brushed the front of her beige-cropped Gorski shearling bomber and gave an exaggerated shudder as she eyed the looming bowling alley.

It looked like what you'd imagine a rundown bowling alley on a street corner would—neon lighting that seemed on the verge of quitting, cracked stone steps, and a door propped open with a bowling ball that appeared to be cut in half. It had definitely never seen the likes of Taylor in her fur jacket and the cream leather Staud boots she seemed to think were appropriate. She said they added a shocking pop of color to her outfit, peeking out from under the hem of her Mother Lasso Sneak straight jeans. I didn't know what look she was going for, but it certainly wasn't *secret bowling alley birthday party*.

"Good thing we'll have a doctor on hand." I narrowed my eyes at her, gripping her arm through the ample fur jacket and hauling her forward.

"What kind of found family scenario am I walking into here? Your two lovers coming together to throw you a birthday party—who would have thought?" Taylor gave another shudder before grabbing my hand with hers, squeezing once, twice, three times. "Don't worry. I'll be on my best behavior. I'll even do my best not to slit brother dearest's throat. But I'm not wearing those fucking shoes."

Tipping my head back in laughter, I gestured our joined hands down to her boots. "Do you plan on bowling in those?"

She pursed her lips, snapping her fingers and taking a measured step over a particular deep crack in the stone steps leading into the building. "I suppose the risk of contracting athlete's foot is the lesser of two evils. I don't want anything to befall these babies. I just got them."

"The horror," I deadpanned, blinking as my eyes adjusted to the on-slaught of fluorescent lighting in the lobby. David had been right—it wasn't busy.

A teenager sat behind the front desk, all cracked padded leather and peeling stickers that at one point looked like they spelled out Lucky Strike, but she was entirely engrossed in her phone. Behind her were shelves of shoes that really did look like they had seen better days. I could practically feel Taylor cringe beside me.

Only a few of the lanes were occupied, and no one seemed particularly concerned that a member of the most elusive dynasty in America just strolled in. The girl's eyes left her phone for just a moment, no flare of recognition behind them, before looking back at the screen and asking in a bored voice, "Name?"

Taylor snorted beside me, amusement radiating from her. I'd only experienced this kind of anonymity in London, and even then, sometimes eyes would stay on me too long, or I'd see someone hitting their friend in the shoulder and gesturing to me.

"The reservation should be under Kennedy?" I smiled, dropping my voice, more out of habit than necessity.

Deacon could probably sprint across every single lane naked, and no one would give a shit.

She didn't bother to look back up when she spoke. "Lanes 21, 22, and 23. Toward the bar."

I was about to say something, confusion etching my features and my lips parting as I looked down at my black Loeffler Randall leather ankle boots, visible under the hem of my own straight-legged jeans. I'd never been bowling, but I was pretty sure there were rules about outside footwear.

Taylor gave my arm a sharp tug before I could say anything, dropping her voice to a whisper. "Don't you dare say anything about those godforsaken shoes. Let's count our blessings—no athlete's foot, *and* there's alcohol."

"I can't imagine the quality of the tannins in the wine here will be quite up to your standards," I muttered, trailing behind her as we rounded the corner.

Our bizarre little found family, as Taylor had put it, was separated from the nearest group by two lanes on either side. David mentioned renting the ones directly beside ours, but maybe it was another sign of good things to come. People were even farther out of earshot.

I was even more thankful for that the minute Taylor opened her mouth. I'd forgotten she hadn't been with Tripp in a social situation since he came back to WH. Any semblance of fondness she was developing for him evaporated quickly when he stood me up at the New York library gala.

Taylor cocked her head, brown eyes sharp the way they only were when she was sizing someone up. "TB. Wondered when you'd crawl out of whatever hole you'd been living in."

"TB?" Tripp arched an eyebrow, giving Taylor a lazy smile from where he sat on the scuffed, plastic bench that made a horseshoe just behind the lane.

Taylor nodded, one of her usual cat-like grins stretching across her face. "TB. Tripp Banks. Tuberculosis. Either or. Take your pick."

"You have the same initials, Taylor," Deacon drawled in a bored voice that would have given the girl at the front desk a run for her money.

Taylor blinked before narrowing her eyes at Deacon. "Speaking of crawling out of holes...how's your hand, by the way?"

My brother was stretched out on the bench across from Tripp, one arm thrown over the back of it, the sleeve of his gray Theory zip sweater bunching against the plastic.

Noa sat just beyond his reach, eyes cutting to him and her features tightening before she looked at me. A smile stretched across her face, and she opened her arms as she stood to hug me. "Happy birthday, Charlie."

I smiled softly, wrapping my arms around her, trying to convey the endless thankfulness I had for her and the sorrow, too, that my brother was practically drowning on dry land. My eyes found David's over her shoulder where he leaned against the bench, one leg kicked up against it and his arms crossed. The sleeves of his light blue Saks cashmere crewneck were rolled up, and it was unfair, really, how otherworldly those arms looked, even in this arguably shitty lighting.

I wrinkled my nose at him, raising my hand in a tiny wave behind Noa before she took a step back.

He winked at me before tipping his chin toward the table in front of the booth where two pitchers of beer sat, perspiring against the scratched table. A stack of red cups that had definitely seen better days sat beside them. There was a glass of what looked like scotch there too, on a napkin as a coaster. It didn't take a genius to figure out who that belonged to, but I didn't care, because everything about this was so beautifully normal.

"Well, happy birthday, Chuck. It's a far cry from themed parties at the sorority house." Tripp leaned forward, taking one of the pitchers and pouring into the questionable red cups. "If only they could see us now."

Taylor's teeth were still on display when she took the cup from Tripp, holding it as far away from her coat as possible, like it might get dirty. "Well, I'm sure it would be quite the surprise to all that someone hasn't simply killed you yet."

Widening my eyes at her, she rolled hers before turning back to Tripp, voice overly saccharine. "It's lovely to see you again."

Tripp raised his eyebrows, handing me a cup of foamy beer.

A small smile played across my face. There was a different version of him that used to hand me cups of shitty beer, not unlike this one, too. Who would have thought?

I definitely wouldn't have thought I'd be ringing in my birthday with a shitty beer, foam sloshing over my hands when all our respective red cups met overtop of the table, that arguably five of my favorite people would be here, despite all reasons they had not to be—they were here for me.

The girl who was never good enough. Left behind and abandoned. The little lost girl. Found family, indeed.

My eyes prickled, tears threatening to spill over, and I scrunched up my nose, willing them away as I finished the last of the beer. It was flat and far too warm, but it made my heart swell anyway.

Deacon dropped his empty cup onto the table, snatching up the scotch.

"That's your second scotch." David's voice was cool, and displeasure evident in the typically beautiful lines of his face.

Deacon snorted, tossing a flat look at David before sitting back on the bench, drink in hand. "Please, it's fucking bowling alley scotch. It's probably so watered down there's no alcohol left."

Noa looked back and forth between Deacon and David, her amber eyes wide and her lips pulled back. She clapped her hands together, a strained look on her face. "Should we bowl?"

Deacon

This heinous bowling alley must have been the entrance to the Twilight Zone.

Or, maybe everyone had a point, and I really had been drinking too much, because just like having my only remaining parent die, I definitely didn't have Charlie, David, and Tripp in fucking stitches over something one of them just said on my bingo card.

Taylor was currently making a show of walking down the lane in those ridiculous Staud boots—even I wouldn't have worn something like that to a bowling alley—and she hadn't even taken off her fur jacket. But somehow, she was fucking winning.

David was a natural athlete, so he wasn't far behind. Tripp hardly deigned to get out of his seat to actually chuck the ball down the laneway, more than content to sit with Charlie and Noa, and have them losing their goddamn minds with whatever dry commentary he was offering up. My sister was pretty hit or miss, either putting way too much force behind the ball or not enough. Noa's usually lost momentum about halfway, and all of mine went into the fucking gutter.

That might have had more to do with the fourth bowling alley scotch I was currently nursing.

My fiancée was hardly speaking to me, and my fucking hand was still killing me. But at least my sister was having fun.

That really did matter most to me at the end of the day. She deserved to be happy, to feel loved and supported, and to enjoy her birthday. Usually, I would have been right up there with Taylor. Rented this entire place out if David insisted on doing something as plebeian as bowling. But I was starting to think maybe a part of me died when my father told me he was going to.

I wanted to get up, to put down this scotch, because it was terrible and to give my sister, my friends, my fiancée, the version of me they deserved, but I just couldn't. It was like all that grief, everything that I'd never dealt with when our mom died, the grief I had for my dad—like it had festered in me and made me so heavy I couldn't even move.

And maybe this is what I deserved, to sit here unmoving, forced to watch the people I loved more than anything enjoy themselves. To be on the outside looking in.

A horribly undignified shriek erupted from Taylor, and she lifted her arms in the air, spinning on the heel of her boot. She'd gotten another fucking strike.

Noa started clapping, her amber eyes sparkling—in the good way, not with unshed tears brought on by yours truly—and she ran forward on those perfect little feet of hers to wrap her arms around Taylor.

"Oh, come on, this is fucking ridiculous." David's nostrils flared, a muscle ticking in his cheek when he bent down to snatch one of the bowling balls from the rack.

Charlie's eyes went wide, and she glanced sideways at Tripp before they both started laughing. "I'm sorry—David, are you mad you're losing at a game of recreational bowling?"

David opened his arms wide, the ball clutched in one palm, and he narrowed his eyes. "She said she'd never bowled before. What is she, some kind of bowling savant?"

"Jesus, DK." Tripp's lips were pulled back, everything about him amused. "I fucking knew you had a flaw, man."

Taylor peered at David over Noa's shoulder, flashing him a grin. "Jealous, David?"

"No," David answered, his voice stubborn and bordering on childlike. "I just think that—"

I didn't hear the rest of what he said. I'd been about to push to stand up, set down the glass of scotch, and go over and join them when Noa's phone started vibrating on the bench beside me.

Her phone rang at a similar frequency to mine. It was constantly going off with social media notifications, emails, texts. In this case, it was a text from her manager, Koa:

> Givenchy fragrance confirmed. Do I need to book you leaving from O'Hare or the Executive Airport?

My grip slipped on the cup of scotch. This wasn't abnormal. She left last minute for calls or shoot requests that took a while to confirm, or another model fell through.

I didn't expect her to put her career on hold. No one knew how long Steven really had. Taylor was particularly tight-lipped about it, saying vague things about the mortality rate for his type of cancer without chemo.

But I hadn't expected her to run back to work the first chance she fucking got.

The thought of being without her right now made it harder to breathe than usual. Instead of the thought of my father dying shredding my lungs, it was the idea that I had become so repugnant to my fiancée that she wanted nothing to do with me.

I could see her walking on tentative feet toward me from the corner of my eye, like she was on her way over here to extend me an olive branch. But I didn't want it, because I'd just fucking break it anyway.

Instead, I pushed to stand, holding her phone out to her. "It really is 'till death do us part. Except in this case, it's not my death."

Noa's bottom lip puckered, and she started to shake her head. She somehow looked both ridiculous and fucking perfect in her tiny white Moncler puffer. "Deacon, what—"

Shrugging, I waved the phone around before tossing it in the air and catching it. "Givenchy. Koa says it's all confirmed. How many days?"

She pulled her head back, blinking rapidly. "Were you looking through my phone?"

"It started vibrating against the goddamn bench! I could see the fucking text on your screen!" I opened my arms, the last remnants of the horrible scotch splashing over the rim of the cup and onto the sleeve of my Theory sweater. Fuck. "You were going to leave without saying anything?"

Noa scoffed, the sound wet with the unshed tears pooling along her lash line. "That's a bit hypocritical, wouldn't you say? I haven't heard a real word come out of your mouth since I got here. You want to talk about saying anything—why don't *you* say something, Deacon? Say anything. Tell me you're mad at your dad. Tell me you're scared. Tell me you're so unbelievably sad, that you feel like a shell of a person, because that's what you *are*. This isn't you!" Her voice rising as she gestured toward the scratched plastic bench I'd been holding vigil at all night. "The you that I know wouldn't sit here all night on the sidelines of your sister's thirtieth birthday. You'd be having just as much fun as everyone else."

Rolling my eyes, I tossed the now empty cup haphazardly down onto the table. "Oh fuck off. I never would have thrown her a birthday party in a bowling alley. I have standards."

Noa's features collapsed, and her lips tugged up into a smile that looked like a combination of rueful and sad; it made me want to fall to my knees and beg for her forgiveness. But I didn't do anything; I was still rooted to the spot by all the things that made me the human equivalent of an anchor somewhere in the ocean, keeping nothing afloat but dragging everything down.

She wrapped her arms around herself and shook her head. "There was a time I would have laughed at that. But I don't think anything about this is very funny."

I opened my mouth to say something back. I wasn't sure what, but before I could, I realized just how silent the whole place was.

People were staring.

Not just my sister, who looked at me like she was in physical pain. Not just Taylor, whose teeth were all on display and looked poised to tear my throat out, or Tripp, who stared at me with that same impassive expression as always. And definitely not just David, who looked like he might actually—*finally*—punch me.

Not just them, the people who I was starting to suspect maybe did have a limit when it came to me—but everyone else in this bowling alley.

No sounds of laughter, of pins dropping from balls rolled down the lane, and it even seemed like the music was quieter.

I wasn't a particularly physical person when it came to violence—too much risk and too many things that could go wrong if you were the one that threw the punch and you had as much money as I did. But I felt like punching David as he walked over, thinly veiled irritation on his face, somehow still as composed and unflustered as always.

"Why don't you take this outside? There's no need to cause a scene and ruin a night that's supposed to be about your sister more than you already have." His words were clipped, and he wrapped his hand around my elbow, like he was going to forcibly drag me out.

Jerking my arm away from him, I rolled my shoulders out and stepped out of his path. As much as I wanted to punch him, I really didn't fucking want him to punch me. He had a solid ten pounds of muscle on me.

Moving toward Noa, I held her phone out. "So, are you going to leave from O'Hare, or do you want the jet?"

Her nostrils flared, and she reached forward, snatching the phone from me and shoving it into the pocket of her coat. She shook her head, her voice cracking when she spoke. "I told Koa I didn't want to do it, Deacon. I have no idea why he went ahead."

I didn't want her to go. I didn't want her to go anywhere. If it were possible, I'd wrap her and all that she was to me around me, like a cocoon I'd never have to leave. My sister was always going on about how David had been her home, what it felt like to feel safe with someone. I'd never understood it until I met Noa, because it had never occurred to me that my sister and I had never been safe. In different ways, but we were both shades of the same coin. Parents could really do a fucking number on their children.

I didn't want Noa to leave me—even for a second. But I didn't want her to have to love this version of me. I didn't really want anyone to see me when I was this fucking hapless, so I shook my head and moved to walk past her.

One of her hands came to my forearm, her engagement ring catching the light, even in this shithole. Her eyes were pleading, and she chewed on the inside of her cheeks. "Stay. Everyone here loves you. We want you here."

Looking beyond Noa to my sister, she wrinkled her nose and tipped her chin toward the exit, mouthing "go." But it didn't feel like a dismissal. It felt like understanding.

Shaking my head, I stepped back, pointing toward her phone. "Call Koa back. I'll be fine. You've wanted to do Givenchy forever. Don't let me stop you."

My words didn't come out harsh, and for once, I didn't mean them to be. But I knew they broke her heart all the same. I felt it weighing me down, too, every single step of the way out of there.

Charlie

The halls of the house were dark, only the flickering sconces that always made me feel like I was stuck in the Regency era were left on. They made everything feel heavier; the silence that always descended on the house more stifling at night than it was during the day.

David and I walked side-by-side, close enough that our arms brushed every few steps, and I could see the way his eyes lit up when he walked under one of the beams of light.

The winding halls didn't feel so lonely when I was navigating them with him.

Noa had followed Deacon out the door only moments after he left, and we hadn't stayed much past that. People started to stare, phones were out, and the anonymous, seedy bowling alley cover was blown pretty quickly.

Tripp opted to stay at his hotel, even though I had invited him to stay here. There were plenty of rooms in the guest wing. He said he'd rather not partake in whatever incestuous living arrangements were happening out in Lake Forest, and he didn't want to risk Taylor scratching his eyes out while he slept. She'd looked particularly proud of that, a glint in her eye at the thought he was scared of her.

She'd left us at the door of the house, going left in the direction of the guest wing when we went straight toward the back of the house.

Everything at the front and on either end was all staged; the only signs a family actually lived here were hidden away at the back of the house where no one would ever see them.

"I'm sorry your brother ruined your birthday. It was supposed to be normal." David's voice was rough when he spoke.

"My brother pitching a fit and spiraling ever closer to his doom is fairly par for the course these days." I looked sideways at David, offering him a wry smile. "It's okay, honestly. I think I have a bit more grace for Deacon right now than everyone else. Granted, I wish he would lay off the scotch. But it's like looking in a mirror...a funhouse one, obviously. I'm far prettier than Deacon."

"I, for one, am very glad you don't look like your brother." David grinned at me, one hand finding the banister leading up the marble steps that would take us to the back of the house and that empty, cavernous hallway my brother and I slept at opposite sides of.

Peering around the staircase, I could see a stretch of light across the polished wood floor. My father's office was back there. Glancing back to David, I offered him a small smile. "You go ahead. I'm just going to go say goodnight to my dad."

Letting go of the banister, David brought his hand to my face, one calloused thumb hovering over the apple of my cheek before he tucked my hair behind my ear. "You'll be okay navigating these empty halls all alone?"

My heart skipped in my chest, beating against my ribcage so desperately, like it could find its way to his hands again. I'd always equated it to this desperate bid to get back to where it belonged, to go home—but I thought about what my father had called him, my lighthouse beam. I didn't really want my heart to live outside my body anymore; my body was my home, my mind was my home, for better or worse. But I liked this idea that maybe my heart sang at the sight of him—because he was the light in all the dark. The reward at the end of a very long trip.

"I'll always be able to find my way if you're the one waiting for me," I said softly, pressing my cheek into his hand where it lingered before taking a step back.

David's eyes roved over me as he took a measured step back and up onto the staircase. "Happy birthday, baby."

"Thank you," I whispered, scrunching my nose at him before turning and padding softly toward the light emanating from under my father's office door. It was probably the place he was most himself, where he'd shared most of himself with my mother, and it was terribly ironic that he kept that hidden and closed away, too.

The door was cracked open, and I hesitated before reaching forward and knocking tentatively. There was a time I probably would have sprinted up the stairs on silent feet in hopes he wouldn't hear me, and now, in whatever world we were living in, I was coming to say goodnight.

His voice was quiet, but there was no hesitation on his end. "Come in."

Pushing the door open, I peeked around it.

He sat at his desk, illuminated by his computer screen. He'd stopped wearing suit jackets at home because they got in the way of his IV, but he was still in a blue Ralph Lauren button-up, perfectly pressed, with the sleeves rolled up to accommodate the butterfly clip. I hadn't seen him today, and his skin looked sallow in comparison to yesterday.

I'd left for the office with David and Deacon around seven, but there'd been another ornate silver tray outside my door with a fresh coffee and a card from his monogrammed stationery that simply read in his messy script: "Happy Birthday – S.W."

Not your typical birthday card, but more than I'd gotten from him in years.

"Hey, just checking in to see if you need anything before I go to bed." I offered him a smile, stepping inside, but one hand still on the brass doorknob.

He shook his head, eyes narrowing momentarily at the computer screen before flicking up to me. "No, thank you. Did you have a nice birthday? Taylor mentioned something this morning about bowling."

"It was good. We had fun but—"

"You don't need to worry about breaking the news about your brother's recent outburst to me. I do have a phone, as did others in that...venue. There are videos." He held his hand up, the ever-present Blackberry that was one of his appendages at this point. "I'm thankful that David didn't throw a punch. It looked rather tense there for a moment."

Chewing on the inside of my cheek, I raised my eyes to the ceiling, focusing on the shadows cast by the light instead of the burning in my eyes. "Please don't be mean to him. Deacon is lost right now. He just needs time. Is there anything I can take on to help? I can do a press conference, I can—"

Leaning back in his chair and crossing his arms with a finesse that made it seem like he didn't even notice the IV anymore, my father studied me before speaking. "There's no need at this moment. There's quite a bit of good press around your return and the idea of sustainable investing. Rebecca has been putting in quite a bit of work for the charity event at the gallery next week. It's garnering quite a bit of interest as well. I suggest you enjoy what remains of your thirtieth birthday. It's Wednesday. You have half a week and the weekend at your disposal."

"Oh?" I arched an eyebrow at him. The idea of enjoying something as frivolous as a birthday was likely as foreign a concept to my father as living in a studio apartment would be. "What would you suggest I do?"

His eyes stayed on me for a moment before finding his monitor again. He shifted in his chair, shoulders rolling slightly. I could tell whatever he was about to say was uncomfortable for him. He seemed like he was rolling the words around before he finally landed on them. "David mentioned a charity surf competition happening back in North Carolina this weekend. Why don't you two take the jet?"

Blinking rapidly, I stood there, gaping at him before finally speaking. "I *just* started back at work. And you want me to abscond to North Carolina for a weekend to watch a surfing competition?"

My father's eyes cut back to me, and it was hard to tell in the light, but they looked softer than usual. "Consider it a birthday present."

Charlie

The Kennedy family home looked the same. Untouched by the time and distance that separated me from the person I used to be, from who I used to be with the boy who grew up here. I watched David from behind my sunglasses, a pair of giant Saint Laurent frames that Taylor and I insisted on stealing back and forth from one another rather than just buying our own.

The muscles in his bicep and shoulder flexed under the cotton of his gray long-sleeve shirt, his hand gripping the leather steering wheel. I wanted to salivate a bit because I was clearly nothing more than a base animal as his fingers released it, and I watched his forearms tense when he parked the truck. It was all that was left at the rental counter when our flight landed.

I hadn't ever actually been in a truck. My life was all sleek SUVs, sports cars, or seemingly anonymous towncars. But I found I liked being this high up, and David looked regular, natural, normal even, weaving the truck in and out of traffic and onto this private access-only island to get to his family home. As normal as someone who looked like that and grew up in a place like this could possibly be.

The engine turned off, and David looked at me, his own eyes hidden behind a pair of Ray Bans. "I'm glad we're here. Taylor has everything in hand, I promise. She won't let anything happen to your dad or Deac. It's almost like she's a literal doctor or something."

My lips twitched, and before I could stop myself, my hand was reaching out, fingers brushing his hair back off his forehead.

We were still existing in a weird in-between space. No sex. No kissing. But we touched all the time. He slept in my bed every night. We fell asleep holding hands or with his arm around me. And despite Taylor's constant bemoaning that we needed to "just bone already," despite how close we came on a regular basis, I was still holding firm. I was the last barrier between us now, what David and I used to have, what we could have again.

There was no ire in his eyes when he looked at me, not a hint of betrayal, mistrust, or hurt. And it wasn't quite like he used to look at me, either. The way David Kennedy looked at me now far surpassed any other look he had ever given me. I thought his eyes were my favorite before. But none of it—nothing—compared to this.

"You in there, Charlie?" David asked, grinning slightly and grabbing my wayward fingers in his. He brought my fingertips to his lips, brushing them gently before dropping my hand entirely.

"Yes. Sorry. I know. I just need to relax. Pretend there isn't a fucking catastrophe waiting for me back in Chicago." My father was just the half of it. Deacon had well and truly gone off the fucking rails.

David looked at me before reaching forward to unbuckle my seatbelt. He leaned even farther, muscles in his back rippling under his shirt as he opened the passenger door for me.

My breath caught, a small gasp escaping me. Because his head was practically between my legs, which I had on good authority as somewhere he thought about being often. My thigh muscles tensed.

David stilled, hand hovering by the now opened door before dropping to my kneecap. I watched him roll out his shoulders before he brought his lips to the inside of my thigh. It was just a brush. And then I felt him smile against the denim of my jeans.

"You want me to go down on you in the driveway of my parents' home, Charlie?" Suddenly, he was sitting up again, too far from me, but one hand still dwarfing my knee. He grinned at me, and I knew underneath the tint of his sunglasses, those eyes were glinting.

"No." *Yes.*

I was certain I wanted David, wanted to be with David like that more than I wanted almost anything. But apparently, I was more stubborn, more petulant than I thought, because I was the one who wouldn't budge. But right now, I wasn't sure why. Taylor was right. I wasn't in the habit of drowning in people anymore, and there was no way he would let me.

"It *can* be just an orgasm, you know. If you want to feel good." David looked at me earnestly, those lines beside his eyes that I loved so much, because they reminded me he was a thirty-one-year-old man and not a boy, crinkled ever so slightly. "I would never push you. Pressure you for it to mean anything more than that."

"I know," I whispered, shrugging my shoulders. "But it would never be just sex with you. And I'm not sure I trust myself yet."

David looked at me, or at least I thought he did behind the sunglasses, with what I assumed was a classic David Kennedy look. One where he assessed me, saw right through me, deep down into my soul, and knew what I was thinking and feeling before even I did. His voice was low, gravelly when he finally spoke. "Do you trust me?"

My lips parted to tell him that of course I trusted him. I had always, would always trust him. My fingers twitched toward his, but I startled when a loud bang came from behind me. I almost fell backward as the truck door was pulled open. I twisted to find the two youngest Kennedy siblings standing there.

Ryan's tie was undone, hanging loosely around the neck of his shirt. Whatever suit jacket he had been wearing, I assumed to match his tailored navy pants, was long discarded. A perspiring beer bottle hung loosely from his fingers. Sophie stood beside him, blonde hair teased, and pulled back into a ponytail that I was sure I had seen Taylor sport on multiple occasions. I recognized the dress immediately—because it was something I would have worn had it not been for the puff sleeves. But the Badgley Mischka Mikado Suit dress suited Sophie more than it ever would have me. The lapel of the white silk top gave way to the constructed black pencil skirt, falling just below her knees. I could see her bouncing back and forth on the balls of her feet, careful not to spill the white wine that danced back and forth in the large glass she held.

David groaned, but it was the kind of good-natured groan that had never existed in my life. His head was against the steering wheel, finally rolling to the side to look at his brother and sister. "Shouldn't you two be at work?"

"We work for Dad. It's Friday. We wanted to leave early," Ryan supplied, a grin not unlike his brother's sliding into place. His blond hair was pushed back, a bit longer than the last time I saw him. But unlike David's, it was straight. Not a single rogue wave to be found.

"Sophie's an intern. She shouldn't be skipping out," David reprimanded, his voice still light. His sister was beaming, honey eyes just like his darting back and forth between us. "And remind me why you two still live at home? Pretty sure Dad told me no one would be here this weekend."

"Are you two back together?" Sophie blurted, continuing to bounce back and forth on her feet, voice practically a squeal.

David's back straightened, and he reached out for me, hand gripping my shoulder. His voice bordered on harsh, the way only an older siblings could achieve. "Charlie needed a change of scenery. I didn't think anyone would be here."

The light in Sophie's eyes seemed to dim, and that made me inexplicably sad. She had always reminded me of Taylor, but a softer version. David had once described her to me as being too good for this world, and I could see that all over her soft features now, her eyes flitting to me, worry darkening them.

I smiled at her and tipped my chin to her wine glass. "I could use a drink. If you're in a sharing mood."

Her smile lit her face, and she nodded exuberantly, offering me a tiny, manicured hand. "For you? My favorite almost sister-in-law?"

"Oh? Do I beat out Victoria?" I looked over my shoulder, eyes widening at David and voice light. Teasing.

"She's such a bitch, man," Ryan muttered over the mouth of his beer, tipping it back. "You beat out anyone, Charlie."

I jumped down from the truck, shoes smacking against the pavement. I felt my spine reverberate, but Sophie's hand was still out, so I grabbed it. She was tugging me toward the open archway that would lead to the pool, to the beach, the ocean, when I heard David. "If that isn't the truth."

I wanted to turn back, maybe tell him I changed my mind, but Sophie's tug was insistent, and she was practically running now, her bare feet surely uncomfortable against the pavement. So I followed her instead, wondering what the fuck I was doing. I'd been waxing poetic with my brother for weeks now about how we waste so much time to not miss out on the opportunity to spend time with our father. That this was all some grand second chance.

Glancing over my shoulder one last time before Sophie dragged me into the house, my heart dropped. It was normal, everyday, and average, the way David grinned at his brother, shoving at his shoulder and hopping out of the truck before bringing him in for a brief hug.

Normal, everyday, and average. But he was beautiful, and I loved him.

Maybe it wasn't a second chance with him, but a new beginning entirely.

It was hard to see all the surfers out on the water, bobbing in the waves, the North Carolina sun beating down unseasonably bright against the ocean. I squinted behind my sunglasses, and even though they were all so far away, looking practically identical in wet suits and zinc smeared across their noses to help with the reflection, I knew exactly where David was.

Sure, he was a shade broader, more muscular than the average build of a surfer, apparently. His hair was certainly messier, and he was the most skilled one out there. But that's not how I knew where he was. I think I'd always know where David Kennedy was—exactly the amount of space he took up down to the centimeter, how the oxygen over there was probably different, because all those stars that lived in his eyes changed the chemical makeup of the universe in whatever space he occupied.

I watched as he swiped a hand through his hair, pushing the wet waves off his forehead. I had no idea how a surf competition worked. I'd never watched one and had certainly never been to one.

He had explained it to me last night, lying beside me in his childhood bed, propped up on one arm, hand mussing his hair up even more, the other toying with the boring, forever paling in comparison straight strands of mine. Apparently, they were all more or less the same, no matter the scale of them—broken down into heats of two to four surfers at a time in whatever the marked competition zone was, and the duration of the heat changed based on the competition, with usually about twenty to thirty minutes to just surf, catch the best waves possible, and get rated on a point scale. They usually only counted the two best waves, and whoever did the best gets to move on. There were some more intricate rules about priority and line-ups, and apparently the judges kept track of that too. The waves were scored on a bunch of things that I never even knew were a factor in surfing.

I wasn't listening the whole time, not because I was bored, not at all. I'd listen to David read from the Webster's Dictionary for the rest of my life. But the way he smiled—the way his eyes lit up—how he was nodding along with the things he was saying, occasionally dropping my hair to demonstrate something with one of those perfect calloused hands—it was hard to focus on anything but how fucking radiant he was.

Sophie had been helpful, pointing to various things or offering information while she sat beside me on the sand. Ryan was down the beach somewhere near the competition tent. He knew a bunch of people competing. It was quite a juxtaposition—everyone on the beach spectating spread out across blankets and in various states of bundled up. It was practically summer for me in comparison to a Chicago fall; I was the only one not in a sweater. Just a long-sleeved black shirt under the Sam quilted down vest. Sophie was overdressed, at least to me. Some sort of pink nylon cropped Prada puffer jacket and mini UGGs made her look like she belonged on a ski hill.

She had gone to get us coffee from one of the tents before the heat started. She said it didn't really matter if she missed it; David was going to win anyway. The way she said it was so nonchalant, like it didn't matter to her, she was just so used to it, that her brother was so good at something. And maybe it didn't matter to her. But it mattered to me. I wanted to see every single second of it. I wanted to watch him and commit every little spray from the waves to memory, to keep them in that extra compartment in my heart that was reserved for David Kennedy.

"Sorry, the line was so long. No wonder, it's fucking freezing." Sophie's manicured hand popped in front of me, holding out a nondescript takeout cup for me.

I raised my eyebrows as I took it, and she dropped beside me. "It's really not."

Sophie shook her head, her slicked-back blonde ponytail moving back and forth while she took a sip of her coffee. "Maybe not for you. But David still had to wear a 3mm wetsuit today."

She gestured with her coffee toward where he was out in the water before tipping her head back and shrieking David's name at the top of her lungs. "He used to hate when I did that at competitions when we were kids. He said it distracted him."

I smiled, the idea of David as a too-serious child warming me. "I can't imagine anything shaking David. He's entirely unflappable, always the calmest one in the room. More logical than the rest of us."

"He was like that when we were kids too." Sophie raised her eyes, smiling fondly and waving toward the water, like he'd be able to see her, and maybe he would in that pink coat. "So serious but somehow so—"

"Childlike? Playful?" I offered, tipping my head to look at her.

Sophie snapped her fingers and took another sip of her coffee. "Yes. You get it. Somehow he's the most mature one in the room, but he'd have no problem pushing you in the pool the second he got a chance."

It was true. My favorite juxtaposition that was David.

"He's like that with us, too. I think Deacon would probably have fallen off a cliff by now, Tripp would have been punched so many times he'd probably need a nose job, Taylor would have no one to rile up, and I'd be..." I trailed off, because I didn't want to think about it, not really. What it was to be without him. I'd been without him before, and no matter the time, distance, and space that separated us, life with David was much better than life without it.

"You'd be?" Sophie tilted her head, a small smile playing on her mouth.

I raised my eyebrows and took a sip of the coffee. There was a time I would have said lost—and I had been a lost girl then. But I wasn't now, and I didn't think I would be again. But I would be so, so lonely without him. Without his love. "I'd be someone missing a very, very vital part of her heart."

"Good answer." Sophie knocked her coffee against mine before leaning back, dropping one hand to the sand.

"Do your other brothers not surf?" I asked, studying her as she puckered her lips and shrugged.

"No, not really. I mean, Jackson and Ryan might fuck around on the water back at the house, but they wouldn't do a charity tournament or anything like this. Nothing David would do. They did a bit when we were all younger, but he was just so much better than them, and it took the fun out of it for two young, ultra-competitive boys really quickly."

That made me smile. I liked the idea that he had something just for him that he excelled at. Nothing he had to share with anyone else. He deserved it. I looked back out to the water, where I could see him pushing down on his board and those fucking arms slicing through the water when he paddled toward a wave. "You know, I have this dream..."

I paused, because it was so like the words I had said to her brother all those years ago when I told him I dreamed about being someone who didn't hurt him, being someone who spent her life making it up to him. He told me about the multiverse—that maybe there was a version of us out there somewhere who were still together. I wanted to be those people so fucking badly; I clung to that maybe he gave me for the better part of two years.

But I was glad we weren't the people we were then, or any of those people out there living together in those other universes. I liked this version of us, where we were at last. A home, but not one built solely on the foundations of one person sitting up on a pedestal. Two imperfect people whose flooring, trusses and framing and siding and windows and doors—they all fit together.

I blinked, Sophie still smiling softly at me, expectantly. "I have this dream. Where I liquidate my shares in WH, or maybe I never had them to begin with. But every day, it's just this. Me and him. Your brother out there doing what he loves. I don't know what I would do, but it's us. Just us...living."

Sophie's voice was quiet. "You wouldn't want to do what you do?"

"I don't know. I like the idea of sustainable investing. It's important. But I don't know if this is what I would have chosen, what choice I even would have made if I was allowed to make different ones. My whole life...you know I'd never been in a truck until your brother rented one? How stupid is that?" I laughed, nestling my coffee in the sand and wiping at my eyes. "Your brother was the first person to see me, who peeled back my skin, flayed me open with all that he is, and took my hand so I could step out of that fucking Winchester suit I'd been wearing my whole life. Maybe that's why I'm so obsessed with him and always will be. Trauma bonds and all that."

"I wouldn't call what you two have a trauma bond. I don't think people who look at one another, who see one another the way you two do, can simply be quantified as a *trauma bond*." Sophie offered, cocking her head to study me. "All of that is true, I can tell. I can see it. Why aren't you two still together?"

I closed my eyes briefly behind my sunglasses, shielding them from the glare and the impending tears. "I hurt your brother. Immeasurably."

"But he hurt you, too." Sophie's voice was low, consoling, and I turned to look at her. She pushed her sunglasses up her face, her nose wrinkling, and those eyes that were so like David's looked endlessly sad.

My voice cracked when I spoke, because it was true. "Yes, very much so."

"We could never figure out...Ryan and I, why he got back together with Victoria. It was so obviously about you—everything my brother does is about you—and it just felt unduly harsh and cruel. To you, and to her. It felt so...unlike him. Not when he's usually so...good."

I exhaled, a tiny puff of air flaring my nostrils. "You know your brother doesn't like to be called good? He thinks it...reduces him to some sort of boring singularity."

Sophie scrunched her nose, shaking her head, and a tiny laugh escaped her. "What book did he read that convinced him he needed to be some morally gray love interest?"

I smiled at that, shrugging, and picking absentmindedly at the lid of the coffee cup. "I'm not sure, but I think some of what I did might have made him think it was a bad thing, to be who he is."

Sophie nodded, taking another sip of her coffee and turned to face me. She tipped her head, all her features impossibly soft. "You hurt him. He hurt you, and here you are...what is it? Three years later, and you still look at each other like that? Seems kind of like a clean slate to me. A fresh start, state of grace...whatever you want to call it."

"Do you really think people get a clean slate?"

I wasn't sure we did, and honestly, I wasn't sure we should. All these things that happened to us in our lives to make us who we are...it seemed too convenient that we could just wipe it all away, and I didn't think I wanted to. I wasn't proud of so many things I had done in my life, but they all led me here.

Sophie puckered her lips again. "Metaphorically, sure. I think people are capable of forgiveness."

She paused, looking at me pointedly before lowering her sunglasses and leaning back on her elbows. "And I think people like you and my brother would be really fucking stupid not to try."

I studied her for a moment longer before turning and looking back out at the water to where David was, back in the lineup now and too far away for me to see those stars, those galaxies that lived in his eyes. But I could feel them winking at me, feel that part of my heart that beat just for him getting faster because he was out there.

He wasn't my friend, not from the moment I met him and his eyes lit up for the first time he heard me laugh, not when I felt those calloused hands on me, and he never had been. And I don't think I wanted him to be.

Charlie

David won. The tournament took most of the day, and he had only run up from the competition tent between heats once, hair plastered to his forehead and sand stuck to his wetsuit, with a thermal blanket wrapped around his shoulders. He stopped to kick sand up over Sophie—entirely childlike—while she shrieked and stood to brush off her pink Prada puffer jacket before crouching down and brushing his thumb across my cheek. He grinned at me, ruffling my hair before jogging back down the beach. It was just a moment—just a minute—but it was stretching, endless like the ocean behind him, which really and truly paled in comparison to David's eyes.

I'd been so desperate not to fall into David, not to drown in him the way I had before; it never even occurred to me that I wasn't the person I was, and neither was he. We weren't those people who fell in love behind closed office doors, who flirted openly in the conference room before fucking on the table after hours. He wasn't someone I felt the need to hide things from, and he wasn't someone I didn't feel good enough for. He saw me then. A different version of me, the one I showed him in an attempt to keep him, but he saw me now, too.

The last rays of sunlight stretched across the ocean, slowly inching backward from the Kennedy family pool. I could see it where I leaned over the edge of the hot tub on the second floor veranda, the warm water bubbling around me. I wouldn't admit it to anyone, resolute that Chicago prepared me for any weather, but it was a nice reprieve from the night air. It was getting cold.

A groan sounded from behind me, and I turned, watching David close the sliding glass door and step out onto the deck, blue Ralph Lauren swim shorts riding up his muscled thighs to reveal a dusting of golden hair. "I'm so fucking sore. I'm getting old, Charlie."

Smiling at him, I raised my eyebrows when he groaned again, stretching his arms across his chest in turn as he crossed the deck.

"Can't hack it with the twenty-year-olds anymore? You are thirty-one, after all. Practically geriatric."

David grinned at me, one leg raising, thigh muscles tensing when he dropped into the water. Another groan, and I watched his throat vibrate, the noise reverberating against my skin, all the way down to my heart, and causing my own thighs to clench under the water. He dropped his head back, arms spread out, and rolled his neck back and forth before looking up at me. "If it weren't for the fact that I wake up every day in your bed with a raging hard-on, then yes, I would have to agree. I'm getting old."

He smiled when he said it, and his eyes lit up in the fading sun, but my heart caught on my ribs. He wasn't old, not by any stretch of the imagination, and neither was I. We were impossibly young, a whole lifetime ahead of us, with these beautiful, sparkling, clean slates just waiting for the next parts of our lives to be scratched, entirely messy, but hopefully not disastrously the way they had been before.

But what hurt was thinking about the twenty-nine-year-old David I fell in love with and those two years, those two birthdays I missed. He was an early July baby, and that fit, because he reminded me of summer—the possibility of a day that stretched forever. I had just left for London both times the date rolled around, nothing to offer but a perfunctory happy birthday text. The first year, the worst year really, when he turned thirty—I paced around my apartment all night, gnawing on my thumb until it was practically bone, until I finally landed on what to say. It was a simple, "Happy Birthday, David." At the time, I wanted to commandeer the next British Airways flight and throw myself onto his doorstep. He said "thank you," because he was endlessly polite, and I spent the rest of the night stalking Deacon's Instagram for a glimpse of him, my glass of wine kept generously topped while my thumb tapped away, story by story by story.

He turned thirty-one when I landed myself at Oxford. It wasn't as desolate, as lonely to be without him. We had talked on the phone while I wandered around aimlessly. He was home—still in his apartment back in New York, drinking a beer by himself and we talked until the clock rolled past midnight.

It didn't hurt in the way it used to; I didn't want to drop down to the center of this hot tub and beg for forgiveness, carve my heart out in penance. It just hurt because David was important. They were dates I didn't want to miss. I wanted to wake up next to him when he turned thirty-two; I wanted to be the first thing he saw to start his year.

I blinked, shaking my head slightly and offering him a tiny smile. "Sorry. I was just thinking. About all those years between us."

"Only three, Charlie," David offered, his voice rough.

I nodded. "Only three, but a lifetime, don't you think?"

David cleared his throat, raising one hand off the back of the hot tub and rubbing his jaw. "When you first came back, came home, you told me you—"

"Had this dream," I interjected, my voice soft. I tipped my head, ends of my ponytail brushing across my shoulder before falling into the bubbling water.

David's eyes moved with it before snapping back to my face. He nodded. "Had this dream. In your dreams, it was just you and me. You didn't do that to me. You spent the rest of your life making it up to me. But I don't think I like that dream anymore, Charlie."

"Oh?" My voice was barely a whisper, hardly discernible above the sound of the jets. We were too far apart.

David shook his head, and leaned forward, resting his hands on his knees under the water. "I don't think I liked it then, but I was too proud to admit it. I have a different dream for us. One where after I've made it up to you, done everything I need to do to prove to you that I'm worthy of *you*, we're on equal footing, no pedestals, no mistakes. Just me and you, the best girl I've ever known."

My lips parted, and I said nothing, gaze tracing every part of him I could see above the water—the ropes of muscle that spanned his bronzed shoulders, the tense lines in his neck while he waited on seemingly bated breath for me to answer, those rogue waves of his golden hair, almost entirely pushed off his face save for one wet strand that had fallen across his forehead. Stubble lining his jaw and the ever-perfect planes of his face. My voice was soft. "That's quite the dream, Mr. Kennedy."

David smiled, a muscle in his jaw feathering before he swallowed. "What do you dream about?"

Him. Always him.

It had never stopped, not really. He was always all around me and always would be. But it used to be this sort of suffocating layer of skin I couldn't get off, all my mistakes pressing in on me and never letting me breathe properly, reminding me that I had David Kennedy and lost him. Now, it was just this. Us, wearing nothing but the way we loved each other, skin truly touching for the first time ever.

I inhaled, my teeth coming to worry at my bottom lip.

David's eyes dropped to them, and I watched his pupils dilate.

Swallowing, I tipped my head. "What I did—what happened between us—it used to be the thing I said if I had one wish, I would take it all back. But I'm not sure that's true. I wish I hadn't hurt you. I'd take that back. But I...now, I dream about this. Just me and you. Always just me and you."

David's nostrils flared, and all that light that lived in his eyes went out; they were impossibly dark. "Come here."

"Mr. Kennedy, that's not very polite. You should at least say please." My words were just a rasp, and David rolled his shoulders, eyes entirely focused on me.

His voice was rough when he spoke. "Baby, over here. Now."

Baby. No billion dollar, just me and him.

Smiling at him, I leaned forward. "I forgot how bossy you are. So controlling, Mr. Kennedy."

I hadn't forgotten, not for one second. And it was taking every ounce of my control not to throw myself at him, to wrap around him and map every inch of him with my hands. The peaks and valleys and all of the muscles that spanned and made up the entirety of him were the same. But they were a path I hadn't walked in too long.

"Charlie." David cocked his head, rolling his shoulders again.

This was my favorite him—not just this, how he was when it came to being with me. Even though I loved it, I did—it was the pieces of him that only I got to see. He was good, so good—too good for this world—but he was endlessly playful, thoughtful and steadfast, and far too controlling when it came to being together like this. Day to day, he'd hold any door open for me, pull out any chair and wait until I sat, drop kisses to my forehead, and look at me with those eyes that saw right through me—but when it came to this, he'd wrap my hair around his fist and fuck me until I couldn't see straight.

So many parts of David were just for me, and they all came together to make this perfect him, but right now, this one was my favorite.

This version of him had my teeth digging into my bottom lip, had me pushing against the back of the hot tub to close the minimal space between us. This version of him had my hands snaking across his chest and his shoulders to wrap around his neck, fisting the back of his hair. My knees came to rest against either side of him—the ridges of his obliques pressing into my thighs.

David's hands found my waist, fingers gripping my skin as a groan left him. Somehow, his pupils had expanded even farther, and he dropped his forehead to mine. His hips flexed upward, like he couldn't help it, and my back arched involuntarily, pressing down into him.

"I love you. I've always loved you." David's voice skittered across my skin until it traversed my ribcage, my heaving chest, and sunk through all my skin and bones, burrowing into my heart. "I'll be whatever you want me to be, baby, but I've fucking missed you, and I've missed fucking you."

Rolling my own hips, I pressed my forehead against his. Our lips were just a breath away from finally, finally touching. I could feel him between my legs, and everything was already hot, entirely on fire. I loved him. I always had, and I always would.

He was David Kennedy, and I was me.

Our lips crashed together at the same time. After all this time, all these years, we were kissing, and it was so fucking different but so fucking perfect.

One of David's hands moved from my waist to splay against my back, pushing me down into him, while the other stayed there, gripping me and starting to roll my hips against his.

I felt a groan reverberate through his throat when our tongues met. It was entirely too sloppy, like two people starved for air finally, *finally*, getting that first breath of oxygen. And maybe that was true. After all this time, we were finally breathing.

David's teeth caught my lower lip as his hand pushed into my back, and his hips flexed upward.

It was too much, him between my legs, his hands all over me, and our hearts beating against our chests in a desperate bid to get to one another. Everything ached, and my skin was too sensitive—the water bubbling against it and the wet material of my bathing suit clinging to me—all the while David's hands, his perfect hands, pressed into my back, pushing my hips down against his and gripped my waist, rolling it against him.

Arching back, a moan fell from my mouth, and David's lips were on mine again instantly, like he wanted—needed—to swallow it, to feel every single noise all the way down to his bones. My teeth sunk down on his bottom lip, and I pulled back for a moment, dropping my forehead to his.

"I love you," I breathed, my voice nothing more than a tiny pant.

David's hands tensed against me, and he paused the rolling of my hips, a low groan coming from his throat. "You're going to make me come."

"I'm not moving," I whispered, fingers twisting and grabbing at the damp hair curling at this neck.

"You don't need to do anything to drive me fucking crazy, Charlie." David's voice was rough, and his hands tensed on me again. Our eyes were so close, and usually, I could still see his sparkling, but they were all pupil, blown entirely wide. "But that, hearing you say that again, after all this time..."

My thigh muscles clenched, and I would have laughed, teased him if we were anywhere else—in any other situation where he wasn't straining against his swim shorts, pressing right against the center of me. If we weren't on the precipice of us, I would have laughed. But there was nothing funny about it. Rolling my hips, I dropped my mouth to his, telling him again, because I did love him. I loved him, I loved him, I loved him. He was David Kennedy, and I was me; that was all there is to it. "I love you."

David's mouth met mine, his lips rough and his teeth scraping against me, like he couldn't wait, couldn't possibly get enough of me. "I'm not kidding. I'll go right in my fucking shorts like a teenager. Let's get you inside."

David's hand left my waist, only for a moment to wrap around my back along with the other one, and in one smooth motion, he stood, pressing me firmly against him. My legs tightened, and David's eyes closed momentarily, nostrils flaring as he rolled his neck. He brought his lips to mine, and they were softer, just a brush this time, and I could barely hear the whispered words, but I didn't need to. I think I'd know David's lips, the way his mouth moved to say "I love you," even if I was trapped in the dark, all senses lost.

Turning, like it was effortless that he was holding all of my weight—and maybe it was because he'd always held all of me any-way—he stepped out of the hot tub, his lips never leaving mine, con-tinuing to move, to spell out all those letters that made up those words, over and over and over again.

The entire way to the still-open sliding glass door, David Kennedy told me he loved me.

His mouth was still moving against mine, articulating the words be-tween tiny kisses, nips of his teeth, and the slide of his tongue against mine when he paused for a moment, one hand dropping to pull the door shut.

"Not going to kick the door shut like in the movies?" My teeth pulled at his bottom lip.

"Hard to kick closed a sliding door, but you tell me to, and I'll shatter every window in this house." David's voice was nothing more than a groan against our still-joined lips as he carried us across the hallway.

His room was at the other end of the stretching, exposed hallway that spanned the top floor of the house, and was entirely visible to anyone walking by on the ground floor or outside really, thanks to the arching, practically floor-to-ceiling windows.

I paused, fingers tensing in his damp curls and pulling my mouth back from his. "Ryan and Sophie—"

David shook his head, one hand fisting in the back of my hair to bring my lips back to his. "Gone. I told them to fuck off. They went to Jackson's for the night."

"Presumptuous, Mr. Kennedy."

His lips spread into a grin against mine, and David shook his head again. "Hopeful, baby."

He paused, pivoting and actually kicking open the door to his bedroom this time. He never wavered, not once, and I didn't slip an inch down the hard ridges of him when he dropped a hand again to slam the door shut.

Our lips broke apart, our breathing heavy as we stared at one another. There were still no stars in his eyes, no sparkling honey, but they were still my favorite eyes on the planet, and those were still my favorite hands holding me.

"It's you and me?" David asked, his rough voice bordering a whisper.

"Yes." The word was out of my mouth before I even had a chance to pause, and there was no pausing, not really. Because it was—it had been from the first moment I grabbed his tie in the office, and he swept everything off my desk and fucked me on it. We were different people then, and I think we were probably each in love with different people then, too. But maybe that was the beauty of it all—some people stayed stagnant, stayed in love with the version of the person they first met, and some people grew together. Some people fell in love with each new version of one another.

That was better than any multiverse version of us that were still there in that old life.

I wouldn't trade this one for the world.

His mouth was on mine, a tangle of tongues, and my hands practically pulled his hair while he gripped my waist and pushed me against him. I felt myself rolling my hips, practically begging for any little bit of friction. His arm tightened around my back, the other dropping and slowly pushing my thigh down, and as it dragged, the center of me dragged against him, and a tiny gasp escaped me, his teeth coming down on my lip with a groan.

Slowly, I dropped my other thigh, pressing into him, and my breath hitched. My hands were still tangled in the back of his hair, my head now tipped up so it could meet his lips.

David's hands found my waist, and I felt his calluses skim against my still-damp skin, a shiver running down my spine. He pulled back from me suddenly, and a small whine left me. He dropped his forehead to mine, lips parting, and all the lines that composed him tense.

"I work for you," he started, his voice entirely too rough, hardly measured at all, like he was losing his restraint. "I work for you, but you remember that in here, you listen to me."

"So bossy," I whispered, but heat skittered across my skin, and my stomach clenched.

David's hands snaked up my waist, traversing my ribcage before one came to the back of my bathing suit top, tugging roughly on the string dangling down from the plain black WARDROBE.NYC triangle top.

I felt as it came undone, the fabric shifting and grazing against my skin, still covering my chest, only because the string around my neck remained tied.

His other hand slid up my side, gripping my ribcage for a moment before his thumb stroked under my breast, moving under the fabric and over my nipple.

My head tipped back, mouth parted. A tiny moan tumbled from my throat as his thumb stayed there for another moment, circling, before his hand came to the back of my neck, where he tugged roughly on the tie to the bathing suit. The damp fabric fell across my chest, landing on the ground between us.

David's hand stayed wrapped around the back of my neck, his calloused fingers gripping my skin. His eyes were dark, and a heavy breath escaped him as they traced my shoulders, down my collarbone, and across my chest. A muscle in his cheek jumped, and I watched his jaw tense back and forth.

"Nothing you haven't seen before," I whispered, eyes practically closing at the feeling of his hand at the nape of my neck.

"Maybe not." David shook his head before releasing my neck and running a hand through his hair before he dropped to his knees in front of me. His hands found my waist, fingers starting to twirl the ties of my bathing suit bottoms. "But every time I look at you, I swear it's like the first time."

Swallowing, I dropped my hands to his shoulders, his muscles tight under my fingers. "Mr. Kennedy, on his knees before me in his childhood bedroom. Whatever would the executive team and the board think?"

David's eyes flashed, his fingers pulled at the ties on either side of my hips, the bottoms coming undone, and he let them fall to the ground at my feet, palms finding my thighs and his fingers grazing my ass.

"Baby." David leaned forward, teeth grazing the inside of my thigh before his mouth dropped to the center of me, tongue running upward. "Who do you listen to?"

My fingernails dug into his shoulders, head dropping back, and another small moan fell from me.

David's tongue dragged upward again before stopping, his shoulders tensing under my hands. His words reverberated against me, another moan, louder this time, coming from me at the sensation of his mouth moving against me. "Fuck. I've thought about the way you taste every day for the last three years."

My breath hitched as his tongue started in slow, deliberate circles, his fingers digging in and gripping against my thighs, bringing me closer to him. I wanted to watch, to look at him, and to memorize the way the muscles in his shoulders looked underneath my fingertips, all that unkempt hair and those rogue waves—the way they looked against my abdomen—how the muscles in his back shuddered, like he was seconds from losing control.

It was too much. Too perfect, too right. His tongue against me, every nerve ending in my body on fucking fire. "David—you're going to—"

"I'd make you come all night if you let me. Every night for the rest of our lives." David's tongue swirled lazy circles for a moment longer, like he meant it. Like this was just the start of it all—the rest of our lives.

"I want you," I whispered, half a moan, while my fingernails dug farther into his shoulders.

David paused, one final drag of his tongue, before pulling back and looking up at me. "You have me."

Shaking my head, my thighs still tense, and all of me entirely aching because of him—for him. "Inside me."

"Come first." His hands tensed against me for another brief moment before he stood, guiding me backward to the bed that took up the center of the room.

Tipping my chin up, I was about to protest. To tell him the only thing I wanted, more than the world, was for all of his weight, all of him—his heart, everything—to be suspended overtop of me, to be inside me. But my legs hit the back of the bed, and in one swift motion, David bent, hands cupping the underside of my knees and practically tossing me backward onto the bed.

A tiny shriek of laughter escaped me, but David was already pulling me toward the end of the bed. He dropped to his knees, grip tightening around my legs, and his eyes flicked up to me.

Pushing up to my elbows, I tipped my head, watching him as he sat there, all of me bare to him.

"I love you." His voice still rough, and the muscles in his shoulders still tense. His pupils were wide, but I could still see them—all those galaxies and all those stars—and I wanted to get lost in them forever.

Teeth scraping against my bottom lip, I shook my head slightly. My eyes burned, and tears started to well because after all this time, we were finally here. Finally home. "I love you, too."

That was all it took, and David's lips dropped to the sensitive skin on the inside of my thigh, tracing up—his tongue there, followed by a scrape of his teeth all the way up, back to the center of me.

My head dropped back, and the breathy noises from earlier long gone—the way his tongue moved against me, the way it had all those years ago but somehow infinitely better, because maybe we were better versions of the people we used to be.

"Louder." His words reverberated against me, having their intended effect, because hearing him, knowing who it was devouring me, the noises coming from me were louder than a moan.

An orgasm was an orgasm—but then there was one given to you by David Kennedy, by the love of your life. I don't think I'd ever felt like this—light and honey and home, and all the good things in the world. My words were punctuated with something between a gasp and a scream. "Don't stop."

His grip tightened around my legs, his words muffled, because his tongue didn't stop. "Never, baby."

I wanted to watch him, to never look away again, because he was mine and I was his after all this time, but my eyes closed, and I think the stars, those ones that lived in him, were exploding behind them.

"Make that fucking noise for me again." David's teeth grazed against my inner thigh again, and his hands finally released my legs.

Tipping my head up to look at him, still on his knees before me, eyes kind of wild to match those rogue waves of his hair, I bit down on my lower lip. "Make me."

That grin, the one that was just for me, split across his face, and he stood, those still-damp swim shorts clinging to his muscular thighs, leaving nothing to the imagination before he pushed them down and kicked them off.

His perfect, calloused hands on my thighs again as he bent over me, dropping his lips to each side of my hips, his stubble grazing my skin, just me and him, nothing between us but the kisses he left there. We said nothing, but my hands tangled in his hair, and I closed my eyes as I laid back against the bed, each brush of his mouth as he made his way up my body—my hips, my abdomen, my ribcage, my chest, my collarbone, my shoulders, my neck, my jaw.

We said nothing, but I could hear all the words echoing between us. *I love you. I'm sorry. Home. Home. Home.*

Suspended over me now, I untangled my hands from his hair, running them over the broad planes of his shoulders before traversing the tapered muscles in his back.

David's breathing was labored, his lips hovering above mine, each brush featherlight but setting every part of my body on fire.

"Condom," I breathed, nails scraping against his back. "I haven't been with anyone since you, but—"

David stilled, the muscles in his arms taut as he was suspended above me. "We'll go get tested as soon as we get back."

"Romantic," I offered through a laugh. But it was, because I couldn't think of a single thing on earth more beautiful than the idea of our skin touching with nothing in between us.

He grinned, rolling his shoulders, and pushing off the bed.

I thought about pushing up again, watching him move through the room like this, but I pressed my hand to my chest instead, where my heart beat against my ribcage, tangling up there just like it used to, but in this desperate beat of happiness instead of grief and sorrow.

I loved him, I loved him, I loved him.

But I loved myself, and he loved me too.

Closing my eyes and smiling through some of the tears that managed to trickle down my cheeks, I felt all sorts of things—but mostly warm all over and entirely loved—as David moved up my body again, smaller, more urgent kisses this time until he was above me.

One of those perfect, calloused thumbs brushed across my cheek, and he dropped his forehead to mine.

Bringing my lips up to his, he stilled before his hips flexed, and he pushed into me, a strangled groan sounding in his throat. We stayed like that for a moment, neither of us moving, but together in all the ways you could be together. Me and him.

Turning and brushing my lips against his inner bicep, my hand wove into the waves at the nape of his neck, and my back arched up to meet him as he started to move.

David Kennedy and me, after all this time.

David

"One more." My teeth grazed Charlie's ear, and I tightened my arm around her ribcage, hand splaying across her sweat-slicked skin. My other hand was between her legs, moving in slow circles, where it had been for the last God knew how long.

Time didn't really mean anything to me anymore. My life split down the middle last night when she told me it was me and her: the time before that and the time after. I was living in a world where she was mine, and I was hers, and that was the only defining feature about this period in my life I needed to know.

"I can't." Her breaths were just these tiny little pants now, probably my favorite sound she'd ever made, second only to her laugh.

"You can." Biting down on her earlobe and rolling my hips upward as I pressed my thumb down against her, a moan caught in her throat. Her head dropped back against my shoulder, her fingers digging into my forearm where I held her up, pressed against me while I fucked her kneeling in the middle of this bed we'd hardly left since last night.

I felt her clench against me when she came, and a groan caught in my throat. I wasn't far behind.

I'd come pretty much instantly after she did all night and this morning. There was probably nothing that felt better to me or turned me on more than knowing how good she felt—that I was the one who made her that way.

My shoulders tensed, and I bit down on the side of her neck, my arm tightening around her. I held her there, her head still back on my shoulder, the column of her throat exposed, and her eyelids fluttering closed as our breathing evened out.

I'd never let her go again.

I would have said the best night of my life was the first one with her, on her desk in the office after hours. That would still be the night my life changed forever, permanently altered and sent on a different trajectory because Charlie Winchester crashed into my life. But it wasn't the best one anymore.

Last night, the start of the rest of my life, would forever be etched as the first chapter in the book of me.

Pressing my lips to her shoulder, I trailed tiny kisses toward her neck before landing on her jaw.

"You alive in there, baby?" I felt her smile, and I didn't have to see her to know it was a real one. A Charlie smile, nothing Winchester about it.

"I should be asking you the same. You have more stamina than a thirty-one-year-old man should. Is this what it would have been like with twenty-one-year-old David?" A laugh tumbled from her, and she finally extracted her fingernails from my forearm.

If I looked down, I'm sure there would be half-moon indents in my skin from her nails.

Her fingers traced the letters of her name, inked on my bicep, lazily, unhurried, like we had all the time in the world. And we finally did.

Pressing one final kiss to her jawline, I grinned against her skin before gripping her hips and slowly extracting myself from her with a groan. "Twenty-one-year-old David probably wouldn't have had a fucking clue what to do with you."

"Oh?" She craned her neck, perfect forest eyes glittering in the early morning light filtering in through the window. "The frat boy version of Mr. Kennedy unable to perform in bed? Too selfish, like most boys that age?"

Shaking my head, my hands tightened on her hips. "I mean, I'm sure I was, but I'd probably have blown it in about 3.5 seconds, leaving you wildly unsatisfied. Girl of my dreams now, and I don't think twenty-one-year-old David could have dreamt you if he tried."

Charlie's hands brushed against mine, slowly extracting herself from my grip, before she shifted toward the edge of my bed, swinging her legs over the side. She reached her arms above her head, all that chocolate hair brushing across her bare back as she stretched.

There was definitely something fucking wrong with me. I'd turned into some sort of predatory animal overnight, because I could feel myself starting to get hard again. Groaning, I palmed my jaw. "Don't do that."

"Do what?" Charlie glanced over her shoulder, hands intertwined above her head.

"Stretch like that." I shook my head, moving forward to wrap my arms around her again. "Your hair moving across your skin like that...I'll have you on your back in five seconds flat again if you keep it up."

Her head tipped back, and a laugh that bordered a cackle echoed across the room. It was so at odds with how she looked right now—practically serene, early morning sunlight dancing across her bare skin, and her lips swollen from mine.

But it made me love her more.

Charlie contained multitudes, whether she always saw them or not, and I loved them all.

"You might *actually* be twenty-one again. Nothing but a sex-crazed frat boy. At least let me shower and make me a coffee before you accost me again." She raised her eyebrows at me, pointedly dropping my hands from where they were gripping her hips again and standing to take a measured step away from me.

Grinning, I held my hands up. "You go take a shower; I'll go make you a coffee."

"Are you telling me there's no fresh, steaming French press of coffee on an ornate, antique silver tray waiting for me outside this door?" Charlie smiled, her voice teasing, and she gestured toward the closed bedroom door.

"Do you want there to be?" I asked dryly, my eyes tracing the jut of her collarbone, the swell of her chest and the taper of her ribcage, all her skin on display, to hips that had no business being the exact size to fit perfectly in my hands. The most beautiful girl in the world.

Wrinkling her nose, she shook her head softly. "No. A nice, normal drip coffee in a nice, normal coffee mug, followed by a nice, normal morning with you, sounds far better than anything left for me on an antique tray ever could."

"Alright baby, a nice, normal morning it is." I stared at her for a moment longer before jerking my head toward the shower, visible through the open ensuite door just beyond her. "I'm serious. You need to get in the shower before I drag you back here, and there would be nothing normal about what I'd do to you."

Rolling her eyes, she crossed her arms, which really only served to accentuate how perfect she looked right now, before turning on the ball of her foot and slamming the bathroom door.

A nice, normal morning. The start of the rest of my life.

But there was nothing normal about Charlie, and I was the luckiest man on the fucking planet.

———

"You call this normal, Mr. Kennedy?" Charlie tipped her head back, leaning against my chest, and smiled softly at me. Her hands were wrapped around a still-steaming coffee mug—a chipped white Ralph Lauren porcelain one that had been shoved into the back of the kitchen cupboards, and the most normal one I could find.

"What? Coffee made by me, not a paid member of family staff, a random blanket I found in the linen closet, an old sweater—" I paused, pulling at the ancient Princeton sweater draped over her shoulders before gesturing to the stretch of beach and the lazy lap of the waves against the shore. "Water, sand. Natural, normal phenomenon of the Earth."

Rolling her eyes, the corners of her mouth twitched up, Charlie looked back toward the water.

We were sitting, wrapped up together, just beyond the boardwalk that led down from the back of my family home, the stretch of private beach empty, save for us.

Pressing my chin to the top of her head, I tightened my grip around her. My coffee was forgotten beside me, the mug haphazardly shoved into the sand in favor of holding her instead.

Charlie brought her coffee to her mouth, taking a small sip before moving one of her hands in a sweeping gesture toward the water. "Oh, yes, nice and normal private beach." Her words were punctuated with laughter, and she ran her fingers across the blanket covering her legs. "What thread count is this? Feels expensive."

Grinning, I shook my head. "Not a fucking clue, but it was folded neatly on the top shelf of the linen closet, so you're probably right. Far too expensive to be on display in the common areas of the home."

I didn't have to see her face to know she was smiling. I could feel it in the way her head shifted against my chest, how her shoulders rolled back against me, far more relaxed than she usually allowed herself to be.

She pointed toward the shoreline with her coffee. "Can you surf here?"

"You might get some baby waves, depending on the time of the year. When I was competing, I'd fuck around out there every morning and just practice different things, nothing crazy dynamic but different pop-ups, different approaches."

Charlie tipped her head back again, blinking up at me. "Is there anywhere in the world that has good surfing all year?"

Nodding, I pressed my mouth to her temple. Not for any particular reason, just because I could. Touching, kissing, sex, and fucking, and all the shades in between were back on the table. Normal for us again. "Kind of depends on the level of wave you're looking for. But Hawaii is great year-round, Bali, South Africa, Australia."

"All nice, normal places." She teased and smiled up at me before leaning back against me, nestling closer under the blankets. Her voice was soft. "Is it wrong that this feels so nice? Not normal, necessarily, because nothing about you makes me feel normal, but...right, perfect. Like maybe everything is as it should be. That everything will be okay."

Frowning, I tightened my grip around her. "Why would that be wrong?"

"I don't know. Nothing should feel okay right now. It would be kind of rude for me to run home and traipse through the halls shouting about how everything is finally working out for us, you know, what with the impending implosion of my brother's life, the malignancy taking my father down cellular brick by brick..." I felt her shrug against me before she continued. "Tripp dragged back here from whatever hell he was living in Boston. I don't know...I don't want to hurt anyone."

There was a time that would have bothered me, bitten at my ego, and sent me raging that he was even a remote priority for her.

But there was nothing like that all over me, under my skin. Just her.

"It's okay to be happy, Charlie. But if you want this to stay between us for a while, that's fine with me. I'll wait as long as you need me to."

Her voice grew raspy, the way it only ever did when she was turned on or teasing me. "Does that mean we get to have secret sex in the office again?"

A grin stretched across my face; it was for her—what she called her classic David Kennedy grin, even if she couldn't see it. "I'm counting on it. It'll make getting through endless calls with self-important shareholders and CEOs much more tolerable if I know I get to lay you out on my desk afterward."

Her hand pressed against my face, and I leaned into it, eyes closing at the feel of her hands on me again after all this time. My favorite place in the world. My favorite person. The start of the rest of our lives.

"I'm not sure your desperate pursuit of normal will ever come to fruition. But if you can settle for things feeling just right in entirely abnormal circumstances, I think we're looking at a pretty spectacular life ahead of us." I lowered my voice, moving my mouth to the shell of her ear.

No one was out here, but the words were just for her.

"Settle? Nothing with you is settling, Mr. Kennedy. Just right, perfect, but entirely abnormal sounds better than anything I could have imagined for myself." Her voice cracked, and I dropped my chin to her shoulder.

"Me too, baby." Just right. Perfect. Entirely abnormal. Whatever it was, I couldn't fucking wait.

Charlie

The hallways of my family home were quiet, just as I'd left them. There were no visible signs of Deacon's destruction, but most of those probably lingered under the surface anyway.

I could see the cracks in the foundation of him as clearly as I'd been able to see my own. He certainly wasn't helping matters—all the scotch and cocaine were probably aiding in the disintegration of whatever my brother was made of.

David had gone to check on him as soon as we got back, partly to make sure he wasn't going through another priceless bottle he'd stolen from our father's collection, and partly to make sure Noa hadn't strangled him yet and didn't need any help burying the body.

We'd parted at the staircase in the middle of the house, only moonlight stretching across the flooring, one brief brush of his lips against mine when he took my bag from me. I went left toward Taylor's room, and he went upstairs toward our wing of the house.

My feet felt lighter as I padded toward her cracked open door. All of me felt lighter. I had endless things to be sad about, all these ghosts to scare me in these haunted halls, but none of it really bothered me tonight. I could deal with my brother and my father, and the general impending doom of our family tomorrow.

Tonight, I wanted to bathe in the light that was David Kennedy just a little longer.

Knocking gently against the heavy door, I dropped my head to the polished mahogany frame. "Hey, I'm back."

One perfectly brushed eyebrow rose on Taylor's forehead, and her eyes flicked up to me. They looked lighter than usual, juxtaposed against the brown silk of the fucking ridiculous Boheme feather-trimmed Sleeper dress she wore. Her fingers paused mid-keystroke, and I watched her fold her hands together, like some sort of movie villain, and straighten her shoulders against the velvet headboard. "Something's different about you."

I shook my head. "Nothing's different."

I was lying. I didn't want anyone to know what *was* different—what changed between us, until I had the chance to talk to Tripp. I should have known Taylor would be able to sniff it out, like some sort of designer-wearing bloodhound.

"Hmm." She pursed her lips, eyebrow rising a fraction higher, before she patted the empty space beside her. "You sure you haven't decided to move to the Outer Banks, take up surfing?"

"I'm sure." I smiled softly, pushing off the door, and padding across the impossibly lengthy floor to drop onto the bed beside her.

Peering over her shoulder to see what she was working on, one of the obscene feather's from her nightgown brushed against the bottom of my chin, and I moved back, swatting it away with my hand. "Jesus, Taylor—how can you sleep with those things?"

Her eyes widened, pillowy lips parting, and she lurched forward, abandoning all pretense and letting her computer fall off the bed as her hands pawed at the hood of my sweater.

"Stop! What are you doing?" I slapped at her wrists, but it was useless. Taylor was fucking tenacious.

Her fingers found my neck, thumb pressing down on a decidedly sensitive spot of skin. A knowing sort of glint flashed in her eyes, and she looked positively feral as her features sharpened into a look of smug superiority I could probably recognize in the dark. "Charlie..." she was practically purring, her lips pulling up into a shit-eating grin that could have rivaled Tripp's. "If nothing's different about you, why do you have a hickey on your neck? Did you fall into a time machine? Go back to when we were in prep school, and it was in vogue to wear your love bites with pride?"

"Stop touching it, you fucking weirdo." I slapped at her hand again, attempting to shove it away from my neck.

Her eyes narrowed in on me, and she finally crossed her arms, one eyebrow rising on her forehead again. "Well?"

My hand found my neck, covering up whatever she could see. I didn't even realize it was there, but the skin was tender. I could feel David's teeth against my neck—but in fairness, they had been everywhere—all over me from the moment we left that hot tub. We had hardly left his bedroom, so it was difficult to know when it might have happened. I certainly wasn't giving any thought to the fact that I was a thirty-year-old vice president at one of the most lucrative holdings in the country who probably shouldn't have hickeys all over her neck. I only cared that it was his mouth, his lips, his tongue, his teeth—him—all over me.

Rolling my eyes, I dropped my hand, fingers fiddling with one another. "Would you like me to recount in vivid detail how I ended up with a hickey? Surely, you know the mechanics behind it all, doctor. When someone sucks—"

"Someone? Someone wasn't sucking on your neck," Taylor interrupted, her voice dropping and becoming uncharacteristically soft. "Unless you took up with some sort of vagrant surfer—it wasn't just *someone* who had their lips on your neck. David Kennedy isn't *just someone*, and he hasn't been since the moment you met him."

"No." I looked up at her, lips pulling in a tiny smile and my eyes stinging. Wiping at my lash line, I shook my head, Taylor becoming just a feathered blur. "Not just someone."

"Tell me everything." Taylor reached forward, her hands that were too rough, too worn from all the hours washing them and all the antiseptic chafed against my skin, but I really didn't mind. It was comforting, probably one of my favorite things in the world. She brought my hands to her chest for a moment, over her heart where those ridiculous feathers were, before dropping them to her lap.

Smiling, thick with tears, I tipped my head to the side, a laugh bubbling in my throat. "Well, when two people love each other very much—"

A grin stretched across her face, and her fingers tightened around my wrists. "You and the golden retriever. The great love of your life. I take it he wasn't very nice if that unsightly mark on your neck is any indication."

"No." I shook my head, smile widening and practically splitting my cheeks while tears rolled down. "He wasn't very nice."

"Orgasms?" Taylor arched an eyebrow, her words a sad attempt at coming off wry, but the excitement that lit her features leaked into her voice.

I nodded, wrinkling my nose at her. "Several."

"Well, it has always been him." She offered, her voice matter-of-fact.

"It has." I nodded again, bringing our joined hands to my own chest.

Taylor smiled at me, a soft one that had no business on her usually sharp face, and if I had been anyone else, any other person on the planet, I would have said it was a trick of the light. But her eyes glistened, and her voice cracked. "I'm so happy. So unbelievably happy for you."

"What? You're not going to tell me not to fuck it up this time?" I asked, a poor attempt at humor.

"No," Taylor answered plainly, but her chin tipped back, her features becoming haughty. "But I do have some choice words for DK."

I clutched her hands to my chest for a moment longer before dropping them. "I'm sure you have a very public...something planned for him. But can it wait? I'm not sure if it's the best idea to make it public knowledge, yet."

"You haven't told Tripp?"

I shook my head, biting at the inside of my cheek. "Not yet. I really want to be the one to tell him. I just—"

"Steven's death gala is in two days, Charlie." Taylor pursed her lips, looking like she was about to reprimand me, before she shook her head and held up her hands. "No, you know what? This is special—this is the thing I have been waiting for since you two started your little...platonic sleepovers. We're getting drunk—let's go steal some of Steven's expensive liquor."

"It seems kind of...gauche to steal from a dying person, no?" I arched an eyebrow, but my smile was still there, unmoving, taking up half my face and maybe just a permanent part of me now.

Taylor's expression soured, and she reached over, plucking her phone from the end table. "Should we make Deacon do it?"

I nodded. "Absolutely. Tell him we need him to bring it to us. He has nary a shred of conscience left. Tell him to grab the Clase Azul and stop in the kitchen for limes."

Taylor nodded, one finger rising while her thumb swiped across the screen of her phone. She snapped her fingers as she finished the text before looking up at me, her smile wide—stretching, endless, like so many things in my life, but this, this was happy. It would be a fond, forever-infinite memory. This moment with my best friend in the entire world, one part of my soul who wanted to celebrate the hickey on my neck.

But it was more than just blemish on my skin, just like David Kennedy was more than just someone. Just like I was more than a rich girl, a lost girl—maybe after all this time, I was just me again. The Charlie Winchester, whoever she was, found at last.

Deacon

Despite my general frivolity, in any battle of wills, I tended to win. In my personal life, in the boardroom—wherever, whatever.

Except there was no way I'd win this staring contest with my phone because there was no way my fiancée was going to text me first. We were barely speaking, and when we did, everything I said made her cry.

It didn't even have to be anything important. We stayed in bed practically all weekend while my sister flitted off to North Carolina, doing whatever she and Kennedy got up to in whatever friendzone they were living in.

Usually, weekends in bed with Noa were my favorite. It wasn't just the sex that would inevitably occur, albeit that was consistently mind-blowing and better than anything I'd ever experienced beforehand. I had mentioned that to David once, early in our relationship, and he'd cut me an incredulous look, asking me if I'd ever had sex with someone I loved before. I said no because I'd never been in love before, and he widened his eyes at me before turning back to watch the hockey game we were at.

It turned out he had a point. Being in love made everything better.

It made staying in bed all weekend, watching cartoon movies—Noa fucking loved cartoons—something I would usually consider to be a huge waste of time, my favorite activity on the planet.

We'd usually accompany those marathons with more bottles of wine than we probably should have, with breaks in between that were just sex and laughter.

But this weekend, we'd mostly slept. Or maybe it was mostly me, curled up on her, like some kind of child and nothing to offer by way of conversation other than to tell her I didn't care what show or movie she put on. Or the sound of me audibly swallowing another Vicodin my dealer dropped off because Taylor refused to write me a prescription for pain meds, and my hand was still fucking throbbing.

Each time I shrugged, offered her some bland or banal response, she looked at me like she didn't even know me. Couldn't recognize this version of me that cared so little about everything in between bouts of feeling entirely too much and lashing out at everyone around me.

I couldn't really recognize this version of me, either.

A knock sounded against the doorframe, and I broke away from staring at my phone. Tripp was leaning in the open doorway of my office. I tried keeping it open today, not that it made much difference when I'd scared everyone away.

Tripp shoved his hands into the pockets of his navy Emporio Armani wool single-breasted suit. Any other day, I'd have been irritated that it was nicer than the one I was wearing. "Ash needs you for a call with Aman at ten."

"He can put it in my calendar." I shook my head, and Tripp raised his eyebrows, pushing off the door frame to leave, but I tipped my chin to the empty chair across from my desk. He was the only one who could really stand to be in my presence.

Saying nothing, he strode into the office, all maddening indifference, surveying the walls like he expected there to be holes in the drywall before dropping down in the chair.

I could see Charlie just beyond the doorway, standing in the middle of the floor, talking animatedly to David. He was smiling down at her, like whatever she'd said was the best thing he'd ever heard. "What do you think they were up to during their little weekend in North Carolina?"

"It's none of my business, man," Tripp answered, but his words felt forced. He rubbed his hand across his jaw before continuing, "She never belonged to me to begin with."

Pulling my head back, my eyebrows came together. "You're telling me you wouldn't have fought for her?"

"I might have entertained it, but come on, you're her brother." Tripp offered me a wry grin that didn't quite meet his eyes, stretching both hands behind his head, leaning back in the chair. "You have a choice, me or Kennedy; who do you really want your sister with?"

My lip curled up. "Fucking neither of you, man. You're both disgusting."

Tripp rolled his eyes before folding his arms over his chest. "What's this art gallery thing your dad keeps going on about? I've gotten like four emails reminding me I need to be there, and I'm expected at the whole event. No absconding back to Boston early. He went as far as to offer me a room in the guest wing at the house for the week."

"Fuck if I know. Steven Winchester, patron saint to shitty Chicago artists." I twirled my phone between my fingers before shoving it in my suit pocket.

Noa wasn't going to cave and talk to me first. Shrugging, I kicked my feet up on the desk. Usually, I would have been worried about scuffing my Ferragamo leather oxfords, but I was tempted to just throw my whole wardrobe out and start again. It had all gone too long without proper dry cleaning or polishing, in the case of these shoes that looked decidedly dull.

I narrowed my eyes at them before flicking my gaze back up to Tripp. "Kind of like you, patron saint to Winchesters in need. First my sister, now me, the office pariah."

Dropping his head against the back of the chair, Tripp let out something that might have been an exhale or a scoff. "You could stop being the office pariah if you'd quit treating everyone like shit. Just because your sister puts up with it doesn't mean she should have to."

"What do you suggest I do? Call an office-wide meeting and make some impassioned speech about how sorry I am? How I'll strive to do better, but I hope everyone understands I'm only human?"

Tripp arched an eyebrow before pushing off the chair to stand. "You seem pretty robotic to me these days, Deac. But I don't know, maybe start with your fiancée."

Narrowing my eyes, I thought about yelling at him. Telling him that he couldn't speak to me like that, but I tried one of those olive branches my sister was always on about. Granted, it was a shitty one. "Steven wants to spend time on Cape Cod for Thanksgiving after the gala. You want to come? That house is probably more fucking haunted than the one in Lake Forest, but it might beat hanging out in SEC Violation Central."

Tripp paused halfway to the door, glancing back at me. "I'm not sure I should be gone for that long. My father's run out of things to bet. Only a matter of time before the house is next. It's his only unfrozen asset, after all."

"Oh, come on, if he loses the house while you're gone, I'll just buy it back for you." It was meant to be a joke, but I must have been losing my touch along with my sanity because Tripp only gave me a flat look before turning back to the doorway.

"I'll think about it." His voice carried over his shoulder, and he raised a hand. "Ash was serious. Ten o'clock with Aman."

I watched him stroll across the executives' floor, the same casual pace he always kept, stopping in the middle where David and Charlie still stood.

My sister's smile grew, and David reached out, clapping Tripp on the shoulder.

She'd arguably made a mess of things more than once, and somehow she'd come out relatively unscathed.

I pulled my phone out of my jacket pocket. Maybe there was hope for me after all.

For the second time in recent memory, I hesitated outside the door to my own bedroom, my hand feathering open and closed uselessly in space before landing on the door knob.

Rolling my shoulders back, I opened the door.

Noa's eyes were on her phone, curls pushed off her face and twisted into a messy knot at the crown of her head. Her skin was bare, cheeks pink, like she'd just gotten out of the shower. Her eyes lifted from the screen and she gave me a small, tentative smile.

It felt like she was waiting on tenterhooks, unsure about which version of me she was going to get.

I fucking hated myself. That this is what I was reduced to—had reduced her to—this tiny, uncertain thing.

Swallowing, I ran a hand through my hair, knocking it loose from the confines of styling gel. "I love you. I missed you today. Will you come over here? I think I need you."

Her face lit up, and a tiny shriek came from her as she pushed off the bed, running toward me and throwing her arms around my neck.

Burying my head in the crook of her shoulder, I wrapped my arms around her, the silk of her royal blue La Perla pajama set soft under my hands and her curls brushing over my face. But I didn't care. Groaning, I pressed my mouth to her bare skin.

One of her hands found the back of my head, tangling in my hair before she pulled my head back and pushed up on her toes to bring her mouth to mine for a brief moment. It was too quick.

Breaking away, she gave me a tiny smile, all full of hope and all the good things that she was made of, and brushed both her hands across my chest before leaving them over top of my heart.

I was never much for metaphors, but it was like I could feel that perfect hand reaching through all the muscle tissue in my chest and cradling my heart for me because it was too fucking heavy for my chest now. I fucking loved her, and I didn't deserve her. I dropped my hand to hers and was about to tell her that when the whole thing splintered right down the middle.

Her ring finger was bare.

"Where's your ring?" I'd meant for my voice to sound even, maybe even rough, but it cracked horribly. Kind of like whatever was left of my heart did at the sight of her empty finger.

Noa tipped her chin up, blinking rapidly at me, her amber eyes growing glossy. "Oh, uhm. It's just on the nightstand."

She gestured over her shoulder, the absence of that stupid fucking diamond cut at me. All those streams of light it usually caught were gone, but they still managed to flay my skin open.

"You haven't taken your ring off since I proposed." It wasn't a lie. That ring went on her finger, and it had never come off. Not even when she was working. She made photographers edit it out during print shoots and refused to take it off during runway.

Her lips parted before she bit down on the full bottom one. "We haven't even talked about the wedding in weeks. I just thought—"

Taking a measured step back, I threw open my arms like my heart wasn't fucking hemorrhaging in my chest. "You do know my father is fucking dying? I'm sorry if I don't want to talk China patterns and centerpieces with you."

"Baby." Her voice went quiet, and she wrapped her arms around herself, shaking her head softly. "Do *you* know your father is dying?"

Tugging on the ends of my hair, I shook my head, trying to keep my voice even. "I came home tonight ready to try, to fucking grovel! I don't grovel for anything, and I never have a day in my life, but I was going to grovel for my fiancée's forgiveness. But can you really be a fiancée if you took the fucking ring off?"

"I don't want you to grovel. I don't want you to be anyone but the person I fell in love with." Noa wiped at her cheek with her left hand, and a visceral hurt cut through my chest. It felt like my knees might buckle. She looked up at the ceiling and blinked rapidly. "Do you even want me to put it back on, Deacon? I'm not asking that to be hurtful. I want to marry you and I love you no matter what, but you aren't yourself right now. I don't know how to help you. I was just trying to take some of the pressure off."

Palming my jaw before scrubbing my hands across my face, I said the only thing I could think of that might spare her from the disaster that was me. "You should go, do Givenchy. I hate you just sitting here, day after day, waiting for whatever version of me that walks through the door that day."

Her voice was small. "I'll miss the gala."

Shrugging, I offered her a grin that I knew she found endearing, like I didn't have a care in the world, even though I had too many, and I was so fucking heavy. But I wrapped my arms around her, crushing her to my chest, and pretended for a moment longer that it was all going to be okay. "I've been to a gala alone before. If anything, it'll look good to shareholders. Like it's not that serious."

"I don't want to leave you," Noa whispered, her fingers digging into my chest. Her shoulders started to shake, and I could feel the warmth from her tears seeping into my shirt.

"I don't know how to keep you here without pushing you away." Dropping my chin to her forehead, my eyes found the hole in the drywall, still untouched. It hadn't grown or changed, but it felt like a chasm, yawning wider and wider each day, and soon it would swallow me whole. I didn't want it to get her, too.

Charlie

David's hands were on me the second the door to our bedroom closed, one wrapping around the nape of my neck and the other tugging roughly at the knotted crepe tie at the waist of my Cinq a Sept Elena Blouson minidress.

"What the fuck is this thing?" His voice was rough with impatience.

Slapping at his hand, I took a tiny step backward, shoulder blades hitting the door. "It's a dress. It's new, and it's one item of Sabine-approved clothing I actually happen to like. So, if you'd like me to undo it, remember your manners, Mr. Kennedy."

Grinning down at me, he pressed his palms to the door on either side of my head, caging me in. "Do you have any idea how hard it was to concentrate today?"

Giving him a flat look, I snatched the hanging tie away from his wandering hands. "How do you concentrate any day, David? I don't think your attraction to me materialized suddenly overnight while we were in North Carolina."

"I don't." He shrugged, his smile turning lazy and those honey eyes growing dark. "I've made some questionable deals for your company in my tenure at Winchester Holdings. You can blame these." One of his hands dropped to the semi-sheer blouse of my dress, tracing over the curve of my chest, his eyes moving with it before coming back up to my face. "And everything in here, and here." He punctuated each word with a brush of his lips: one to my forehead and the other right above my heart.

Wrinkling my nose, my heart beating erratically in my chest, I shook my head. "How do you go from practically a feral animal to a man who was surely written by a woman?"

One eyebrow lifted, and he grinned at me before dropping his lips to my jaw, his stubble brushing my neck in a way that had my hands finding his shoulders and nails digging in through the jacket of his charcoal Canali suit.

His mouth moved across my skin. "Easily. There's nothing about you that doesn't do something for me."

Dropping my head back against the door and angling it to give him better access to my neck, my eyelids fluttered closed.

His lips trailed from my jaw, down the side of my neck, where they paused against my shoulder.

I brought one hand to the back of David's head, twisting in the waves that had gotten progressively messier over the course of the day. Mine to touch and tug forever.

I wanted to remember this forever—the first night in this room that had become ours, where David Kennedy cradled my heart, let me cry, slept beside me, and held my hand when it all threatened to fall apart. Ran a bath for me because he had nowhere better to be, even when he did.

Someone had pulled back the curtains, leaving them tied off with silk on either side of the French doors that spanned the back of my room. During the day, the gentle slope of the lawn was visible. You could see the entire property when the sun was out, and at night, you could sometimes see the outline of the boathouse, silhouetted by any sailboats dotting the lake. But tonight, the entire structure was illuminated from within.

Splaying my palms over David's shoulders, I knit my eyebrows. "There's a light on in the boathouse."

"So?" David's words were muffled against my neck, where his teeth nipped at my skin, followed by gentle swipes of his tongue. "You can be concerned about the wasted electricity later."

"Only one person goes down there." I pushed into his shoulders, and he lifted his head, eyes cutting to the doors where the light could be seen flickering out there in the darkness.

Letting out an exasperated sigh, he shook his head before tugging on the ends of his hair. "I'll go."

Shaking my head, I offered him a tiny smile. "No, let me. I don't think Deacon needs tough love right now. I think he needs someone who understands. Someone like him."

A dubious look flashed in David's eyes, like he didn't quite believe my brother and I could possibly be similar. Our coping mechanisms might have differed greatly, but underneath it all, we were made of all the same things—the distance that stretched across our family, the ghosts that haunted these halls, and the cracks in the foundations of us we were born with.

It was just me and him against the world, after all.

———

The grass crunched under the soles of my sneakers, the frost glittering under the strips of light cast by my phone. I could have found my way down to the boathouse with my eyes closed—but I didn't particularly relish tripping and falling to an untimely death when a whole lifetime with David was waiting for me.

I took the stone path that ran alongside the house, cutting across the lawn where it evened out after the slope and rounded to the rocky shore that bordered the beach. The stone ledge, where I'd sat by myself, with Tripp, with David, over the years, was right there. I once thought of it as the scene that precipitated my great downfall, the beginning of the end. But maybe it was more of a tripwire—for all the things to come, both good and bad.

We hadn't kept boats here in years, not since before my mom died. I had memories of us sailing, the four of us out there on the lake, and there were photographs, so I knew they weren't figments of my imagination. But she died, our father grew too disinterested in maintaining them or too distant from the person he used to be. Deacon did sometimes, but mostly he sloughed all the responsibility of having a sailboat on employees at the yacht club. I always thought it had more to do with his commitment to and mastery of avoidance, but he was the only one who ever came down here.

The memories couldn't have been that bad if it was where he sought refuge.

It wasn't even really a boathouse in the traditional sense of the word, and it never had been. A dock did stretch out onto the lake on the other side, where our father kept whatever sailboat he was using at the time, and there was a smaller building where all the necessary maintenance supplies were housed, but I highly doubted they were tools Steven Winchester ever used.

Walls of windows stretched around it, between panels of polished black wood, revealing the room illuminated inside. It was more like a lounge than anything—a wet bar in the corner, padded leather chairs, smooth granite countertops, artfully arranged bottles of any type of alcohol imaginable, and a wine fridge built in underneath.

A buttery leather couch spanned practically the length of the boathouse itself. It had been custom-made by some designer years ago, specifically for this space, to exude comfort even on a property where there was none. A gas fireplace sat in the center of the back wall against a towering dark stone outcropping in the middle of the glass windows looking out onto the lake.

And through the sliding glass door, I could see the back of my brother's head where he sat on the couch—straight hair unkempt and tumbling over his ears, his shoulders swallowed by a too-large heather gray Ralph Lauren hooded sweatshirt he hardly ever wore, occasionally bringing a glass of scotch to his lips. His eyes glued to whatever ESPN replay he had on the TV mounted high on the wall, above the glass doors surrounding the other side that looked toward the water.

Knocking gently on the sliding door, I pulled it open, stepping through on tentative feet and closing it behind me. I couldn't remember the last time I'd been down here.

Deacon glanced backward, eyes dull under the low lighting, and turned back to the TV.

It wasn't a dismissal, and I wouldn't have left, anyway—the pain radiating off him was palpable, so I walked around the outrageous length of the couch to drop down beside him. Glancing up at the TV, I was going to ask him some inane question—who was playing, what was he watching, did he want me to stay, when I turned to look at him.

He was twirling Noa's engagement ring in his fingers, the diamond hardly catching the low light from the flickering flame, like the whole thing had dulled.

My heart plummeted through my ribcage, dropping down into my stomach. She wouldn't have left him. There was no fucking way. She was too good, too pure, too in love.

Lurching forward, I grabbed his forearm. "Deacon, why do you have that?"

He turned his head, and despite the uneven stubble peppering his usually sharp jawline, everything about him looked childlike and small.

Chocolate strands of hair falling over his forehead, and those forest eyes that were so like mine were entirely bloodshot. "I told her to go."

"Why?" I whispered, dropping his arm and rubbing my chest absentmindedly, like that would help the ache there. Watching my brother self-destruct had been one of the more painful things in my life, like watching a funhouse version mirror of me in the past make all the same mistakes in different fonts.

What was probably supposed to be a dry, irreverent smile crossed his features, and he looked at me for a moment longer before his eyes went back to the ring. He said nothing, staring at it—all dull and empty—so unlike what their love used to be, before he shoved it in the pocket of his sweater, like it wasn't a priceless, one-of-a-kind diamond, like it belonged there instead of on Noa's finger.

He took a measured sip of scotch, his voice rough when he answered, "You know why, Charlie. I'm drowning, and I'll fucking drag her down with me. I love her enough to make sure she stays on dry land in the sunlight where she belongs."

"The people we love, who love us, wouldn't let us drown, Deacon," I murmured, echoing Taylor's words, dropping my head to his shoulder.

He said nothing, occasionally swirling the amber liquid, the melting king cube knocking against the crystal.

I sighed through my nose, about to push back, to sit up and beg him to come back to the house with me, tell him that there was nothing he couldn't make right if he didn't try hard enough, that it would work out for him in the end the way it had for me.

But my brother spoke first and shattered my heart into pieces. "I don't want him to die." Deacon's voice cracked horribly, and I felt his shoulders shudder beneath my cheek, the first rasp of a sob catching in his throat.

My throat burned, and I pressed my eyes closed, the tears spilling over anyway. "Me neither." Pulling back, I wrapped my arms around his middle, burying my face into his back. My own sobs started to wrack my body, the two of us dissolving into nothing more than the two children we used to be and maybe still were—crying and crying and crying with no parents to comfort us.

"I don't want to be alone." Deacon buried his face in his hands, a choked sob catching in his throat.

Moving to sit back, I wiped at my cheeks, taking a shuddering inhale.

My brother's sobs echoed throughout the room, against my eardrums, and reverberated through the very center of me.

Reaching forward, I pried his hands from his face and gripped them between my own.

He turned to look at me, hair falling across his forehead, and his face that was so like my own, wet with tears, his mouth parted, and everything about him entirely hopeless.

"You're not alone." My words were small as I shook my head, gulped in air, and brought his hands to my chest. "You're not alone, Deacon."

And he wasn't.

Neither was I, and I never had been.

Charlie

The mist hanging off the lake had become a permanent feature the closer we inched to December. It was already what I would have considered winter in Chicago, but my father was still insistent on taking his breakfast outside. He'd at least started wearing a wool jacket over his suit.

I don't even know why he wore one every day. It's not like he ever took video calls, and even though he was no longer under strict orders not to go into the office, he'd made very clear his intentions to sue any reporter who took a photo of him with an IV pole until they had nothing left. The grounds for that would be shaky at best, but he didn't particularly relish looking weak in public either, so at home he stayed.

"Morning." I smiled softly at him, wrapping my arms around myself, the chill from the air permeating, despite the Sam vegan leather and down jacket I wore.

He glanced up from the stack of paper he held loosely in his left hand, the other wrapped around a steaming coffee mug. Judging by the thick, cream paper—they were WH financial statements. Steven Winchester preferred to preside over his wealth in a tangible format. No excel spreadsheets for him.

His eyes were back on the paper before he spoke. "How was North Carolina?"

"Good," I answered, pulling out my chair.

The staff had started leaving out two additional place settings each morning. One for me, one for Deacon, though his went untouched each day. I don't know if our father formally invited him the way he did me—an Outlook invitation sent for the next morning—or if he just hoped Deacon would show his face.

His eyes flicked up to me again. They always looked more gray than blue in the early morning sunshine, but today, they looked duller against the circles under his eyes. "Good? That's rather vague."

Shrugging, I flipped over my mug and poured my own coffee from the still-steaming press. "It was warmer than here, if that's what you mean. David won the tournament and gave the prize money back to the charity. It was something for turtles."

"Turtles," he repeated, one eyebrow lifting wryly.

"Turtles." I nodded, leaning back and tipping my chin up to the sky.

It was all mottled hues of gray, the clouds tumbling along ominously, but my heart floated in my chest, suspended where it was supposed to be instead of beating itself bloody and snagging on my ribs, while I bled out internally because the love of my life wasn't with me.

But he was with me.

My father said nothing for a moment longer, and I heard the papers rustle before his words. If I hadn't known better, I would have thought there was humor hidden there. "I was at the hospital with Taylor yesterday for a scan. She neglected to mention anything about turtles, but she seemed to think it was far better than *good* and shared far too much information with me. Including the fact that you two saw fit to empty what was left of a 15th-anniversary bottle of Clase Azul in celebration of just how *good* the weekend was."

The coffee burned my throat as I swallowed prematurely. Eyes watering, I dropped the mug and pressed my hand to my chest, like that would help my surely scalded skin, or the fact that my best friend couldn't keep her mouth shut and saw fit to discuss my sex life with my father.

"What are you two talking about?"

Whipping my head around, I was thankful for my brother's interruption until I saw how awful he looked. His hair fell across his forehead, pieces at the back sticking up every which way, and the bags under his eyes rivaling the permanent circles on our father's.

He still wore the same sweater from last night, looking decidedly rumpled, hands shoved into the pockets of his black Stefano Ricci jogging pants. They were tapered, so I supposed it elevated the look a bit, but not by much. He was usually long ready for work by now, and he certainly wasn't schlepping around the house with unkempt hair and last night's clothes.

He tossed himself down into the chair across from me, the place setting and steaming press waiting for him finally put to use.

Something flashed behind our father's eyes before they were back on the reports. "Your sister and David. It seems they've reunited."

Deacon jerked his head toward me, hurt flashing behind his eyes. "What? You didn't say anything last night."

"You were a little distracted." I widened my eyes at him, reaching out and grabbing his arm. "I would have told you. Apparently, Taylor likes to talk when she's supervising CT scans."

Deacon stared at me for a moment longer before a grin split across his face. It didn't quite meet his eyes, but I could tell he was trying. "About fucking time. Someone call down for champagne."

He grabbed the back of my head roughly, kissing my forehead. He dropped back in his chair, one arm thrown across the back, looking ever the quintessential billionaire boy without a care in the world. But I could see his broken heart all over him.

Our father cut him a look. "There'll be plenty of that at the gala this evening. You're both due back at the house by three p.m. Sabine and Rebecca want to get press shots before we leave."

A childlike noise rose in my throat. Press shots typically meant gold, fringes, and sequins. "It's a charity event at some new art gala. I don't think whatever she'll have picked for me is appropriate. Can you ask her to just bring over something plain?"

Finally setting down the report in favor of his daily glass of juice, our father took a measured swallow before speaking. "Sabine is under strict instructions to let you choose your own dress. She'll bring over whatever she has, but that's where her services end for the evening."

"Do I get to pick my own dress, too?" Deacon tipped his head to the side, his voice dry.

Rolling my eyes, I was tempted to reach out and pinch his arm, but the door to the terrace swung open again.

Taylor wasn't wearing her scrubs, but it was hard to tell what she was wearing underneath what was a wholly unnecessary calf-length black Moncler puffer coat that made her look like she was working at a remote research station in the fucking Arctic Circle. Her eyes swept between my father and me, a soft smile tugging on her features before her gaze snagged on Deacon.

Her lips curled up. "Look who decided to re-enter the land of the living. And all alone! No fiancée making sure you're functioning properly. To what do we owe the pleasure, Deacon?"

Widening my eyes at her, I began making a cutting gesture with my hands, but Taylor was laser-focused on my brother.

Deacon didn't bother to look at her, or anyone really; he simply stared out at the lake for a moment before swallowing. "Noa left last night."

Our father's features tightened, but he waited, saying nothing and appraising his only son.

"And where the fuck does she think she's running off to?" Taylor's eyes narrowed, her features turning predatory the way they only ever did when someone she loved was hurt. She might be furious with Deacon, and Noa might be her friend, but if she thought Noa did something to hurt him, she'd turn on her in a second. Our fucked-up childhood triad came first.

"Settle down." Deacon gave her a flat look. "I told her to go. For work. But it's nice to know there's some semblance of affection for me still living in that sterile heart of yours."

Pursing her lips, she marched across the terrace, coming to stand behind me and dropping her hand to my shoulder. "That was a stupid idea. You're liable to hurt yourself if left to your own devices."

"Well, it's a good thing I have you, *doctor*." He raised his palm, the angry red welt flashing in the early morning sunlight.

I pressed my hand to hers, worried I'd have to physically restrain her before changing the subject. "What are you doing? It's your day off."

"It is." Her voice sounded strained, so I tipped my head back, and she offered me a tight smile. "Steven, are you free to come back to the hospital with me? I'd like to repeat your scan. I called in a favor, and I can have the machine cleared for you when we go. The radiologist on-call sent me the images from yesterday, and they aren't as clear as we'd like. They're a bit shadowed."

"What does that mean?" Deacon's words were sharp, but I could hear all that hurt, all those tears and sobs we shared last night just underneath them.

I turned to face her, one hand gripping the back of the chair.

"Probably nothing," Taylor answered, her words softening when she continued. "Honestly. It just means there are some shadows showing up on the scan. Imaging can look off for a thousand reasons. It's just a precaution."

Turning back to my dad, I blinked, offering him what was supposed to be a reassuring smile but probably looked as pathetic as it felt.

If he was bothered, he didn't show it. Checking his watch—his preferred vintage Audemars Piguet—he glanced back at Taylor. "I have a call at 9:30. Afterward?"

Taylor nodded, smiling at him. "Sure. Whenever. Call me when you're done, and we can head over together. I'll just be in my room. I want to finish up some notes from last night."

He raised his eyebrows in response, and I waited for him to reach for the reports in a clear dismissal, but he cleared his throat. "Thank you, Taylor. On your way down, can you buzz the kitchen? Have someone on staff send up a bottle of champagne and orange juice. Whatever vintage is fine."

Her eyes widened, and her usual catlike grin stretched across her face. "Oh, are we celebrating the hickey on Charlie's neck as a family? How sweet. Who knew the golden retriever had it in him."

"Before I change my mind about the scan, Taylor," he stated, voice flat before he picked up the reports again. His voice was quiet as she left, sidestepping my attempts to elbow her or toss my scalding coffee on her, stopping once to ruffle Deacon's hair. "Though I do find my daughter's happiness and love a cause for celebration, yes."

―――――――

In my wildest dreams, all the years I'd fantasized about it, yearned for it—it had never occurred to me I might hate it. Fucking loathe and abhor it.

I had no idea how to pick my own dress.

"Help me," I hissed, tossing Taylor a pleading look.

Her feet were kicked up on the chaise lounge from where she lay spread across my floor. She claimed it would give the messy ponytail her hair was twisted into more volume. The Kiwi Carolina Herrera strapless column gown she was going to wear in front of the French doors. It was a bit bright for late fall, but something like that would never stop Taylor.

"Charlie," she rolled her neck so she was facing me, "the world is your oyster. Just pick the dress you like best. Try whatever on. They're all in your size."

"That's the problem." I whined, lifting one of the garment bags before letting it fall helplessly. "I have no idea what kind of evening gown I'd like best. I've never even been allowed to look through the racks before!"

"Poor little rich girl," Taylor crooned before offering me an exaggerated eye roll. A belabored moan came from her, and she swung her legs off the lounge and pushed to stand. "You know what you like, Charlie. You're just projecting because you're worried about your brother and nervous about your father making his first public appearance. Nothing's going to go wrong. I made sure he was chalked full of fluids and enough vitamins to probably cure one of Deac's hangovers."

Taylor came to stand beside me, dropping her chin on my shoulder, and lacing our fingers together. She squeezed her hand around mine *once, twice, three times.* "And when in doubt, just pick whatever you think David would like."

A snort escaped me. "That's hardly helpful. He liked that fucking Ralph Lauren sequined monstrosity Sabine made me wear to that yacht club event! The one that made me look like a mermaid?"

"Hey—I liked that dress. So some might say he has great taste." Taylor squeezed my hand again before beginning to look through the rack of gowns. "There's nary a sequin to be seen, that should make you happy."

I gave her a flat look before moving around to the other side of the rack and pulling the zipper on the first gown hanging there—a sheath of black velvet spilled out. Flicking my eyes up to her, I moved to the zipper on the second gown. I liked this one. "Will you wait for me to try some of these on?"

She smiled at me—it was one of those catlike Taylor grins, but the way her eyes shimmered, it was something only a best friend would be able to see. Like the looming idea of me with choice, agency, feeling entirely at home in my own skin at an event, made her happy. "Who am I kidding? You out from underneath Sabine's Oscar de la Renta-loving thumb? I've been waiting for this moment for practically my entire life."

***

In a bitter twist of irony, the gown I liked ended up having ruffles. But they were contained to the skirt. The Zac Posen Midnight tiered ruffled gown had more movement than I was accustomed to—the corset-inspired, sweetheart neckline bodice wasn't suffocating me. The dress even had thick straps.

I certainly didn't take up any extra room in the back of the stretch town car. It wasn't quite a limo. My father avoided those whenever possible because he considered them to be the height of tacky, but it might as well have been one; there was enough space for practically the entire leadership team.

He actually had Rebecca stagger the entrances that way. Guests, like Taylor and her parents, interspersed with members of the WH Executive team. Seeing as she managed to have everything timed down to the millisecond, David and Tripp should have just stepped out of their car with Ash as ours pulled up to the curb.

We would be the last ones to enter.

Even dying—the man still wanted to make an entrance.

"Where the fuck even are we?" Deacon's lips curled back, and he craned his neck to peer through the front window. "I don't think I've ever set foot in this part of the city."

"We're in the arts' district, Deacon." I widened my eyes at him, waiting for some semblance of recognition to flash behind his eyes, but none came. "Pilsen, Deacon. You know, the neighborhood? There's like thirty galleries between 18th and Halstead."

He blinked, and I waited for a snide remark for him to say that he considered the neighborhood to be undesirable, but he tugged on the black bowtie around his neck before turning to our father. "What's with the vested interest in the arts? This some new world for you to conquer? What's next, you'll buy a theater and become a thespian?"

Our father's usually impassive face looked strained for a moment. His fingers even drummed on the armrest. "No, but I did have a long vested interest in your mother's art. This was a...dream of hers, before I suspect she stopped dreaming at all. It's for her as much as it's for you two."

"What are you talking about?" Deacon's voice was flat, and his face paled.

We'd never even been able to find a companionable middle ground as far as our mother was concerned. I'd started to equate it to two islands without a bridge in between—one inhabited by me and the glimpses of our mother's ghost that grew more and more frequent, more welcome. And the one inhabited by my brother, an adamant fortress bolted so tight, without so much as a window for a spirit to slip in during the night.

I'd never really been sure where my father lived, assuming he was just in some tiny slice of land somewhere out in the sea while the world raged on around him, and he felt nothing—until I'd seen those small tributes to her, hidden in plain sight. Her favorite bistro set. Her art, lovingly kept and preserved.

I shook my head, lips parted, and entirely unsure what to say. I had no memory of my mom ever talking about supporting a gallery or even being a patron of the arts' scene in Chicago in general. It wasn't like she needed to worry about the money, she could have done whatever she wanted.

Saying nothing, our father cleared his throat and straightened the lapels of his custom Ralph Lauren tuxedo. The car had rolled to a slow stop, and he was already swinging his legs out of the door that was opened for him.

Deacon's nostrils flared, and he shook his head before ducking to follow our father out of the car.

I was always the last one out. Usually because whatever dress I'd been stuck in took the longest or required the most fussing to straighten before it was photo-ready. My brother usually waited for me so he could block any last-minute adjustments I needed to make.

But I stepped right into his back when I tried to leave the car, because he hadn't moved at all. I braced his shoulders to keep from stumbling. This wasn't a good place for a fucking photo op.

I pinched the back of his arm before taking a smooth step around him, plastering one of my more demure Winchester smiles on.

Cameras were flashing—several of them. But my brother wasn't looking at them.

He was looking at the sign for the gallery, the soft lightning illuminating it from underneath.

The beautiful penmanship, I recognized, from the corner of countless paintings, blown up and painstakingly etched on a sleek, white sign hanging above the glass doors.

The Claire Winchester Center of Art.

"Move Deacon," I hissed under my breath, firmly pushing my palms against his back. His feet were rooted there on the sidewalk just beyond the town car, whether by his own accord, or the hands of all his ghosts had finally caught up to him and held him there. "You have to move."

Cameras continued flashing, and I kept my smile plastered across my face like nothing was wrong.

Like we'd known our father was about to drop a bomb on us in the form of a newly minted art gallery that looked to take up every floor in a converted, three-story loft, dedicated to our mother, after never so much as speaking her name out loud for the better part of a decade.

My heart beat erratically in my chest, my throat felt like it was closing in, and I wasn't sure there was any air left in my lungs.

Giving my brother one final shove, I brought one of my hands to grip the crook of his elbow, pressing firmly through the jacket of his navy textured wool Corneliani tuxedo.

Deacon glanced sideways at me, the set of his jaw tense before he schooled his features, his lazy, billionaire boy smile falling into place. It didn't meet his eyes, but I wasn't sure any of his smiles had reached them in a long time.

The walkway to the gallery entrance wasn't long—our father had already reached the door, shaking hands with a photographer I didn't recognize before stepping into this gallery, this testament—whatever you wanted to call it—that he'd built for our mother.

Raising my hand toward the still-flashing cameras one last time, I gathered the tiered ruffle skirt of my gown and directed my brother in through the still-open door.

The doorman shut it behind us, effectively sealing us in with our father in the entryway and whatever parts of our mother he'd imbued into these walls.

A family of four again, after all this time.

The dim lighting overhead cast shadows across the three of us, and an unattended front desk with distressed leather padding sat pushed up against the wall to our left, where the same sign with the gallery name was hung on the wall behind it. A dimly lit hallway with strategically hung Edison bulbs and wall sconces opened behind our father, and I could make out the faint din of chatter rising from where I assumed the main room of the gallery was.

Ripping his arm from my grip, Deacon rolled his shoulders and neck before turning to our father, his words biting. "A little heads up would have been nice."

Our father simply cocked his head, surveying Deacon, like he was a particularly interesting opponent in the boardroom. "And had you known, would you have come?"

Deacon's nostrils flared, the muscles in his neck tightening.

"I thought not." Our father continued after a beat of heavy silence. "This is for you both, as much as it is for your mother. Do try to enjoy your evening."

Folding my arms across my chest, my voice cracked horribly when I looked at my father, tears threatening to spill over and ruin the painstakingly applied makeup. "What is this, Dad?"

"A gallery," he offered dryly before clearing his throat and continuing. "It's ultimately yours to do with what you please. But it was an idea of your mother's, a very long time ago. A place for her work to hang permanently, to feature other local artists to build their profile and provide exposure. I've hired a curator who will be responsible for acquisitions, and I've left it up to the two of you whether you'd like to turn this place into something profitable. For the next six months, all proceeds, other than the commission that belongs to the artists, will go to various community mental health programs around the city."

"I need a fucking drink." Deacon palmed his jaw, shooting our father one last look of disdain before turning on the heel of his Gucci loafer, and stalking down the hallway into the crowded reception room.

We both watched him go and whatever invisible string that tied us all together again—father, mother, sister, brother—snapped when he stepped into the other room, that fake smile falling into place again as he greeted a passing waiter with a tray of champagne.

"This is lovely," I murmured, looking up at my father through eyes that were clouding over by the minute. Swallowing, I shook my head. "I just wish it'd come sooner."

My father stared at me for a moment, and if it hadn't surely been a trick of my own blurred vision, I would have thought his eyes might have misted over, too. "As do I."

He cleared his throat before extending his elbow to me. Offering him a soft smile, I stepped forward on tentative feet to place my hand in the crook of it.

I'd lost count of how many galas and events I'd attended with my father. But I could count on one hand how many of them we walked into together—as a family, as a father and a daughter, not as a dutiful child following along and trailing in the wake of a man she didn't quite understand—one.

This one.

Tripp

I recognized the signature from the gallery sign in the corner of some of the paintings interspersed throughout the gallery. Claire Winchester.

"Her signature looks almost exactly like Deacon's." David gestured with his champagne flute toward the painting in front of us. It was abstract—with four distinct swirls of emerald that I was fairly certain were supposed to represent Charlie and Deacon's eyes.

Squinting, I nodded. "It does. He's always had freakishly neat penmanship. You know their mom was such an artist?"

I'd known her for longer than him, something that used to be a point of pride for me, somehow justifying whatever base need I felt around her. But I'd never known that.

He nodded, swallowing a sip of champagne. "Yeah, Charlie showed me some of her work a few weeks ago. She was talented. Apparently, Deac can actually draw, believe it or not."

"And there's Chuck. She can barely even write her signature neatly. It's—"

"Just like Steven's," David finished for me, tossing back the rest of his champagne and setting the empty flute on the passing tray of a server. He shoved one hand into his classic black Armani A-line tux and tipped his chin toward an empty cocktail table nearby.

Swallowing the rest of my champagne, I dropped the flute on the same tray and followed after him, careful not to catch the toe of my Prada loafer on the stone floor. It wasn't nearly as polished as the likes of the marble in the Winchester Holdings' offices.

A muscle ticked in his jaw, and he looked like he was seconds from pushing onto the balls of his feet to get a better look at the crowd. He was looking for Chuck; it would be obvious to anyone who knew him. She was like a fucking homing beacon for him and always had been.

It made me uncomfortable, just another reminder of all the things I'd done that had nothing to do with him, nothing to do with Charlie, and everything to do with whatever was broken inside me. As a thirty-two year old man, I shouldn't still be blaming my actions on my upbringing. But the sterile environment I was raised in didn't lead to much personal nourishment. I'd been taught my whole life if you wanted something, you took it. And I'd wanted her.

I cleared my throat. "How was North Carolina?"

His eyes did one more sweep of the party for her before he looked back to me and nodded, those unshakeable manners falling back into place. "It was good. Thanks for asking, man. Everything okay at home?"

Ignoring him, I arched an eyebrow and knocked my knuckles against the white table cloth, "You win?"

David gave me a flat look. "Of course I won."

"Jesus, first the bowling, now this. I had no idea you were so fucking competitive." I shook my head, raising my other hand to the nearest server, weaving through the crowd with a fresh tray of champagne.

He shrugged, eyes cutting to the doorway again, like Chuck might suddenly materialize. "I started competing when I was eight years old. Hard habit to break, I guess."

I said nothing, pulling my phone from my pocket again to check it, even though I hadn't felt it go off. I wasn't even paying attention when the two new glasses of champagne were left on the table. But that was one of the perks of having Kennedy around—he might be the love of your dream girl's life—but he'd never forget his manners when your own were severely lacking.

His thank you was entirely genuine, and he went as far as to clap the server on the back before handing me the crystal flute. His eyes narrowed as I shoved my phone back into my pocket. "You've checked your phone ten times since we got out of the town car. Everything okay?"

I debated lying, brushing it off the way I had whenever anyone other than Steven Winchester asked me that question. I don't know if it was the fact that he was dying, or maybe he'd always been like this and was just too stubborn to show any kindness, lest it be misconstrued for weakness—but he'd checked in almost every day since the charges were filed.

But all that lying, everything I did that made me a lesser person over the last three years and even before that—the fact that I had my hands on someone he loved when I had no right to, and he was still showing me kindness—had me shrugging and taking a sip of champagne instead. "My dad's under house arrest. And before you ask—multiple SEC violations. Only kept out of the press due to the generous reach of Steven Winchester's arm."

David nodded, a crease forming between his eyebrows before he looked at me with what might have actually been concern. "That's where you've been? That's why you gave everything up? For a man who can't even abide by the fucking rules set out by the Securities and Exchange Commission?"

The words hung between us. We both knew what everything meant.

I shrugged again. "A lot of people don't abide by those rules, DK."

But he shook his head, like he couldn't possibly understand who'd pick anything, anyone, over Charlie Winchester. "What's done is done, Tripp. What are you doing still wasting your time back there with him?"

"Making sure he doesn't get desperate and gnaw his ankle off in a bid for freedom," I answered dryly before staring down at the bubbles breaking through the surface of my champagne. "Blind loyalty. I don't know anymore. There's nothing for me there."

He looked like he was about to say something, and knowing DK and his impeccable fucking manners, it was probably some impassioned speech about how there was something for me here, and there always had been.

But for the first time in my life, I was grateful for the arrival of Taylor.

"Boys," Taylor purred, practically floating to our table. She held a sequined Bottega Veneta clutch between her hands, and the lime green column gown trailed behind her, fluttering in an invisible wind. The color wasn't in season at all, but on her, it looked good.

David grinned at her, throwing one arm around her shoulder and bringing her in for a hug. She leaned into him, smiling, before she looked pointedly at me, her features pinched as she spoke, overly saccharine. "TB."

"Doctor." I inclined my head, that same lilt to my voice that always annoyed Chuck, finding its way out to annoy her, too.

Taylor narrowed her eyes, but before she could share whatever retort she'd surely been storing up all day, David's eyes snapped to the right.

I didn't have to turn to know Charlie was there, but I did, because maybe I was a masochist and wanted one last look at her that no one else would be able to see.

She always looked beautiful, but tonight, there was something special about her. She wasn't fidgeting or pulling at the neckline of her dress. Her hair was parted down the middle, teased ever-so-slightly at the crown of her head to give it a bit of volume, and tucked behind her ears to reveal a pair of pearl earrings I recognized immediately.

They were the same ones she wore to that New York Public Library event back in New York. I recognized them from the photos I'd seen online of her and Kennedy, all moony-eyed and staring at one another. I'd committed them to memory, because I noticed the sheer size of them right away and wondered if it were those pearls crushing my windpipe for a moment, not my shattered, stomped-on heart.

Deacon was only a few steps behind her, one hand shoved into the pockets of his pants, the other clutching a scotch. Charlie raised a hand before turning and practically dragging him toward our table.

He looked like he'd seen better days, that was nothing new, but everything about him looked dull—like a fucking light had gone out. And maybe one had. "Where's Noa?"

Deacon made a non-committal jerk of his head before tipping back his scotch. "Milan."

Something like pain flashed behind Taylor's eyes, a rare instance of humanity, before one of her wide smiles spread across her face, and she snapped her fingers. "This feels familiar. Like déjà vu, perhaps. There was another time we all stood around a cocktail table like this." She paused, snapping again before pointing at Chuck. "I know. After the Forbes party. You were in feathers, and you—" Her gaze landed on me, and she lifted one shoulder before continuing, "—were also there."

Charlie cut Taylor a look before giving an exaggerated shudder, a tiny smile playing on her lips when she glanced back to her brother. Probably the one person on the planet she loved more than David Kennedy. "Sometimes I can still feel those feathers against my skin. Fucking horrifying."

"We can toast to those feathers being forever immortalized on the cover of a magazine. Tequila?" Taylor leaned forward, dropping her chin to her elbow, drumming the fingers of her other hand against the table.

It was subtle, but when Taylor leaned forward, I could see that David had rolled his shoulders back, his arm casually outstretched behind her to find the curve of Charlie's waist. The way his finger and thumb rubbed the material of her gown—it wasn't friendly.

Neither was the small intake of breath, the way she swallowed, these tiny movements most people wouldn't even be able to see.

I blinked. It didn't hurt as much as I would have thought. I was probably happier for her than anything. I'd like to think I knew Chuck better than most people, had the distinct pleasure of knowing more than one version of her too, and I couldn't think of anything she'd ever wanted more than him.

It was there, though—a spurt of blood through a tiny hole in my heart, dull pain thudding in my chest. A small wound, ripe for infection and rot, but it was nothing the tequila wouldn't be able to fix.

Charlie

Sabine finally extracting her claws after all these years and allowing me to pick my own dress probably didn't include me accessorizing it with my leather jacket to shield against the unforgiving cold coming off the lake.

She also probably wouldn't have been too fussed about me compromising the integrity of the gown by sitting on the stone ledge overlooking the water, either. But it wasn't the first time I'd sat out here, staring aimlessly at the stars rippling across the surface of the lake, listening to the waves lapping against the shore.

Not the first time—but I hoped it would be the last.

I wasn't sure why I came down here when we got back. Our father had stayed away from us most of the night, save for when he wanted to introduce us to an artist, and Deacon had done a passable job of feigning interest. You'd only know it was faked if you knew him well at all. His smile never seemed forced, and he knew enough about art to carry on a conversation about different brushstrokes and mediums.

But his eyes lacked that usual effervescent sparkle.

He'd pointedly ignored our father and dragged Tripp back here with promises of alcohol that would far surpass the quality of any he'd find in the minibar of his hotel.

They'd all gone down to the boathouse, but I'd excused myself and said I'd be down in a minute, ending up here, staring at the water. There was a painting hanging at the gallery that looked similar to this, at least I thought it did—all swirls of midnight and cobalt blue, eddies of yellow interspersed in a way that made me think they were the stars reflecting off the surface of the lake, and shades of gray around the edges that looked like the worn rocks that lined the shore.

Maybe my mother had sat here, just like me—in a different designer gown, in a different life.

The grass was covered in frost, and I heard the crunch of footsteps cresting down the hill. I knew they weren't David's footsteps—they weren't steady, unfaltering. These steps were lazy, unhurried, and could only belong to one person.

Glancing over my shoulder, Tripp raised his eyebrows before stopping beside me and tossing his legs over the stone ledge to sit beside me.

"It really is déjà vu from the Forbes party." I glanced at him, offering a wry smile. "Just sans feathers."

"I fucking hope not." Tripp's lips curled back. "I'm not proud of that, Chuck. I shouldn't have done that to you. Kissed you when you weren't mine to kiss. I'd take it back if I could."

Turning my head, his profile was thrown into sharper contrast by the moon hanging low in the sky—sharp jaw, dusted with dark stubble and frozen eyes. He looked almost the same as he did when he careened back into my life, and I upended the whole thing. "I wouldn't."

"You fell back in love with him while I was gone." Tripp's voice was quiet, but it wasn't strained. Everything about him looked resigned—even the creases in his suit jacket seemed tired.

"I was never out of love with him," I answered softly, looking out at the water. It seemed endless without any flickering lights from distant boats. "But I was never out of love with you, either."

I could see Tripp shake his head out of the corner of my eye. "But it's not the same."

"No, it's not," I murmured.

The words were true—all of it was true. But it hurt, my heart beat a little bit faster, and the back of my throat ached. After all this time, after everything that happened between us, I didn't want to hurt him. I'd used a lot of adjectives for Tripp finding his way back into my life over the last three years—weaseled, wormed, slithered. None of them had ever fit; they were just awful words of anger thrown at him because I didn't like what he reminded me of, how lost I was.

But if this body, this heart, this life were home—he had a place on the mantle of me, too.

"Would it have ever been us?" His voice was rough.

"Maybe. Yes. No. I can't answer that because that's not what was meant for you and me in this life." Turning to look at him again, I cocked my head. "Did you want it to be us?"

Tripp shrugged, tossing me a lazy grin that looked more rueful than anything. "I thought I did. But I think I was too busy taking what I thought I was owed for having a life that felt shitty and empty most of the time. It didn't occur to me that you might have been owed something better too."

My shoulders collapsed and I reached out, grabbing one of his hands in mine. "You helped me get something better, Tripp. In your own way. I think I owe you. All those years ago. Sitting here—me trimmed in ostrich feathers. If you hadn't kissed me…if I hadn't let you. I wouldn't be the person I am today. I wouldn't love myself the way I do, the way I deserve. I never would have found my way home." Shaking my head, I brought his hand to my heart before gently letting it go. "David and I would probably be married to entirely different versions of one another. I'd still be at WH in a job that wasn't meant for me. I wouldn't have you back in my life. I wouldn't trade any of it for anything."

Glancing down at his hand, he flexed his fingers before turning to me, those eyes unthawed and earnest. "Does he still make you sleepy?"

Smiling, I shook my head as tears started to track down my cheeks. "No, he makes me feel alive."

We stared at one another, and he offered me a resigned grin, eyes tracking my tears. His shoulders tensed under his suit jacket, like he might want to reach forward and wipe them away.

I knocked my shoulder against his. "Funny how things work out."

Tripp exhaled, his nostrils flaring, and he looked like he was steeling himself, preparing to air some sort of unpleasant truth. "Your dad kept my dad out of jail. He paid an exorbitant amount of money to pull strings only a man like him would have at his disposal. He said he was doing me a favor, but I don't really think it was just for me. I think it was for you, too, Chuck. He didn't want it to hurt you—your career. Being tied to me. It's why I left...why I couldn't be there for you. It's where I've been all these months—wasting away in that fucking house with people who are practically strangers."

There was a time in the not-so-distant past that I wouldn't have believed that—that any of my father's decisions had anything to do with me. I would have sworn up and down that it was a move made wholly for himself, so it didn't reflect badly on WH, solely so he could cash in on a favor owed to him at exactly the right time.

I would have refuted that any decision made by Steven Winchester was for my benefit.

But I knew better now.

My eyes burned. For me, for my father, for him and the hell he'd been living in all because I think, at the end of the day, he was like the person I used to be—I don't think he liked himself very much. "Why'd you stay there? Why do that to yourself?"

Tripp scrubbed his face before shrugging a shoulder. "I don't know. Maybe I thought it would be penance for all the ways I've been a shitty person. That it's what I deserved."

"You're not a shitty person." My words were sharp. "You should stay. *Here*. There's plenty of room for you in the house. They don't deserve you, Tripp. Stay here, with us. In our little fucked up found family, as Taylor likes to call it. I'll pay you."

He cut me a sideways look, his words dry and the lilt rising in his voice. "You already pay me."

"I'll pay you more." I tipped my chin up, grabbing his shoulders and shaking him like a child throwing a tantrum might.

"At least come to Cape Cod for my father's weird little pilgrimage back to the place my mother took her last breath."

"I'll think about it."

"I think you're my best friend. Don't tell Taylor." I leaned forward, whispering conspiratorially. It was sort of a joke, but he was an important part of me.

"Wouldn't dream of it, Chuck." The ghost of a smile flashed on his face before he pushed to stand, holding a hand out for me.

Taking his hand, I held it up, pointedly looking at it in the moonlight. "Are you sure you don't get manicures?"

Rolling his eyes, he jerked his hand back when I stood and shoved it into his pocket, tipping his chin toward the boathouse.

"Deac said something about *keeping the party going* down here if you want to have a drink."

"Oh!" I raised my hands, a laugh tumbling from me. "I didn't realize the gala held at the art gallery our dying father christened for our already dead mother was considered a party, but sure. A drink sounds great."

The grass crunched under our feet, the heels of my Nudistcurve Glitter Stuart Weitzmans barely sinking into the frozen ground. The dull thud of the TV grew louder, and the light shining from the boathouse grew brighter, stretched across the grass.

Tripp paused just before the door, his features thrown into shadows.

It was all there, hanging around us, between us, and all over us—the people we'd been and the people we were. He wasn't someone I'd have pictured to be standing beside me at the end of the day, but I was eternally grateful he was.

Sticking out my hand, I smiled up at him. "Friends?"

He cocked his head, eyes impassive for just a moment before all that ice melted. He smiled softly at me and looked like the boy I used to know. And when he met my hand with his, I think we were back there—just two kids with whole lives ahead of them that would become so intertwined—but I was so fucking happy we ended up here. "Friends."

Rolling his shoulders back, he let go of my hand, pulled open the sliding glass door, and gestured for me to step through.

Melodramatic, emo acoustics sounded from the speakers.

Deacon's choice. His taste in music didn't match his taste in suits.

My brother was behind the bar, barely sparing us a glance, his eyes only for the bottles of scotch he was pilfering through. Taylor was perched on one of the bar stools opposite him, fingers drumming impatiently, and David was seemingly ignoring them both, sitting on the couch and his eyes on the TV, a football replay. He craned his neck, leaning back over his shoulder when Tripp pulled the door closed.

"Everything okay out there?" Taylor cocked her head, her features settling into that predatory stillness she only ever reserved for the moment before she was readying herself to tear the throat out of someone who threatened anyone she loved.

"Yeah, just celebrating the fact that these two finally worked it out." Tripp gestured between David and me before quite literally sauntering over to the bar where she sat, arms crossed, and lips pursed with eyes that were probably lasers boring into him. "You're welcome, by the way."

"What the fuck did you do?" Deacon raised his eyes from where he'd been intently staring at the scotch he was pouring.

"Brought excitement to all your boring lives. How dull would things be if I never showed up?" Tripp dropped into the leather barstool beside Taylor, offering her a lazy grin.

Taylor scrunched her nose, winking at me before grabbing the seat of her chair and attempting to shuffle it away from Tripp.

David's eyes were still on me, one arm slung over the back of the couch, a glass of scotch dangling lazily from his perfect, calloused fingertips.

Smiling softly at him, I bent down to undo the clasp on my heels before kicking them off. The restored wood floor was cold under my feet, and I practically sprinted across the floor to wrap my arms around him.

His words were low, one of his hands coming to rest on my shoulder. "You all good, baby?"

"Yeah." I dropped my head against his, eyes fluttering closed. I splayed my hand under his suit jacket, pressing it over top of his heart. I could feel it beating there, just under the expanse of muscle in his chest—these parts of his body that made up him, the love of my life, and I could hear the laughter of all my favorite people on the planet. "I think I'm all good."

Deacon

"Did you know he had the pool filled in?" My sister glanced sideways at me, her hair whipping across her face in the wind blowing off the bay. She wrapped her arms around herself, and the shiny material of her coat caught in the sunlight, practically blinding me underneath my Ray Bans. It reminded me of something Noa would wear, and I didn't like it.

I scoffed, staring at the expanse of white-washed wood that lined where the pool used to be, connected to the rest of the deck that stretched off the back of the house like it had always been there. I needed a fucking drink. "No, but I can't say I'm surprised."

Our mother died in that pool—and our father had it filled in and encased with fucking concrete—laying down sheets of wood like none of it had ever happened.

It felt like a slap in the face, the last insult he could offer the woman he loved, the mother of his children. Looking at it, the proverbial gravesite filled with concrete and wood that was carefully selected by whoever he kept on speed dial for interior design. It made me want to hit him, actually.

But then I caught my reflection in one of the wraparound glass windows, and even though the armor I built around myself—all the ways I kept my mother out—wasn't real, I could see it all weighing me down, staring right back at me.

I was no better than him. I hadn't literally buried the last place she breathed, covered it up, and moved on like he had, but I'd turned away from her and never looked back.

"I'm not sure what I was expecting." Charlie shrugged, worrying at her bottom lip with her teeth. "I mean, it's not like we were all coming back here for a fucking pool party, but whatever I expected, it wasn't this."

I nodded, saying nothing, eyes sweeping over the fresh expanse of wood one more time, the fireplaces dug into it, and the black stones sparkling under the sunlight before looking out to the gentle slope of the lawn that led to the beach.

We'd flown in this morning, and it was a generally miserable flight for me, considering I typically used any excuse to take the jet due to the more-than-comfortable amenities. I didn't know how to speak to my father—where to even begin. I'd been pretty close to apologizing to him, throwing myself at his feet and sobbing like nothing more than a child who wanted his parent, but that was before he decided to open that stupid gallery without telling us.

I thought about asking Taylor what she made of it—this constant tug of war in my chest between grief and anger, what that said about someone like me, but she'd sat beside David and Charlie, and then fucking Tripp had sat across from them, and I'd been stuck sitting across from my father. Steven had the audacity to look less-than-composed, his leg bouncing up and down, and his knuckles practically white against the armrest of his seat. He didn't speak to me once, staring out the window the entire three hours from takeoff to landing.

I'd left my phone on, stupidly thinking that Noa might text me, but we'd barely spoken since she left, and I'd ignored her last three calls.

The fully stocked bar had served me well.

It felt a bit like a funeral procession—leaving the plane and ducking into the waiting SUVs with their tinted windows and freshly waxed black exteriors, driving through the tiny towns and the winding streets until we all arrived at this place none of us had set foot in for close to a decade.

I'd thought it looked the same until Charlie and I walked around the side of the property, past the two-bedroom guest house and the shining windows, like we were making some silent pilgrimage to see our mother's grave, and then we saw the pool had been filled in.

Our father had gone right inside to answer a phone call, and David, Taylor, and Tripp had gone down to the short boardwalk to the beach to give us some semblance of privacy. I was probably supposed to feel more than I was—but the only thing I wanted was a glass of scotch and a line.

I wanted my fiancée too, but I'd driven her away, and I hated the feeling of the empty space beside me, so much that I'd reached out my hand instinctively to grab hers when I saw that the pool was gone and she wasn't there.

I didn't like it.

I didn't want to feel anything anymore.

Clearing my throat, I jerked my chin toward the beach. "You were never going to get over him, were you?"

She shook her head, rubbing her lips together before a tiny smile pulled on them while she looked beyond the seagrass, swaying gently in the breeze toward where he stood. "No, I don't think I was."

"New York was just a giant love letter to him, wasn't it? You two...looking back. It was never getting untangled, was it?" I gestured toward them, to Taylor tipping her head back and cackling shrilly at something Tripp had just said, to David where he stood, hands in the pockets of his chinos and a smile on his face. His eyes were hidden behind his sunglasses, but I knew they were on my sister.

"No," she said, her words simple. But they were true.

I turned, narrowing my eyes on her from behind my sunglasses. "What was Tripp, then?"

She seemed like she was chewing on her words, and then the corners of her lips twitched in something like fondness. "A lifeboat. But not in a...diminishing way. I loved him, too, you know."

"But not enough?" I asked quietly.

"Not the same." Charlie turned to look at me, her words soft. "Have you called Noa?"

I cut her a look, my silence offering more of an answer than I could. The thought of Noa made my throat feel like it was closing in, like I might collapse from the sheer weight of it all. But I wasn't going to be able to keep her happy, and despite the general consensus, I wasn't selfish enough to make her miserable for my own benefit.

"Don't waste time. Not the way we did." She gestured to David before glancing back at the house, the stretch of glass between the wood paneling and the intentionally worn shingles, to where our father was, somewhere on the phone, pretending nothing had changed.

Charlie pushed her sunglasses up, offering me a watery smile, and I could see the tears pooling behind her eyes, glistening under the sunlight. Holding out her hand, she continued to smile expectantly at me. "Come on, let's go down to the water."

I eyed her outstretched hand, the literal one in front of me and the metaphorical one she'd always held out for me, even when I didn't deserve it.

I could hear her words from the other night, when she held me as I cried like the fucking child that I was, telling me over and over that I wasn't alone. And maybe I wasn't.

But our mother had been alone.

And I'd left her ghost alone, too, so I shoved my hands into the pockets of my Tom Fords, tipped my chin toward the beach, and pretended I didn't see my sister's heart break behind her eyes.

———

The numbers on my black Centurion card blurred in front of me, and I paused as I cut through the tiny pile of coke I had spread out across a white flat stone table in the living room of the guesthouse.

The practically pure white interior looked almost pink in the last rays of the setting sun, streaming through the same floor-to-ceiling windows that lined the main house.

I could see my sister and David in the distance still down by the water, the seagrass blocking some of what looked like a game of tag—David would go one way, while Charlie bounced back and forth before sprinting off and trying to outrun him. He caught her every time, arms wrapping around her stomach as he spun her around, and she tipped her head back in laughter. I couldn't hear it, but I could imagine what it sounded like: unburdened. Happy.

All the things she deserved to be, and all the things I wasn't.

She was down there on a private section of beach, making use of the fifteen-million-dollar slice of real estate with the love of her life, and I was in the guesthouse racking up a line while Tripp fucking Banks sat next to me, looking vaguely disgusted.

"She fell in love with him, and it was the beginning and end of everything." I glanced sideways at Tripp, and it was kind of annoying really.

He looked as impassive as always—one eyebrow rose on his forehead, barely sparing me a look before bringing the glass to his mouth. I didn't know what I wanted, but I wanted something. My sister had this theory that ever since our mother died, drowned, left this world by choice—whatever you wanted to call it—she and I were constantly trying to drown everyone else around us, too.

Maybe I wanted Tripp to drown with me. His ship seemed primed to tip over along with mine, which was fucking upside down and leaking from the hull.

He said nothing, and I shook my head as I chalked up the line spread across the table. I leaned forward, the edges of the bill sharp against my nostril when I inhaled. It was fucking bitter. Maybe I was fucking bitter because I looked at him and decided to shoot a canon through the wood panels of whatever boat he was floating on. "You didn't stand a fucking chance."

Tripp turned to look at me, everything about his gaze flat. I held out the bill and shoved the tray toward him. His eyes closed briefly, and he shook his head before knocking back the rest of his scotch. His voice was flat, practically devoid of life. "Grow up, Deac."

"Fuck off." I rolled my eyes, pinching my nose and inhaling.

His glass dropped to the table, echoing as it rolled for a moment before stopping. He cocked his head, and his words weren't as harsh as they should have been. "Why are you making this about me? About me and your sister and Kennedy? When it's clearly fucking about you and whatever daddy issues you—"

Throwing the bill to the table, I turned and pointed at him. "Hey, you fucking work for me. Don't talk to me like that."

Tripp brought his hands together in a slow clap, like I was a child who did the bare minimum, before leaning forward and crossing his arms to rest on his knees. "You're right. I do work for you. But you know what else? Once upon a time, we were friends. And I thought we were still friends now, so let me do you a fucking favor and tell you to stop acting like you're twenty, to smarten up, and to be there for your fucking sister, because she deserves it."

I grabbed my own glass of scotch, previously abandoned in favor of drugs. "What is it about her anyway? Has you and Kennedy in fucking knots? Some sort of magic—"

"Finish that fucking sentence, Deacon—and not only are *you* going to regret it in the morning, but there's going to be nothing left of you when David's done with you."

He was right, but I wasn't about to tell him that. "Oh, you going to tattle on me? Not going to stand up for her? And come on, you think Mr. North Carolina, with his fucking manners, is going to punch his best friend?"

Tripp scoffed, tossing a flat look at me. "He's practically from the Outer Banks. Trust me, the golden retriever with his secret cigarettes can throw a fucking punch."

I shoved the tray toward him again, and he shook his head. I probably shouldn't have done another line—but I wasn't sure I had a fiancée anymore. I didn't have a mother, and soon, I wouldn't have a father, either—so what did it really matter? I leaned forward and snorted again before flopping back against the couch. "Ah, that's right. I forgot he decked you...all those years ago when we caught you kissing Charlie at the Northwestern Memorial gala."

"I didn't," Tripp answered, voice dry. "And all those years ago? It's barely been three."

"Feels like a fucking lifetime, man." I shook my head, palming my jaw and closing my eyes, waiting for the coke to take over and stop the spinning from all the alcohol. "Your parents can't live far from here, thinking about paying them a visit? Checking in to see if the house has been bartered?"

"No."

Digging the heels of my palms into my eyes, I groaned before rolling my neck against the back of the couch and looking at him. A muscle ticked in his jaw, and he stared into the dregs of scotch left in his glass where it perspired on the table. "Does this mean you're staying? Plenty of room in the old Winchester Homestead for you."

Tripp rolled his eyes before reaching forward to grab the remnants of his scotch. "I can find my own accommodations. Pretty nice suite reserved for me weekly at The Waldorf."

"You aren't going to stay in a fucking hotel, man." I shook my head, lips pulling back. "How fucking sterile. You're not my father."

Pushing to stand, Tripp swiped the bill from the table, like he was robbing me of my only available drug paraphernalia. He said nothing until he pulled open the sliding glass door, one eyebrow arched. "I'll leave the hotel when you call Noa."

Flicking my middle finger up, I waited until he closed the door before pulling out another bill from my wallet.

Tripp

It was a beautiful property—the type of place my father would salivate over. Not even the actual architecture, though that was impressive: wall-to-wall glass windows and sliding doors surrounding the main level of the home, offering an unobscured view of the beach and the bay, the traditional intentionally worn shingles and slats wrapping around the house, and the white wood-paneled walls and shockingly modern interior, open concept and white with pops of color to remind you where you were.

The whole thing reeked of old money. And death.

It was a once-in-a-lifetime property, but I couldn't understand for the fucking life of me why Steven didn't sell it.

And I couldn't understand why he'd been so adamant about coming back here and dragging all of us with him. He'd been upstairs almost the entire day, presumably fielding phone calls, or maybe he was simply sitting out on the wraparound terrace that led off all the rooms, staring out at the ocean.

Taylor had gone up there a few times to check on him, but she said nothing whenever she came back outside where we were all camped out, despite the chill in the air.

It was too cold to sit out there all day. Still, Deacon and Charlie didn't seem to relish being locked in the house with their dying father and whatever memories they had of their mother, and fucking Kennedy had come to the rescue and built a literal fire on the beach, never mind the fact that sunken fireplaces lined the deck.

We'd sat out there for most of the afternoon, huddled around the fire that he knew exactly how to keep properly stoked, despite the breeze off the water, wool blankets spread out on the sand, passing around a bottle of scotch, Deacon intermittently getting up to go get high, until Taylor brought glasses and a bucket of ice back from the house.

It was nestled in the sand beside her now, an empty bottle discarded beside it. The sun set hours ago, but no one moved to go back into the house. Steven hadn't even come down for dinner, and we'd all stayed out here, circled around the fire, each on our respective wool blanket. Charlie wasn't even sitting with David, which I guessed was for my benefit but was wholly unnecessary. I was going to have to get used to seeing it, and maybe I already was.

There was something about them that made sense—probably more sense than we ever made. He tempered her, grounded her, kept her safe and made her laugh, all the while holding the weight of the world up for her.

The whole afternoon and evening had been companionable, despite the loud snorts and sniffs coming from Deacon, who seemed to finally be coming down from his high. He hadn't been back up in the guesthouse since I'd left him there, and he was lounging on his blanket, propped up on one elbow, staring at the fire.

I watched as he took an overly large swallow of his scotch, his eyes finally swinging between all of us. "Should we play a game?"

Charlie gave him a sideways look. "And what game would you propose we play, Deacon? None of your faculties are operating at one-hundred percent at the moment, so I can't imagine you have the reflexes for a nighttime game of badminton."

Narrowing his eyes at her, he raised his glass. "Never have I ever slept with more than one person in this circle."

Chuck didn't even look hurt; she just looked tired. Her shoulders fell, she brought her knees to her chest, and dropped her chin there.

Kennedy, on the other hand, looked like he was seconds from ripping Deacon limb from limb and tossing him into the fire. A muscle twitched in his jaw, and I think a fucking vein popped in his neck.

I didn't really relish the idea of having to split them up should things turn physical, and I wasn't too fond of Deacon's chances, so I turned to Taylor, offering her a grin. "Care to change that, doctor?"

Taylor pulled her head back, a look that could only be described as a combination of horror and disgust playing across her face. "Absolutely not."

But her eyes softened as she said it, like she didn't hate me as much as she usually pretended to.

Deacon rolled his head back and forth, the wisps of his hair flopping across his forehead. "What if he was the last man on Earth?"

She shrugged, tipping her chin up. "I would, as they say, let the human race die."

The corners of David's mouth twitched, and even Deacon looked poised to laugh, though his eyes appeared good and dead.

Charlie's smile was tired, and her words were quiet as she stood. "I'm going to check on Dad."

"Why?" Deacon scoffed, staring intently into what was left of his glass of scotch, like it held the secrets of the universe. "He couldn't even be bothered to come down for dinner."

Charlie turned, her features softening, and I could see her eyes glistening, even though the fire was causing shadows to dance across her face. "Because he's our father, he's sick, and he's probably grieving our mother."

Shaking her head, she wrapped her arms around herself and trudged through the sand toward the house.

"Say goodnight for me," Deacon called after her, practically baring his teeth in what was probably supposed to be a smile. He swirled his scotch before draining the rest. "I'm going to bed."

"Good luck with that." Taylor smiled, but really it was all just teeth too, before she pointedly tapped her nose.

Rolling his eyes, Deacon tossed the glass down into the sand, like it wasn't Waterford crystal, before shoving his hands in his pockets and following after his sister. His retreating silhouette was followed by the distinct sound of a sliding glass door slamming shut.

David groaned, running his hands over his face before pushing to stand. "I need a fucking cigarette."

"You shouldn't smoke," Taylor reprimanded, pursing her lips as he walked by her.

He raised a hand over his shoulder, two fingers up in acknowledgment, before jogging up the small stretch of beach toward the boardwalk.

Silence fell between us, just the crackling fire and the steady lap of waves on the shore as I watched her stare into the flames.

"Have we ever been alone together?"

Taylor's eyes sharpened, and her lips pursed in that fucking pinched, annoying way only she could ever achieve. She was objectively beautiful—entirely different from Chuck, all sharp edges, a voice that usually cut across my skin and not in a good way.

One eyebrow rose as she considered me, crossing her arms over her oversized pink Alexander Wang hooded sweatshirt. That was one thing I would give her credit for—she had great taste.

"I suppose we haven't. But I try not to spend my time around people whose initials are akin to a communicable disease." She swung her legs underneath her, and sat straighter on her wool blanket.

Swirling my scotch, the ice knocked against the crystal, and I rolled my eyes. "Same initials, Taylor."

She shook her head, practically tipping her chin upward so she somehow managed to look down at me, even though I was still about a foot taller than her sitting. "I go by my full initials. TCB."

She didn't. I had the misfortune of knowing her for three years, and I'd never once heard her go by anything other than Taylor or Dr. Breen, and Chuck would have mentioned it. "What's the C for?"

With no shame, an emotion I wasn't even sure she was capable of to begin with, Taylor pursed her lips again before answering. "Cressida."

"Of course it is." That was fucking fitting. I shook my head and brought the glass of scotch to my lips.

Her voice was sharp when she spoke. "Oh, and your middle name is better? Your parents are the type of people who named their children Post and Tripp. I'm sure it's as pretentious as they come."

It wasn't much better, and I usually wouldn't have given her the satisfaction of answering. I would have gotten up and topped up my scotch, gone to find Deacon, or to my own room in this godforsaken death house we were all stuck in while Steven played Daddy, but I didn't want to risk walking by their room.

"Benson."

A derisive sort of cackle sounded from her, and she tipped her head back for a moment before she looked back at me. She stilled, almost predatory in how quickly she changed tunes. I'd seen her do it before a million times when she swung back and forth between being Team Me or Team Kennedy. She was like a mean, exceptionally well-dressed wrecking ball. Taylor cocked her head, and it was probably a trick of the light, but her brown eyes seemed to melt, soften, just for a moment, and her nose wrinkled. "When did you know?"

"Know what?" I asked, voice bland, like I didn't have a clue what she was talking about. But I knew.

I wasn't the one, and I never was.

Her voice was soft, uncharacteristically so, and she tipped her head even farther, that annoyingly messy ponytail moving with her. "That it wasn't you. That it was never going to be you."

My nostrils flared, and I looked away from her, back at the ice floating aimlessly in the amber liquid. I didn't want to see the sympathy—the pity emanating from her; pity and sorrow for me, that I would have ever been stupid enough to think I could have been David Kennedy to her. "The second I got back."

"And you still stayed?"

"What can I say? I'm a sucker for punishment." I knocked back the rest of the scotch, the ice clinking against the glass, and I wished there was more.

Clearing my throat, I continued. "It was at the hospital. The second he came back into the room, I could see it. Her shoulders slumped, but not in...defeat or sadness. She relaxed. Just by walking in the room, David fucking Kennedy took whatever tension she was carrying around, untangled whatever permanent knots live in the muscles of a Winchesters' back, and they were just...gone. It was like he took all the worlds, all the weight that she carries on those bony fucking shoulders, and just...held it for her. Held it all for her so she could breathe."

A small breath came from her, and I looked up, because I was a masochist and had probably done plenty of things in my life that would mean I deserved to feel like shit when someone pitied me.

But Taylor's lips pulled to the side, and she shook her head softly. "It was never going to be you, Tripp. Even when it was you, it wasn't you. No matter how much...fun you had."

Tossing her a wry smile, I shrugged. "Just because we fucked well together never meant I was the one for her. You can't manufacture what they have, and all the chemistry in the world can't create it. Whatever that is, seeing each other in the way only they seem to...it comes around once in a lifetime."

Taylor said nothing; she just continued eyeing me shrewdly, and I wasn't sure I liked it, so I cocked my head and asked a question I didn't really want the answer to, but anything was better than this—having her look at me like I was some sort of interesting specimen spread across a slide under a microscope. "Did she ever tell you who was better in bed?"

One eyebrow rose on her forehead. "No. I don't think there was ever a comparison to be made, because I don't think you ever existed on the same plane as he did for her."

A scoff sounded from my throat, and my fingers tightened against the glass. That was harsh, even for her.

Her voice was quiet, and she leaned forward, offering what was probably supposed to be an encouraging smile but looked odd juxtaposed against the rest of her angular features. "To be fair, I don't think anyone ever has, and no one ever could."

I let out a low whistle. "Careful, Cressida, or I might tell everyone you're being nice to me."

"No one would believe you." Taylor raised her eyebrows, smiling at me. But it was still soft. I watched as she pushed to stand, entirely engulfed by that huge sweatsuit, the pink making her look less abrasive and less sharp than she would ever be. "Goodnight, Tripp."

I arched an eyebrow at her, eyeing the slowly melting ice cube, debating pulling a Deacon and drinking myself into oblivion. The guest rooms were all at the same end of the house, and passing out seemed preferable to hearing Charlie and David. She wasn't exactly quiet.

Taylor had taken a step toward the path back to the house, but she wrapped her arms around herself and looked back over her shoulder. Her stubby fingernails were the only thing about her that was never entirely calculated, entirely put together. Her lips pulled into a smile that felt sort of quiet, somehow. "You'll get over her, Tripp. It'll be okay."

"I know," I answered, my voice nothing more than a pathetic whisper. And I did know. I did, and I was on the way. I just wasn't sure how long the journey would be. "Don't worry about me, Taylor. I'm not going to pull a Deacon and need to be picked up off the floor tomorrow morning."

She grinned, tipping her chin toward me. "Oh, I would never be worried about that. Brunello Cucinelli doesn't belong on the floor. Even if it's a floor in the Winchesters' house."

I glanced down, plucking at the gray cashmere sweater. "No one could ever accuse you of having poor taste."

"Doubtful, seeing as I've spent the last twenty minutes willingly talking to you." Taylor scrunched her nose, before smiling softly again. "Goodnight, TB."

"Night night, Cressida." I raised my empty glass at her when she turned away toward the house.

Her hand rose above her head, and I thought for a second she might have been waving goodnight, but that was her middle finger stuck up, resolutely over her head of annoyingly crimped hair and that pink sweatsuit as she disappeared down the boardwalk.

A laugh caught in my throat. I watched the flames licking toward the sky, the occasional crack of an ember spilling out toward the sand, the abandoned wool blankets, and empty bottles. It wouldn't be the worst thing in the world for this to be my life. The five of us, existing like this.

It was a life without Chuck, sure. But not really. She was still my friend, probably my best, and that might have been the way I'd always loved her if I really looked back, opened up all those old, forgotten doors in my mind where I kept those old versions of us. It would be a life without her—at least the way I thought I wanted her, needed her—but it didn't seem empty when I thought about it. Her as my friend, nothing more and certainly nothing less. Deacon needed the supervision of at least two adults at all times now, and he would surely find endless ways to fill any void before it managed to creep up on him, or anyone else for that matter. Taylor would always be a bitch, albeit a slightly more enjoyable one, and Kennedy would probably forever remain a righteous prick—entirely unflappable and worlds more mature than the rest of us.

I could go home—back to my parents and to the fucking bank and to Post, a righteous prick for entirely different reasons. I could sit there while my mother smiled blandly at all of her nice things and patted my father's hand when he got angry, while he wasted away in front of the TV, wishing he could place a bet or arrange for someone to deflate some fucking footballs. That's what life would be with my family—full, because they were all living and breathing, but fucking desolate and empty the way it always had been.

But this life, the one from this evening—with the girl who was probably my best friend, her disaster of a brother, a doctor who wore too many sequins, and someone who smoked more than they should—didn't seem particularly empty at all.

Charlie

It was easy to remember why I loved this place so much. It wasn't just the backdrop of the sparkling water, how different the air felt against my skin, how much easier it was to breathe out here. Sure, there was sparkling water and the rolling expanse of an enormous, manicured lawn back in Lake Forest, but this place had been so unburdened, once upon a time.

Even the house itself, the wall-to-wall windows and all the sliding doors, the open concept, white interior with the gray-washed paneled walls, had always felt lighter, less suffocating than the dark, winding, desolate halls back in that other home of ours, if you could call it that.

And even now, despite the shadows crawling across the walls, stretching along the flooring—when I was alone with the ghosts that surely lived here too—I felt like I could breathe.

The crack of the sliding door sounded from behind me, and I glanced over my shoulder, expecting David or Taylor—even Tripp, who'd been known to follow after people into the night.

But it was my brother closing the door, stepping into this house where, even though I could breathe, he looked like he was struggling for every molecule of oxygen.

I wrapped my arms around myself. "Are you going to bed?"

Deacon raised his eyebrows as he nodded.

We'd have to walk up the same staircase to get to our rooms. This house was far more open-concept than any other property we frequented.

"Why don't you come with me to see Dad?"

My brother cut me a flat look.

"You'll never regret being nicer to him, Deacon." Shrugging, I held out my hand like he used to do for me when I was small, and I fell off my bike because our parents certainly weren't watching us, or when I was scared at night because that house was so dark, had felt so big and vast, filled with all their expectations, and I wasn't allowed to have a nightlight.

He didn't take it, but he fell into step beside me up the staircase. What had been our parents' room was at the end of the hall, a faint light emanating from underneath the door. It was on the corner of the house, offering a direct view of the bay, all those other multi-million-dollar homes and their private sections of beach, and any boats bobbing in the water.

"Enter."

Deacon and I looked at each other, mouths practically gaping, and some of that light that lived in him waking up. It was still dim, but he looked a bit brighter. Rolling his eyes, he pushed open the door.

Neither of us paused to survey our surroundings. I didn't want to know what he'd changed in here, where one of the beds they used to share lived, if he'd gone as far as to fill in the pool.

The sliding door to the balcony was open, our father standing just beyond it, still in his suit, but his jacket gone and the sleeves rolled up his forearms. There was no IV pole, but I could see the gauze wrapped around his arm to protect the line.

He held a glass of scotch in one hand, the other resting on the balcony railing.

"Hi," I offered quietly, coming to stand beside him. "We just came to say goodnight. See how you were feeling."

"Both of you?" One eyebrow rose before he glanced between the two of us.

Cutting my brother a sideways look, I widened my eyes.

Deacon rolled his, tipping his chin toward our father. "Yeah, how are you feeling?"

"I feel fine, thank you." Taking a sip of his scotch, he cleared his throat. "I apologize for my absence today. Being here one final time was...more difficult than I'd anticipated. It wasn't intended to isolate you, though I acknowledge I've done my fair share of that."

I wrapped my arms around myself, smiling tightly. "We're used to entertaining ourselves."

It wasn't meant to be a dig, but it was the truth. Because he had left us alone for years, and now he'd leave us in the most permanent way there was.

"It looked like the five of you were having fun." He tipped his glass toward the opposite end of the balcony. You could see the fire still burning there, where we'd all been sitting, running around, and playing like children on the beach all afternoon. "It's a shame Noa couldn't be here."

"Do you ever wish you were a different man?" Deacon blurted. His voice was small—a question from a son to his father. His eyes looked pinched, and he palmed his jaw, shaking his head. "That you'd done things differently?"

Considering his question, our father nodded, weighing his next words. "Hindsight is, as they say, 20-20. There are very few moments over my life when I've wished I was different, that I'd done something differently. Perhaps an unpopular thing for a dying man to say, but it remains true. I wanted, so I worked. I earned. I took. But I regret what some of those decisions cost me. I regret that they cost me your mother. Cost me your happiness and, at times, the both of you."

"What are we supposed to do without you?" A sob escaped through my clenched teeth, no longer a prisoner, but free and out here with us in real life, exposing all the hurt, all the festering, open wounds that were ravaging my body at the thought of a world without my father.

Deacon's shoulders shook with a shuddering inhale, and he pressed his palms to his eyes.

"Be happier than you were when you were trying to live up to astronomical expectations I never should have set." He gazed out at the ocean for a moment longer, at the stars reflected in it.

It all seemed so vast—and for a moment, it was easy to believe that maybe our mother was out there, just beyond it all, waiting for him to come home.

He turned back to me, raising his glass—priceless, vintage Waterford crystal and amber liquid sparkling under the starlight.

"And know you have far surpassed them."

The sound I made would have woken my poor etiquette instructor from her grave. Guttural, unfettered—the wail of a child without her parents. First a daughter without her mother, and now a daughter without her father.

"And you—lay off the drugs. Call your fiancée back. Make me proud like you have." Grabbing Deacon's shoulder, he looked like he wanted to shake him, but his grip just tightened before he let go, turning back out to stare at all that empty nothingness, all those stars.

A normal family might have hugged, one sibling under each arm of their father, their last remaining parent.

But we weren't those people, and we never were. And maybe we'd never really been a family; we'd always just been three people linked by nothing more than DNA and circumstance and whatever swirled in the stars to drop us all off here, in this life we'd been in together.

So we stared out at the ocean, not one step behind him like usual, but Deacon and I on either side, our father in the middle, and maybe our mother out there somewhere.

And he had the last word, because he was still Steven Winchester, after all.

"Be good to the people around you. Be good to each other. Be better than me."

David

Charlie looked beautiful all the time. Even when Sabine shoved her into what might as well have been sequinned Saran wrap—she looked beautiful.

I had a thing for the ocean, so seeing her silhouetted by the moon and the bay sparkling just beyond her, elbows propped up on the wooden balcony railing and all the chocolate hair blowing in the breeze, was a dream I didn't even know I had.

She wasn't angelic—she swore far too much—but she looked ethereal, and I was scared that she might vanish into nothing, like I'd really and truly made her up all those years ago. I practically tip-toed across the floor and out onto the terrace.

"Everything okay?" I dropped my chin to her head, winding my arms around her.

She leaned back, her shoulders softening with a measured exhale. "I think so. We talked, but no one hugged. That would certainly be taking it too far. But I think...I think it was good. For all of us."

I pulled her in tighter. "You once told me this was your favorite place on the planet."

Charlie nodded, tipping her head back and blinking up at me.

"I did say that, yes. I recall it was after you'd fucked me thoroughly on the high-pile rug in my old townhouse in Lincoln Park."

I loved that townhouse.

Grinning, I dropped my mouth to the crook of her neck. "Where's your favorite place now?"

"You smell like cigarettes." Her voice was petulant, and I could feel her purse her lips, even though I couldn't see her. "As disarmingly and unpredictably sexy as watching you smoke may be, please stop. I don't care if it's just once in a while. I've had enough malignant cells for a lifetime."

"I'm sorry," I whispered, lips moving against her skin. And I meant it. I'd hurt her enough, and I'd never fucking do it again. "You can stomp all over my last pack with your Jimmy Choos first thing tomorrow morning."

"I didn't bring heels to the beach, David. I'm not Taylor." Her voice was light, and I pressed a kiss to her neck. I could feel her pulse just beneath her skin, that thing that kept my favorite person in the world alive and breathing.

I'd do anything for her.

We were silent for a while. My head buried in the crook of her neck, and her just staring out at the same ocean as her father. And if I knew her brother as well as I thought, that's where he'd be too—on his balcony, staring out into the abyss.

I felt her throat move as she spoke, and she brought our joined hands to her lips, murmuring against them, "My favorite place is anywhere with you."

———

Steven was already at the head of the table when Charlie and I made our way down there for breakfast. Taylor was there too, seemingly content to sit beside him, curled up in her chair with a steaming mug of coffee in one hand and her phone in the other.

His IV pole was noticeably absent this trip, but I had it on good authority from Charlie that Taylor checked him over thoroughly every morning.

He raised his eyes from behind the paper he had spread out in front of him. "Good morning. Did you sleep well?"

Charlie nodded, brushing her hand over his shoulder and bending to kiss his cheek in an uncharacteristic move before settling into a chair beside Taylor.

"David?" he asked, eyes back on the paper.

"Yeah, great. I could fall asleep anywhere by the water." I winked at Charlie, dropping my arm over the back of her chair when I sat beside her.

Steven made a noncommittal noise and didn't look up from his paper again until Deacon and Tripp descended the stairs.

A feline smile split across Taylor's face. "Benson, there you are. I was concerned you might have drank too much scotch and accidentally fallen into the fire. What a shame that would have been."

Tripp smiled lazily at Taylor, pulling out the chair across from her. "Cressida."

"Who the fuck are Benson and Cressida?" Deacon's lips curved into what I could only describe as a sneer when he dropped down across from me, the backdrop of the paneled wood wall making the pallor of his skin look questionable for someone who was known to keep a tanning bed in their apartment.

Charlie pointed toward them both. "Their middle names."

He snorted, shaking his head before narrowing his eyes at Taylor and Tripp. "Oh, come on, don't tell me you two stayed up too late and things got carried away. That would really be taking the definition of *sharing* too far."

"Enough." Steven interjected, but he sounded vaguely amused. "I thought today we could take the boat out and—"

His words cut off mid-sentence. He swallowed before clearing his throat.

"Dad?" Charlie's eyes flicked up, her hand pausing, outstretched and reaching for the steaming carafe.

He shook his head, holding up a finger. Clearing his throat again, his eyes pinched closed. The muscles in his neck popped.

Deacon's eyebrows came together, his mouth parting. "Dad?"

Steven said nothing, reaching forward for the glass of freshly pressed juice—that thing he couldn't start his day without—and his knuckles knocked into it while his hand opened uselessly in space, sending the whole thing crashing to the floor.

Charlie pushed back from the table, her chair making an ungodly scraping noise that sounded more like it was ripping through the fabric of whatever was left of this family.

"Daddy?" Her voice cracked, sounding impossibly small, and at that moment, she didn't look like the woman who turned my earth on its axis; she looked a bit like the little girl she was supposed to be once upon a time.

And maybe there was really a tear through the whole thing—because Steven brought his fist to his still-closed mouth, a horrible choking rasp catching in his throat—and when he pulled his hand back, it was covered with blood. He blinked, eyes coming together, and his usual shrewd expression passing over his face before he stumbled forward to his knees.

Taylor was already on her feet, hauling him up by his shoulders while his head lolled from side to side, like a broken marionette had taken up residence in his body instead of the harsh, unwavering, steadfast person that usually lived there.

"Steven?" Taylor snapped her fingers in his face, his eyes sliding in and out of focus before a bubble of blood burst on his lips. "Deacon, call 9-1-1."

Charlie lurched forward, knocking over her coffee, scrambling toward them.

Grabbing her around the middle, I pulled her back, away from where Taylor was sweeping her hands through Steven's mouth, her fingers covered in what looked like a blood clot when she took them out. Droplets sprayed off her hand as she shook it, peppering the formerly pristine walls. She tipped his chin up, all clinical precision, to get a better look inside his mouth before her hands, covered in what felt like so much more than just his blood, started pumping up and down on his chest.

Charlie's feet lifted in the air, swinging wildly, and her hands clawed at my forearms, that same skin she usually traced with loving reverence, her nails were now digging in, piercing through it, while she tried to get to her father.

Tightening my arms around her felt unnatural. The idea of caging her in—denying her what she wanted—felt like a noose around my neck. Pressing my lips to her ear, I murmured, even though I didn't think she could hear anything. "Baby, let her work. It's going to be okay. It's fine, he's fine."

It didn't feel fine. It certainly didn't look fine.

"9-1-1, Deacon." Taylor's eyes snapped up, her hands unwavering as they pushed against his chest.

Deacon blinked, like he wasn't sure what he was looking at, and a stupid expression came across his face as he slowly shook his head.

His phone was sitting there on the table, like it usually was, face up, waiting for Noa to cave first and to call him, when Tripp reached over the table, snatching it, and started dialing.

Taylor's lips moved with the count of her compressions before she dropped her mouth to Steven's, trying so hard to give him oxygen again, while Deacon stumbled backward, face pale, sliding down against the wall, and her best friend clawed at my arms for her father's life.

———

There are moments in history everyone remembers—people tell you exactly where they were when it happened. What the sky looked like. What the air smelled like.

There are moments history itself remembers because eventually people grow old and die, and stop telling the stories. But the exact minute was written down somewhere because enough people cared about it, because it was important in some capacity.

At about 2:20 a.m. on April 15, 1912, the last of the Titanic sank.

World War I ended on November 11, 1918 at 11:00 a.m.

On January 28, 1986 at 11:39 a.m. the Challenger exploded.

And at 10:17 a.m. on December 4, Steven Winchester died.

History would know he died. The fucking stock market would know he died.

But they wouldn't know what time.

I would.

Because I felt the world teeter off its axis when he took his last breath and left his two children behind. Left my best friend and the girl I loved more than anything on the planet.

Something like that, a catastrophic event—like an earthquake, a hurricane, a tsunami, the end of their world as they knew it—you'd think would be loud, that it would make a lot of noise.

That their grief might scream, beg the world to stop, to hear it.

Because their father just died, and even when they fucking hated him—they loved him.

But it didn't make a sound, and neither did they.

Deacon's eyes flashed, the muscles in his neck went tense, but he nodded when the doctor stepped out from behind that curtain where they'd been trying to save him. Charlie's left knee wobbled for a minute, and she took a tiny step backward, away from the doctor, away from the bed Steven laid in, until Taylor grabbed her hand.

She said nothing, but she blinked slowly and only twice. Her body swayed side to side, and it looked almost involuntary.

They looked like children.

I pressed my palm into her lower back, the other hand finding Taylor's shoulder. She was blinking rapidly, her chin tipped in the air, all that cool medical precision from earlier gone.

The doctor, whose name I didn't even hear, offered them what was probably supposed to be an apologetic smile. "I'm so sorry. It was likely a terminal hemorrhage. It happens when a patient has advanced cancer, and a tumor invades a blood vessel leading to—"

"I know what a terminal hemorrhage is," Taylor snapped, hand firmly wrapped in Charlie's and the other on Deacon's shoulder. "He is—*was* my patient. You just send me all your labs and paperwork, and I can take it from here."

"When can we take him home?" Charlie blurted. Her voice was so fucking small that I cringed, wanted to pick her up and carry her away from it all. I would have brought her somewhere nothing could hurt her, but I wasn't sure there was anywhere on this planet the loss of her father wouldn't find her.

Tripp cut me a sideways glance before taking a measured step beside Deacon, like they needed to be surrounded from all sides, bubble-wrapped and protected from a world that was surely going to eat them alive.

"Home?" The doctor tipped his head.

"Him." Charlie gestured toward the curtain that stretched around the hospital bed, keeping Steven's body hidden from view. "We can leave now, right? With him?"

He pulled his head back, shaking it slowly. "You should consider an autopsy so we can be certain about the cause of death."

"No. That won't be necessary." Charlie shook her head. The gesture looked resolute, but her face was blank, and she was blinking too much now. "He'd hate that. Please just...discharge, release his body, whatever you call it, and we'll take him home to Chicago."

With an air of maddening patience that made me want to punch him a bit, he sighed, raking a hand through his short, salt-and-pepper hair. It was oddly reminiscent of Steven's haircut. "It's not as simple as that. We have procedures to follow, it can take time to arrange for transport—"

Something like life flashed behind Deacon's eyes. He held up his hand to cut the doctor off. He might have leaned forward, but Tripp dropped his hand to his shoulder, like it was a casual gesture of reassurance, but I think he was keeping him upright, too. "Do you know who we are?"

Exhaling through his nostrils, he blinked. "Yes."

Deacon held his arms wide, shouting, but his voice cracked. "So do what she's asking, or I'll buy this fucking hospital, and the first thing I'll do is fire you!"

Taylor glanced sideways at Deacon, her features indignant, like she was about to tell him that you couldn't just buy a hospital the way you could a Porsche, but she rolled her shoulders back and turned toward the doctor. "I'm his primary physician. You can transfer his—*him*—to me. We can discuss arrangements."

The doctor nodded before tipping his head; everything about him resigned. "Would you like to see him one last time?"

"No, thank you." Charlie shook her head, smiling blandly at him, like he'd asked her if she wanted a fucking glass of water.

"Charlie," I leaned forward, one arm wrapping around her to bring her flush to my chest, "are you sure?"

"Yes. I don't need to. I like...I like the memory of him from last night. I think I'll keep him that way." Her voice cracked, and it felt like the first sign of a real, live person under there.

"Deac?" Taylor dropped Charlie's hand, her voice softer than I'd ever heard it. She reached out and brushed her thumb across his cheek. "I'll go with you if you'd like to see him."

Deacon's eyes swept across the hospital room and the banal decorations, like he was checking to see if there was anything of note, before they landed on that drawn, navy curtain. He swallowed, and it looked heavy, like the entire world, the one that had just tipped off its axis, tipped onto his shoulders.

"No."

He didn't even spare a glance for the curtain, for his father, before he turned around and walked out of the room.

Charlie barely even turned her head, hands wrapped around my forearm, staring out the window into the unseasonably bright morning.

"I've got him," Tripp said, his voice low before he followed Deacon.

The words were just for me. Taylor was talking to the doctor, wiping at her cheeks when she thought no one was looking.

He had him, and I had her.

I could count on one hand what I was thankful to Steven Winchester for. At one point, it was just my job, the opportunities he'd given me. And then it was for his daughter, despite the fact that he had little to nothing to do with her turning out the way she did, and now, it was for bringing us all back together—the five of us, whatever this was.

Maybe he'd known his children after all.

Tightening my arm around her, I dropped my chin to her head, holding her while she stared out the window into that whole new world, the one without Steven Winchester, that waited for her out there.

She felt smaller in my arms, different, and maybe she was—nothing more than a fawn without parents on spindly new legs that might buckle at any moment. But I had her. I'd keep her upright as long as she needed, and she'd never be alone.

Charlie

The sun still rose each day. The mist still hung suspended above the lake. The water still rolled against the rocks dotting the shore. The halls of this house were still winding, still empty, and still full of ghosts all at the same time.

The stars still burned in the sky, and the universes and the galaxies they lived in existed on.

This world still turned.

My heart still beat, and my lungs still filled with air. Each beat, each breath, hurt more than I ever would have imagined, but my body lived on.

All those things happened, just without Steven Winchester.

That thought alone sliced through my skin, snipping all the carefully sewn sutures that my hands chafed and bled for, all in pursuit of making myself whole, a real girl at last. I think my chest cavity was open for the entire world to see now, even the air pinching the raw, exposed nerve endings of me.

All these things that hurt me—the idea that I was breathing in a world where my father wasn't—continued on.

But the quiet, beautiful, and good things did, too.

Taylor was marching around this house like she was in charge. She'd stolen her Gucci sneakers back, which felt so decidedly normal that it almost made me cry. Tripp was here more often than not, mostly to serve as a drinking buddy for my brother, but the five of us would pile into the theater or go down to the boathouse to watch whatever game was on.

Things didn't feel as empty with them around.

David Kennedy was still in my bed each morning.

He was here now, grinning at me, lazy and eyes all sparkling honey in the sunlight streaming through the paned windows. "What are you thinking about?

Gesturing vaguely toward the ceiling, I smiled softly at him. "The vastness of it all. But mostly thinking about asking you to stay in bed with me today."

He groaned, rolling over and propping himself over me, the striations of muscle in his shoulders tensing. "Baby, no. I have to go to work."

Deacon and I were on strict orders not to show up at the office until Rebecca deemed our mourning period "suitable." She thought we should be waiting another week after the funeral before showing our faces at the office.

I didn't have the heart to tell her that, based on experience, your mourning period for a parent never really ended. You just wore the grief differently.

Deacon was working more hours than he ever had, permanently supplanting himself in our father's office and doing more drugs than you probably should off a desk that was, up until very recently, occupied by your newly dead father. The stock had taken yet another alarming dip when the board released a statement announcing his death, which was to be predicted.

But someone took a photo of us outside the hospital on Cape Cod, hugging—both our hands fisted into each other's sweaters, heads buried into shoulders, and then another when we finally pulled apart, faces wet with tears and ripe with anguish.

It was a moment of unfettered, raw, sharp, visceral grief that had just been meant for the two of us.

It hurt me that it was splashed across every news outlet and tabloid. To see it used for headlines and the grief of the two richest orphans in the world—their words, not mine—to be nothing more than a tool to sell copies and get clicks.

But it had an unanticipated impact. Public opinion of us had never been higher. Everyone seemed to forget that they once called me a whore, and that my brother had recently thrown a public fit in a bowling alley, that he'd smashed a champagne glass and sprayed blood all over the table of a fine-dining establishment.

It was horribly ironic—our father had been so resistant to demonstrating humanity publicly and privately for fear that it would make him seem less than unwavering, unfaltering.

And that tiny moment that was just meant for my brother and me was what steadied the ship. What saved his empire from crumbling.

Blinking at David, I tipped my chin up, all petulance. He'd worked from home more than he should have with me this week until Rebecca called and told him if he didn't show his face, she'd come down to the house and drag him out herself.

No one wanted to see her monochromatic outfits stalking the halls, so they went in, and Deacon and I stayed here.

"Five more minutes, then," I whispered, brushing my lips against his.

I felt him grin against my mouth, and his words as they whispered back. "Five more minutes then, baby."

It was just a brush, a tiny moment and a tiny kiss where my heart didn't feel as heavy; my lungs didn't burn.

Just a tiny little promise that maybe, just maybe, it would all be okay.

———

I heard Taylor's voice before David pushed open the heavy door that led to the breakfast room.

She'd taken it upon herself to run things around here, even though nothing really needed running. The staff had worked for my father for decades, and this house, with all its halls, all its ghosts, and all its pretentious lighting, kept running after he was gone, too.

No one sat at the head of the table where my father would have, his chair pushed in and the ornately carved wooden arms touching matching edges of the table. Ready and waiting forever for its sole occupant to pull it out, fold himself down there, and wait for his paper, his glass of juice to be poured and for his day to begin.

We hadn't touched the chair, the staff never laid down a place setting, and the days began anyway.

Taylor pointed at Deacon, her chin tipped in the air. "You are cut off from drugs. I've spoken to your dealer, and to be honest with you, Deacon, I believe Tripp when he says his father knows a lot of frightening men in Boston. We aren't above calling them."

"And you—" Taylor narrowed her eyes on me, "are cut off from sex."

"That's not why we were late for breakfast," David answered, pulling my chair out for me before tugging up the sleeves of his charcoal Theory suit and folding his arms across the back of it.

"David," Taylor held up her hand to silence him before continuing, "I don't care how much she begs. There will be no unhealthy coping mechanisms taking over in this house on my watch. You know what, as of this moment, you yourself are also cut off."

Taylor rounded on Tripp, appraising him with a shrewd look that could have rivaled my father. My heart ached, pressing against my ribcage. I rubbed my chest absentmindedly while she drummed her fingers against her chin before speaking again. "And you—you are the only one doing their job around here. So, kudos to you, and thank you for holding down the fort."

Arching an eyebrow, Tripp offered her a mock salute. His eyes landed on the Rolex on his wrist. "Speaking of, DK, we should go. Ash wants to meet with us before that call with Halton."

David's hands pressed into my shoulders, and I could feel him hesitate before he nodded

Despite the threat of Rebecca, if I turned around and asked, he'd stay with me.

"I'll drop you two off. I need to be at the hospital soon." Taylor pointed her finger at both of us before standing. She brushed off the front of her scrubs before throwing one final look at us. "Behave."

David brushed a hand over my head, dropping a kiss there, and Tripp offered me a wry smile while he clapped my brother on the shoulder before they followed Taylor out of the still-swinging door like they'd been instructed.

"And then there were two." Deacon raised his coffee to me before leaning back in his chair, an almost undetectable slump to his shoulders. All of him looked wilted, in desperate need of sunlight and water and love.

"Have you talked to Noa?" I asked quietly, looking like I was significantly more interested in pouring my coffee than watching his reaction.

But I could see it, the measured swallow and the tick of his jawline—his broken heart, worn in between the creases of his sleeves.

Deacon shrugged. "A bit. I told her I'd let her know when to come back. No sense coming here before the funeral. I might not be going into the office, but it's a fucking mess. You're lucky you're still doing discovery shit."

I was. It was all endless research and emails and phone calls before we made our first investment. It had timed out well, if there was such a thing—for your father to entrust you with an entirely new direction for the investing structure in his multi-billion dollar holding, for him to die suddenly because of a hemorrhage no one saw coming, and for the head of public relations to ban you and your brother from showing your faces at the office.

Glancing up at my brother over my carafe, I arched an eyebrow. "And she's listening to you?"

Deacon stretched his arms out, tossing me a wry smile that didn't meet his eyes. "Would you want to spend extra time with me?"

"Yes. I think you're great," I answered, tipping my chin in the air, a sorry imitation of Taylor earlier. I didn't think I was very capable of standing up straight, all of me weighed down by such a heavy heart and shredded lungs.

"That makes one of us." Deacon rolled his eyes before his features softened. "Do you think he knew?"

He could have been talking about any number of things. There were a whole host of things our father kept from us, as it turned out. But I knew what he meant. "About a random hemorrhage that no one could have seen coming?"

Deacon shrugged, a jerk of his shoulder, like we were discussing the weather. Something casual. Certainly not about our last remaining parent and the way they'd both left us behind. "Yeah, like, on some innate level, knew that the hands of the clock were almost at midnight, and he wanted to go back to where she'd last...where Mom died?"

The second scan Taylor took confirmed the new growth of tumors in his lungs. She saw it too late, but it wouldn't have mattered. There was no way to know what would happen and that it would happen so quickly.

I'd begged her to tell me the minutia of it all—the physiology of how, even though she told me I didn't need to know, and most importantly, I didn't want to know.

He'd bled to death, essentially, albeit in a matter of moments.

But because the hemorrhage had happened in his lungs, she said sometimes it was akin to drowning.

There was something ironic there.

Wiping at my cheeks before taking an undignified exhale, I looked up at my brother through watery eyes. "I wasn't able to read his mind in life, and I certainly can't now that he's gone, but I have to say...this isn't how I thought the story would end."

"No? You thought he was going to somehow come out on top?" Deacon's voice rose like he wanted to sound dry, irreverent, but a horrible crack lurked there, just below the surface.

A wet laugh bubbled in my throat. "Quietly. Maybe. I don't know. I kind of thought that maybe it was black sludge coursing through his veins all these years. Definitely not real, life-giving blood. And certainly not enough to kill him when it made him bleed."

Deacon looked down at his coffee, swirling it once, twice, like it was a scotch he'd pilfered from our father's stores. "I guess that turned out not to be true, after all."

"I thought maybe he'd spend his last days here, the three of us watching movies in bed or something. That he'd lament, tell us how he missed our mother, and that we were the best things that happened to him—" I inhaled again, offering my brother a tiny shrug.

He tipped his head, lips pulling into a resigned smile. "This isn't Hallmark. That wasn't in the cards for us, Charles."

Resigned, I leaned back in my chair and blinked up at the vaulted ceiling, wishing with all my heart it looked like one of those cloudless morning skies out on the terrace with our father.

"I have to go. I have a call I need to prep for." Deacon's voice was rough as he stood, pushing away from the table. He paused, one hand coming down to grip my shoulder. "If there had to be only two of us left, I'm glad it's me and you, Charles. Us against the world."

Reaching back, I wrapped my hand around his wrist. "Promise me you'll call Noa. That you won't leave it too late. That you won't waste time."

His fingers tensed against my shoulder before he left, his parting words fractured and quiet. "I'll think about it."

I wanted more than anything for him to know he was okay—that he'd be okay—the way I was okay, because I had David.

I had Taylor. I had Tripp. I had him.

And he had me.

We'd never be alone, and we'd never been alone, not from the moment we'd met as children. There weren't many photos to capture whatever that homecoming had been like, but I imagined there'd been a recognition between two infants, two souls, of the way it would always be.

Me and him against the world.

Deacon

My father's funeral was soon. Too soon.

In a lot of ways, but mostly because it was tomorrow.

There was a child somewhere in me, crying after a long, tired day where they'd played and laughed and ran through a field barefoot—sobbing when they were put to bed because they didn't want the day to be over. Because they hoped tomorrow never came.

I hoped a lot of things would never come, but I'd delayed this conversation for long enough. Too long, probably. Noa was back from Milan, and she'd been in New York, back in that apartment that had been hers and was only ours for not even close to enough fucking time.

My eyes closed when I heard it, fingertips biting against the edges of the diamond in her engagement ring I'd taken to carrying around in my pocket.

Her voice. The voice I'd have crawled on my knees to hear. Begged for it like someone might beg for water, for food, for sustenance. Begged for a millisecond of her attention to be on me. Begged to be bathed in the sound of it—of her.

The voice I'd paused meetings for. The voice I'd probably hear echoing in my head until the day I died.

The voice of the person who deserved so much more than I could give them.

She sounded a bit breathless, a bit exasperated, but a bit hopeful—like the sight of my name on her phone was sunshine on a rainy day. It was pathetic that I'd been reduced to that, to being so unreliable and unpredictable that something as simple as a phone call would brighten her.

"Hi, hi—I'm so sorry I didn't call earlier. I'm back at home now. I'm packing, and I need to check the time of my flight, but I'll be there. The shoot went long. It was that same art director from when—"

Interjecting, I swallowed and rolled the engagement ring back and forth over my knuckles. "You need to do me a favor, baby."

"Hmm?" She sounded distracted, and I could picture her—all flushed and eyes sparkling, her teeth coming down to worry on her bottom lip, and all that hair curling around her face, still damp from the shower, while she tried to pack her bag, open on the bed that was ours for not nearly enough time—never enough. She'd worry about what to wear for the funeral. Not because she cared what anyone thought, not because she particularly cared about clothes, but because I did, because she cared about me.

"Don't come home."

I said it before I could change my mind, and I hung up before I could hear what those words did to that voice, that person, that fucking girl, on the other end of the phone.

Exhaling, my cheeks puffed out as I watched the setting sun catch against the diamond I was still rolling between my fingers.

It was sparkling again. I hoped she sparkled again. She didn't deserve to be dulled by the likes of me.

I pitched my arm back, the ring sailing in an arc *up, up, up,* over the rocky shore before it hit the water somewhere out there on the lake.

The ripples were small, because even though it had been giant by diamond standards and represented something so much bigger than that—something that was infinite and would forever echo out there in the lake while the ring sank to the bottom—I watched them for a moment, stretching out but never quite reaching the shore.

And then they were gone.

Charlie

The lights around my vanity were too bright. I blinked, dabbing the makeup sponge under my eye. I'd been here for the last thirty minutes, painstakingly applying what I hoped was enough concealer to hide the bags under my eyes. It likely called for a professional, but I didn't really feel like having a stranger poke and prod at my face today.

I'd left the door to my room ajar—just enough that my brother could come in if he needed me. Even though I knew he wouldn't. When it pushed open, I was expecting David or Taylor. I certainly hadn't been expecting to see Sabine in her classic black jumpsuit, pushing her rack of dresses in.

Shaking my head, I looked back to the mirror and kept blending my concealer. "No one cares what I'm wearing to my father's funeral, Sabine."

She paused, glancing over her shoulder as she straightened the hangers on her rack. "Sadly, Charlie—they do. They care very much."

Dropping the sponge, I leaned back in the chair and crossed my arms. "Who is even paying you?"

"Your father. He arranged this with me before he died. He didn't want you to have to worry, Charlie, about what they're all going to think. He was just trying to take care of you both, perhaps the only way he knew how."

Oh.

A few extra pounds were added to the weight I'd been carrying around in my heart, and a few more fires started in my lungs.

My voice cracked when I spoke, wiping my lash line as I watched Sabine in the mirror, rifling through the dresses with the same thoughtful precision she had for years. "I suppose this is it then. Our last hoorah."

Sabine paused, tapping a manicured finger before taking the Givenchy Dress in Tweed off the rack. It was something I would have picked for myself—houndstooth pattern, a boat neck, and tiny sleeves, with a flared skirt that hit mid-thigh. She glanced up at me, raising her eyebrows, and for the first time in her career, waited for my approval.

I nodded softly at her, and she turned to her accessory trunk and pulled out a pair of opaque Falke tights before laying them on the chaise lounge at the end of the bed.

The heels of her black Manolo Blahnik pumps sunk into the plush carpet as she came to stand behind me. In an uncharacteristic display of affection, she dropped her hands to my shoulders and smiled at me in the reflection. "You have a standing appointment with me for the rest of your life. You call, I'll answer. Though I doubt you'll call."

I shrugged one shoulder, blinking at her. "You never know."

"It's been a pleasure watching you grow up." Her voice sounded wistful, and her brown eyes sparkled under the light of the chandelier, unshed tears pooling on her lash line.

"You're barely ten years older than me," I said, voice thick with tears.

I'd been wanting out of this routine, my most loathed and abhorred duty as a Winchester, as my father's daughter, and now, the finality in the air felt suffocating.

"I didn't mean numerically." Sabine shook her head, taking a steadying breath. "May I make one final suggestion?"

I nodded, watching her through lashes heavy with tears. She scrunched her nose, and her fingers braced on my shoulders before she let go, turning and grabbing something else from the still-open trunk.

She smiled, a black velvet headband held in her hands.

"That's pretty," I offered quietly, picking up the sponge again and dabbing uselessly at my face before dropping it.

Setting it down beside the makeup spread across the table, Sabine dropped one hand to my shoulder. "It'll give your hair a bit of a lift."

I nodded again, because I wasn't sure what else to do. We just stared at each other in the mirror, watery eyes and years stretching between us. It really was the end of an era.

A knock sounded on the door, and both of our eyes cut to it, that string that stretched there finally snapping.

David leaned in the doorway, one hand shoved in the pocket of his black Prada suit pants, the other holding a takeout cup. "Latte. Non-fat milk with one pump of sugar-free vanilla syrup."

Sabine pressed her hand into my shoulder, giving me one final smile in the mirror before pointing at the coffee. "Drink that before you get into the dress. If you spill, that will be a nightmare to get out of the tweed."

"Noted," I whispered, smiling at her in return, some of the tears sneaking over my lash line and spilling down my cheeks. "I'll see you later? At the funeral?"

Nodding, Sabine took a tiny, shuddering inhale before clasping her hands in front of her chest. "Just remember to pair that with a platform heel. Closed toe would be best."

"Sure." My voice was small, raising a hand to her in farewell.

She smiled at me, tears falling down her cheeks now, too, before she did the same.

David stepped away from the door, and Sabine brushed past him into the hallway.

I offered him a small smile before taking a measured exhale and turning back to the mirror. There were tear tracks through my concealer.

"Baby." David dropped the latte beside my abandoned makeup sponge, wrapped his arms around me, and buried his face in my neck. His lips brushed across the pulse point, dropping right on top of my heartbeat before he looked up at me in the mirror. "Are you crying because it's the funeral, or because it looks like you just broke up with your stylist?"

"Can't it be both?" I asked through a wet laugh, dropping my head against his.

His arms tightened around me. "Do you need anything?"

I shook my head.

"I've got a flask in my suit jacket in case it goes south." David grinned at me, his eyes lighting up for a moment. "Is there anything else I can do to get you through the day?"

Closing my eyes, I wrapped my hands around his arms. I was heavy. So, so heavy. But when his hands were on me, I think some of the weight was held by them—those perfect, calloused hands that I loved and that loved me. "No. I think I have everything I need."

———

I'd always equated walking down the sweeping staircase in the center of our home as marching toward uncertain doom in some way or another—whether it was to an event my father was hosting in the foyer of the house, outside on the sweeping lawn, or if I was just expected to make a grand entrance to something.

But it all paled in comparison to this—walking down these stairs, my hand in David's, toward my father's funeral.

I didn't want to look up to the bottom of the staircase where my brother would be, to where my father's ghost probably waited like he had time and time again when he was a living, breathing human. So I looked at our joined hands instead. I'd always been taught to watch each step I was taking in case I tripped and fell or did something human, like make a fool of myself, but it was David Kennedy's hand I was holding, and he wouldn't let me stumble.

I was keenly aware of the sound from the platform of my heels. I'd listened to Sabine, grabbing a pair of black velvet Jimmy Choo sandals from my closet. But they were echoing substantially more than a pump might have, and each step down, each reverberation up the platform, through my leg, went all the way up to my heart.

It was like the tick of a clock, maybe the same one that had been moving its hands inside my father's body; each step was one minute closer to the end, the final hour where I'd have to say goodbye.

David's fingers squeezed mine before he stepped down from the stairs, lifting our still-joined hands to help me take that final step. I finally brought my gaze up to him, smiling softly, and noticed we were short one person.

My brother's back was turned to me; his hands shoved into the pockets of his custom black Stefano Ricci suit that he only wore on the most important occasions. His head was tipped up, hair immaculately styled into place, and looked like he might be staring at the face of the antique grandfather clock by the front door.

Taylor fiddled with the collar of her Alice + Olivia Wynell Tipped dress in the reflection of her cellphone before she dropped it back into her black Aquazurra Twist satin clutch.

Tripp stood just to the side of her. One eyebrow lifted as he watched her, arms crossed across the front of his black Brooks Brothers suit.

I looked back and forth between them. "Where's Noa?"

He rolled his head back, grimacing.

Taylor widened her eyes at me, leaning forward with arms crossed over her chest, like it should have been something I ignored, pretended wasn't staring us all in the face.

My brother turned, shrugging with a rueful smile and eyes that looked like he'd been up all night. "Not here."

Dropping David's hands, I walked on tentative feet toward him, ignoring the resounding sound of my heels. "What did you do?"

Deacon looked at me before running a hand over his jaw. "The right thing, for once. She deserves something I can't give her. She deserves better than me."

Grabbing his hand in both of mine, I pressed my thumbs into his palm. "You are the best, Deacon."

"Charlie, we both know that's not true." His voice dropped, and he wrapped his hand around my wrist before letting it go and clearing his throat. "You ready?"

"No," I rasped, placing my fingers under my eyes to catch some of the tears before they tracked down my face.

Deacon shook his head, extending his elbow to me. "Me neither."

"You shouldn't do this alone, Deacon," I whispered up at him, placing my hand in the crook of his elbow. My big brother. My favorite person on the planet and the other half of me, all broken and without the person who made his heart whole.

Deacon jerked his head backward. "I'm not alone. And neither are you."

The smile he tried to give me was strained, a muscle jumping in his jaw, and tears lined his bloodshot eyes.

Swallowing thickly, I nodded, blinking and dropping my head to his chest as those hands on the clock ticked down, and we had to take those last few steps toward our new world together.

Deacon

My father's funeral differed vastly from my mother's—and how lucky was I to be in the minority of people who could even make that kind of comparison?

My mother died in the spring. It had been a gray day, but there was a warm breeze. I remember that much. I thought about it, the way it felt against my face as I sat there earlier in that stifling church, shoulder to shoulder with my sister, like dutiful children as the minister droned on and on.

My father wasn't a religious man; I think he'd only really believed in himself and the vast reach of his wealth, but there wasn't much talk of a greater power in the speech anyway.

It was a lot of vague platitudes about grief and love, and there wasn't a moment of the service that felt warm. Nothing like that breeze on my face ten years ago.

And that's not to say my mother had been a particularly warm person. I don't think she was, looking back. But I think that maybe I was different, colder now. Maybe all those years that chased my sister around finally caught up with me.

It would be ironic, the kind of thing you'd read about in a book—the lost daughter returns home and finally lays her ghosts to rest, but they claw and scrape their way out of their graves and come for the wayward son at last.

I felt oddly detached the entire time, if I was being honest, like I was floating above the whole thing watching it happen. Maybe that's because the person who'd anchored me down, kept me in this atmosphere and made sure everything felt like it would be okay wasn't there. I'd sent her away. It had been for her own good, but it hurt all the same.

My cheeks burned from forced smiles of thanks and pleasantry, and my eyes felt like fucking sandpaper.

And the worst part was, we'd have to do the whole thing again in a few months because the fucking ground was frozen. We hadn't been able to bury him. There would be no laying our father to rest just yet.

The thought of his body on ice for the foreseeable future, preserved in some sort of industrial freezer, made my fucking skin crawl. I wore that knowledge all day—that the pristine, oak casket was actually empty—like a second suit I'd put on too tight.

I was still wearing it now, walking beside my sister down the lawn to the boathouse. Yanking on my tie, I closed my eyes, breathing in and out.

A hand brushed my elbow, and my sister whispered to me. "The stars are beautiful tonight."

Flicking my gaze up, I saw she was right. They were beautiful, objectively. But it all seemed bleaker than it should. The sky I saw was probably different than the one she did—she had the love of her life, and her two best friends beside her. People who saw her, truly saw her, and loved her unapologetically.

I think my sky was just three separate black holes, where the most important people should have been. One for my mother, one for my father, and one for Noa. They were man made, created by me and all my inabilities and failures, up there yawning open, wider and wider, eating up all the light that was supposed to shine down on me.

I said nothing, offering her a strained smile and pulling the door to the boathouse open for her. The lights were left on, but dim, casting eerie shadows that looked like they might reach out and wrap their claws around my legs and drag me out through those floor-to-ceiling glass windows and drown me in the lake.

Charlie kicked off her heels, wrapping her arms around herself, and padded on light feet towards the bar. An awkward, wet sort of laugh tumbled from her as she surveyed the bar and wine fridge, while Taylor, David and Tripp filed in behind us.

We'd been spending a lot of time down here, this place that had gone unused but become a refuge for the five of us. Whatever we were.

"What does one do after their only remaining parent's funeral?" Charlie's eyes were wide, sweeping across the shadowed room before landing on me.

Taylor practically pushed past me, and usually her take charge attitude was one I could do without, but I was a bit astray right now. I could probably use all the guidance she offered.

"I say we have a toast." She tipped her chin in the air, pulling open the wine fridge and grabbing the first bottle of champagne she saw—a 1961 Krug Vintage. My sister's eyes cut to me, and her cheeks twitched with the ghost of a smile. It had been our parent's wedding wine.

Fitting, to toast with it, to send them both off, out there and into the ether. Maybe they were together again.

I glanced back out at the water, watching the rolling waves through the windows, illuminated by the dock lights. I vaguely heard the cork pop—and then Tripp was shoving a crystal flute in my hand.

Blinking, I turned back and raised my eyebrows. Taylor leaned over the bar counter, head cocked to the side, waiting for me, and David was behind my sister. The five of us. All that was left.

Taylor raised her glass, tipping her head, eyes moving over me before she smiled softly. Like she could stitch me up, fix me the way she couldn't fix my father. "To Steven."

David's arm wrapped around Charlie, pulling her flush to his chest, murmuring the same words and raising his own glass. She leaned her head back, eyes fluttering closed, and her shoulders softening in an exhale. I think the sight of her, happy, content—all the things she deserved to be—chased some of that blackness in my sky away. My sister would be what I held onto from now on, the only person who would never leave me. The light in all my dark.

Tripp eyed me for a moment before swallowing and raising his own glass. His words were weighted. My father had saved his father, even when he didn't deserve it. Probably showed him more care and consideration than his own family.

All these people who owed Steven Winchester something, who loved him. I loved him, I did. But I think I fucking hated him, too. I couldn't tell.

They all smiled at me like they were feeling something—some greater sense of purpose, comfort, finding love in grief the way you're supposed to. I didn't really feel anything.

My heart thudded in my chest, sure. But it was hollow, dull. Forgotten. Still here even though the two people who gave it life were gone—one nothing but dust and the other with ice inching over their skin, to keep them preserved until the spring had thawed the world enough for us to properly say goodbye.

I didn't want to let him go. I wasn't ready. I raised my champagne, murmuring my father's name along with the rest of them, the only people I had, and I pretended it was goodbye. It wasn't really, because he was in a freezer, my mother was already in the ground and one day soon, when it all softened and the wind stopped biting at exposed skin and raw hearts, I'd have to face it.

But I hoped that day never came.

Charlie

I finally had to ditch my leather jacket earlier this week. The wind had been far too unforgiving for too long, but I kept wearing it despite the fact that we were well into winter now.

It reminded me of my father—a bit because he hated it, and I could picture him clearer than usual, one salt-and-pepper eyebrow rising on his forehead when he'd see it before he'd look back at his paper.

"If it's too cold for me to walk aimlessly around the streets of Chicago, David, it's certainly too cold for you." I folded my arms, glancing sideways at him before gesturing to the empty sidewalk before us. "We're the only ones out here. That should tell you something."

He grinned, and I could see the corners of his eyes wrinkle from behind the pair of battered Ray Bans shielding him from the winter sun. He plucked at his gray Thome Browne jacket. "I'm fine, baby. You're the one bundled up."

"That coat cannot be warm enough." I rolled my eyes, tugging the strings hanging down from my Mackage Nefi puffer jacket.

David shrugged. "It's a wool blend."

I snorted, shaking my head. "You've been spending too much time with Taylor and Tripp. Three months ago, you wouldn't have been able to name the different types of fabric used to make coats, let alone name them."

"Oh, come on." He laughed, reaching an arm around me and bringing me into his chest. "I've been friends with your brother for long enough to at least know a high-quality material when I see one."

Smiling, I wrapped my arms around him, trying to keep up with his significantly longer strides, the toe of my Chloe Shearling Leather boot nearly catching on a crack in the pavement. "Where are we going? You've been looping us around random streets for like thirty minutes, ever since we left the gallery."

I spent most weekends there. Art had never been something I thought would play a pivotal role in my adult life, but I liked it, being surrounded by those pieces of my mother, lovingly kept and curated by my father.

It was a quiet sort of joy I never would have anticipated, overhearing a stranger whisper about how talented my mother was, even my brother, because I'd stolen some drawings he did back when we were in prep school and hung them beside hers. My father had apparently kept those, too.

I'd never so much as scribbled on a sheet with a crayon as a child, at least not created anything worth keeping. But he had kept my first publication from my master's thesis. He had a paper copy and an original print of the journal. I wasn't sure where to hang that, so I left it in his desk drawer, the place I found it.

"Helen called me into her office the other week," David answered, his voice rough. I felt his hand tighten through the ridiculous sleeves of my jacket. "She had a question about something that was directed to you in the fine print of your father's estate."

His steps slowed, and he gripped both my shoulders with those perfect hands, a softer smile playing on his face, before he spun me around and brought me flush to his chest.

We were outside my old townhouse, the stoop only feet away.

David pressed his lips to the side of my head before dropping his mouth to my ear. "He bought it back from the people you sold it to."

"Why would he do that?" I whispered, taking in a horrible gulp of the sharp winter air.

There were always tiny fires burning in my lungs, the loss of my parents, the life I never had, and the loss of one that I did, crackling away, tiny embers flying off the logs of our past and burning me from the inside. They weren't wildfires; they were just there—little flames flickering. But today, that cold, shredding air gusted through, and the wind picked up all those embers, and all of me went up in flames.

Sometimes it hit me all at once—not the loss of my father, but the fact that I'd never get to know him in his entirety.

David shook his head against mine, pulling me tighter to his chest. "I don't know why he did most things, baby. But we can go inside if you'd like? I have the key."

"Helen just gave you the key? That feels questionable in its legality." I laughed, but my voice shook.

I felt David grin against my ear, his hands squeezing my shoulders before he let go. One hand found mine, and he interlaced our fingers. "Do you want to go inside?"

I nodded. "Yes."

There was something about seeing David, after all these years, pulling out a key to that old townhouse, walking up the stoop, and opening the door.

The door creaked open, and nothing was different, and everything was the same. But it wasn't. Not at all.

Wrapping my arms around myself, I took a tentative step into the hallway. And then another. And then another. I knew this house like the back of my hand, and even though it was empty, I could picture it like it used to be.

The photos on the wall from all the places I ran to when I was running from home. The high-pile rug in the living room. The vintage leather couch. The sideboard along the wall. The empty rack for stemware underneath the cupboards.

The terrace above us where David and I became the us we would be for the last three years.

But none of those things were here anymore, and I was glad for that.

David cleared his throat, running a hand through his hair. "It can be yours, or ours, if you'd like it to be."

"You want to move in here with me? Back where it all started?" I asked, looking up at him.

"I'd live in a cardboard box if you asked me to." David shrugged, his eyes wandering around the empty kitchen. "But this place doesn't really feel like it used to, does it?"

I shook my head. "No, it doesn't."

And it didn't. I always expected this house would feel a bit like a tomb, all the hope and promise and possibility of what could have been sealed away in here, left to wither and fade away into nothing.

But the sunlight stretched from the paned window at the back of the kitchen across the island, touching those honey eyes looking down at me, and when that first ray hit me, the fires in my lungs banked.

David cocked his head at me before swallowing, a muscle in his cheek jumped. Unflappable, unwavering David Kennedy looked nervous as he reached into the pocket of his wildly impractical jacket; big, perfect, calloused fingers fumbling over something as he pulled it out.

It caught in the ray of sunlight reaching across the room, and I blinked for a moment before I realized what it was.

My mother's ring.

His voice was rough when he spoke. "Apparently, Steven left this to me. But I think you should have it. You can give this back to me someday, if you'd ever like me to use it."

With those perfect fingers that belonged to those perfect hands on my favorite perfectly imperfect person, David set the ring gently down on the granite countertop. The noise it made was jarring, just a tiny clink from that one-of-a-kind diamond when it touched the stone, but it sounded a bit like the wind chime outside your childhood home on a perfect spring day. The kind where you woke up and the sun shone on your face through the window in just the right way, and you were quietly happy, content.

I nodded, scrunching my nose at him. Tears tracked down my face. Some of them were sad, some of them were happy. But I meant what I said, because the future was impossibly bright, and for the first time in my life, there was something I was running toward. "Someday."

He grinned at me, and his honey eyes sparkled. His heart whispered to me the way it had from the day we met all those years ago. I could hear it through his shirt, through his chest, and all that muscle tissue.

But it was his words that I held on to, that gently blew out all that was left of that burning in my lungs, that reached down and held my impossibly heavy heart so I could breathe.

"Welcome home, baby."

Four Months Later

If I angled my head properly, moved my chair to the right by just a few inches—and if it wasn't a particularly busy day on the executives' floor—I could see clear across it and into my father's old office.

It was empty, save for everything he left behind, so not really empty at all by the definition of the word—but entirely empty because Steven Winchester was gone, and nothing would ever take up space the way he had.

Unflinching. Unyielding. Entirely cutthroat and brilliant. Domineering and brash, and probably leaving most of the business world glad he was gone. To be missed, but not really deep down.

But I missed him, not even all that deep down. Just all around me. In usual, nondescript moments.

It wasn't like I had an entire arsenal of happy memories to choose from, but maybe that's what made the little moments of humanity my father exhibited—that I kept close—all the more special. They were the Steven Winchester version of human moments—freshly squeezed orange juice. An Audemars Piguet watch. A folded copy of the Tribune.

He was probably still there—a freshly delivered Americano in his left hand, one salt-and-pepper eyebrow rising as he looked on at everything.

But I couldn't see him, not in this life, in this world anymore.

It wasn't a quiet day on the floor, anyway. It was Friday, and as per the tradition my father started, it was the weekly executive briefing. Ash kept that tradition, as he kept most things my father put into place—down to not touching anything in his office—all the way to his wayward son.

Casual Friday, which really wasn't all that casual, was still around. But my leather jacket, really bordering on too worn now, hung over the back of my chair. I guess I kept some things the same, too.

Squinting at my computer, my lips started to move as I silently read the email on my screen. I owed Ash an update on my latest conversation with an up-and-coming ESG policy think tank. I owed it to the rest of the executive team and my brother, too—the only person with enough shareholding power for it to really make a difference, to really matter. But Deacon didn't care about much these days.

A knock came from the door, and I flicked my eyes up, lips tugging into a smile that was anything but small, anything but Winchester fake—but entirely overlarge, so big my cheeks hurt—because David Kennedy was standing in my doorway.

He was leaning against it, arms crossed and the top buttons of the slim-fit white shirt undone, revealing a sliver of his tanned chest. The sleeves were pushed up his forearms, cords of muscle even more prominent from the way his arms were crossed—and on his bicep, the way the midday light was shining through the floor-to-ceiling windows, I could just see the faint outline of the black ink there. My signature. Me on his skin.

David grinned at me—my grin—the only one that really ever mattered, that could light up a room and pull back the curtains on all the windows in the rooms in my heart, my lungs, my soul, the home inside my body. The house I lived in. The home I loved.

One rogue wave curled across his forehead, and he looked almost the same, standing in the doorway of that same office, that same building, and that same city from all those years ago.

Three years. It wasn't that long, not really, not in the grand scheme of things—nothing but a blink, a millisecond of a life lived.

Not that long. But forever, stretching and endless. Honey eyes. My brother's laugh. Taylor, one eyebrow rising. Noa, smiling and too good for this world. Someone entirely thawed. My father. My mother's memory—not a ghost—but something else entirely. Something lovely. Too many sequin dresses and tan suits to count. A friendship formed and kept after all these years. David Kennedy and me.

All these bricks and mortar and pieces of foundation I used to build my new home. All the pieces of me.

"Hey, baby. You almost ready?" David's voice was the familiar creak of the stairs, the breeze that comes through the window during a fall morning, the stretch of sunlight across crisp, freshly washed sheets.

"For a casual Friday executives' briefing?" I raised my eyebrows, leaning back in my chair and crossing my arms over my white Armani t-shirt. "Of course."

David was still grinning, but those honey eyes—anything but sweet—briefly dropped to my chest. He arched one eyebrow at me, pushing off the door frame, his long legs crossing the floor in a moment. He paused beside me, leaning against the edge of the desk, one calloused hand shoved into his navy suit pants, and the other dropping to my thigh.

His fingers skimmed my knee, and I could feel the heat on my skin through the thick wool of my tights before he grabbed the hem of my Theory Trouser-Front skirt and rubbed it back and forth between his forefinger and thumb.

David's eyes flicked up, not sparkling, but his pupils wide and entirely dark. "I didn't realize fancy, important, majority shareholders, Vice Presidents of Sustainable Investing, wore miniskirts to work."

"This one does," I offered quietly, heat flaming across my cheeks when David's hand slid under my skirt, grazing the inside of my thigh. "Easy. I can't spend my days bent over your desk. I have big, important vice president things to do."

David raised his hands, both palms facing me, and that grin, that entirely radiant smile, stretched across his face. "Far be it from me to distract you. At home then?"

Home. That townhouse I shared with him. The one that my father kept for me.

"At home." I raised my eyebrows. "What are you doing here? Did you come down here to kidnap me before the executives' meeting?"

David grinned, holding one perfect, too-calloused hand out to me. The hand that would hold mine for the rest of my life. Reaching forward, I interlaced our fingers.

He pulled me up, the heels of my Staud boots hitting the floor, and his other hand coming to the small of my back, warm and pressing me flush against him.

"I'm sorry—" I burst out laughing, one hand coming to his chest. "Do you have a boner?"

David dropped his lips to my forehead briefly. "I like your skirt."

"Yeah, well, I like your pants, too, but we have a meeting to get to." I pointedly pushed him back a step, narrowing my eyes. "Can you be trusted to follow me down the hall? Or do you need a few minutes for the blood to return to your head?"

"Going to need a few minutes. I've spent too much time in that briefing room with my blood flow diverted. But you go ahead. I'll follow you."

David's hand dropped over mine, where it was pressed to his chest. He held it there for a moment, and I could feel his heart, just through his shirt.

"You'd follow me, Mr. Kennedy?" I asked, just a whisper, my eyes wholly on his.

David's voice was low when he spoke. It wrapped around me, poured itself into the cement foundations of my home, reinforced the trusses, opened the windows to let all the light in, and knocked gently on the door. "I'd follow you anywhere, billion dollar baby."

"Anywhere?" I whispered, fingers tightening against his chest.

"Anywhere." He stared back at me, eyes crinkling at the corners, those lines of age I loved to run my fingers over. "Say the word, and we're out of here. We can sail around the world."

He leaned forward, his lips brushing mine for a moment—just a moment, but a lifetime, an eternity.

I would have stayed there kissing him in this office where we met, lifetimes and homes, and the people we were stretching between us—taken any scraps, any moments of attention he would give me—but they weren't scraps; none of it was fleeting. It was forever. We were forever.

David's hand splayed against my back, bringing me flush against him again—against his astronomically inappropriate office boner—and I felt his teeth graze my lip, his tongue sweep forward against the seam of my mouth.

"Okay!" I planted my hands on his chest, pushing him backward. I shook my head, throwing him a look and pursuing my lips before smoothing my shirt. But I was smiling. I smiled a lot now.

He grinned, palms up in the air again. "Sorry, sorry. You go ahead."

Pointing at him, I stepped aside, and he threw himself down into my chair. "Make all the...adjustments you need. I'll see you down the hall."

David winked at me before stretching his arms up behind his head and leaning back.

The sound of my heels clicking against the marble was drowned by the sounds of the office, most doors open, and everyone talking, laughing, living their lives, and actually enjoying their day at Winchester Holdings.

Most doors, except my brothers. The door to Deacon's office was firmly closed and usually remained that way until he deigned to grace everyone with his presence. The nameplate on his door read "Chief Financial Officer" now, no longer "Vice President," and there was no light emanating from underneath it.

But he was in there—he was never late for work, no matter the time he dragged himself out of bed—his or someone else's. But he would stay there, behind the door, shut off from the joy the life out here used to give him, the life he used to love until he was done with whatever wake-me-up he needed—Hydra-V, coffee, cocaine. It varied day by day.

I had stopped throwing open the door and dragging him out about a month ago. He would dig his heels in—both literally and figuratively. It wasn't worth the scene he'd cause, the further damage to his reputation.

My lips twitched, pulling down, and I folded my arms across my chest, fingers fluttering uselessly, because I wanted to go throw the door open. But I turned, walking by instead.

The boardroom was empty—save for an occupied seat across from where I typically sat.

The fabric of Tripp's powder blue Hugo Boss shirt stretched across his back, and his hair looked decidedly unkempt, particularly for him. At least from the back—because his forehead was firmly planted against the mahogany table.

"Ew, get your forehead off my conference table." I wrinkled my nose and pulled out the ostentatious, high-backed leather chair across from him. All of my father's original furnishings remained, too, but they were growing on me.

He lifted his head, icy eyes serving me a flat look before he leaned back in his chair, scrubbing at his jaw.

"You look horrible," I offered, arching an eyebrow.

"Your brother had me out until four a.m. last night." Tripp's voice was practically a groan, and he ran a hand through his hair, somehow making it worse.

"You could have sent him to my place. Saved yourself a terrible headache. He'd just drink himself into oblivion alone on the terrace."

Tripp gave me a wry look before slinging an arm over the back of the chair. "Someone had to make sure he didn't end up in the lake. Besides, you're busy playing house with Kennedy in Lincoln Park."

My lips pulled, about to offer an indignant response when I realized Tripp was sitting in the same chair my brother had been three years earlier—when I heard his name for the first time in almost a decade.

I paused, a tiny breath escaping me, and my cheeks started to burn with the start of a smile.

And here he was, one of my closest friends, a central figure in our little fucked-up found family—a phrase not-so-lovingly coined by Taylor, but now adopted by all of us.

I wanted to reach out across time, through the years, wrap my arms around that old version of me, whisper to her, to let her know that it would be okay. That something wonderful, magical, beautiful—a life full of love and starlight was waiting for her on the other side of it all.

Titling my head, my hair falling in a sheet over my shoulder, I smiled softly at Tripp. "You want to come for dinner tonight then? Taylor's off. We can share Deacon duty."

Tripp appraised me, lips pulling to the side. "You're not cooking right?"

"Excuse me?" I asked, eyes wide.

His nostrils flared, and a choked laugh caught in his throat. "Chuck, you're the only person I know who had a meal service in college, and we went to Brown. That's fucking saying something."

"Hey—I can cook." I slapped a palm to the table but was cut off before I could continue.

"Baby, you can hardly boil water for pasta." David dropped beside me, one arm lazily extended over the back of my chair.

"Oh." I carefully extracted myself from under David's arm and rolled my eyes at him. "Did you fix your little problem then?"

"For now." David grinned, eyes wandering to my lips before he rolled his neck against the back of the chair and tipped his chin toward Tripp. "My dad had some lobster shipped up yesterday. I'll cook that if you want to come over?'

A groan, entirely undignified, left Tripp, and he crossed his arms, nodding. "Yeah, alright. That sounds good. The lobster here fucking sucks. Don't count on Deac, though. Says he has a date."

My lip curled back. "Who this time?"

Tripp shrugged. "Some twenty-four-year-old. Not nearly as intelligent, nor as nice as Noa, so don't worry, Chuck. He'll come to his senses soon."

"Not soon enough," I muttered, dropping my head back against the chair.

"Give him some time." David's voice was gentle, and his hand wound around the back of my neck, lifting my head back up for me. Carrying it so I didn't have to hold it alone. "Have you talked to Noa?"

I nodded, biting down on the inside of my cheek. "Taylor and I were on FaceTime with her the other night. She's in Australia for the next while."

"How's she doing?" Tripp asked, a pained look on his face.

I raised my eyebrows. "I think she'd be better if she wasn't forced to see photos of her former fiancé with someone new each night splashed on every tabloid across the United States."

"Wouldn't we all?" Tripp's voice was dry, and he spun around once in his chair. "What time do you want me to come over? Maybe we can cut out of here early, the game—"

"No one's leaving early." Ash threw open the glass door to the conference room, a thick stack of papers tucked under one arm. It seemed like he tried to give us all a sharp look before his gaze softened on me, the corners of his eyes wrinkling, and his mouth twitching. He paused behind my chair, rapping his knuckles once against my head, like he did when I was a child.

He avoided the chair at the head of the table, leaving it empty, because it belonged to my father, and for better or worse, no one would ever be like him again.

His eyes narrowed on the empty chair beside Tripp. "Where's Deacon?"

"Jesus Christ, I'm right here." Deacon held up his hands as he strode through the doorway. He didn't look particularly worse for wear—his hair was immaculately styled, perfectly pushed back, and there wasn't a crease in his suit. Even his shoes were polished.

But I could see it all over him—all the grief he carried weighing down his shoulders, and no one helping to hold it for him. I think his chair sank an inch lower than everyone else's when he dropped into it.

He swiveled back and forth for a moment while the rest of the table filled up, ever the irreverent billionaire boy, and when he stopped, he offered me a rare, real-him smile. Nothing Winchester, nothing fake about it, but he looked impossibly sad all the same.

I leaned forward. "Dinner tonight?"

He gave me a flat look. "Can't. I have a date."

I widened my eyes at him, kicking out under the table to find his kneecap. "Cancel it. David's cooking. Everyone's coming over."

"Ouch—Jesus fuck, fine." His lip curled, and he shook his head at me, but I think he sat up straighter.

I hoped so. David was holding my weight, so I could hold some of his.

"Charlie, if you're ready, you can get us started." Ash didn't look up from the paper he was rifling through, gesturing vaguely toward me.

It was the one tradition of my father's he let go—none of us had to stand at the front of the room to present. It used to bother me. It felt too much like I was on display to be judged, measured, and ultimately found wanting. It wouldn't have bothered *this* me, though.

I'd been many versions of myself in my life, and maybe that was normal. But it was odd for so many of them to have lived in this conference room, to be able to see them all like that if years were people gathered around a table—a little rich girl, desperate for a home, for love, trying to claw for approval anyway she could; a lost girl who couldn't stop running.

But I think my favorite version of me was the one I was now—*found*.

Acknowledgements

I'll try to keep this short because if you're reading this, you've been through at least two of my long-winded acknowledgement sections.

It's hard to believe I'm writing this, here at the end of Charlie's story—this idea that was conceived in the midst of the pandemic on my old MacBook with a hard drive that had already crashed twice. This story was once a standalone, once only two books, and eventually it became three. It had an entirely different name, and so, so many things were so very different.

Once upon a time, Tripp was never even going to show his face again after the end of Rich Girl—and how boring would that have been? Deacon was never supposed to be engaged, and Steven was never supposed to be, well, Steven.

I struggled writing this book, and I've been open about that. But it's here, in your hands, and for that, I'm endlessly thankful to so many people.

Thank you to my editor, Krys, for your belief in these characters and this series. To my beta readers, Christina, Esther and Danielle, your attention and thoughtfulness means so much.

Christina, we've been doing this together for a long time, and I hope there are many more swapped manuscripts to come.

Esther, I love you, and it's funny how someone whose DMs I slid into would suddenly occupy so much space in not only my virtual world, but my real one. My appreciation and love for you is endless.

Danielle, I love you too, and not only has it been a joy to be your friend, it's been a joy to watch your storytelling grow and flourish. Thank you for sharing your time, energy, and your work with me. It's a privilege I don't take for granted.

To Benjamin, for peeling me off the proverbial floor and reminding me that standards shift, and that's okay. It's actually a good thing.

And a very, very, endless, eternal thank you to each and every one of you. There are people who believed in this book from the very beginning, and have been with Charlie since the early days, and to you—I am so grateful. Vanessa, Shannon, Ashley, Kat and Kayla—you've been with these characters forever, and my appreciation for that cannot be over-stated. You've kept me going.

To every single person who took the time out of their day to send me a message and tell me they loved these books, this series, these charac-ters—those messages always seemed to come at just the right time. For your time and energy, I'll never be able to repay you. You have no idea what those words meant to me, and I'll never forget them. I'm so grateful to have been able to give you words that meant something to you, too.

And finally, to Charlie, Deacon, David, Tripp, Taylor and Noa—thank you for being the first characters I dreamed up after such a long time.

Until next time.

Xoxo,

Haley

About the author

Haley is an almost-academic who traded peer-reviewed manuscripts for stories about flawed people falling in love against the backdrop of popular genres and tropes. Dubbed a "rom-traum" author by her readers, she loves to write about messy people making messy decisions as they move through one of our ever present companions in life: grief.

A big fan of her dog, horror movies with a splash of comedy, and the millennial peace sign, Haley is usually researching her next travel destination, consuming urban fantasies (give her a magical school or a vampire with a cellphone any day of the week), and concocting the most gut-wrenching scenes she can drag a reader through on their way to a HEA while she does reformer Pilates.

Self-deprecating to a fault, Haley actually wants nothing more than for her readers to find a home for all their flaws, mistakes, and baggage in her characters so they realize that they, too, deserve a love the likes of which could only be found in a book. You can find her on Instagram as @haleylwrites.

More by Haley Warren

Near Miss

Life in November

Bad Daughter

<u>Winchester Holdings</u>
Rich Girl
Lost Girl
Found Girl